Just Watch Me

Also by Peter Grimsdale
Perfect Night

Just Watch Me

PETER GRIMSDALE

First published in Great Britain in 2009 by Orion Books,
an imprint of The Orion Publishing Group Ltd
Orion House, 5 Upper Saint Martin's Lane
London WC2H 9EA

An Hachette UK Company

1 3 5 7 9 10 8 6 4 2

A CIP catalogue record for this book is
available from the British Library.

ISBN (Hardback) 978 0 7528 9082 1
ISBN (Export Trade Paperback) 978 0 7528 9083 8

Typeset by Deltatype Ltd, Birkenhead, Merseyside

Printed and bound in the UK by CPI Mackays, Chatham ME5 8TD

The Orion Publishing Group's policy is to use papers that are natural,
renewable and recyclable products and made from wood grown in
sustainable forests. The logging and manufacturing processes are
expected to conform to the environmental regulations
of the country of origin.

www.orionbooks.co.uk

For Lydia

Prologue

It was too perfect. That should have been a warning.

Something in the silence, like the voice in my head that had helped me stay alive this far. But I was in new country, unfamiliar terrain. Not listening.

The bed was the biggest in the hotel but Sara had laid claim to most of it. She was sprawled out as if she'd just landed from a great height, her arms thrown across the mound of pillows, her black hair spread out like a fan. Her strapless white satin dress clung to her, mermaid-like, the silky sheet, half thrown back, forming a great fin that cascaded onto the carpet. I stood a few feet from her, watching. With each blink I half-expected to find her gone, just a dream. So I stood, as she slept, as if the longer I looked the more real it would all become.

The stillness – just the hushed breath of the air conditioning: that could have alerted me. Silences were suspect: after a barrage, a deserted village, the freshly dead. But I had put all that behind me. That was the plan.

I'd been told to take my time. Not to plunge into anything too serious. 'It's a jungle out there; watch your back,' said the regimental shrink with dead eyes. I didn't interest him because I hadn't cracked. 'You may be home but in your head you're still in Afghanistan. Don't bother explaining it to your bird; she won't have a clue what you're on about.' He didn't say it – they don't – but I could tell he didn't fancy my chances. I'd prove him wrong. *Just watch me.*

Sara sighed and her mouth parted slightly as if waiting to be kissed again. Between each breath there were huge intervals, long enough for me to imagine the knifing fear of her dead.

I wrenched my eyes away from her and pulled back the curtains, exposed myself to the icy hug of air lurking behind them. The windows were still wet from the storm that had woken me. A monochrome London roofscape, a coat of half-hearted snow, cloud thick as smoke from an oil fire. I looked at my watch. Twenty minutes to pick-up. Any sane person would call in sick. I didn't do sick. That stuff they'd implanted in our heads that switches off common sense, which kept us solid and kept us killing – it was still in there.

I'd got out of the Army just in time. You only have so much luck and I'd used up all mine. I needed a clean break. I could have gone into IT, or back to college. A headhunter took me through some sensible options, registered my indifference and passed me Trent's brochure: *Integrated Strategic Solutions.*

'Spot of surveillance, protection – might suit while you find your feet.'

A no-man's-land full of lads like me, not quite ready for the real world – until Sara, that was.

I turned back just as her eyes opened, wide and surprised. They hovered uncomprehending on the champagne bottle in the bucket by the bed, drifted to the bouquet, compliments of the manager, swept round the sumptuous room then settled on my gaze and smirked. 'It's rude to stare.'

'Can't help it.' I stepped closer. 'Anyway, you were asleep.'

'I could feel your eyes.'

She widened hers, and there it was, arcing between us, high voltage, invisible current.

Five weeks. That was all it had been. I'd just come off a thirty-six hour shift in the bowels of a car park, watching a Chrysler no one came to collect. Either way I needed coffee, a shower and a shave. I was in no condition to pull. The café was part of a theatre, not my kind of place but close to the job.

She was alone at a small table, coat over her shoulders, arms folded, leaning on her elbows, cradling her gorgeous face. She looked up, eyes shining, dark as rock pools. My pulse shifted gear. There were other empty chairs but I ignored them.

'Can I?'

She nodded at the script in front of her. 'I'm trying to concentrate.'

'I promise not to put you off.'

I scraped my eyes off her face and glanced at the pages in front of her. *Denial*. Two parts: Jim and Cassie.

She shook her head and sighed. 'I've got five minutes to get this off by heart.'

She stared at the words then closed her stunning black eyes.

I scanned the upside down page then looked back at her.

'"Whatever you're thinking, forget it. It's not going to happen." Then Jim says, "I know what I think—" But then Cassie cuts in. "You think you're in love with me but you're not. You're in love with an idea of me. What you see is just an image."'

Her eyes widened as I recited the words. She opened her mouth but I put up a hand. 'And then Cassie says, "I'm a hologram. I walk and talk but that's all. The 'me' is somewhere else, sealed up safe where no one can get at it. No matter how long you hang around, I'll not give anything away. I may as well be invisible."'

'Wow.'

I had all her attention now. I shook my head.

'What?'

'I think you could do better.'

'How do you mean?'

'A better part. This one's not for you.'

A woman with a clipboard came into the café, an old walkie-talkie swinging from her belt. 'Sara Harding?'

No one moved.

'*Sara* Harding?' The woman sighed. 'OK. Abbie Franks?'

Another woman got up and followed her out.

'I'm Dan.'

She extended her hand, eyes on full beam. 'Sara Harding.'

Some of the pre-dawn light spread into the room. She raised herself up on her elbows and frowned. 'You're dressed.'

'I know.'

'Haven't you forgotten something?' Predatory look.

'You're the one who fell asleep.'

'I could seek an annulment. Technically, the marriage hasn't been consummated.'

I moved nearer, breathed a breath of her scent. I sat down on the bed and put a hand on her abdomen.

'Bit late for that.'

Two hearts beating. Twins ran in my family.

She lifted her arms and hooked me towards her lips. 'I wish I had your discipline.'

I felt her breath on my eyes, felt every muscle engage.

'Come on. You know you want to.'

Five weeks since our café encounter. Four weeks, six days and twenty-three hours fifty-nine minutes since I noticed I was in love. *A whole minute. What took you so long?* Three days since she told me she was pregnant.

4

'What are you going to do about it?' She'd said, mock stern, hands on hips.

'Marry you.' One shot. No hesitation, no risk assessment, no question. What was there to think about?

She returned fire: 'There's an "if".'

I waited for it.

She blinked slowly and her eyes flashed. 'We do it now.'

And that's what we did. I took the next day off. She found the dress, found me the suit. In the rain, no umbrella, my coat round her shoulders. We recruited two witnesses off the street outside the register office, West Indian sisters, Myrtle and Jean, who doubled up when we asked them, cried copiously when it was done and smothered us in kisses.

'Stay.'

I shrugged. 'I can't let the lads down.'

'But I'm your wife now. You must obey.' Her eyes were all over me, melting my resolve. *Make love to my beautiful new wife or sit in a Transit van with a reeking Sanilav and an undiagnosed psychopath?*

'It's just a few hours.'

A tremor of fear passed across her face, then she shook her head and pouted. 'I may not be in the mood by then.'

My phone buzzed. A text from the Trent driver. *Outside.* I unplugged the camera chargers and dropped the batteries into the bag.

'Shoot me.'

'*What?*'

'Take one. Now.'

I hadn't brought the camera to the wedding. Cameras were for work. She felt for her bag, found a mirror and touched up her lipstick in two expert sweeps.

I pulled out the Nikon. It was cold, slightly greasy. I

5

swapped lenses, and looked into the viewfinder. Seeing her in the cross-hairs, I shivered. She looked even more beautiful, black eyes glistening, black hair in a sweep across her bare shoulders, slightly lifted on one elbow, a hand on her cleavage and the silvery folds of her dress. As I squeezed the shutter, she mouthed *I love you*. 'Remember this always, whatever happens.'

Not acting now.

The snow had turned to sleet. The Transit was parked opposite the clinic, squeezed between a Nissan and an Audi. The sides of the van were plain, just a faint square where they'd painted over an old logo. A ladder was lashed to a couple of roof bars to help the disguise.

I crossed the road and peered through a fogged window. A ghostly glow from the laptop lit Greg's face. He looked up and grinned.

'Surprise.'

He pulled off the headphones, reached over and unlocked the passenger door. A fetid waft of food, smoke and shit hit me as I climbed in.

'What happened to Vic?'

'Swapped shifts. Thought you'd like to see a friendly face.'

'Always thinking of others.' I nodded at the Sanilav. 'No one ever teach you to flush?'

He smirked. 'No toilet training remember?' Three KFC boxes were wedged between the windscreen and the top of the dash. He swatted one towards me. 'Breakfast?' His bloodshot eyes fixed on me like a dog's. Expectant. I hadn't told him about the wedding.

Since Afghanistan he'd put on weight. The poppers on his denim shirt strained against the flab. And he'd started a beard that just seemed to exaggerate the babyish roundness his face had always had.

I settled into the seat, took out the camera and replaced the long lens.

'They brief you?'

'What d'you think?'

I nodded at the laptop. 'Anything logged?'

He shrugged.

I sighed. 'At least *pretend* to take an interest.'

'OK, OK.' He tapped the keyboard. Scrolled down the notes.

'Yesterday. *15.35: Base to chemist. Prescription package. Dry cleaners.* Wow, this is fun.'

'Just go on.'

'*Tesco's: Papers and cat food.*'

He let out a knowing laugh. I groaned. 'He does have a cat.'

'Right. *Observed target's Lexus – scrape on the nearside rear door. T and W examine.*' He frowned at the screen.

'Tariq is Waheed's driver.'

'What's a raghead doing cruising London in a chauffeured Lexus?'

'Gift from a Saudi benefactor.'

'Thought he was an exile.'

'So you do know something.'

'Yeah. That much.' He pressed a thumb and forefinger together. 'I operate on a need to know basis. And I need to know shit.'

He turned his attention back to his laptop. Since his teens he'd prized ignorance like a badge of honour. As if knowledge would fill his head up and leave no room for the murky stuff that interested him.

I let the silence run on. He'd have to know sooner or later. I opened the window to let in some air and rain.

He closed the laptop and started on a joint, spreading out three papers.

'Tell me it's worth it. Tell me he's Bin Laden's man in

7

the UK, plotting to turn the London Eye into a Catherine wheel.'

The sleet came on harder, carpeting the street with a greasy grey nap. I shut the window.

'He's never been connected to any terror group or plot. He's a scholar, comes from Jeddah. Fought the Soviets in Afghanistan, but slagged off the Saudi Royals, so they won't have him back.'

'A suspect though.'

'Low to zero. Anything higher, this job wouldn't have been outsourced.'

'What's he do all day, apart from eat cat food?'

'Prays, writes pamphlets. He's got no phone, no computer, doesn't do email. Does everything by messenger, wants to turn the clock back to the pre-oil days.'

He sniffed the air. 'Quite an expert, aren't you?'

'It's all in the brief if you bothered to look.'

He nodded at the clinic across the road. 'What's this about?'

'Dodgy kidneys. Today's his monthly check-up.'

Greg groaned. 'I can't wait.'

He had been discharged just after me. I was hoping he'd go his own way, fend for himself. But once he found out I'd gone to Trent's he got himself hired as well. 'We gotta stick by each other.' At least, that was how he saw it. But he wasn't taking to the job.

Because of Afghanistan, Trent had us on extended probation. A year at the lower rate. I'd tried arguing: 'What are we, war criminals?' Trent had given me his long, fuck-with-me-and-you're-out-now look. 'If you *were* war criminals, Carter, you'd only be on six months.'

Ten weeks on surveillance, he told us; if we didn't screw up we'd get something more active. But it had been five months now. I wasn't bothered – the less action the better,

8

as far as I was concerned. But Greg needed distraction and wasn't getting it.

'Why bother with this dude?' He sprinkled some hash into the tobacco and grinned. 'I'm taking an interest, like you told me to.'

'It's box-ticking. So the spooks can say they've got everyone covered. The more people they watch the easier it is to justify their budget.'

'Cheaper to hoover up him and his mates and ship 'em home. Better still, line 'em all up and slot 'em.'

I looked at my watch. I'd only been here ten minutes. I should have stayed in bed.

'If he's not a terrorist, what's he doing here then?'

It was raining hard now, drumming on the roof of the van.

'Maybe the urologists are better here.'

I looked down at the screen on the back of the camera and replayed the images of Sara in her white satin. Beamed myself away for a moment. Twenty minutes to go till Waheed was due. Twenty minutes to fill. Then another wait – however long the appointment took, then a bit of following, then back to Sara. Hardly a lifetime to wait, even if it felt like it.

Greg wound down his window and spat.

'So. Good day off?'

I left it a beat. 'OK.'

The joint flared as he lit it. 'There's a rumour going round that you got yourself hitched. I told them it was bollocks.'

I put down the camera. I didn't speak. Didn't need to. He looked like a man awaiting sentence. After a full half minute he let out a long sigh, like an old steam engine.

'Well fuck you very much.'

He rubbed a hand across his face and wagged a finger my way. 'You know Trent's rules – no dependents.'

'I'm quitting.' Another bombshell. Might as well get it all over with. 'Friday's my last day.'

He stared out of the windscreen, looking at nothing. 'I promised your mum I'd keep an eye on you. Her last words: "Keep him out of trouble."'

'I'm not in trouble.'

He swallowed. 'You really fucking went and got it done, then?'

I looked down at the camera. 'It was a wedding, not an execution.'

He turned and waved a finger at the space between us. 'Next thing you know she'll want a—'

I smirked.

His mouth dropped open.

I put up two fingers. 'Twins.'

'Jesus Christ all-fucking-mighty.' He hit the steering wheel with a palm and shook his head slowly. 'You poor fuck.'

His reaction was no surprise. Nothing in his upbringing – if you could call it that – would have given him any incentive to be a parent. His mother had used him like a punch bag. He never found out who his father was. I looked across at him. Under the scrubby facial hair was the same thirteen-year-old I'd come home from school and found in our flat watching telly. He had got in through the window over the sink and was just sitting there in front of *Grange Hill*, holding a slice of cold pizza he'd found in the fridge. The way he just looked up and said 'hullo', I could tell he'd done this before, not with any great thought, just taken refuge, hoping we might not notice, or better still, just let him stick around, like a stray.

He stared at the furnace on the end of his joint, glanced at the thin band on my finger, and shook his head again. He'd need to look out for himself now.

I gave him a winning grin. 'You'll be fine.' He'd have to be.

He let out a long sigh, reopened the laptop, which was wedged between his stomach and the steering wheel, stroked the touch-pad with the side of his thumb and clicked on a file. I gazed up the street. A couple came towards us, a child between them hopscotching her way over the paving stones, her wellies sliding in the slush.

I glanced back at him. He was staring at the screen, mouth open.

'Sex or violence?'

'A beheading.'

I knew I shouldn't have asked.

'US Marine. Truck caught an IED north of Kabul. He was the only survivor.'

He raised his eyebrows and gestured at the screen with a sweep of his hand as a waiter might over a cheese board.

'Thanks, but not before breakfast.'

He looked perturbed. 'It's not very high res: the blood's a blur.'

He angled the screen my way. I kept my eyes on the windscreen but he'd already clicked Play.

'He's telling his kids he loves them and then – SHUNK!' He sawed his neck with the side of a flattened hand. 'With a fucking breadknife.'

I looked at him, sighed. 'N.O.'

He looked grey.

'I'm only saying.'

'Saying what?'

'Could of been one of us.'

The words of an interpreter in Kabul floated back out of the library of unwanted memories in my head. A father of three, telling me between sobs why he had to get out of the country he loved. *Children – they make cowards of us.*

Greg pulled the headphone lead out of the laptop. The

van filled with a metallic stream of high-pitched pleading, a scream and then a silence, followed by some rapid words in Pashto in praise of Allah.

I reached over and slammed the lid shut. I glared at him, the chilling sounds reverberating in my head. 'You don't need to go there.'

Despite all the crap he'd put up with in his life, he had a fatal attraction to the macabre.

'We're home. Time to move on.' *Like me,* I didn't say.

He looked at me, blinked, sucked on his joint, the question in his eyes. *Where to?* He shrugged. 'Whatever. I've forwarded you the link.'

For some people there's only so much you can do. I'd already done more than I should. In Afghanistan, I'd protected him like I had back home. It had become a habit – one it was time to kick.

I took out my own laptop, hooked up the camera, squirted the shots of Sara across and filed them under Pictures. There was only one other shot in there – from the scan I'd insisted on. Two butter beans dancing in space. Five-week-old life.

'Does Trent know?'

'Not yet.'

'He won't be happy.'

'I'm not here to make him happy.'

'He won't give you a reference.'

'Don't need one.'

He gave me a panicky look from under his eyebrows. 'You really are clearing out?'

'End of the week.'

He sucked on the joint. 'Well I'll be fucked.'

The radio squawked. Wez, in the Merc. 'He's mobile.'

Greg leaned forward. 'Copy.'

I switched the camera to Standby and laid it ready in my lap. Greg shook his head. 'We were a team.'

I shrugged. 'Sorry, mate.'

He went silent, just stared at the road ahead, the view blurred by sleet crystals. Then he shrugged. 'Should get myself a girl I suppose.'

I gave his shoulder a brotherly squeeze. 'There's an idea.'

He nodded, but the fear was still in his face.

Waheed's journey from his flat in Highbury to the clinic took about thirty minutes. I looked at my watch. Twelve minutes since Wez's call. I stared into the rear-view mirror, trying to cling on to some of the magic of the last twenty-four hours, another planet from the reeking Transit.

The sleet came down harder now, turning the street a dull grey and muting the sounds. Greg tapped the wiper stalk. One sweep cleared the view. On the opposite pavement fifty metres away, a couple of schoolgirls in purple uniform skipped ahead of a woman with a blue scarf over her bowed head. Nearer to the van two youths in hoodies were bearing down on an old lady. A man kissed another woman under her umbrella and stepped into the road to cross. A lowered Honda with skinny tyres on chrome rims came past slowly, the driver's head bobbing to the throb of his sound system, his gaze on the girls. A third woman with a trench coat over her head shoved a plastic recycling box towards the kerb with her foot. Greg nudged me and pointed.

'She's fit.'

'What?'

'The one on the left.' He pointed at the schoolgirls.

'Get a grip.'

'OK, her then. Bird in the scarf.'

He pointed to the woman with the blue pashmina-type scarf over her hair, shadowing her face. She had on a short leather coat, a laptop case under her arm. She had stopped just short of the clinic, and was looking past our van, down the street behind us. I glanced in the mirror again. It was blurred by the sleet. I wound down the window to clear it, heard the squeal of tyres, a scrape of metal, a shout. I craned round. Waheed's Lexus. Four minutes early, accelerating past thirty. Tariq never went above twenty. The car fishtailed wildly. Out of control? Evasion? We'd driven like that under fire.

A motorbike was alongside the car, its rider in a black helmet, an arm extended, pointing. There was only one person in the Lexus.

A dull thud, but a big one, then a much sharper *thwack* as the nearside front corner of the Lexus struck the tailgate of a parked truck. A spray of plastic splinters from the car's front end collided with a shower of window glass. As the Lexus recoiled from the impact, a black missile with flailing wings soared over its roof and landed, tumbling along the tarmac, shiny round end coming towards me. The rider. The car did a hundred and eighty degree pirouette and stopped, sideways across the street. I saw the deep scratch on the nearside door.

Trent's Rule One: 'In the event of anything – ANYTHING – do not get involved, do not engage. You are not there for that. No one knows you are there. You're deniable. Leave the van and we wash our hands of you.'

I was out of the van. Waheed was in the driver's seat, draped in the dead airbag, blinking at me. The first time our eyes had met. His shirt was gone, his chest all blood, smoke swirled around him. I went for his door but he shook his head. Then he cupped his hands and held them up in front of his face. I looked over to the rider, on his back in the road, still. My foot struck something. I looked down. An M79 sawn-off. *Stray firearm – leave it.* That's the drill. That's what's in the manual. I glanced back at Greg, through the open Transit door, frozen, mouth open.

I didn't like unattended weapons, never mind the rules. *If you don't pick it up someone else will.* That's what I'd learned. I picked it up. Still hot from discharge, the shell case still in the barrel. I took another step towards the Lexus.

The blast knocked me back against the Transit. The gun flew out of my hand. When I looked again the car interior was a ball of fiery smoke. Nothing to do there. I crouched over the biker, felt for signs. Eased off his helmet. They tell you not to, but how else can you give mouth to mouth? His face was lean, skin stretched over prominent bones, strong brow, a gash on the bridge of his nose, an old scar bisecting his left eyebrow. A warrior's face. I puffed and pumped the life back into him, willing him back. His eyes flickered – then stared full into mine.

The second blast was bigger, slamming me against the van again. When I came to, a column of blue-black smoke gushed from the Lexus. I got up and fell down again. I looked round for the biker. He was gone.

Hospital smells mingled with the residue of petrol and burnt plastic in my nostrils. All I heard was the ringing in my ears from the blast. There was something over my eyes. My face felt twice its normal size, pulsing with half-sedated pain. My hands were dead weights.

Sara. I had to get back to her.

I drifted away again.

There was someone in the room. Another smell, after-shave and old cigarette smoke. Sharp breaths, tense. Older. You can tell someone's age by the sound of their breathing. And squeaks. Rubber soles on vinyl floor, pacing.

A sigh.

'Fucking bollocks.'

Trent's voice, just a whisper, but enough to identify it.

A great weight was holding me down, chemical, not

physical. The front of my face felt numb. I was sinking again.

Where was Sara?

A door opened. A squeak of shoes. Lighter steps, two sets. Cold damp air dragged in on coats. There was a gruff greeting from Trent, almost inaudible. For a few seconds no one spoke. Just atmosphere. Someone came close; I felt his breath on my chin.

Trent spoke first.

'No sign of the Met?'

'We've held them off. MOD's bomb people have the car.' A toff voice, full of authority.

'It's the Met's turf. They'll want transparency. Remember Menezes?'

'I'm not even going to answer that.'

'If this is down to your lot—'

The toff cut in. 'Credit us with a little more gumption, Jack. What's his name?'

'Dan Carter. I've got his file here.' A third voice, younger, eager.

A grunt from Trent.

'Oh sorry, Jack. Stuart Holder. Our "care in the community" man.' A snort of laughter. 'Stuart'll mind Carter once we're sure he's going to play ball. What's the hospital say?'

It was Stuart's turn. 'Concussion, broken nose, bruising, swelling ... looks like he was hit by debris, some burns from the blast. With a bit of luck he won't remember a thing.'

The toff again, peeved. 'The sidekick said he got out of the van. I thought your people—'

Another grunt from Trent.

'He's got to be briefed before the cops get anywhere near him. No loose ends.'

I wanted to move, get back to Sara. Should never have

left her. But even thinking was an effort.

'The other one stayed put?'

'Kept his head down like a good lad. He'll keep to the script.'

Something tapped my foot. 'And this one?'

'Let's see.'

Stuart piped up again. 'Soon as we can we'll get his version. Maybe he can throw some light—'

The toff interjected. 'That's for later. Right now it's what it *looks* like. We're dealing with perceptions here.'

Trent cleared his throat. 'Far as I can see, it was a crash job, last minute, stop him whatever. Someone unaware of our surveillance.'

There was an awkward silence.

'Thanks for your insightful analysis, Jack. We'll handle this from here on, OK?'

No one moved. Trent hadn't taken the hint.

The toff again, testily: 'Carter's our problem now.'

'Have it your way. There's just the question of—'

A weary sigh from the toff. 'Ye-es, we'll pick up the tab.'

The door opened and closed. The toff groaned. 'What a relief.'

'Why do we use him?'

'Because he charges a fraction of what it would cost us, because he's that bit more deniable. Because there's no one else.'

Neither of them spoke for several seconds.

'Any theories?'

'Too many.'

'What's being given out?'

'We're going with botched suicide bombing.'

'Is that going to stick?'

'Fucking has to.'

'And the cops?'

'They'll have to go along with it.'

The bed moved slightly. One of them had perched on the end.

'When he wakes, should we get his version?'

A hint of irritation in Toff's reply. 'We don't need *his* version; he needs *our* version and he needs to stick with it.'

'File suggests an awkward streak. Some trouble in Afghanistan.'

'There's always trouble in Afghanistan.'

Something tapped my ring finger. The toff lowered his voice. 'We have the wife.'

They must have noticed me tense. No one spoke for a few seconds. I felt breath on my cheek again. A face close to mine. 'Carter? Raise your hand if you can hear ... Well that's something. Carter, we're here to help.'

The sedation was starting to wear off. Steady hammer blows were pounding in my forehead.

'We'll take this one step at a time. Don't try to talk. Just nod, OK? You were a witness. A witness to a car bomb. You saw who was in the car? Nod if you did.'

I nodded.

'Waheed, right? Good.'

'You witnessed him blow himself up.'

The only sound was the hammering, louder and faster.

'Where's my wife?' The voice exploded inside my head. It was a second before I realised it was mine.

'Ah good, we have communication.'

'Where is she?'

All the moisture had gone out of my mouth. I felt a pair of hands pressing my shoulders back down on the bed.

'Don't move, just listen. Your wife is fine. Naturally she's very concerned for your welfare. You'll be able to see her once we've got through this.'

I didn't speak or move. Just felt the wave of rage sweep

through me, engulfing everything, even the pounding.

'Getting back to what you saw. You got out of the van to try and help, after the car crashed. You saw Waheed. And then he exploded.'

All I could see was the biker's eyes staring, absorbing all he could of my face.

'In fact you saw Waheed pull something. And then the car exploded.'

I didn't move. There was a big gap in this I didn't like.

'Come on, soldier. You're our star witness. Last man to see Waheed alive, you saw him do the business.'

The look he gave me. The shake of his head. 'He cupped his hands.'

A phone buzzed, Stuart answered. 'Just a sec.' I heard the door. I was alone with the toff.

I felt his face close, a gust of tea and smoke breath. His voice dropped to a whisper. 'Carter – there's no time to piss about. We both know the chap on the bike; he's not going to forget your face. Whoever sent him, they won't want any loose ends here any more than we do. So I rather think you need us even more than we need you. Your family certainly will. Oh, and congratulations by the way.'

He was silent for a few seconds, letting the words sink in.

'So, Carter, you're with us?'

All I could think of was Sara, her face. A shadow over the light in her eyes.

'Do I have a choice?'

One

Sara shook me awake. She was holding the digital clock in front of my face. She had no make-up on. She was furious.

'You set it for five. How *could* you *do* that? Today of all days.'

Emma was already crying on the landing. Charlie was shouting something about his pants, his voice all nasal with sleep.

'The flight's not till eight-thirty. Gatwick's only forty minutes.'

'Check-in's two hours before.'

I levered myself up. 'We'll be fine.'

This was Sara's worst nightmare. She had prepared everything so there would be no panic. The two big bags had been packed and put ready by the front door the night before. She had hung the children's travelling clothes on their radiator and adjusted the heating to come on early, laid the breakfast table, poured out their choice of cereal the night before with saucers over the bowls to keep it fresh. The hand luggage had everything for emergencies: spare pants, plasters, Calpol, plastic bags to isolate anything that got sicked on, sun protection, crayons, little spiral drawing pads, every recommended anti-bug concoction. These bags also stood by the front door, unzipped in readiness for toothbrushes and other last minute items to be dropped in as we left. She had gone about it all with a tense manic energy that had alarmed me. Perhaps once we got there the Caribbean sun would force her to relax.

I went into the bathroom, confronted my ghost in the mirror. We exchanged withering looks.

The trip was my idea. We needed one badly. At first Sara had just snorted. 'They'll never let us.' But I was determined. I'd put it to Stuart, our careworn handler. His eyes had widened as they usually did with my demands. His stock response, always with a chuckle, was 'That's a bit off-piste', or when I got more demanding, 'That's *really* off-piste'. But this one, a family holiday to Tobago, was 'Really very off-piste, Dan.' It was a place I knew Sara had always dreamed of. 'Either this or I'm bailing out.'

I made it sound as if I meant it.

When I'd flourished the new passports in front of her, she had smiled briefly, but her reaction was hedged with buts and what-ifs, the spark dying as it was lit. She had opened the back page and examined our cover names: Paul and Sara Mandler. Would we ever be ourselves again?

I splashed cold water on my face which brought some of the colour back. I could hear Sara downstairs arguing with the children about some last minute toys they wanted to bring.

We'd been in the Scheme since Waheed. As soon as I was on my feet, we had been spirited away to a smart penthouse in Brighton 'just till the dust settles.' I'd watched the fall-out on TV: demonstrations in Riyadh when the body was flown home, extremists vowing revenge, Western embassies attacked in five capitals, British and American flags burned. Martyrdom had transformed Waheed into a global hero. The suicide bomb story, instead of damping things down, merely heightened speculation about his death.

But for Sara, once she knew I'd be OK, it was an adventure. The idea of living undercover amused her. When I warned her it could go on a long time she just shrugged and pulled me towards her. 'What's it matter when we've got each other?' She patted her abdomen. 'And them.'

When her bump started to show, Stuart told us we were being moved to 'something more suitable' – a big detached house along the coast on the edge of Worthing, a seaside town I'd never heard of. I'd had my doubts but Sara settled right in.

She was happy and that's what mattered.

But six months ago, there had been a change. There was no incident, no row. Just as if a light inside her had been switched off. She denied that anything was wrong and told me to ignore it. I knew the Scheme would get to her eventually. She had been so supportive at the start, as if the sheer force of her enthusiasm for our life together would overwhelm the limitations placed on us, but it had beaten her.

It wasn't what she did so much as what she stopped doing – less eye contact, fewer touches, a force field repelling me when I came near. I just backed off, hoping the holiday would bring her back to me.

'Pleeaase don't take your shoes off! I've just put them on.' Downstairs, Sara was shouting at Charlie who was still crying.

'I want flip-flops.'

'Not till we get there.'

'Let him wear the fucking flip-flops.' I said to the bathroom mirror. The last four days had been unusually tense, Sara swooping down on the children and barking at them for minor misdemeanours. I decided to stay out of it. One good thing was that after the initial doubts, she had embraced the trip as her own project. It was good to see her engaged. But the night before, I'd found her curled up, streaked with tears. I'd taken her in my arms and she'd sobbed into my shoulder, gripping me as though her life depended on it, repeating my name over and over. 'It's going to be fine,' I promised her.

I shrugged at my reflection, doused my face with cold water and searched for my toothbrush. Sticking out from under the bin was Sara's pink 'Sleepeezee' inflatable collar that I had bought her for the trip. The children usually deployed it as a bath toy. Downstairs, I waved my discovery at her in triumph. She snatched it from me.

'Can we just get going?'

By the time I'd reversed out onto the drive, she and the kids were on the front step. Charlie, keen to help, picked an unzipped bag up by one handle and marched forward, emptying it on to the drive.

'Fucking hell.'

'*Mummy!*'

Sara scooped up the contents and hustled the children towards the car.

'I'm tired,' Emma said.

'You'll be feeling a lot worse than tired if you don't get in *right now*.'

I let out a long sigh. Sara shot me a frosty look. 'Thanks for the help.' She slammed their door and climbed in beside me.

Charlie was grunting behind. 'I can't do my belt.'

'Just pull. It's trapped under your booster.'

As Sara reached into the back to sort him out, I caught the smell of sick on her breath.

'Are you all right?'

She didn't answer.

I floored the accelerator and pulled the wheel hard right. The Range Rover drifted in the gravel until the tyres bit and we surged forward.

'Da-aad.'

'For God's sake,' Sara muttered in a loud whisper.

'Stop arguing!' Charlie particularly hated any parental discord. We drove in silence.

Maybe that's how it was in normal families, pre-holiday nerves. How would I know? There was nothing normal about us. Getting the trip at all had been a small triumph, the rules we lived under temporarily suspended. We should have been excited. Our first holiday. A milestone. The children had never travelled more than ten miles from home before.

'When will we get there?'

'Emma ...'

'Whe-en?'

It was Charlie's turn. 'I want to see zebras.'

Sara put her face in her hands. I looked over my shoulder at him. We had only told them last night where we were going. 'There are no zebras in Tobago, sweetheart. There's lots of other things, like hummingbirds and lizards.'

'But I want to see zebras.' He looked crestfallen.

Sara covered her face. 'Eyes on the road, *please*.'

'Can we have a CD?

'If you can agree on one.'

'*Jungle Games*!'

'*Pony Club*!'

'OK, *Jungle Games*.' It wasn't my choice of sound track for a dash to the airport but I had developed the ability to screen out even the most insistent kids' entertainment. I could even read them a story while thinking about something else.

Still dark, the roads were deserted. We passed the Downs and hit the A23 in minutes. Not long now. The speedo surged past a hundred.

'Dan – please.' Sara put her face in her hands.

'You were the one in a hurry.' I eased back. And shot between two cars in the fast and slow lanes. Sara turned her head away in a theatrical gesture of desperation.

The Gatwick slip road came into view and I overtook two more lorries before making the exit as late as I could. The Range Rover heeled over as I tackled the roundabout. We swept on to the Departures ramp like VIPs.

'You get out and I'll park.'

Sara went for a trolley. I opened the tailgate and hefted out the bags. When she came back she was sucking on a cigarette. I hadn't seen her smoke in the morning in a long time and never in front of the kids. She let it drop and ground it out under her boot.

'No comment,' I said and lifted the bags onto the trolley.

Emma said she needed a wee. Sara gathered up Charlie. 'See you at the check-in. Zone D.'

The sky was lightening to the east behind the cutout shapes of the airport buildings. I watched the monorail sliding between the terminals. As a kid I'd fantasised about living in a world with monorails. A world without disappointment. At least the monorails were real; that was something.

I drove into Long Stay. The day was brightening and the puddles on the tarmac reflected the pink fluffs of cloud that dotted the sky. It would get better. How many times had I heard myself say that? I squeezed the button on the key and the locks clicked. I turned towards the terminal.

I found them in a snaking check-in queue. Sara was already near the front, looking round for me, documents in her hand. The children were laughing and trying to walk on each other's feet. Only then did I register that we were on a charter flight.

'Who the hell are Sunkiss?' The tickets had only arrived the day before, and Sara had taken charge of them. For some reason I'd assumed we would have been put on British Airways.

Sara ignored me and shuffled forward. The attendant's

hair was bleached and gelled up in a swirl, which did nothing for my confidence in Sunkiss. He examined the tickets and passports Sara handed him. He looked up at me.

'And yours, sir?'

I glanced at Sara.

'With the others.'

He held up three passports and pursed his lips.

I felt a hot pain spreading through my chest. Sara dropped to a squat and started going through the hand luggage. I patted the pockets of my jacket, knowing it wasn't there, then bent down to help her as she tore into the bag, her face burning red. 'See what happens when we rush.'

The children had picked up that something was wrong and stopped their game. Someone behind sighed loudly.

'Maybe it's in the car. I'll go back and check.'

I sprinted back. Not panicking. I don't do panic. Nothing to be gained, plenty to be lost. Stay focused. I lifted the tailgate. Nothing. I checked under the seats, all the cubbyholes and compartments, all the time imagining it on the front step. I checked the time. Not enough time to go back. Even if it was there on the drive I'd never make the flight now. If I'd set the alarm for earlier ...

I slammed the door with far more force than it needed, took a few steps away then smashed my fist on the bonnet. A family of five gave me matching frowns as they wheeled their bags toward the terminal.

I went to Lost Property. There was no one on the desk. I pressed a buzzer several times. A man with the absent look of someone who had fielded every insult imaginable appeared from behind a frosted glass door.

He listened, shaking his head. 'Nothing this morning. They tend not to get handed in ... if you know what I mean.'

Sara was standing near the check-in, a solemn child in each hand. 'That's it then. We'll just have to go home.'

She looked at the ground, trying not to let the children see her tears.

I put my anger on hold, pulled her towards me. 'Look, these things happen. You go on. I'll get it sorted.'

I'd call Stuart. *Hey, you're not gonna believe this …* He'd sigh, a collective sigh for all the times I'd laid at his door problems I wasn't allowed to solve myself. He'd fix it, sort me another passport, get me on the next flight. He knew how much was riding on this trip for us.

I saw the fear in Sara's eyes. For four years we had never had a night apart, never been more than a few miles from each other. She pushed me away.

'I can't do this. Please don't make me.'

'You can. Let's not let the children down.'

A burly man behind us already in his beach shorts gestured at the check-in. 'Can we just get to the fucking desk?'

I bent down and took a child in each hand.

'Daddy's gone and lost his passport. I'm going to sort it out. You go with Mummy and you'll see me very soon.'

They both looked doubtful. I wanted to be the magician in their lives, the one who made everything perfect, but it was as if they already knew the truth. I was just a conduit, passing requests on to Stuart who would always 'see what he could do'.

Sara's face started to crumple. I could see Charlie's alarm. He had never seen her cry. He gripped my forefinger hard. I knew they would cope, but at four they still believe their parents are infallible.

We moved towards Passport Control. I had a child in each hand. Emma, looking cross, twisted hers in mine.

'Too tight!'

'Sorry, darling.' I loosened my grip.

'Too loose!'

A game we'd played since she was very small. She sneaked

a smile up at me. It was her way of telling me it was going to be OK. From early on I had always sensed she knew what I was feeling and was always keen to make things better.

Outside security I crouched down and took each of them in my arms. The inside of my throat went hard and dry. Every night, even when I'd got back after they were asleep, I had kissed them goodnight. Wished the same wish, that they would have long lives, come to no harm. Every morning I had been there when they woke up. I gave them gentle reassuring pats and happy smiles that they were already too smart to take at face value.

'I'll see you very soon. Promise,' the words whispered, my voice ready to crack.

Charlie looked doubtful.

I glanced at Sara and shrugged. 'Just one of those things.'

She turned her eyes to me and for a second I saw a look I hadn't seen in her face for some time, the one that had convinced me we had to be together. She clung to me and we kissed, her eyes tight shut, her cheeks burning. Then she pushed back from me and with a hand on each child's shoulder turned towards the gate.

She didn't look back.

Two

I took my time driving back, let my body slow down, put away my rage. By the time I pulled on to our drive it was just starting to get light. It was a Sunday and the street had yet to wake up. I switched off the engine. There was no passport on the drive. I turned off the lights and sat there, my chin on the wheel, staring at the house.

Things happen. That's all that could be said. There was no logic, no meaning. I'd learned that in the Army. Everything could be going fine and then – craziness. And afterwards the search for someone or something to blame, the ifs. If we'd gone left not right, down this alley not that, if he'd kept down. If I'd stayed in the van ... A pointless exercise.

I let myself in, punched in the alarm code and raised the shutters that covered every window. The house was a seized asset; it had belonged to a fugitive drug trafficker who had heavily fortified it – a feature that had appealed to Sara. I looked for the passport in all the rooms, in the unlikely event that one of the children had got it out. I even checked the filing cabinet where what documents we were allowed to keep were stored.

I came back outside, looked again. There was no sound except the ticking from the car engine as it cooled. I dialled Gatwick Lost Property. The same man gave the same answer.

I took a deep breath and called Stuart. It wasn't that I was afraid, certainly not of him. It was the admission of defeat, that we'd screwed up, the humiliation.

We were supposed to go through the switchboard, but I'd squeezed his mobile number out of him during some previous crisis. The ring tone indicated he was abroad. Some of his other people were 'billeted offshore', defectors, informers, high-value asylum seekers, closeted away by Her Majesty's Government, all expenses paid.

It went to voicemail. I broke another rule and left a pleading message for him to call, then with a sinking heart, rang the office line.

'Yes?' Three equally sour assistants manned the line round the clock. Linda, the senior assistant, was the worst.

'Good morning Linda.'

'Yes?'

If Stuart was too obliging, too long suffering, Linda more than compensated. For her, the fact we were in the Scheme meant we were at best suspicious and at worst criminals or terrorists, spongers living it large, courtesy of the British taxpayer.

'I need to contact Stuart. It can't wait.'

'Mr Holder's not available at this time. What is it you need?'

Plumbers, babysitters, window-cleaners, gardeners, electricians, they all had to be ordered through Linda's team. Anything more complicated was always 'One for Mr Holder'.

'When will he be back?'

'He's gone for the week.'

'Where is he?'

'That's not for me to say. Perhaps you should explain what it is you're calling about.'

'There's a problem with the trip.'

There was a long pause.

'I have no information about that.' She hadn't been told. He said he had bent all the rules to let us go. 'You are aware it's a Sunday?'

'Could you get him to call me as soon as possible? Please?'

'If he rings in.'

'Thank you so much.'

Just to be sure, I texted him as well: *Passport problem. Help!*

Then I sent a message to Sara. *Txt wen u land.* Then, as an afterthought, typed *Love you.* I stared at the message for a few seconds, as if it was a foreign language, then pressed *Send*.

A second later my phone buzzed. It was Stuart. Airport sounds in the background.

'Hey, soldier, what's up?'

There was no point trying to make excuses. I told him what had happened. I heard a sympathetic chuckle. 'Dear oh dear. What can I say?' Unflappable.

'I think *fucking* and *idiot* could be the words you're groping for.'

He sighed. 'Hey ho, these things happen.' The resigned tone, so familiar. 'What about Sara and co?'

'I told them to go on ahead.'

'Right. Hang on a mo.'

The phone blasted with the sound of a taxiing light plane. I pictured him, tropical suit, briefcase under his arm, hurrying for a flight, trying to corral wisps of sandy hair with his free hand.

'Where are you?'

'Gibraltar.' A weary tone.

'That bad?'

'A Ukrainian ex-arms dealer assaulted a woman in the vet's where his poodle suffered liver failure. I'm on my way to spring him from custody. How's that for work of national importance?'

'Sorry I asked.'

'What do you want to do?'

'I promised Sara I'd be on the next plane.'

He let out a low whistle, his trademark distress call whenever I wanted something difficult from him. 'Had a feeling you'd say that.'

I had leaned hard on him to get this trip. He knew how much store I'd set by it.

'Should be a seat this time of year.'

'We still have to pay for it, *plus* the replacement passport.'

There were ways of getting round him, one of which was a bit of kidding. 'If it helps there's a bloke in Brighton could run one up for me. I could flog a car and get a ticket. You could deny all knowledge.'

'As it is, if my masters find out about this jaunt I'll be in so much shit.'

I let the silence do the pleading for me. He exhaled a lungful of air that ended in a groan. 'OK, let me make some calls. If I don't get back to you, it's because I've got the heave-ho.'

Any formality between us was long gone. His exasperation with the job had soon showed through as he recited the menial tasks he had been forced to do for his more demanding charges, whether it was sourcing fetish garments ordered by a captive Uzbek software genius who was threatening suicide, or arranging rehab for a Croatian former warlord's self-harming daughter. 'Imagine if it got out – what the taxpayers would think.'

What had caused him to drop his guard with me, I didn't know. We came from different worlds; his diplomat parents had billeted him in a series of boarding schools from an early age, where he buried himself in his studies. While I was skipping school and nicking cars he was honing his gift for languages in extra lessons. While he was avoiding bullies, I was giving it to who ever looked me in the eye too long. Becoming a spook was where he finally got to break a few rules, while the Army was where I finally learned to follow some.

What we had in common was Afghanistan. He knew my story and he had read the files. When he probed I had clammed up and he had the decency to back off. I'd figured that something bad had happened to him out there as well. Whatever it was that had shunted his promising career into this siding, looking after the likes of me, it had been while he was stationed in Kabul. 'An operation that got out of hand,' was all he said, with a nervous wave of his hands to show he was doing his best to forget it. Without exchanging a word we had arrived at an understanding that Afghanistan was a no-go area for both of us, which was fine with me.

My phone buzzed again.

'OK, we're sorted.'

'How soon?'

'Couple of days, max.'

I felt another surge of frustration, but it was futile being angry. It wasn't his fault. 'OK, I'll try and amuse myself.'

'Just relax. Enjoy the peace and quiet.' He was always telling me to relax.

'Hey, thanks.'

He snorted. 'Amigo, if you knew how rarely I hear that precious word ... Stay put OK? Just chill.'

The house was eerily still. I stood, listening to the silence, looking out at the sky. Nothing more I could do now except wait.

It was the first time I had ever been alone in the house. *The* house. Not *our* house. Certainly not *home*, not to me, anyway, despite Sara's efforts. It was bigger and fancier than anything I could have dreamed of, but that wasn't the point. I turned away from the window and surveyed the room as if it was hostile terrain. Without the children filling it with sound, it felt even more alien.

What had made it all right was that Sara had loved it at first sight. 'My dream home,' she called it, before she had even got out of the car. Inside it was all hard edges and cold marble but she wasn't deterred. She strode round it opening every door and drawer while I hovered in the hall, doubtfully. After a whirlwind tour she came back to me, her eyes locked on to mine shining with joy. 'I'll make you love it; you'll have no choice.'

My warnings that it wouldn't be for ever went unheard. She had made up her mind, just as she had made up her mind about me. Our new life would begin here.

As soon as we were in she started collecting swatches of fabric for curtains, and painted squares of colour on the walls before settling on a choice. 'I have to see the daylight *and* artificial light on them first,' she said, as if she was an old hand at this sort of thing.

When she had made her choices I got to work with a roller and brushes, covering the hard white with the warmer shades she had chosen. She got rid of all the furniture the drug trafficker had left, swapped the brothel-like white leather sofas for a pair with leaf patterns, exchanged the stained white rugs for blue wool. In the months leading up to the birth, this was her focus. I loved her for her industriousness and determination. What mattered was that she was happy, and I was grateful that she never blamed me for landing her in this artificial life. She had made the house her own. But I couldn't stop thinking of it as a disguise; despite her colours and fabrics, the rooms still vibrated with the indecipherable whispers of its dodgy past.

But that was all in my head. And outside, no one noticed.

'We're no different from them really,' Sara said one night, standing in the front window of our living room, a few weeks before the twins were born. She swept a hand in the direction of the other houses in the street. 'Detached, double-glazed, alarmed, sealed from each other: that's how everyone lives round here. For all we know they might well be in hiding too.'

Maybe she was right, but I wasn't convinced. To passers-by we might look like residents; I knew we were inmates.

I glanced at my watch. Eight-forty. They would be in the air now. Like an amputee still feeling the itch on a severed limb, I couldn't reconcile myself to the idea of being apart from them. Maybe I shouldn't have made her go, but I couldn't let the loss of my passport be a defeat for all of us.

I went into the kitchen, bypassing the breakfast mess and put on some coffee. The sound of the machine filled the silence. I dropped a slice of the children's favourite white bread into the toaster, put on the radio, punched through several stations, couldn't find any music I liked and switched it off again. I found the TV remote, aimed it at the set. The picture appeared but there was no sound – it was jammed on mute. I threw the remote across the room and rubbed my neck and flexed my shoulders to smooth away the tension. I took a carton of orange juice out of the fridge, poured a glass, picked it up, looked at it.

Then it was gone. Bits of glass were scattered over the sink and the floor. A streak of orange dribbled down the side of the kitchen unit, a small crescent-shaped dent where the glass had hit.

I hadn't even seen it leave my hand. Didn't remember the decision. I clutched the counter, giddy from the sudden outburst. Then I drove my fist, still aching from contact with the car bonnet, into the door of the fridge. Stupid. I picked up another glass, poured more orange and drank it down slowly as if this would somehow cancel out the first.

I had to get out of there.

What did other men do when they suddenly found themselves alone? Call their mates, play some sport, get pissed? I stared out at the lawn. The guy opposite, Andy Rudney, was struggling to fit a pair of roof bars to his people carrier. He saw me watching and waved. A windsurfer lay on the drive, waiting to be loaded. When we moved in he'd asked me if I was interested in joining a five-a-side team; I told him I had a knee injury.

Every interaction with the rest of the world involved some lie or another. Once it was clear that our time in the Scheme would be 'ongoing', as Stuart put it, we were sent for training. A florid-faced man with all the smarm of a chat-show host tried to make it sound like a game.

'Rule one. Less is best. Avoid eye contact. Smile though. We don't want to come over all shifty. Never make conversation unless you have to. Rule two, try not to attract unnecessary attention. Dress down, no outlandish make-up. Try to make yourselves as unmemorable as possible.' When he said this his eyes slid towards Sara. 'Though in some cases that could be a teensy bit of a challenge.' And then with a smirk at me he added, 'Make your own fun, as they used to say before television. Focus on some domestic pursuits. Hobbies are handy. Make the most of each other's company.' He winked. 'At least what you get up to in the bedroom is your business; just try not to wake the neighbours. Anyone you have to establish a rapport with, other mums, neighbours, anyone you can't keep at arm's length, notify us and we'll give them a quick vetting, just for safety's sake. Generally other chaps aren't a problem. But the ladies ...' He glanced at me with a weary face. 'And once their imaginations get going ...'

As he spoke, I'd felt the world around me start to mutate into something horribly familiar. This was like Afghanistan

– proceed with caution, on constant alert, everyone a potential threat.

'Each time you have to tell a little lie, keep a record – so you stick to your story as you build it up. After a while it'll be second nature; you won't even know you're doing it.' With a creepy wink at Sara, he'd added, 'Just like acting.'

Rudney wasn't getting anywhere with his bars. I opened the front door and went across to his drive.

He looked surprised. My usual interactions with him amounted to no more than a wave from the other side of the road. Suddenly I was on his territory. He gave me a warm smile as if to say, I knew you'd give in sooner or later.

I lifted one end, walked it round to the other side of the vehicle and slotted it into the roof. Inside the house a row was under way between his wife and one of their kids. He rolled his eyes. 'Cheers.'

He was shorter than me, compact but stocky, the kind of build that came from real training, not the gym. I knew he had an IT business but he looked ex-military, the sort of guy I would have been glad to know.

I repeated the action with the other bar, then helped him lift the windsurfer.

'Got shot of them?' He nodded at our house. 'Lucky bugger. What wouldn't I give for a bit of time out.'

I grinned and nodded. Was that what Sara and I really needed, a bit of time out?

'Only a couple of days – then I'll be joining them.'

'Somewhere hot?'

I nodded. *Don't say where.*

He opened his mouth for his follow-up question just as his wife appeared with a coffee. She was several years older than Sara, ample, with a put-upon, round-shouldered look. She stopped when she saw me and frowned. 'Well this is a pleasant surprise.' She straightened herself and jabbed at her hair with her free hand.

I smiled. *Always smile.*

She shook her head and nodded in the direction of the kids' voices. 'They're back on the bloody Wii. Tell you what, I've had it with that thing. One day I'm going to disappear and see how long it takes anyone to notice.'

I nodded, grabbed at a harmless response. 'I hear they're pretty compulsive.'

At times like this I felt like a newsreader, with a voice in my ear telling me what to say.

She rolled her eyes but continued to look surprised by my presence, so I went on. 'My two aren't quite there yet. Guess it won't be long.'

Mention of the twins softened her expression. 'Now *they* are *angels*. I see them going down the road with you, skipping along – if only mine could be like that.'

I shook my head. 'It's all Sara.'

She wagged a finger. 'Oh come on. *I've* seen you. I *know*.' She nodded for extra emphasis.

When in doubt, keep smiling. I braced myself for what was coming.

She shot her husband a venomous look. 'A father who makes that much time for his kids. Need I say more ...?'

Rudney was already shaking his head. The look on his face suggested he had heard this line before.

'Yeah well, I'm sure Paul's got better things to do with his Sunday than listen to your sermon.'

Paul. We'd never exchanged any first names, real or false. He smirked. 'If I was married to Sara I think I'd be in a lot ...'

She swatted his cheek before he could finish, then frowned at me. 'You should look after that young lady, she's been looking very tired lately. Is she all right?'

I nodded, mechanically. 'She's just a bit tired.' *Time to pull out,* said a voice in my head.

'If she ever needs a hand, I'm always here, tell her.'

I gave her a big warm smile, one I'd been made to practise on the training, and patted my hips.

'Sure you won't have a coffee?'

'Thanks, but I've got to be somewhere.'

In the sky, a clear and dazzling blue, a plane was climbing over the Channel curving away towards the Atlantic.

'Thanks for the help.' He stroked the windsurfer. 'Ever done this?'

'Not me,' I lied.

He opened his mouth – maybe he was about to extend another invitation, but I gave him a wave and headed back up our drive.

I'd got to be somewhere.

I picked up my running kit, locked the house, got in the Range Rover, changed the CD, opened the roof, put on my sunglasses and pretended to be on holiday.

I headed down to the sea. Even though Sara had never spoken to her, nor to my knowledge even crossed to her side of the street, the Rudney woman had seen the change in her. What else had they noticed? That she'd stopped looking me in the eye when we spoke, that she never smiled or laughed when I tried to humour her? If they had been able to peer across from their upstairs into our bedroom they could have seen that not only had we not had sex for months, we barely touched – the bed that had once been our private island now like a partitioned state.

I pulled into a space just east of the pier, where a kink in the coast line had been shored up with a pile of grey rocks. A universally ignored sign leaned drunkenly. *Danger. Keep off.* The tide was right out, leaving the great stretch of wet sand where I regularly took the twins to explore the pools that formed round the sea defences, and make dams with the water draining off the pebbles. I changed in the car, then started walking across the rocks where I sometimes allowed the kids an illicit climb – determined not to be cowed by their absence, refusing to admit how crippling it felt.

When Sara told me she was pregnant, I never showed her my fear. She needed to know that it would be fine, that whatever happened I wanted her for ever, that she could count on my protection – for her, for them. The responsibility felt crushing, nothing like I'd ever known, but then I thought it would be OK, that having children, being a father, would reinforce the break with everything that had happened before. There was nothing I needed from the past. I embraced the future, and as Sara withdrew from me I sought refuge even more with the kids, playing the model Dad card, not for brownie points but for consolation. I read to them every night, whisked them to the beach regardless of the weather, or up to the Downs to have battles amongst the trees around the earth circles that a thousand years ago had been fortresses against invaders.

'Why's Mummy sad, Daddy?' Emma was the first to pick up on the change in her mother. I'd told her Mummy needed a rest and would feel better soon. Emma wasn't convinced. *Don't patronise me, Dad. I may only be four but I know when you're shitting me,* her look seemed to say. Charlie had his own interpretation: 'Mummy's just cross with the world.'

'Why do you say that?' I asked him.

'Because she is.'

Nevertheless, it didn't seem to get in the way of their capacity for fun, and I absorbed as much as I could get of them, like a heavy user. I knew them so well, could guess their moods and anticipate their wants. I knew that they'd be sitting on that aeroplane, wondering when they were going to see me.

I broke into a jog and pounded the splashy ridges of sand along the edge of the water. The sun was still quite low in the east and I ran towards it feeling the warmth on my face despite the March chill.

Usually a run improved my spirits but it wasn't working today. I slowed at the second pile of rocks just below the Half Brick pub and turned back. And then, as I faced my shadow, came the realisation that had been chasing me, that I'd been refusing to acknowledge: I knew the children much better than I knew Sara.

The 'Life Audit' was part of the Scheme training: an intensive two-hour one-to-one interrogation about my past by a small bald man with the thick neck of a rugby prop and hands to match, who, after a breathless introduction, dispatched his questions in rapid bursts.

'Friends, family, acquaintances, enemies, any unfinished business that might cause someone to come after you. Don't be backwards coming forwards. We'll need it all one way or the other.'

I'd wondered what 'the other' way was and imagined his hands round my neck wringing out the last detail. I laid it all out for him. When I'd finished I thought how little life I'd actually lived.

'Keep a lot close to your chest, don't you?'

I shrugged.

'Maybe just as well.'

He wrote something in a file and closed it, then opened another. 'Need to visit your mum's grave?' he'd asked, casually, as if he was offering to open the window.

'She was cremated.'

'Father?'

'Died in the Falklands. Never knew him.'

41

It was all in the file, but he asked anyway, keeping his eyes on me all the time, watching the spaces between my words.

'Mum have any boyfriends? Bosom buddies? Just because you don't have any family doesn't meant there isn't someone significant.'

We spent some time on Greg. 'Someone you might want to seek out at some point?'

'I wouldn't call him that.'

'He would.'

'Maybe.'

He glanced down at a page of close type. 'Seems as though you were inseparable.'

'It looked like that.'

'But it wasn't?'

'Well we're separate now.'

He put his head on one side.

'Bit of a liability, would you say?'

I shrugged.

'You covered for him in Afghanistan.'

I didn't respond.

'Very loyal to him aren't you? Any unfinished business there?'

'Not for me.'

He gave me a thin smile and I gave him one back.

'Anything else you want to say? It's all for your own protection, remember. What we don't know about we can't help with.'

'Renouncing the past and all my earthly possessions, it feels like I'm joining a cult.'

He raised his eyebrows and looked at the ceiling, digesting the thought, then he nodded and replied without any trace of irony. 'Actually that's not a bad way of looking at it.'

They put Sara through the same process. I wasn't allowed

to be with her. When she came out she was white; it was the first time I had seen her rattled by the requirements of the Scheme. I was furious. Stuart was full of apologies. 'They're very anal about detail. I promise you only have to go through it once.'

Earlier, just before the wedding, when she said she wanted it to be only us, I had asked her about her family. Her face went blank. All I knew was her mother was dead and there was an older sister she'd not kept up with. Nothing about the father. I could tell by the tone of her answers that it was a no-go area. There had been plenty like her in the Army, fugitives from unhappy situations. With my parents long gone, and no brothers or sisters, there was no one for me to miss either. But I wanted her to know that it was safe to talk, when she was ready.

She drew me in, laid her head on my chest. 'Give me time, OK? After all, we've got our whole life together.' Then for punctuation, as if to close the thought, she looked up and kissed me. 'And we don't want to run out of things to say.'

I climbed up the beach near where I had parked. A café at the top had just opened. A woman in a ski jacket was putting out chairs. She looked up and smiled. 'Summer's coming.' Then she laughed and looked round. 'Where's those darlings today?'

'On their way to somewhere warmer.'

She looked put out. 'Oh, so Worthing not good enough for them any more.'

'A break for their mum.'

'Well don't get in any trouble while they're away.'

I ordered a black coffee and a glass of water, turned a chair to face the sun, and sat down. She put a coffee in front of me. 'You want a paper?'

A *Mail on Sunday*. I hesitated, then I unfolded it,

knowing it was the anniversary, knowing there would be something. Under a grainy portrait was the headline: WAHEED: TIME TO COME CLEAN. *'New broom'* *Met chief orders reinvestigation.*

Below was a picture of the new commissioner. *Henshaw: Call for transparency.* Further down was a smaller headline. *Witnesses to be reinterviewed.*

It was pretty much the same line every time. Nothing changing, the police trying to sound like they were still on the case. No end in sight.

I felt the 'ifs' raining down on me like hostile fire. *If* I'd stayed in bed. *If* I hadn't got out of the van. *If* I hadn't revived the gunman.

I folded the paper. I needed some other distraction. Now.

Greg's number wafted through my head, stuck there like the jingle from an ad. I took out my phone again, debated whether to call. Someone in a listening station somewhere kept a log of all our calls. 'Just a formality,' we'd been told. This wasn't the day for breaking any Scheme rules. I didn't want anything to get in the way of my passport or ticket.

I finished my coffee. There was a call box near the pier.

It wasn't that I missed him, but the habit of looking out for him had got ingrained. When my mum let him stay with us, I'd been a bit pissed off. But I could see the difference she made.

I thought of him more often than I expected to. As the last known witness to my previous life, the one before the Army, he still counted. And he'd never had anyone like my mum, who was attracted to creatures that were a bit damaged and needed fussing over.

A few months ago, right around the time Sara started to change, he showed up – the first and only time we had a 'breach', in Scheme jargon, when someone from our old life stepped through the invisible curtain around us.

I'd heard Sara calling the kids inside and for me to come downstairs 'Now, please.' I looked out of the window and saw a Subaru Impreza with a big wing on the back.

Greg was leaning against it, arms folded, gazing up at the house and shaking his head. I went down to greet him. He made a gun with his finger and pointed it at the house. 'Landed on your feet.'

I nodded at the car. 'You too.'

He patted the bonnet. 'Zero to pussy in three point eight.'

He was thinner and fitter-looking than he'd ever been in the Army. The beard had gone, his leather jacket gleamed and creaked, a flash watch was on his wrist. He looked like the 'after' from a TV makeover show.

He nodded at the passenger seat. A woman in a leather skirt grinned and waggled long-nailed fingers at me. She was rocking slightly to whatever was playing on her iPod. 'It's all right. She doesn't even know *my* real name. GFE.'

'What?'

'"Girlfriend experience." Escort – the ones that don't just fuck – though she'd happily do that all day.' He wagged a finger at her as he might a pet. 'Stay.'

We sat in the garden. His eyes swivelled up to the house every few seconds. He was waiting for Sara to show.

'Thought I should check up on you, see you're not going off the rails.'

'How did you find me?'

He smirked. 'Last time the Waheed cops got me in, the driver had a list of addresses – all the witnesses and where they had to be collected from. As they say, I eliminated the others from my inquiries. Paul Mandler ...' He shook his head. 'The names they come up with.'

He lit up and tapped his lighter on the patio table. 'Thought you'd have got a message to me.'

'Verboten. Scheme rules.'

'There must be exceptions.'

There were, but he didn't know that.

He gestured at his clothes and jangled his watch. 'Bet you didn't expect to see me like this?'

'You've done well. Good for you.'

He glanced at the house and sniffed. 'And you?'

'What?'

'All right?'

'It gets easier,' I lied.

'You look tired.' A line my mother had been fond of.

I shrugged. 'Kids – you know.'

He had gone part-time with Trent. 'Freelance opportunities,' he said, with a wink. 'Cut out the middleman.' He leaned over to me. 'Maybe when all this is over we could go into partnership.'

I smiled. 'When or if?'

He dropped his voice.

'Trent says they're going to wind up Waheed.'

'What does he know?'

'He hears stuff.'

'It's not going away like they hoped. As long as they can say it's "ongoing" they can hide behind that.'

'You were always the optimist.'

'I defected.'

Sara appeared at the French windows. I nodded and she came towards us, wary.

'*Wow*,' Greg said under his breath.

I introduced them. Sara asked if we needed anything.

'We're fine,' I said, before Greg could make a request.

'Good score.' He gave me a heavy wink as he watched her step back into the house.

He showed me a picture of his project, a dilapidated farmhouse. As long as I had known him he'd fantasised about living on a farm. It was less than twenty miles away.

46

'Very nice. What you always wanted.' He'd never had anything you could call a home.

After he had gone I'd found a mobile number scribbled on his empty fag packet next to the words *In case of emergency.*

The first call box was trashed. I walked into town and found another. A selection of postcards offered ludicrously inflated women with Barbie faces.

I picked up the receiver, put in a pound and dialled, listened to it ring.

No answer.

There was no one else, so I dialled Ross.

'You in?'

There were several wheezy breaths before he answered.

'Where else?'

'Sounds like you should be in bed.'

He covered the mouthpiece and coughed. 'Not gone then?'

'Change of plan.'

There was a knowing silence at the other end. He'd always doubted that the trip would happen.

Three

Ross was sitting in the stripped-out interior of a late-fifties Citroën DS, stirring the wand-like gear lever that stuck vertically out of the steering column. He let out a low groan that finished in a cough. 'Prick in a bucket.'

I got in beside him, leaned under the steering column, found the small toggle beneath the dash and shifted it into the lock position. The lever sprang to attention. 'Immobiliser, 1950s-style.'

'Fucking French, taking the piss. Any more crap from this, it's going in the crusher. End of.'

'This one was built by Brits. In Slough.'

'Spineless fucking collaborators.'

'In 1959?'

'Whatever.'

For each nationality of vehicle he had his own customised contempt. German engineering was 'fascist shite', anything Italian was 'mafia crap', Japanese: he mimed a Samurai swordsman beheading all comers; and for British cars he reserved a forlorn silence climaxing in a slow motion shake of the head. But his real loathing was reserved for anything American. The hatred burned deep. Ross was a Northern Irish Protestant who regarded US bankrolling of the IRA as instrumental in prolonging the conflict that had put him in the Scheme.

He coughed hard and long into his fist. 'OK, Maigret, so how do I start the fucker?'

'Watch and learn.' I leaned over and turned the key. The lights on the dash glowed foggily. 'Switch on and just push the stick to the left. First is towards you, second away, third and fourth off to the right.' I moved the lever left. The starter caught and whirred, then faded.

'Very clever.' He let out a few hen-like clucks, which was the closest he got to a laugh. 'Tea break.'

He lifted himself out of the car. On the stairs up to the office he paused and coughed heavily.

'You seen the doc about that yet?'

He ignored the question and heaved himself forward.

Ross came with another concession I'd wrung out of Stuart. Something I learned in the Army: no matter how well you get on, there are limits to how much time you can spend in the same company. However devoted I was to Sara and the children, I needed somewhere else to be and something to do with my life.

Stuart's solution was another seized asset, an old boat-builder's premises by Shoreham Docks. Inside, several once-glamorous cars squatted on flat tyres on a puddled floor. The previous owner, a former property developer turned fraudster, had stashed his collection here. The damp salt air had not been kind to them.

Ross was part of the deal. His creased face had only one setting: gloom.

'Give him time,' Stuart advised. 'He's been on the Scheme a while.' For the first few weeks, I kept my distance while Ross kept his head under a bonnet. I unloaded the least ravaged car at an auction and used the proceeds to get spares and materials for the rest. He acknowledged this initiative with an almost imperceptible nod. The arrangement was all right with him. The less he had to deal with people the better. I became another shield from the rest of the world, while the new role offered me some new human contact.

Eventually the ice around him melted. I warmed him up with tales of my teenage joyriding and he told me about lethal illicit bike races round country roads in Ulster. We weren't supposed to discuss the Scheme or why we were there.

'Since it's Sunday – what about a bag each?'

He was hunched over a pair of mugs, moving the teabag from one to the other.

'When I was a lad, one of these had to last a week.'

'When you were a lad the tea bag hadn't been invented.'

He brought the bag to the surface, pressed it against the side of the mug with the back of a spoon. Dark dense liquid oozed from it.

'Waste not, want not.'

I liked the view from the office. I imagined a steely-eyed boat-builder's clerk with a green eyeshade monitoring progress from up here. Once we'd fixed the roof, cleaned and tidied the space and started on the cars, it looked like a going concern. It wasn't what I'd envisaged doing with my life but it filled a void.

He stirred his tea, his eyes occasionally swivelling my way. He wasn't expecting me today.

'I lost my passport.'

'Right.' He carried on stirring.

Like an archaeologist collecting shards of pottery from a ploughed field, I'd pieced together the rough outline of his past. In Belfast he had worked in an RUC police garage, maintaining their fleet. He had married a Catholic and through a relative heard about an IRA plan to blow up police cars. He thought he'd done the right thing when he told his foreman. Several people went to jail. But word got out that Ross was the source. He was a marked man, in the Scheme for life.

'All in the past,' he'd said with a shrug, a man whose pain was scored into every fold and wrinkle of his face.

He turned away, coughed, and wiped his chin discreetly. But I saw blood on the tissue.

'You're ill.'

'Bollocks.' He pushed a folded copy of the *Mail* towards me. 'Your trip cos of this?'

I left it where it was, the peaked cap in the photo of the new commissioner just visible.

He snorted. '"New broom". In the end it all goes back under the carpet. Take my word for it.'

He opened it and spread it out on the bench. A double-spread photo of the Lexus, a sheet over its wrecked cabin and a shot of a pro-Waheed demonstration in Birmingham.

'It's not going away, is it?' Pessimism was his default mode. He studied the pictures. 'Worried?'

'If it prolongs things.'

He squinted at the text. 'Ever told you what I want on my gravestone?'

'No.'

'"You can't be too paranoid."' His gaze moved back to the paper. He shook his head. '"Transparency."'

The word seemed to catch in his throat. He started to cough. He got up to turn to the sink, then sat down again, holding a fist to his chest, his face reddening.

'I'm calling the doc.'

I reached for the phone but his hand got there first. 'Leave it.'

I could feel the heat coming off him. I took out my mobile and dialled the doctors' line. The number went through automatically to whichever approved GP was on duty. One of the perks of our confinement was twenty-four-hour medical help. The Scheme didn't want us exposed to the NHS unsupervised.

Helen picked up. Her voice was breathy, as if she'd not been up long.

'Hey, aren't you supposed to be—'

I cut her off. 'I'm bringing Ross, he's not good.'

'So what else is new?'

'You've got ten minutes to work on your bedside manner.'

I bundled Ross into the Range Rover and drove back along the seafront towards Worthing, the sun bouncing off the sea. Helen's surgery was opposite the beach in a sun-blasted building that had once been a guesthouse. She was unlocking just as we pulled up.

'So what happened ...?' She gestured with her chin at the sky.

'Don't ask.'

She was dressed for the gym, her hair pulled back in a ponytail.

'Sorry to spoil your Sunday.'

'You owe me.'

Ross was taking his time getting out of the car. She shook her head. 'I don't have a good feeling about this.'

She made him lie on her couch and opened his shirt.

'Been a while since a girl's done that.'

'Mm, what a surprise.'

She listened to his chest without expression, grey eyes darting as she listened. She had one of those workmanlike tans that come from spending a lot of time on boats; her dusty blonde hair had a weathered look, as if her natural home was the sea. She frowned. 'Christ almighty.'

'Is that a diagnosis?'

She nodded. 'What else can you say about fifty a day for five decades?'

'Six,' Ross croaked. 'I started early.'

'Yeah, in the womb.'

I wondered how this attitude went down with her female patients. I had never seen her with Sara. Despite this brusqueness, she had a soft spot for Ross. One day she had shown up at the wharf unannounced, inspected the cars and put a down payment on a pretty Lancia roadster we had just finished. I told her we didn't do private customers – all our cars went to auction. But she ignored me. 'Got to live before you die.'

She told Ross to cough. 'Any blood?'

'Nope.'

She glanced at me. I nodded and mouthed *oh yes*.

She looked at the thermometer and winced.

'Right, young man. A & E for you. '

I drove them to the hospital, where we put him into a wheel-chair and steered him straight past reception, Helen leading the way. I waited, watching a cross section of human life pass through the waiting area: a surfer with a huge gouge in his back from a propeller, a skinhead who had been bit-ten by his own Rottweiler, a tiny old lady with a black eye, carried in by a large policeman, cradling her as he might a baby. And a small unconscious girl, Emma's age, for whom everything stopped, her ashen parents hurrying behind the stretcher. I texted Sara again. *U there yet?* Then dialled her. No ring. No voicemail. *The Vodafone number you are calling may be switched off. Please try later.* I didn't even know if her phone worked overseas.

I closed my eyes, dozed and had a garbled dream in which I was telling Sara it was all going to end soon, then catching myself in a mirror, old like Ross. The shock woke me.

I took out Ross's *Mail*, which I'd stuffed into my coat and read the article again. Nine months ago it had looked like the story was going away. I was invited to a briefing from one of Stuart's 'masters', a man with shiny bags under his eyes who nodded a lot. 'We can envisage a point not too far down the line when we release you back into the wild,' he said. 'Not to get your hopes up too much but we could be talking less than a year,' But there had been no follow-up.

When I mentioned it to Stuart he put on his grim, bad-news-bearer smile and shook his head. 'Possibly they jumped the gun.'

The sky outside was turning pink by the time Helen re-appeared. She had her professional face on.

'He's been sedated to allow his lungs to relax. They've had to put a drain in so he's going to have to stay put for at least a night.'

'He won't like all the strangers.'

She sighed. 'He's got no choice.'

We went through double doors out into the sunlight.

'What are his chances?'

She blinked at the sun. 'You don't like to give up hope do you?'

'That's not an answer.'

She looked into my face. 'Honest?'

'Honest.'

'He's had enough. He wants out.' She sighed. 'What now?'

'How about a drink?' I heard myself say.

The light came back into her eyes. 'I'd thought you'd never ask.'

Four

I drove Helen to her flat, in a new block overlooking the
sea. The sun was horizontal, hovering above the waves,
bathing the buildings in a pink glow, and for a moment
the seafront looked almost exotic. She made me wait in the
car.

'It's a mess up there.'

I looked at my phone. No messages. I dialled Sara's
number again. ... *Please try later.*

Helen returned, transformed, in boots, jeans and a leather
jacket. She pointed at the Lancia.

'You drive.'

She unravelled a scarf, which she wrapped round her
hair, and started to unfasten the roof.

The Lancia was a delight. Nothing power-assisted, sharp
responsive controls, a tribute to Ross's care and attention.

She was watching me as I drove. 'How do you let your
hair down?'

I glanced at her, unable to think of an answer. 'I'm a
parent, remember.'

She frowned. 'Must be so wearing.' She shook her head
– or maybe it was a shudder. 'That feeling that you can
never totally relax and let go, that part of you is on duty,
twenty-four seven.'

'But you're a doctor, isn't that how it is for you?'

'It's different when they're not your own. You do what
you can. If it works, they live. If not ...' She grimaced. 'All
that business, nappies, being woken at three, picking up
socks ... Bet you leave all that to Sara.'

'Actually, I'm a model father.'

'That's what they all say.'

She hunched over to get some shelter while she lit a cigarette.

I had a whole speech ready about the unexpected joys of parenthood. To be able to make things all right for them, to be needed and adored that much, there was nothing better. Charlie and Emma made it all worthwhile. Not to mention the bready smell of their cheeks, their charm, their tears, their sense of fun, their innate capacity for wisdom about the world, despite their few years. They shone light into my darkest places and saved me from myself.

But she didn't need to hear all that. 'I do my bit,' I said, and left it at that.

She chose the Maison du Temps, a vast anonymous conference hotel the other side of the A27. 'A patient-free zone: some of them don't understand the concept of off-duty.'

'Like there's that many Scheme patients loose in Worthing?'

'I'm not exclusive to you lot. I help out at other surgeries, even do the odd shift on A & E. When all the Mummy and Daddy GPs are tucked up on Saturday night, I'm pumping stomachs and setting busted noses.'

The hotel smelled of saunas and coffee and could have been anywhere in the world. We settled in a curved booth in a corner of the bar.

I ordered a lager. She asked for a Virgin Mary.

'I feel like a traitor.'

She frowned. 'Why?'

'This is the first time since I got married that I've had a drink with another woman.'

'Don't worry, I won't jump you.' She clinked my glass. 'Wrong gender.' She gave me a wink. 'Now Sara ...'

'Oh please.'

She giggled wickedly. 'I thought you boys like the idea of two girlies ...'

The drinks arrived. She clinked my glass. 'Here's to liberation. Let yourself go.'

I glared at her.

'Oh come on – bit of space, a breather from the family bosom, some clear blue water ...'

My stomach tightened. Thousands of miles away now ...

She sighed. 'OK, OK, but you need to lighten up, get some serotonin flowing.'

She rolled her eyes at my blank look. 'When you're happy you release serotonin – it makes you happier, it's an upward spiral.'

'And without it?'

She drew a downward spiral in the air.

I sipped my drink. A couple in the next booth leaned across and kissed, cheeks hollowing as their mouths opened.

'See – the serotonin's practically spurting out over there.'

I looked into my drink. 'They said it would get easier, being on the Scheme.'

She shook her head. 'They actually believe that. And then they're dismayed when people freak out.'

'Does it happen much?'

She screwed up her eyes. 'Three or four a year. Last year a bloke strangled his three kids, topped the wife and jumped in front of a train. In his farewell letter he said he wanted them to be safe.'

'Jesus.'

'Most people complain. The ranters aren't the problem. They're pissed off; you're the first to hear about it. It's the quiet ones you have to look out for. Devoted loving father and husband, his notes said.' She shook her head. 'It's the loss of control, the powerlessness. That and all the free time, plus the worry about what might be coming round the corner.'

'Maybe it would be simpler if we all took our chances in the real world.'

She wagged a finger at me. 'Gosh, common sense? Can't have that. Oh no. Budgets have been allocated, targets set, processes set in motion, goals to be met. The state has a duty of care to all Scheme residents – don't you love the word *residents*? Its all laid out in thick ring binders for which entire forests have been felled. In fact the entire planet is a degree warmer so Scheme guidelines can be distributed to sit unopened on our shelves.'

'You're not a fan.'

'Don't get me started.'

'You're worse than Stuart.'

She frowned – mock indignant. 'What he puts up with … the man's a saint. Either that or a fool.'

'He deserves a proper job.'

'Don't we all.'

'Why do you people do it?'

'Same as what you joined up for – adventure, money, Queen and country.'

I took out my cigarettes. She pointed at the *No Smoking* sign.

'You really don't get out much, do you?'

I put them back.

'So why are you here?'

She frowned at the question. 'It's Sunday night, a girl can relax.'

'I mean why aren't you heading up a unit in some big London hospital?'

'What's wrong with Worthing?'

I gave her a look.

She sighed, looked into her drink, swallowed, looked away. 'I helped myself.'

'To what?'

'The whole pharmacy pretty much.'

'How did you get clean?'

She gazed into the gloom of the bar. 'Ten weeks' detox. Then NA three times a week.' She shivered. 'My crowd were all heavy users. Afterwards, it was like being a nun at an orgy. I had to move away.'

'Why did you ... indulge?'

'Why does anybody? Because they're either fucked up or bored.'

'Which were you?'

She gave me her bad-girl smirk. 'Both.'

Her gaze drifted off to the other side of the room. The couple in the other booth were snogging shamelessly. 'I keep a photograph, just a reminder. The police mugshot from when I was picked up. If ever I feel like relapsing I take it out.' She drained her glass, set it down on its coaster. 'On the bright side, there's the extra money for dealing with you lot, "Hazard Allowance", "Confidentiality Supplement"...' She snorted. 'Don't you love their euphemisms? Anyway it helps pay for my boat.'

Her eyes lit up briefly.

'How far do you go?'

She shrugged. 'Brighton Marina or down to the Solent. Never out of sight of land.' She stared off into the gloom again. 'One day ...'

The waiter drifted past. I ordered another round.

She sighed. 'Trouble is, we're all winged. Not just you lot. Me, Stuart. He ever said how he ended up looking after you?'

I shrugged.

She leaned closer, lowered her voice. 'Girl trouble, in Afghanistan, I heard.' She left a silence for me to fill, hoping for some details.

'He hasn't said.'

She raised an eyebrow. 'I thought maybe you had something on him – you know, getting the big house, holidays.'

'*A* holiday – one I don't seem to be on yet. Maybe it's because I keep my nose out of his business.'

She glared at me. 'You're good at all that.'

'What?'

'Not talking – not prying.'

'It's a bloke thing.'

'Or a Scheme thing.' She picked at her coaster. 'Who *do* you talk to? Sara?'

A warning light flashed somewhere in my head. 'Why?'

'Ross. He's dying and just now he was telling me he's worried about you.'

'He likes to worry, it occupies his mind.'

'He thinks you're heading for trouble. Before I left him. He said I should watch out for you. Should I?'

I shrugged. 'He doesn't have anyone else to worry about.'

'That's not an answer.'

I exhaled a long breath. 'It helps when there's light at the end of the tunnel. Trouble is they keep extending the tunnel.'

'You've been good for him. Before you showed up they were going to put him on suicide watch.'

'I prefer it when people stay alive.'

She leaned a fraction closer. 'I've seen your psych file. You saw more than your share didn't you, soldier.'

I let her words hang there while I took another sip. I was beginning to regret this drink. 'There was a war on.'

'Ever talk to anyone – download a bit?'

I felt my shoulders stiffen. 'Nothing to say.'

She groaned, 'Yeah, right. You turned down a medal.'

I put my glass down on the coaster. I wasn't going to be spooked by her. 'Killing a kid isn't the sort of thing you want to be decorated for.'

She put her a hand up. 'OK. Point taken.'

The snogging couple got up and left. The bar was empty now. I looked at her again. 'Where did you train?'

'Aldershot then Bosnia.'

My eyes widened. I should have guessed.

She grinned and nodded. 'Battle hardened, just like you. I've sewn back every body part you can imagine – and some you'd prefer not to. You just had to hope you were stitching them back onto the right patient.'

The waiter returned with our drinks.

She clinked her glass against mine. I still wasn't clear what her agenda was. She pressed on. 'Do you miss it?'

'What?'

'The action. Battle.'

There was something energising about her bluntness.

'When you've been in a fire fight, in the cold, in the dark, wet through, on an almost vertical rock face with no cover against an enemy with more bullets than you, eager for Paradise with all its virgins, and your mate's been blown into so many bits there's nothing to bring back. And when daylight comes and for reasons you don't understand you're still alive. And you've done the same five nights running – you feel like the fucking Terminator. And that's not a good thing if you've got any designs on a normal life. You feel very alive, not knowing if you'll be dead the next minute. Dangerous drug.'

She sighed. 'You're one of the lucky ones – with the gift.'

'What's that?'

'Maximum threat situations or real wipeouts send most of us mere mortals into shock. Those with the gift can shut everything down, give themselves extra focus. To be able to switch, just like that, it's very useful.' She glanced at me. 'Some people think it's a lack of imagination.'

'There may be something in that.'

'Did anything scare you?'

'They had bigger spiders out there.'

'Oh ha ha.' She laughed briefly then switched to serious again. 'What about those moments – decision time?' She drew a circle in the air in front of her face and crossed it. 'Seeing the target in the scope, so close you can see their blackheads, before you pull the trigger. Those faces haunt you?'

I had the answer ready. 'You're so far away, most of the time they don't even know you're there. They're gone before they know it.'

'And when they do see you?' Her eyes flashed at me again.

I didn't answer that one.

She shook her head. 'You snipers are such cold-hearted fuckers.'

'You don't let up, do you?'

She shrugged, slapped her hands down on her thighs. 'Let's go for a smoke.'

We sat on a patio bench among some freshly planted saplings. The brand new hotel, fringed with lights, and a high fence, looked as if it had just been unpacked and assembled from a kit. A breeze from the south made the air salty, which mingled with her scent. The chill made her eyes moisten. An emergency vehicle, sirens blaring, went past on the main road.

I gave her one of my cigarettes and lit it. She took a big lungful and let it out slowly. 'In Afghanistan, what really happened with the boy?'

I looked at her. We'd inhabited the same world. She had seen it all. 'It was him or Greg. I had about a tenth of a second to decide.'

She raised an eyebrow. 'There's a suggestion in the report that you covered up for your mate.'

Another set of sirens blotted out all sound for a few seconds. I didn't answer.

'Your vehicle hit an IED. You and your pal Greg, you two were on the back – got blown off. Everyone else, killed. The radio was shot. You went up the ridge to get a signal on your phone. Greg went walkabout, shocked or stoned, who knows? A few people came out from between some buildings. A boy with a gun, aiming at Greg. You looked round just in time.' She opened her eyes. 'But that's not the full story, is it?'

I didn't respond. I'd shut down.

'An appendix to the report contains an alternative scenario. Did you know that?'

She waited for me to react but I didn't. 'It suggests that the gun was Greg's. Your mate had left it, and the lad picked it up.'

'So?'

'Greg would have been in very big trouble for leaving his weapon, is what.'

She took a long drag on her cigarette. I hoped that was the end of it, but it wasn't. 'Must have taken some bottle.'

I didn't answer.

'The kid saw you.'

I felt the air in my lungs chill. 'Is that a question or a statement?'

'Which would you prefer?'

I looked blankly at her.

'Most snipers I've debriefed rely on the idea that their victims don't have time to react. They never see what's coming. One second the target's picking his nose, the next ...' She snapped her fingers. 'The tricky bit's if they see you, when they realise you're locked on and their last second is looking at you.' She aimed a finger at me and pulled an imaginary trigger.

This had gone way further than I'd imagined. I turned

away, studied the end of my cigarette, watched the paper flare and fall away round the embers.

'How old was he?'

'Maybe twelve.'

'Plucky little thing – grabbing the gun. Daring.'

I shrugged. 'They're a fearless lot.'

'But you had no choice.'

I took a long drag on the cigarette, watched the furnace flare. I felt a stab of rage but I wasn't going to show it. Again, I didn't answer. She moved so she was in my eyeline. Her voice much softer. 'Sara would surely understand.'

'Why burden her? It's not part of our life.'

'But it's a big part of yours. Maybe her burden is *not* knowing what happened to you.'

'What's this about?'

She gave me a weary look. 'I think you know.'

A bleeper went off in her bag. She ignored it. 'You know what happens when you don't talk about stuff? My grandad survived Dunkirk – just. My mum thought it was completely normal for Daddies to howl in their sleep like trapped dogs – every night.' She leaned closer. 'You get scary. That's what happens. You don't talk about what you can see in your head every day; it starts to come out some other way. And your loved ones get the brunt of it. In my case it was the booze and the smack. Others get violent.'

I stiffened. 'You trying to send me a message?'

She reached into her bag, took out her phone, examined a text and sighed. 'Just when this was getting interesting. You mind making your own way back?' She held out her hand.

I didn't move. 'Is this what tonight's been all about?'

She pecked me on the cheek. 'Ignore me. I'm just a nosey old dyke with not enough to do. Thanks for the drink.' And she went towards her car.

*

64

I walked back through the town, my head pulsing with two lagers and too many thoughts. I found my car and unlocked it. The interior lights went on, but then I turned and walked towards the beach. The tide was up but there was no wind. I walked down to the water's edge. Apart from a thin fringe of froth where little waves broke against the shingle, the sea was a vast expanse of oily blackness.

I'd packed Afghanistan away along with all the other stuff from my previous life that was no longer required. But Helen had unlocked it and there it all was, in sharp focus, as if projected onto the blank blackness of the sea. Until the incident with the boy, it was everything I'd wanted. The excitement, the challenge, the danger, a sense of purpose I'd never known before. It was life in high definition. We didn't question what we were doing. We kept solid, for ourselves and for each other. I knew I was finding it easier than the others. The extremes – the cold in winter, the stifling heat of the summer, the hard terrain, the crap food, the unpredictable relentless enemy – 'You get off on it, don't you?' That was Greg's assessment. He was right.

But after the kid, it all changed. I kept going but the spark was gone. I needed to get out.

Sara had never questioned me about it. She had accepted what little I told her about the Army, never probed me, not even a single question. For her, it was part of the past. 'BU', she called it: 'Before Us'.

I took out my phone. Still no message. Was this some kind of punishment for making her go without me? More than twelve hours had passed since we'd said goodbye at Gatwick, the longest time we'd ever been apart.

I went back to the car and headed home, music on loud to drown out my thoughts. Our road was quiet. Everyone tucked up. I pulled up on to the drive, sat for a moment looking at the empty house in the dull orange glow of the streetlights. Our first night apart.

A light in the kitchen was flickering. The TV was still on. I was in no mood to go to bed. I went inside and put on some coffee. For something to do I started clearing up the remains of the children's breakfast. Chunks of cereal were fused to the bowls. I left them to soak while I swept a hot sponge over the worktops.

My phone buzzed in my pocket. Sara at last?

Not Sara. Helen. I thought about letting it go to voice-mail. Just before it did I pressed Accept.

Her voice was small, all the brisk confidence gone from it. 'I don't know how to say this.'

'You're forgiven. I'm sure you meant well.'

There was a pause. 'You better put on the news.'

I turned and faced the TV. A wide shot of a police launch bobbing on a bright sea. The shot changed to close-ups of a taxiing airliner. At the bottom of the frame were white letters on a red strip: *Missing jet search*. On the tail plane, in orange on red, was the logo – Sunkiss.

Five

Taped to the Gatwick Departures information desk was a hastily scrawled sign in dayglo magic marker, *Sunkiss: Enquiries This Way*. It reminded me of signs put up for children's parties. Another arrow pointed to a set of double doors. Beside them stood a woman with a fixed expression of concern and a couple of heavies.

'Sir, would you mind giving me the name or names, as well as yours?'

I looked at her.

'Who are you here for?'

She wrote them down.

'You should have a list.'

She nodded. 'I know, sir; I do apologise. It's on its way. Would you mind stepping to the side a sec?' One of the heavies came forward with a security wand. 'Airport policy, I'm afraid, sir.'

She looked into my eyes briefly, as if she wanted to say something more but didn't have the words.

There weren't any.

At the end of a long grey corridor was another set of double doors. Behind them I could hear a hubbub of voices interspersed with forlorn wails. I took a breath and pushed open the door.

It was a vast windowless room. There must have been two hundred people, in huddles or alone, clutching themselves, or staring at nothing, frozen in shock. There were couples holding each other, groups clustered round officials, engaged in loud exchanges. Several nurses were on hand, one kneeling in front of a woman who was bent almost double, rocking. A litter of paper cups was building up on the carpet. The air was hot and smelled faintly of sick. I had never seen grief on this scale.

'This is fucking ri-*dic*-ulous,' a posh man's voice rose above the others.

I stood behind a crowd clustered round an official with the face of an undertaker. He made push-up movements in the air as if trying to separate himself from something. 'Soon as there's anything ...'

A tall fair-haired man suddenly let out a cry as his face crumpled up. A woman who could have been his daughter reached up and held his face.

I turned away and exchanged a look with an older man in an overcoat who was holding a notebook, too old to be Press. He shook his head. 'Load of bollocks.'

He sighed and jotted something down, then pulled out a BlackBerry. He met my gaze. 'They're keeping something back.'

'What makes you so sure?'

'For one thing, no one seems to have a passenger list. There's a whole set of procedures for this sort of thing, none of which are happening.'

'Like what?'

'Well, for one thing they should be arranging for us to go to the crash site – those that want to.'

His phone buzzed. 'Frankland.' He listened for a few seconds, nodding. 'And I'm telling you it's an obligation. Go back and tell them.' He rang off. 'Fucking shambles.' He then launched into a description of the procedures for major incidents. He was so matter of fact that at first I thought he was here in some sort of professional capacity, until he revealed that his daughter had been on the plane. His businesslike approach made me less self-conscious about my own blankness. I let him talk on. He claimed he knew all about 'multiple fatalities' and explained how there were whole manuals now on coping with the aftermath of disasters and managing mass bereavement. I was beginning to wonder if he was some kind of fanatic, when he thrust out his hand. 'Frankland. Detective Super – Retired.'

His eyes narrowed when I gave him mine. He studied me for a few seconds, checking his mental files for any Paul Mandlers he had fingered in his time.

Two other men, apparent strangers who had arrived a few minutes after me, were clasping each other's arms, crying openly. One of them was making an unattractive whinnying sound. Frankland rolled his eyes. He wasn't going to do that. Nor was I. We were comrades in the cause of restrained grief.

My mobile rang. Stuart. I turned away from Frankland and answered.

'I don't know any words ...' I could hear his rapid breathing.

'What *do* you know?'

'About the plane? No indications of foul play.'

'This isn't a fucking football match.'

Stuart swallowed. 'Look, I know what you're thinking. Don't jump to any conclusions. None of us are going there. It's confirmed there was no threat report, no alert. Try to keep it in perspective.'

'That doesn't make them any less dead.' A couple of people near me looked round as I spat out the words. I moved further away.

'Dan, don't do this.' He broke off; when he spoke again his voice was cracking. 'I just want to say—'

I cut him off. 'Save it.'

'Where are you?'

I told him.

'I'm sending someone.'

'I don't want anyone. I want a passport.'

There was a silence at the other end.

'You're getting me a replacement run up, remember?'

Another silence.

'I'm going out there.'

'Dan, that's out of the question.'

I lowered my voice. 'You want the truth about Waheed in tomorrow's papers? I've got nothing left to lose now. Make it happen.'

I rang off. Frankland was still there, watching.

Six

The sun had just slipped into the ocean. I watched it drop out of the sky until the last splinter of fire was doused by the sea. In an otherwise featureless sky, a pair of frowning, eyebrow-shaped clouds turned pink and for a few minutes the moisture in the air glistened, bathing the cruise ship in a ghostly glow. It may have been beautiful. I couldn't tell. The deck was almost deserted. The other mourners had retreated either to their beds or the bar. Just one figure towards the stern: a woman at the handrail, watching the same sunset from her own space. She lifted her hand to sweep back a strand of hair. I couldn't see her features. She was just a silhouette. For a fraction of a second I thought – no.

Sara was gone.

I looked away.

They'd put us on the BA flight to Barbados. Sunkiss must have assumed we wouldn't travel on one of their own fleet. Now we were en route to the crash site in a cruise ship. A painfully slow twenty-four-hour sailing. I'd hardly spoken a word to the other mourners. It wasn't difficult. Most of them observed a respectful distance. One or two had bonded, comforting each other as their sorrow boiled over. Maybe they would be the ones who would recover best.

In the afternoon I had a few Scotches and dozed briefly in the bar. When I woke, one of the counsellors was speaking softly at the next table:

'Losses at sea are particularly hard for the bereaved.

There's nothing to see. No aftermath, no one to bury. There's no tangible proof of what happened. Nothing may be recovered. No body to lay to rest.'

I went out on deck and stared at the water until all the reflections of the day had dissolved into an inky gloom, broken only by the wash from the ship. For a second I felt a spasm of vertigo as I imagined the distance between the surface and the seabed, a lightless landscape populated by whatever life survived there. The grey shape of a fuselage started to form in my head.

I blew a plume of smoke at where the sun had been and dropped the cigarette into the water, watched it disappear. I gripped the handrail, felt the rhythm of the engines.

Out of the gloom came a fragment of memory: a driver in Afghanistan, his wife, his children, his brothers all gone. I'd asked him what kept him going. He shook his head. 'I keep alive to keep their memories alive. If I died, who would there be to remember them?'

I couldn't even see their faces properly. Only flashes, fragments. A sound, a plastic spoon against a bowl, a giggle, the squeeze of a whole small hand around my forefinger, the screech of a felt tip across paper.

I had seen people alive one second, dead the next. I had touched bodies still warm, looking for life signs, and others stiff and cold; corpses without a mark, the life punched out of them by shock. Others in too many bits to clear up. But the sheer absurdity of the idea that Emma and Charlie could be anything other than alive ... Or Sara. This was all wrong: we'd agreed, we would be together for ever.

I looked away from the water. The woman near the stern was still there, now perched on the handrail. I turned away and started to make my way forward to where my cabin was, but after a few steps I stopped. Perhaps it was the parental antennae, still functioning, sweeping the area for all dangers. I turned. Her mouth was open but no sound I could hear was coming out.

And then I was running, arms outstretched like a sprinter at the tape. As I closed in on her I saw how tensed she was, her torso lifting with each rapid breath, preparing to spring. She slipped off the handrail just as I got there. I saw her head twist towards me and her astonished glare as my arms clamped around her. For a second I thought I would go over too as I struggled to keep my grip on her and the rail. I hauled her back and we fell on to the deck in an unseemly sprawl.

I gripped her wrist, in case she had another go. She took several breaths and tried to reach for the rail, then gave up and glared at me with the sort of affronted disgust I associated with being rebuffed after an unwelcome pass.

Her eyes were pale blue and furious. I helped her up, taking her other hand. It was completely cold. She flinched, as if my touch scorched her, and shook free of my grip. Still breathing hard, she steadied herself, adjusted her top and smoothed her skirt.

'It won't be how you think.'

She glared, then looked away.

'You'll be hoping it's quick; I promise you it'll be long and messy.'

She pushed a hand through her blonde hair. 'What?'

'Well the drop is just the beginning, unless you're lucky enough to get knocked out by the propellers. Don't underestimate your subconscious instinct for survival. It's more powerful than you can imagine. The adrenalin blocks your negative emotions so you'll lose touch with what drove you to jump. Your body will go onto autopilot and fight to keep you afloat whatever you try to tell it to do. The sea's quite warm, so no chance of hypothermia. Exhaustion won't set in for several hours. It's a long wait, unless the sharks get you. Trust me.'

'Why should I?'

'Jumpers who've survived usually say they regretted it the second they let go.'

I stepped back to give her some room, took out my cigarettes and shook two from the pack.

'I've given up,' she said, taking one.

Her fingers were shaking so much I had to steady the tip to light it. She inhaled deeply and lifted her face to where the sun had been. Her complexion was ghostly pale. She breathed out the smoke in a long sigh and braced herself against the handrail.

She looked at me full on and I saw what looked like a flash of pure fear, as if some terrible secret was trying to escape from her. Her gaze shifted to the gloom where the sea was. 'God I'm a mess.'

'Aren't we all?'

She took another long pull on her cigarette. I felt my pulse slowing.

'What's your name?'

'Jane Cochran.'

'Paul Mandler.'

She smiled briefly. 'Good name.'

'What do you mean?'

She became lost in the turmoil of her own thoughts, clutching herself as if there was a chill. Her eyes darted in every direction as if she was at a loss to know what to do next.

We stood a few feet apart. Everyone on the ship seemed to be at pains not to intrude on each other's private grief.

She looked down. 'I'm not very good at this.'

'Who is?'

'I'm afraid of myself.' She glanced out into the gloom where the sea was. Eventually she turned. 'I need a drink.' She started towards the stern, her fingers trailing along the handrail as if for balance. She had already had a few. She paused at a cabin door. 'I can't face the bar.'

74

She perched on the corner of her bed while I poured us each a large Scotch from a bottle she pulled out of her luggage. She smiled faintly, then frowned into her drink, took a sip and closed her eyes. A minute passed while she repeated this routine. The air conditioner stirred the moist air and the fittings in the cabin vibrated to the pulse of the engines. She lifted her face and swallowed as if preparing for a speech.

On the bedside table was a small silver picture frame. A man my age with a military haircut, a regimental pin in his lapel. Face full of focus and direction, comfortable with certainty, hard to imagine dead.

Eventually she spoke. 'We were separated. He was with someone else.'

She looked down and smoothed the sheet with her hands. My eyes settled on the plain bands on her ring finger. She saw me looking at them and folded her fingers into a fist. Little white dots appeared on her knuckles. 'I'm pathetic, I'm just so sorry for myself.'

'That's the shit of being left behind.'

She was suddenly vehement again. 'You won't under-stand, nobody understands.' Tears were coursing down her cheeks. They made a quiet 'pock pock' sound as they hit the sheets, like distant gunfire. She was taking deep breaths and for a moment I thought she was preparing to make a lunge for the door – and the water.

'They say talking is better than not.'

She shook her head. 'I wouldn't know where to begin.'

I tried to imagine her on a better day. She looked early thirties, smart, independent, used to attention but not cor-rupted by it. One of those faces that didn't need make-up. She ran the ring finger under her eyelashes and gathered up some loose strands of blonde hair. As she composed herself her features came into focus. Her eyes flitted towards me and away, like birds, unable to settle for long. She shivered despite the heat and folded her arms.

'Don't ask me any questions, OK? Let's just agree we don't have to go through that "who are you here for" shit.'

'Fine with me.'

I glanced at the window. Other than the glow of the deck lights it was black outside.

She picked at a nail. 'Aren't you angry?'

'I'm not there yet.'

'So where are you?'

I shrugged. 'Just numb.'

I didn't say that for the last five nights I'd had the same splinter of a dream: diving down to the fuselage, its nose speared into the seabed, climbing the seatbacks like a ladder, searching among the drifting bodies, believing they might be holding their last breath till I got there to release them. And then waking bolt upright, my lungs bursting, covered in sweat.

She sighed as if trying to exhale some tension. 'I'm so sorry for your loss.' The formality of her words jarred.

'They're all dead. Nothing can change that.'

Each time I said it, it sounded more convincing. Maybe that was the path to accepting it.

She snorted. 'You make it sound so simple.'

I didn't respond. Let the inappropriateness of her remark hang there. She pressed a fist into her forehead.

'Sorry, I'm a bit drunk.'

She swallowed some more Scotch, nodded at the ring on my left hand.

'Was she the love of your life?'

There was a trace of sarcasm in her question. Maybe it was the Scotch. I looked at her steadily and took a breath.

'I thought we weren't going there, but since you ask, yes.'

I felt a sudden urge to talk about Sara, to defend her honour.

'There was no one else?'

I gave her a look.

'Sorry. Inappropriate.' She shook her head and shuddered.

'She was the only one.'

She nodded, but with a slight frown, as if she hadn't heard anyone say such a thing before.

'Is that so strange?'

She shrugged. Maybe in her world it was. She wound a handkerchief round her fingers. 'But were you happy?'

There was a beat before I spoke, which in its own way was an answer.

'I was.'

'Ever lie to her?'

'No.'

'Did you trust her?'

I felt myself bristle.

'Howard said trust was the cornerstone of a marriage. If I couldn't trust him I didn't love him. After he left I discovered he'd had a whole other secret life.' She shook her head. 'So you trusted her – your wife.'

'I didn't have a reason not to. Why do you ask?'

Tears filled her eyes again. 'Because you can't trust anyone. Not really. Trust is just one of those lies you tell yourself.'

'My wife's dead.'

There was real terror in her eyes. Perhaps I'd glimpsed what had driven her so close to jumping. She shook her head. 'You can't trust the dead.'

She went on shaking her head, her eyes tight shut as if she was trying to banish a terrible thought.

'You should try and get some sleep.'

Her face was still but there was movement under the

surface as if tiny electrical charges were pulsing through her muscles, working to keep her composure. She stared at the window. There was no sound other than the whirr of the air conditioner. 'I don't know which is worse, knowing too little about someone – or too much.'

'Is there such a thing as too much?'

Grief is like a kind of madness; it possesses people and contorts their faces and their minds, suppressing rational thought. Her appearance, how she carried herself, her taut, toned body – she looked like someone who under other circumstances was good at managing herself.

Suddenly I wanted to be alone. I had no desire to have my feelings for Sara scrutinised by a stranger. But she looked like she was in no condition to be left. I wondered what sort of a man would leave a woman like her, though there was something disturbing, more than the grief – madness? Her eyes flashed with such intensity, as if she was battling some hostile force that had taken hold inside her.

I followed her gaze to the window. The moon was up, sliced in half by a sliver of cloud. She put a hand up to her neck and massaged it.

'You should have let me go.'

'I've had enough of people dying around me.'

She emptied most of the remaining Scotch into her tumbler and didn't bother with ice.

Her voice softened. 'Have you got anyone, I mean some-one to keep an eye out for you, a guardian angel?'

It was Stuart who floated into my thoughts. He would do what he could, like he always did. It was his job. Greg? He'd like to think he was. Ross – I didn't even know if he was still alive. I downed the rest of the Scotch and stared into the empty glass. 'I look after myself.'

She cried some more, holding my hand, then lay back on the pillows. I started to get up but she tightened her grip, her face full of fear again.

'Just a bit longer, I don't want to be alone.'

There was a pleading, desperate look in her eyes.

I sat back down on the edge of the bed. The Scotch bottle was empty. Just as well. I lit a cigarette and smoked, more for something to do than any pleasure. I let down the mosquito net and draped it around her. She was on her back, her face drawn and pale.

She felt under the net for my hand and pulled it gently so I was half lying, propped on an elbow. I manoeuvred myself into a position at a polite a distance as was possible on the small double bed and turned off the light.

Seven

'Don't die before me.'

I lowered whatever I was reading and looked at the face by the bed. Emma had already grasped the concept of mortality and all its ramifications.

'Promise, Daddy.'

She settled her chin on my arm. I could smell the soap from her bath. The low light from the reading lamp made her complexion glow. She moved her face so close to mine it was almost out of focus. 'I don't want to miss you.'

I put down the book and cupped her face in my hands. 'But if you died, I'd miss you.'

'But you're a grown-up.'

The cabin was ablaze with sunlight. As my eyes opened the shock of remembering shot through me like a jolt of current. How many more weeks or months would it take before that stopped?

Then the night before came back into focus. As my eyes adjusted to the glare I saw Jane's arm, covered with a forest of fine colourless down. Each hair cast its own miniature shadow from the horizontal sun, which illuminated the drifts and dips of her sleeping form. I could just make out the rhythm of her breathing above the steady beat of the big diesels down below.

I'd gone the whole night beside a woman I'd just met. As I moved off the bed she rolled over and stirred, slowly at first, the lids of her eyes lifting like blinds being furled. Then they snapped open so wide that her pupils floated in a sea of bloodshot white as if she had no recollection of why I was there. She shot upright. 'Jesus.'

She turned away and hid her face. I stood and busied myself with trying to brush the creases out of my clothes. The full force of the morning sun was overwhelming.

'I've made a dreadful fool of myself.' She glanced at me, then looked away again.

'It's allowed.'

'Whatever I said, just forget it.'

I gave a shrug. 'Consider it forgotten.'

'When do we get there?'

I looked at my watch. It was still on UK time. 'Couple of hours.'

I moved to the door. She looked up. Her eyes flitted over my face. That intense gaze again, a mind in turmoil. Something she couldn't articulate.

'I have to go.'

I stepped out into the sun and the blast of hot sea air. The blazing brightness of the day seemed so inappropriate. It was still early. The deck was deserted except for the bulky silhouette of Frankland, the retired cop, striding away towards the stern. I watched him until he disappeared down some stairs.

The covers of the bed in my cabin had been neatly turned down at the corner. It was hot and stale in there so I left the door open to let in the morning sea air. The framed photos I'd brought were set in front of the mirror. I moved them away so I wouldn't have to see myself as I looked at them.

One had been taken on the twins' last birthday. The two of them with Sara poised over a birthday cake. Eight candles. Four pink, four blue. Sara is smiling but I can detect the irritation in her eyes as I delay the proceedings for this picture. The children want to arrange themselves both with rosebud lips, ready to blow out the candles, but every time they try they start laughing. 'Cat's bottom!' Charlie shrieks pointing at his sister's pursed mouth. I'm laughing too. Sara just wants to get on with it. Her black hair is pulled tightly back from her face and there is something tired about the shadows round her eyes. 'Grow up,' she's saying to them.

Not the best picture, but the last.

The other one – just Sara, the morning after the wedding, barely awake, her mouth slightly parted, eyes shining.

There, in my hands, like a certificate. Confirmation, should anyone be in any doubt, of the feelings she once had for me.

I showered in the tiny bathroom. By the time I'd finished with the towel I was sweating again. The overhead fan stirred the damp air and a grille over the door exhaled gusts of moisture. I glanced at myself, ghostly in the condensation on the mirror, closed my eyes, tried to imagine Sara as she laid her hands on my shoulders, pressing herself against my back. *Talk to me.* But there was nothing except the low rumble of the engines and the slapping of the sea against the hull.

I shook out the creased suit, pulled on the trousers and a shirt and hung the jacket over my shoulder. I put on my sunglasses and stepped out onto the deck.

I wasn't hungry but I needed something in my stomach. The heat hammered down, but a steady breeze from the west tempered it. A middle-aged woman with a tight perm was being sick over the side. I touched her shoulder, which immediately tensed.

'Is there anything I can do?'

She didn't answer, looking straight through me, lost in grief. Her face was blotchy and peeling with eczema, a lump of tissue was balled in her fist. Her eyes refocused and she shook her head.

In the lounge, passengers either sat apart or in twos; several were clustered around a giant TV.

Some were twitching and fussing – engaged in mundane activities with their belongings to displace their grief. Others sat very still, semi-sedated on double doses of whatever had been prescribed for them. I saw the man I had sat beside on the plane, still reading the same copy of *Classic Car* that had occupied him all through the flight. He was sweating heavily under an ancient tweed sports jacket. He nodded at me and carried on reading through rimless half glasses. When I'd shown some interest he had talked to me in terrifying detail about his vintage MG. Maybe it was all he could find to distract himself.

Frankland sat alone, his BlackBerry clamped to one ear, his glasses perched on the end of his nose. Once he'd caught my eye, he beckoned me over. I lingered in front of him and took off my sunglasses. I wanted to be distracted. He gestured at the vacant chair next to him. I sat and listened to his end of the conversation. Whatever he was hearing wasn't pleasing him.

'No. No. *You* listen to *me*. First of all there are two boxes and neither of them are black. The cockpit voice recorder should have the last thirty seconds of communication and the FDR has the flight parameters. Flight Data Recorders, yes. It's all in your major incident manuals if you could be bothered to read them. The seabed is a thousand metres and the only people with the gear to go down that far are the US Navy ... Listen. *Listen!* ... No they won't do it for free. The airline's registered in Panama for fuck's sake. Someone has to contract them. I don't care about your public holidays. And I don't care about jurisdiction in international waters. There are British passengers down there and you need to get a handle on this.'

He clasped his forehead and shook his head. 'We've been flown halfway round the world and sailed another hundred miles to be at the crash site and you're still on your arses in Bridgetown. You should *want* to be on top of this. I'm not emotional, I'm fucking furious. There are a hundred and fifty people on this boat who all want to know— I know. I *know that*. The equipment *is* available. I've already checked. It's sitting on a dock in Florida and I've a good mind to hire it myself and send you the bill.'

He took the phone away from his ear and looked at it in disgust. 'He hung up.'

Frankland wasn't going to be deterred. He punched the green phone button to redial and unfurled a chart. His breakfast table had become a one-man incident room.

He was through again. '... No I won't apologise and I'll tell you what else. I'm calling every member of the Cabinet and every national newspaper editor ...' Maybe that did the trick. He listened for a while. 'No. *You* call *me* back. After the service.' He looked at his watch. 'Two hours. Yes. Thank you.' He snapped his phone shut.

'Dear, dear.' He folded his map and focused on me. 'Good night?'

I looked at him and shrugged. 'You?'

'Can't complain. I was on the phone most of it.'

He rubbed his chin.

'Are you getting anywhere?'

He puffed out his cheeks. 'There's a row going on about whose jurisdiction it is and who's going to pick up the tab, would you believe.' He shook his head. 'None of them give a shit about what's actually happened.'

At Gatwick, after several hours, we had been briefed: Barbados Air Traffic Control reported that the plane was a hundred miles off course when it hit the water. Sudden loss of cabin pressure was suspected, causing the crew and passengers to lose consciousness. There had been no mayday, no communication with the ground.

'Is there anything more?'

'A fault on the cockpit fuel gauge reported by the crew on the inbound flight two weeks ago. Nothing about whether

84

it was fixed. Other than that – just a lot of speculation.' He studied my face. 'What do *you* think?'

The worst, I wanted to say, but I just shrugged.

Frankland went on. 'This is what we've all got to live with now. Once upon a time we'd have said, "Why would anyone blow up a plane full of holiday makers?"' He sighed. 'Not any more. We're all combatants now. All fair game.'

Perhaps in his world all incidents, like all crimes, had to have culprits. He needed someone to hold to account for his daughter's death, whether it was an inexperienced mechanic, a careless pilot or a suicide bomber. And the steely energy he gave off suggested he wouldn't give up until he found one.

I looked at him. A hasty shave had left sprinklings of silver stubble on his chin and neck. His shirt looked like it wanted changing. At a distance he was an old man in need of a tidy, but up close his face was bright and alive, and his squat, square frame showed no sign of wilting. Retired or not, he was all cop, smelling blood. If I was going to find out the truth, he looked a better bet than Stuart and his people.

A steward appeared and poured me a coffee without asking. I took a sip. It felt like poison in my stomach. My mind drifted back to last night and right on cue, Jane came into the dining room. She had on a silver grey cotton suit over a thin muslin shirt. Her eyes were covered in big square sunglasses. Frankland watched her go by.

'Business kept you at home?'

'What?'

He looked down at the papers in front of him. 'Your family – you weren't with them.'

I told him about the passport. He listened in that non-reactive way policemen do while absorbing interesting information.

'Your lucky day.'

I gasped at the inappropriateness of the remark. His eyes roamed around as if he was lost in his own thoughts. 'Did it turn up?'

'I got another.'

He raised an eyebrow. 'Friends in high places.'

It felt like time to change the subject. 'Was your daughter with anyone?'

'Berk she'd fallen for at work. His parents are over there.'

He gestured at an elderly couple with identical dazed expressions and matching beige jackets.

'Were they … ?'

He closed his eyes and nodded.

'Honeymoon. Muggins was paying.'

'What about your wife?'

He shook his head. 'Long gone.'

'Any other kids?'

'No, just the one.'

He blew out a gust of breath, which ended in a cough. 'We had our ups and downs.' He glanced at me and sighed. 'You know how it is.' He took off his glasses and polished them. 'You were in the forces.'

'Is it that obvious?'

'Police and Army, worst offenders on the family front.'

'That's why I got out. I wanted a normal life.'

He nodded at nothing in particular. There was nothing normal about my life.

'You miss it – the job?'

He dismissed the question with a shrug.

There was a flurry of activity near the TV as the news ran the same picture package of Sunkiss tail planes and search craft.

'Pathetic really. Because there's still no passenger list, they can't give up hoping for a mistake, that their loved ones'll magically turn up at another airport like lost luggage.' He shook his head. 'Terrible thing, hope.'

'What's taking so long?'

'Authorities claim they've still not found all the next of kin.'

'That's possible, isn't it?'

'Should have done it by now, or at least issued a partial list. Usual problem, no one in charge.'

I looked back at the screen. A shot of Waheed appeared, followed by the talking head of a senior policeman in his peaked cap. After a few seconds it cut away to the familiar shot of the Lexus. The least of my cares now.

A silence settled over us. I gazed at the charts spread on the table. A thousand metres ...

A couple approached and asked him how he was getting on with his inquiries. Their faces were crumpled masks of grief.

'We're so grateful for your efforts.'

Frankland shrugged. He was enjoying his new status as self-appointed investigator – he'd found a role that kept him distracted from his own loss. I envied him that. The couple were about to sit down when he turned to me.

'Stroll?' He stood up and gestured at the deck, shuffled the charts and papers together and slotted them into a lumpy briefcase. The couple backed away.

Frankland strode forward, his hands thrust into his jacket pockets. Although he was sweating steadily, like an old colonial it didn't seem to bother him. The reflection from the sea and the white paint of the ship blasted us with light that blotted out everything else, a prison of glare.

'Until they find the black boxes, what else is there?'

'Well there's that lot.' He gestured at the lounge and rubbed his hands together as if relishing the prospect of a mass interrogation.

'Couple of years back, a Palestinian put his wife on a plane to Tel Aviv, sent her off with a bomb in her suitcase. *And* she was pregnant.'

I took out my cigarettes and offered him one. He looked dismayed, as if small gestures of generosity were unfamiliar to him. We smoked in silence for a minute, in the shade of the bridge.

'You think your perpetrator would make this journey?'

'Murderers are drawn to crime scenes.'

'How likely is that?'

He gave me a weary look, like a disappointed teacher. 'Likely doesn't come in to it. You want to know what happened? You have to look at all possibilities. Rule nothing out, no one above suspicion. You, for example – not getting on the plane.'

I didn't know whether to laugh or be angry. 'Why would I want to kill my family?'

'Most children are killed by one of their parents. Husbands are the commonest killers of wives.'

'If you believed this was down to me you wouldn't be telling me.'

He let out a short laugh. 'Don't bank on it. I've had a lifelong weakness for speaking my mind. Caused me all kinds of trouble.' He laughed again, then his face changed. 'You and your wife – you were getting on? No infidelity?'

'You haven't retired at all.'

He smirked. 'Can't help what comes naturally.'

'A man wanting to get rid of his wife and kids would destroy a planeload of people?'

His eyes darted about, his brain busy with ideas. 'An ex-soldier, struggling with life outside, stuff in his past, pressures at home ...'

This was a game I suddenly didn't feel like playing. I turned away but he gripped my elbow. 'This passport. How did you lose it?'

'I don't know.'

'Bit careless. Where did you last see it?'

'My wife had all the documents.'

'So it was down to her?'

'I can't say.'

'Was it with the others?'

'Of course.'

'But only yours disappeared.'

'This isn't going to get you anywhere.'

'Was she a careless person?'

I glared at him. 'Absolutely not.'

'You're very defensive of her.'

'She's dead, remember?'

He smiled grimly. I looked away.

The sea flashed like beaten metal. I recalled a detail from a TV programme about a woman whose parachute didn't open. *The speed she was going, the surface of the sea would have been as unyielding as steel.*

'What will you do if it turns out to be a mechanical fault? No one to blame?'

'There's always someone.' He shoved his hands into his jacket pockets. 'A plane crashed in Albuquerque because of a four millimetre crack in one turbine blade. It had showed up on a maintenance X-ray but the radiographer who examined it had had a row with her boyfriend that morning and left her contacts in his bathroom.' He let out a long breath. 'There's always someone.'

'How long will you give it?'

He looked out at the blazing sea. 'As long as it takes.'

I gestured at the lounge. 'And how do you check them all?'

He brandished his BlackBerry. 'Cyberspace. The final frontier. It's all there. Everybody's behaviour down to almost every minute of their lives. Every card transaction, where they ate, where they stayed, what they bought in

89

Sainsbury's, every phone call, every text, all their movements, hour by hour, street by street on CCTV.' His eyes were alight now, fired by an almost childish wonder. 'Every email, every search, every visit to every site. Without even clapping eyes on them you can know whether they're responsible, faithful, fanatical, philandering ...'

'How wonderful for you.'

He shook his head. 'Not without the manpower to process it all. That's the trouble with the surveillance society. We're drowning in data.'

'So what happens?'

'Look for the gaps.' He stood, legs slightly apart. I imagined him in an incident room, addressing his team. 'Find what's *not* there, what's *missing*.'

He tossed the butt of his cigarette into the water. 'Take you. Paul Mandler, householder, on the electoral roll, joint bank account with your wife, your own car, registered in your name, all paid for. You've got NI numbers, kids in a local nursery, you pay council tax and your other bills by direct debit, you've not racked up any debts.'

He paused while I digested this.

'What's missing so far? There are no debts, no late payments, not even a traffic violation.' He smirked. 'You've done a great job of living a blameless life. The trouble is we don't live in a blameless world.'

'So?'

He threw his hands out as if the answer was obvious. 'So look a bit further. What else is missing? This trip to Tobago – your first family trip abroad?'

'It's not easy travelling with small children.'

'No debit for it in your account. A processing delay? Or maybe it was a present, or you won it in a competition. Keep looking for gaps. Something else: your driver's licence. Only goes back four years. You don't look like someone who learned to drive late. Same with your NI number, and your bank account. As if Paul George Mandler fell to earth four years ago.'

There was a gleam in his eye as if he'd just reprised an old party trick. He pushed the sweat off his forehead with the back of a thumb.

A cormorant drifted above the ship, barely moving its wings. Another came near and together they peeled off, losing a hundred metres in a matter of seconds until they skimmed the surface of the water.

When I looked back his eyes were still scanning me, on full alert. For a moment I envied him, his head brimming with facts and details, no empty spaces.

'You done?'

He chuckled. 'Oh, I've hardly started.'

Eight

It was getting hotter by the minute. A huge white awning had been stretched over the deck. With the elaborate displays of tropical flowers and the string quintet, the occasion could have been mistaken for a wedding. On a raised platform were ministers and representatives from several different religions, even a Quaker. The chief executive of the airline, dressed in the Sunkiss livery perhaps to distinguish himself from the mourners, spoke first. He asked that we all, regardless of our beliefs, support each other through the service.

Several mourners stood with their wreaths, ready to send them overboard. Some carried soft toys with messages. There were a few children, a couple of whom had started a game further down one of the decks. The adults tried to keep them under control without success. I was grateful for this display of life going on until one of them called 'Daddy' in a voice so like Charlie's I moved away.

I had nothing to throw into the sea, though part of me wanted to be down there with them. In fact I would have paid to be in the craft that would go down to search for the black box. I'd only come on this trip for some sort of confirmation that the plane was there. Maybe only then, I told myself, would I start to believe they were gone.

The airline boss handed over to an English woman who seemed to have nominated herself chief mourner. I tuned out when I heard the phrase 'at rest'. I had held men as the life drained out of them, seen the shock on their faces as they realised their future was gone. Is that what Sara went through? Emma and Charlie?

The woman took her time, carefully enunciating her words as if for the hard of hearing. As this was going on a cellist sawed gently through some Brahms. I scanned the group from my vantage point at the back. I caught sight of Jane, behind her big black sunglasses, looking in my direction.

I turned away. I should have been thinking about Sara and the twins in the way I most wanted to remember them, but what kept replaying were the last minutes in the airport, her face tight with a mixture of fear and anger. Over the last months, she had become obsessive about the children's safety. She had given up the part-time job she had in a shop. She insisted on ferrying them to and from nursery herself, a task I had been happy to share. She had got rid of Karina, the nanny provided by the Scheme who the children adored.

We had been warned about 'Scheme blues' in the induction sessions. I hadn't confronted her. It wasn't what we did. Instead, I put all my hopes into the healing potential of the trip.

The man who had been reading the car magazine was still in his Harris tweed jacket, his face wet with perspiration. He was facing in the opposite direction from the rest of the group. I watched him move very slowly away to the side of the ship, a trancelike expression on his face. The cellist stopped and a man in uniform stepped forward with a trumpet. When I looked back, the Harris tweed man was craning over the rail. For a second I thought he was going to jump and started towards him, but then he stretched out an arm. I moved closer to see what he was pointing at. He let out a high-pitched wail that rose above the trumpet. Everyone looked round.

Bobbing in the water, about fifty metres from the ship was a half submerged row of airline seats. Around them were smaller items, which I couldn't make out at first. The trumpet died away and I felt the jostle of the other mourners gathering at the rail. A breeze was carrying the seats slowly towards us. A dark fish-shaped object floated nearer the ship – a surfboard still in its cover. When I looked at the seats again they were surrounded by a slick of small, brightly coloured shapes, items from exploded luggage.

'I've seen this sort of thing before.' Frankland was at my elbow, casting his professional eye over the water. 'Crash scenes. The whole road carpeted with belongings, far as the eye can see.'

Several people were crying. I put my arm round a tiny, birdlike elderly woman who pressed her hot damp face into my chest.

Something caught my eye, floating among the cases and items of clothing – Sara's pink Sleepeezee inflatable collar.

Nine

'Do not expect this to be a quick process,' said a counsellor who addressed a group at the stern of the ship. It was a few hours later, on our return journey. She was a large Asian woman swathed in an electric-blue sari, like an exotic butterfly. The colour alone projected some kind of hope.

'Do not blame yourself if you don't feel the things you think you should. People talk about getting over the loss of loved ones.' She gave the words 'getting over' extra emphasis. 'It's not like that. Not now, not tomorrow, but over time you will *grow into* the idea of their absence. You will come to celebrate the memory of them and cherish good moments, value the days they were alive. There's no easy way to this, no short cuts. Drugs and alcohol, I promise you, will not help in the long run.'

I watched the ocean, gripping the rail near the stern. The ship was headed back, its frothy wake stretching almost to the horizon, where we had left the flotilla of debris. A pair of seabirds, black against the hot sky, glided like outriders behind us. I watched them for a while. When I looked round, Jane was at my side. She took off her sunglasses and rested her wrists on the rail. 'You saw something – earlier. In the water.'

I nodded.

'I'm so sorry.'

'Maybe it helps, makes it more real.'

The breeze caught the lapel of my jacket. She smoothed it down. 'You were so kind to me last night. I was completely out of order. I owe you.'

I waved her apology away. Her face was calmer today, almost dreamy, and I saw properly now just how beautiful she was under all the grief. She leaned closer; the shoulder of her jacket brushed my arm. 'It's not how I am really.'

'There's no need to apologise. We're all struggling.'

Her eyes widened. I could feel her breath on my cheek. 'Please, if ever, if there's anything ...'

Her face was close to mine, closer than was natural for two people who had only just met. The intensity in her eyes was there again, but different. Not frantic now but still alarming. She was looking at me as if she had known me a long time, shared all my secrets. She put a hand on my chest, went up on tiptoes and kissed my cheek.

I heard familiar heavy footsteps approaching. Frankland coming to my rescue. She pressed a card into my hand.

'Ah, there you are.' Frankland's face glowed with energy as if the day had recharged his detective batteries. Would he ever grieve? Maybe never, as long as he had something to get to the bottom of.

I turned back to Jane to introduce him but she had walked away.

He looked in her direction. 'Did I break something up?'

I ignored the question.

'The deep-water search craft's on its way – finally.'

'Well done.'

'And the CAA and the NTSB are forming a joint task force.'

'Is that good?'

He opened his arms as if preparing to greet an old friend. 'Two agencies, competing teams jostling for position, withholding what they know from each other, trampling over crucial information, spinning and leaking and counter-leaking. Draw your own conclusions. Meanwhile ...' He glanced at me. 'There's a complete media blackout.'

'Where's that leave you?'

He grinned. 'Makes no difference.'

He glanced in the direction Jane had gone.

'Oh, I almost forgot; your passport's turned up. It's at Gatwick.'

Ten

At Barbados I left the queue for the flight home and bought a ticket for Tobago. I'd had enough of the group mourning experience. I wanted to be alone with my thoughts, unmolested by other people's grief, or Frankland's speculations. I wanted to finish the journey we had started, see the beach where we would have played.

The twin-engine Fokker skimmed the sea, now darkened by a threatening bank of cloud to the west, which blocked out the sun. I pulled down the blind, shut my eyes and tried to conjure up Sara. I replayed my favourite memory of her, waking up the morning after our wedding as I was trying to leave for the van and Waheed.

Shoot me.

Framing her in the viewfinder, seeing her mouth the words as I took the picture. *I love you.*

Remember this always, whatever happens.

I was trying.

But something was wrong. The image seemed fogged. I couldn't bring it into focus. Frankland had set me thinking and now another face was calling me to attention, one I hadn't thought about for some time.

'Forget about the guy on the bike.' That had been Stuart's advice. 'Pretend he was never there. Just a small lie to keep us all out of big trouble. It's in the national interest, just like when you were on tour in Afghanistan.'

I wasn't persuaded. But I was learning to live with lies. I

was telling lies every day to keep up appearances. That part had got easier.

'You're a natural.' Stuart had congratulated me as if I'd won a Scheme merit award. Part of his job, he said, was to 'keep me credible'.

'When the cops talk to you, be yourself. It's not as if we're asking you to do something out of character.'

I'd asked him what he meant.

'Well you're a man of few words, eh, soldier?'

The police had questioned me three times, the first when I was still in hospital. The young spiky-haired detective who smelled strongly of aftershave and kept his overcoat on was no challenge.

'Just do what you can,' he said, and made a few notes on a pad.

The second time was more detailed. An older, more senior, cop with a pretty young female detective who smiled a lot and wrote out everything I said in longhand on a big pad. Some CCTV footage had been found of the moments before the blast. They played it to me. The camera angle was from the end of the street where the Lexus had entered. It showed the car broadside in the road, the Transit door open. My head and shoulders were just visible above the roof of the Lexus. There was no bike or biker visible. The only place he seemed to exist was in my memory, the inert leather-clad body lying on the street, his eyes snapping open as I pumped the life back into him.

They played the footage a couple of times. 'Can you establish for us your presence at the scene?'

There was only one figure in shot.

'Just point, sir.'

I did.

'Thank you.'

I waited for the next question. There wasn't one.

Then I was taken to a vast hangar outside Croydon, big

enough to take a jumbo jet. Under a gantry of arc lights was a collection of vehicles, and in amongst them a team in white overalls studying laptops, taking pictures, talking into phones. It looked like a film set. Waheed, the movie. The Transit was there: the same registration, same ladder on top, the same plastic hubcaps scored and chewed from contact with kerbs. Its passenger door open just as I had left it. Even the KFC boxes were still wedged between the top of the dash and the windscreen. I hoped they'd emptied the toilet.

The Lexus had a sheet over the passenger area. A couple of men in overalls pulled it off. The roof had gone, leaving just the stumps of each door pillar, as if it had been pulled apart by a furious giant. The smell of burned plastics still lingered. The dashboard was almost completely melted away. Globules of charred plastic lay clumped in the footwells. The steering wheel, a crater in the centre where the airbag had been, was reduced to a thin ring of corroded metal. All that remained of the driver's seat was the mechanism of the armrest, the seatbelt anchorage points and bits of the seat frame.

I'd seen the aftermath of suicide bombings, knew how to read them. Damage, whether it's on paintwork, brickwork or human flesh, can be read like a map, the marks radiating out from the centre of the blast. The closer to the site of the detonation, the less remains intact. Scars in the paint on the Lexus bonnet indicated the trajectory of debris originating from the driver's position.

The nearside front was stoved in from the impact with the truck. Tiny fragments of glass still lay in the headlamp housing, along with pieces of orange plastic from the indicator. The front wheels were at exactly the same sharp angle they had been when the car had come to rest. But the dent in the offside door that had been recorded in the log was not there.

It was a similar car, very similar, but not the same car. Stuart had hovered in the shadows watching me as I examined it. Afterwards he grinned conspiratorially. 'They've done a lovely job, haven't they?'

'Why bother?' I asked.

'Shows how seriously we're taking it, if anyone wants to know. Also, if there's an inquest, we'll need our ducks in a row.' He clasped my shoulder and winked. 'Let's hope it doesn't come to that.'

In my head, it didn't go away. All through the first year in the Scheme, I replayed the images of the biker, the gun, Waheed's look, the shake of his head, the cupping motion he made with his hands.

When I quizzed Stuart for more details, he wafted my questions away. 'That's sixth floor stuff. All I know is that it was a big bloody embarrassment. No warning, no trail. And right in our own backyard. Our job's to contain it.' He gave me a warning look. 'We don't need to know any more.'

I started at the library. There was a computer at the house but it was linked to the Scheme's mainframe. I didn't want my searches monitored. I waded through the thousands of Google listings of news stories on Waheed. He was labelled an extremist, a zealot, a jihadi, a fanatic who wanted to turn the clock back to a time before oil and arms dealers. But there was nothing that confirmed any connection with a terror network, nothing that pointed to anyone who might want him dead. He had fought the Russians in Afghanistan like Bin Laden, but he had refused to condone 9/11. He made no attempt to disguise his opposition to the Saudi Royal Family, who had sent him into exile. But he posed no threat to them.

From a payphone, posing as a student, I pestered a *Guardian* journalist who had upset Waheed's supporters by rubbishing their assassination claim. He was weary of being challenged. 'Show me a viable culprit who'd go to the bother of mounting a hit in the middle of London. Until then – there's nothing more to say. Goodbye.'

I traced an academic, the author of a paper, 'Waheed al Amarir, the Conscience of Islam'. He recited a long list of opponents Waheed had acquired, but he agreed with the journalist. 'In my circles he's seen as pretty marginal, a harmless old theologian. It's only his death that's made him a celebrity.'

The next time I saw Stuart I grilled him. 'You must have some idea who. The Saudis?'

He shook his head rapidly, as if the idea made him shudder. 'Good God no. He was a thorn in their side, but he served a purpose as the acceptable face of opposition, a safety valve. If the finger of suspicion pointed at them all hell would break loose. And the last thing we or the Yanks want is them upset.'

'So who are the suspects?' I asked.

He gave me a desolate look. 'I'm not party to that. My job's to make sure you keep singing from the same sheet as everyone else.'

'Until ...?'

He put on his concerned face. 'Look, I know you're stuck in the middle of this for – well for the time being, but if it went public that he was killed on our patch, never mind who did it, the Saudis would be obliged to act.' He shuddered. 'Think of the consequences if they suspended cooperation on intelligence or started cancelling valuable contracts. Have you any idea of the impact of that on our economy?'

He slapped his thighs to signal he'd made his final point, but I wasn't finished.

'If I'm the only one who saw how he *really* died, why don't you shoot me and have done with it? Why go to all this trouble with the Scheme?'

He grimaced, then gripped my shoulder. 'Dan, you need to keep this in perspective. And don't forget, you're one of us after all.'

I stepped out of his grip. 'Answer the question.'

He went silent for a moment, shaking his head. 'Look, *I'd* be shot for saying this but ...' He leaned nearer and lowered his voice. 'If the other powers – the Yanks, the Saudis – if it turned out they *did* have some hand in it or knew more than they're telling us but aren't saying ... If it all went pear-shaped and fingers started getting pointed.' He gripped my shoulder again. 'Well, we've got a witness who *really* did see what happened ... we've got one over them. It'll help keep everyone in line. You're our great asset. You're *very* valuable.'

'What about the police? They buy into all this?'

He looked at me for a few seconds, while he chose his words. 'They don't have much choice.'

'For how long, though?'

He gave me a glazed look while he searched for a stock response. 'Remember, we're all part of the same family. Sometimes we have our differences, the odd spat, but basically we're family.' He could see I wasn't convinced. 'Dan, don't forget you're not alone. We've got three, maybe four hundred like you squirrelled away round the country. People who need protecting because of what they know, who've done stuff for us. That's how we do business these days. If we don't protect you how will we get anyone to cooperate in the future?'

He clamped his mouth so his lips disappeared, made an apologetic smile, and slapped my knee. 'What matters is you're all safe. You've got your lovely wife, beautiful kids – and a not entirely insalubrious residence.' He gave a short laugh. 'Who's going to look for you in Worthing for God's sake?'

I let it go, but I was still no nearer to knowing who killed

Waheed or why. Still the face of the assassin came back. We had looked into each other's eyes. He would remember every detail of my face, as I remembered his. I'd saved his life. Now I was paying the price.

The plane bucked sharply. I lifted the blind. Visibility was nil. *How had it been in the plane on their flight?* My stomach twisted as I imagined the children, sensing danger, looking up at their mother for an explanation. That's what they do at that age. Any trouble, check the parent's expression. What was on Sara's face? Suddenly I saw her clearly – at the airport the look of panic as I urged her towards the departure gate. How did they cope in those last seconds? I'd never know. I wasn't there. The sky lightened and suddenly we were out of the smoky cloud into dazzling sunlight.

The cab was a white Chevrolet Impala that must have been thirty years old. The driver, twice its age, slowed almost to a standstill over each bump in the road.

'She likes to take them slowly, the old lady,' he explained. His name was Gerald. He wore a spectacular shirt of surfing scenes and a straw trilby with a tiny brim.

I told him to drive me around.

'We have many fine hotels here, sir.'

'I'm not here for the fine hotels.'

We stopped at Pigeon Point, a beach. I took off my shoes. The sand was hot. I walked to the edge of the sea. It was pale blue. Two white kids were arguing with their parents over a huge inflatable dolphin. The mother, broiled red, had her fists pressed into her waist.

'You'll get carried out and you'll drown.'

I came back to the car.

'Everything all right, sir?'

'Why?'

He laughed. 'You look like you just saw a ghost.'

I got in the front beside him.

'How far is Starwood Bay?'

He shrugged. 'An hour.'

'Let's go.'

We drove up the windward side of the island. Big rollers crashed against the beaches. 'Good fishing off here.' He recited a long list of fish names I'd never heard before.

'Are you married, Gerald?'

'Widower.'

'Me too.' There. I'd said it.

'Mine's been gone thirty years. Not a week goes by I don't weep for her.' He shook his big head slowly, then glanced at me conspiratorially. 'But you're a young man.'

'Can we have some music?'

'You bet.'

He jabbed at the chrome push-button radio and it sprang into life, gentle reggae, anaesthetic for the ears.

I watched the sea flashing behind the wide drooping banana leaves, a hummingbird hovering over a flower, a group of lizards scattering into crevices of a wall. I'd promised Sara we'd come here one day. Now I was here, alone.

In the tourist office Gilda Benson peered at her computer screen. The fan by her desk wafted the plastic chain that hung from her glasses. All I had was a name: Sea View. 'It was recommended. I thought if I could take a look while I was here ...' She shook her head very slowly. I waited. It was a small place. I'd find it even if I had to go door to door.

She drew in a breath and let out a long sigh. 'Been a lot of cancellations, dear me.' She glanced at me over her glasses. 'You heard about the plane, Mr Carter?'

I'd given her my real name. I'd had it with Paul Mandler.

She tapped her screen with a top of a pink pen. 'Sea View. That was one. Mr and Mrs Mandler, rest their souls. Another couple in there now.'

It wasn't what I'd expected, a small cove between rocky outcrops, buffeted by the sea. I listened for a while to the rollers sucking the water away, rearing up and crashing it back down. Sea View clung to a rocky outcrop at one end. Some narrow steps with a flimsy handrail led up to it. A small white jeep stood on a gravel apron.

I tapped the edge of the screen. The door was open. A half-unpacked bag lay open. A woman in her early fifties came to the door. I apologised for the intrusion and said I was looking for somewhere to rent in a few weeks' time. She was German, walnut-tanned, wrapped in a batik sarong held together in a big knot between her breasts. Her husband's tiny trunks did nothing to conceal his ample grey pubic hair. They were delighted with their retreat.

'We are on an escape from the children. Last minute. We are so lucky there was a cancellation.'

Her husband chipped in. 'Our second honeymoon. Were you looking for something similar?'

The tiny balcony just had room for a table for two.

'Maybe.'

'Have a good look.' He gestured at the solitary bedroom. It was hard to imagine us all crammed into the space. This couldn't be it. I turned to go.

'Have a glass of champagne with us.'

The wife waved a glass in my direction. 'We'll toast the Mandlers.'

I looked at her.

She gestured at a half-case of bottles and dropped her voice to a whisper. 'It came for the people who cancelled.' She smiled guiltily and put a finger to her lips.

The balcony jutted out over the rocks. I looked down at

the wooden staircase and the beach battered by powerful Atlantic breakers. No place for children.

I waved. 'Sorry to have disturbed you. Enjoy your holiday.'

I settled back beside Gerald.

'Did you find what you were looking for?'

'I don't know.'

Eleven

Gerald dropped me at a big hotel near the airport.

'Will you be needing me tomorrow, sir?'

'I'll call if I do.' I handed him the fare and a tip. He examined the money. 'You not making a mistake here?'

I smiled and shook my head. He reached over and we shook hands.

'You take care of yourself, sir.' He frowned. 'For a young man you got an old face.'

After I'd checked in and showered, I tried to switch my brain off with a few Scotches in the bar but it didn't work. The lost passport at Gatwick, the unsuitable Sea View ... None of it made sense. Jane's words surfaced. *You can't trust the dead.* Small electrical charges in my tired brain arcing and shorting. I'd come here to be alone with my memories, but they'd been crowded out by questions.

I went to the room and lay down, listened to the air conditioner competing with the cicadas, and in the distance the breakers. I replayed the moment at Gatwick, the farewell. Sara's words.

I can't do this. Please don't make me.

Sara had wanted to stay. I urged her to go. I didn't want us to be defeated by the passport. I didn't want the children to be disappointed – their first trip abroad, first time in an aeroplane.

You can. Let's not let the children down.

She could have argued: *I don't want to go without you. We've never been this far apart. I need you beside me. Always. That's what we promised each other.* She could have reached up and taken my face in her hands. *Let's do this together.*

But she hadn't. She had resisted and I had insisted. That was how so much of our communication had become. Terse exchanges, expressing nothing but frustration.

The knocking was very soft. I looked at the bedside clock: 03.20. I closed my eyes again. More knocking. I went to the door and listened. Another knock and then a whisper. 'Dan?'

It was Stuart.

I flung the door open and turned back into the room. 'For fuck's sake.'

He spoke to someone in the corridor. 'A few minutes, OK?'

I went into the bathroom, ran the cold tap and splashed my face.

He appeared behind me in the reflection. 'I'm truly sorry.'

'About what exactly?'

He was panting, as if he'd jogged all the way from London. His face was pink under his freckles, which, together with the short-sleeved shirt and loosened tie, made him look even more boyish than usual. A hand went up and swept his sandy hair off his forehead. His eyes were bloodshot from too much flying.

'Look, I know how you must be feeling—'

I put up my hand. 'No you don't.'

He clamped his mouth shut so his lips disappeared and shook his head at the ground. He steadied himself against the doorpost. 'Had the devil's own job finding you.'

'Yeah, there's lots of empty rooms on the island – for some reason.'

His arms flapped at his sides like useless wings. 'Dan, please don't.'

'What's the latest on the plane? I heard there was a fuel gauge problem.'

He looked at me, his face grey. 'Not now.'

'Just tell me.'

He let out a long sigh and rubbed his face with the side of his hand. 'OK. The crew on the inbound flight the day before complained that the cabin was cold. Temperature reduction can be an indicator of pressurisation problems. The heat exchanger had been replaced a couple of weeks before following a hard landing in Costa Rica. It was in-spected at Gatwick during the turnaround and pronounced servicable.'

He swallowed. 'The fact that the plane travelled for some time on auto pilot after contact was lost suggests it was – the crew suffered – hypoxia. That's consistent with loss of cabin pressure.' He blinked heavily. 'At least they'd have felt nothing.'

'How come no one noticed on the ground?'

'Local air traffic control operators don't monitor the progress of every flight. If it was maintaining altitude on a seemingly steady path, even if it had gone off course, well – it wouldn't necessarily have attracted anyone's atten-tion.'

'So, just a crap airline cutting maintenance corners. Why did you pick them?'

He kept his face angled away. His tone was official now. 'The Scheme has a budgetary ceiling for extraneous com-passionate expenses, but it's modest. Pooling the allowance for the four of you, it was just enough for the package without me having to refer the decision up. A scheduled flight would have been excessive. My masters would have told me to forget it.'

'Excessive. A plane that stays in the sky?'

His face suddenly reddened. 'For God's sake, Dan, how do you imagine *I* feel?'

I took a deep breath and told myself to leave off. The trip had been my idea. I had pressured him into letting us go. 'You're in the shit for this?'

He waved a flattened hand above his head. 'Up to here. I'm finished.'

Part of me wanted to take it out on him; instead I pulled him towards me. I held him for a second, gripped the back of his neck, and gave him a couple of comradely slaps on the back. He felt hot and tense. When I let go he looked embarrassed. Not the done thing in his world, perhaps.

He held my gaze for a few seconds then sat down on the edge of the bed, as if all his strength had suddenly evaporated. He put his face in his hands. 'God I fucking hate this job. You stick to the rules, everyone hates you. You try bending a few ...'

Whose life was weirder, his or mine? For four years he had been the main conduit for all our needs, however trivial, and the butt of all my frustrations with the life we had been condemned to. I wouldn't have picked him for a friend, but having been thrown together by the Scheme, in the hours we had clocked up in each other's company, some kinship had taken root. He genuinely seemed to care about our welfare.

He started to shake behind his hands, heaving gasps of despair, as if he'd unleashed something he couldn't control. His voice turned into a shrill whine. 'Everything I touch turns to shit.'

As suddenly as he'd started, he stopped. He sat up, let out a big breath and wiped his face. 'God, embarrassing. Sorry about that.'

His phone chirped. He moved over towards the door while he took the call, hunched over, fingers pressed against his forehead.

I went over to the window and slid it open. Warm salty air rushed in. Black silhouettes of palm trees waved, leaves rattling. Behind them was the sea. The moon was out, and in a pool of silvery water I could see the outline of a fishing boat, a plume of exhaust bending in the breeze.

His call finished, he came over and stood beside me. 'If anyone asks – what shall I say you came for?'

I looked at him. He had no children. Could he understand?

'I thought being nearer, where the plane finished up – it might make a difference.'

'Has it?'

'Not yet.'

Images of the breakers and Sea View's treacherous steps crowded back in. 'I went to where we were supposed to be staying.'

He had put on his concerned listening face, waiting.

'It wouldn't have worked.'

He frowned. 'How do you mean?'

'Place too small, beach too dangerous. No good for the kids.'

He stood up, looked at his watch. 'Shall we ...?' He gestured at the door.

'You have to be kidding.'

'There's a plane waiting.'

'Another four years? Fuck off.'

'I've got to send you back. I don't have a choice.'

'*I* do. I can walk out of this door and never see you again.' I felt another wave of anger.

'What would you do?'

I hadn't got an answer for that. I hadn't thought that far. I felt the energy drain away. What was there to do?

He wiped his face with his palm. 'Plus the Met will want to see you again. There's a new team on it. They'll review the whole case.' His face brightened a little. 'This could be the end of it.'

'You said that last time. And what if it is? The light at

the end of the tunnel's just turned into a fucking void.'

There was a soft knock on the door. He went over and opened it. A minder was standing there, holding a phone. 'They want to know how much longer.'

'Few minutes, OK?'

I gestured at the door. 'What's the goon for – in case I don't come quietly?'

'He'll have to see you home – they've given me another stop to do.' He slapped his sides helplessly, like a flightless bird.

'No.'

'Dan, please.'

He put on another sombre face and looked down.

'Please, no more sympathy.'

'Actually, I was thinking about Ross.' He paused, breathing in. 'He's been asking for you. He's not got long.'

Twelve

We dropped through thick banks of cloud towards Gatwick. Everything beneath was reduced to monochrome, a joyless empty world. Nothing there for me.

I had slept in bursts, dreamed I was back on the beach in Tobago, calling Emma and Charlie away from the breakers, then dragging them up the steep steps, Charlie protesting that he hadn't seen any zebras, each of them clutching one of my fingers so tightly that when I woke I was sure I could still feel a trace of their grip.

'Good sleep?' Bill, the minder, emerged from under a blanket, stretched and burped into his fist.

We took a side route through immigration. Bill, leading the way, waved a document at a woman in the booth. She examined it and nodded in the direction of some seats.

Anne Lapper stood up, smoothed her skirt and came towards me, a concerned smile fixed on her face. She was encased in a high-buttoned suit. A cloud of scent surrounded her like a shield. She put out her hand and drew me in, offering a heavily made-up cheek.

'It's OK, Bill, we'll take care of him from here.' And then with a tight smile, 'He is one of ours.'

Bill looked off into the distance, like a man who didn't do eye contact with women, especially when they were pulling rank. 'He's on his way home.'

Anne looked at me while she replied. 'I think Dan would like us to bring him up to date with developments.'

Bill pulled out a phone. 'I'll have to make a call.'

As Trent's HR Director, Anne had only two modes: caring and stubborn. Today she was in caring mode. 'We're all so, so very sorry for your loss. Jack wants to give you his condolences in person.'

'That's thoughtful of him.'

'And give you a briefing.'

She gave a little nod for emphasis. The caring bit was over.

She led me to a Mercedes with tinted windows that smelled strongly of smoke. The driver, with shaved head, shades and earpiece, looked too big for his seat. Bill got in beside him.

'What developments?'

'Not yet.' She put a hand on my arm. 'How are you coping? I expect you're better equipped than most.'

'One from your HR handbook of silver linings?'

She glanced at me warily. 'Your sense of humour's still intact, I see.'

The Merc surged forward. Trent's building was on the Gatwick perimeter road.

'How's business? Any good coups?'

She smiled at the windscreen. 'Still mostly outsourcing for HMG. No one else does what we do for them.'

It sounded like a line from their sales pitch. I wondered what she was like off duty, if she ever was off duty. She was another one like Stuart, living the job, always on call.

'Greg still with you?'

'Occasionally. He's freelance now.'

'Does he – know?'

She nodded. 'He's hoping to see you – Scheme permitting, of course.'

'Of course. Whatever we do, let's not upset the client.'

Trent's building was a converted hangar. Outside, a Land Rover with all its glass gone, a big rip in the side and a wheel missing, was being inspected by a man with a clipboard.

'Land mine?'

'Animal liberationists.'

The foyer had a new pair of black leather sofas, which almost obscured the shrunken maroon carpet tiles beneath.

'Take a seat. We'll be right with you.'

On a coffee table was Trent's latest brochure. I flipped it open.

- *Supporting global stability for a safer world.*
- *Turn-key solutions for all threat environments.*
- *Hand picked teams optimised to deliver results*
- *A full suite of protective and security services.*
- *Discreet, comprehensive, conclusive.*

Under a photograph of a small jet, plain white, no markings, was a caption: *Twenty-four-hour on-call rescue and repatriation with full medical back-up.*

A receptionist appeared, furling an umbrella and clutching a large McDonald's bag. She gave me a nervous look.

'It's all right, Kirsty, he's with me.' Anne glided back into the reception area. I pointed at the picture of the plane. 'You've gone up in the world.'

'Jack's new toy.' She gave me a wry smile. 'We have to move with the times. Come through.'

I followed her down a corridor. Outside a pair of large double doors she paused and turned, her face grave.

'Dan, my advice to you here is to let him have his say. He, ah, needs to get some things off his chest. I apologise in advance for any inappropriateness and hope you won't … overreact.'

'It's OK, I'm not armed.'

The walls of the conference room were hung with a set

of staged photos of paramilitaries in action poses, leaping from helicopters, storming a pockmarked building, setting up a grenade launcher. Above the head of the table was a black and white blow-up of a young captain astride the bonnet of a lightweight Land Rover, fists on hips, chin jutted forward as if about to lead a charge. Except for a meanness in the eyes, there was nothing to connect the ambitious-looking captain with the figure seated beneath. Trent's round form rose behind the table in one continuous curve, his head hunched low over a spreadsheet. What was left of his hair was shaved close so the shiny pink flesh of his scalp showed through. A pair of glasses clung to his forehead. Small lively eyes peered out between folds of skin. His jacket was off, braces loose round his shoulders. A cigarette burned in the sort of extra large ashtray pubs used to have.

He looked up and frowned. 'Thought you were my lunch.'

He picked up a phone, jabbed the buttons and shouted into it. 'Where's my fucking—? Well bring it now. Yes NOW.'

The door opened behind us and the receptionist tottered in with a Big Mac box and a large Coke. Trent grabbed them without a word and rummaged in the box. He pulled out the burger, studied it for a second and took a large bite. Once his mouth was full he spoke again.

'Carter: here.' He snapped his fingers at an adjacent seat and lunged again at the burger. Anne sat opposite, knitted her fingers together and leaned forward. 'Mr Trent was very sorry to hear about your bereavement.'

He frowned for a couple of seconds until what she was saying registered then nodded vigorously while he finished the mouthful. He took a swig of Coke.

'Awful, yes ... Anyway.'

His eyes swept to me and back to the spreadsheet in front

of him. 'There's nothing I hate more than having to rake over the past, so let's get on with it.'

He tapped the glasses on his forehead so they dropped down like a visor, and studied the spreadsheet in front of him.

'You may not be aware, Carter, that under the terms of our agreement with MI5 we are liable for half the cost of your ah – protection. Do you know how much that is?'

I shrugged.

'Four hundred and fifty thousand a year.' His face reddened suddenly as if the figure caused him physical pain. His eyes blazed with rage. 'I also don't need to remind you that technically the moment you tied the knot, you were in breach of your agreement with us.'

In the corner of my eye I could see Anne's hands clench. 'I think this isn't quite the moment—'

He used the interruption to bite into his burger. Ignoring her, he continued. 'You also failed to adhere to specific mission procedures by exiting a surveillance vehicle.' He prodded a piece of paper in front of him. 'Under the terms of your employment agreement with us, in normal circumstances you would have effectively dismissed yourself. *Twice.*'

He gave a couple of nods for emphasis. 'But unfortunately for me, because of the small print in the contract, and the client's ludicrous obsession with political correctness, not only are we obliged to keep you on our books, we've had to stump up for half of this four-year holiday for you and all your dependents.'

His complete lack of grace was almost cathartic. I smiled. 'I think you'll find I just got a whole lot cheaper.'

Anne's gaze drifted towards the ceiling. I looked at them both: Trent, mouth open, breathing quickly as if trying to lower his temperature; Anne, sphinx-like, tight lipped, trying to project calm into the room. Eventually she spoke. 'Is there something you'd like to tell us?'

'Like what?'

'Anything we don't know? If you're keeping stuff back it makes it harder for us to help you.'

Trent cleared his throat. 'This Tobago caper ...'

Anne raised a hand and started to speak, but he jabbed a finger at her. '*I'm* talking. Were you trying to do a runner? Our spook didn't seem to know about your trip.'

'Maybe your spook hadn't talked to my spook. Why would I be doing a runner?'

He exchanged a glance with Anne, pushed the spreadsheet away and focused his attention on a model of his new plane mounted on a stand in the middle of the table.

'We have a problem.'

He made a sound somewhere between a sigh and a groan. 'A valuable client, a very important influential client, has given us the boot.' His face grew redder, as if he was struggling to keep his composure. 'As you know, Carter, we have an unmatched reputation for discretion. For some time, and for some not inconsiderable remuneration, we have undertaken discreet assignments on behalf of our Arab friends, in particular when their visiting subjects succumb to temptations on offer in our decadent capital.' He flattened his hands and laid them on the table. 'Contract terminated. No warning, no notice, no explanation. Who else is going to clear up their sick, Allah, be praised, only knows.'

His eyes closed for a moment. 'Naturally we had to know why. Had we underperformed? Has our service ceased to give satisfaction? No reason, they say. Well there's always a reason.' He took off his glasses and laid them on the table. 'And for the reason – there's a price. And I have to open my wallet.'

Anne glanced at me and raised a finger. 'I think Dan understands the gravity—'

Trent's hand shot up to cut her off again. 'We put our

man in Riyadh to work. He does a few checks, crosses a few palms. The problem? Our old friend Waheed, or more precisely his cheerleaders, the Brothers of the Martyr. They've banged on all this time about him being topped without a shred of evidence. Until ...'

He pulled a manila folder towards him and drummed his fingers on the cover. 'One of their crew boasts to his brother's cousin's concubine's father-in-law, who happens to be an associate of ours, that Allah has blessed them with some evidence that's going to screw the suicide bomb story for good. An Egyptian journalist has shown them a picture purporting to be of the "assassination" but he wants an over-the-top price for it. One of the Brothers – no surprise here – is also in the pay of Saudi intelligence who detain the journalist and seize all his worldly goods.' Trent paused and took a swig of Coke. 'I go back to the chap who's just terminated the contract. I say to him, "We know what you have. At least allow us to verify it for you."' He reddened again. 'I am doing my level best to forget the "fee" I had to pay for sight of this.'

He flipped open the folder and held up a fax. 'Recognise anything?'

It was a black and white photograph, very low resolution, almost certainly taken with a phone. A wide shot, the car and the figure in the centre of the frame no more than silhouettes.

I shrugged. 'What do you want me to say?'

Trent's face reddened again. His voice dropped to a whisper. 'What don't I like about this picture?'

He tapped the silhouette of me with the tip of a pencil. 'What's in your hand? What do you appear to be pointing at the car?'

'The gun was on the ground.'

'And you picked it up.' The pitch of his voice rose as it got louder. 'You got hitched, you got out of the van, you picked up a fucking weapon. It was Kensington, for fuck's sake! Not Kandahar.'

Anne opened her mouth. Trent's hand shot up again. 'Not *now*.'

He glared at me, waiting for a response. I couldn't think of one. He snatched the picture back. 'For four years, four long expensive years, we have kept up this charade of the botched suicide.' He shook his head.

'Who else has seen this?'

'We don't know. My former client let it be known that his people are still considering their options. If they're sensible they'd destroy it and all trace of it. Is that likely? No. Will they use it to exert some pressure on the Brits? Probably. Will it leak? Very likely. And let's just imagine the consequences, shall we? The Saudis will be compelled to cover their arses by accusing the Brits. The Yanks'll most likely side with the Saudis. The media will have a field day, Scotland Yard will leak that they were leaned on to keep quiet. The media will go bonkers ...' He lowered his head onto his hands.

I folded my arms and leaned over the table. 'Maybe the Brits have already seen it.'

'Except I don't yet hear the pitter-patter of shit raining down on our roof. So this is what we are going to do. HMG is our meal ticket, our main client. We lose them – we may as well fold our tents and head for the hills. It doesn't bear thinking about. They rely on us; they also expect us to keep them in the loop if we come across anything we think they might like to know. So we are going to be men and do the decent thing. *We* are going to show this to them, but we need to have done our homework first.' He picked up a phone and jabbed some buttons. 'OK.'

A few seconds later the door opened and a man with a paunch and a droopy moustache entered, a laptop under his arm.

'Evening all.'

Trent rolled his eyes. 'Enright was with the Met. He served on the first Waheed inquiry, before we headhunted him.'

Enright plugged his laptop into a lead and pointed a remote at the wall behind Trent. A white screen descended.

He smoothed a hand over his moustache and pressed a key on his laptop. The image from the fax filled the screen. Projected, it seemed to be breaking apart into indecipherable blobs.

'And enhanced.' Enright tapped another key. The picture sharpened up. The car became the Lexus, the figure became me.

'The firearm appears to be an M79—'

Trent cut him off. 'Never mind all that. What you're here to help us with is where the fuck this image came from.'

I stood up and walked over to the screen. 'The angle's too low for CCTV. It's head height. Someone must have taken it. Judging by the quality, with a phone.'

'Right. And that's what we need when we talk to HMG, because if this is from a phone then there's someone out there who took it, who could stand up in court, point at you and say that's the man.'

He left a couple of seconds for the rest of us to absorb this.

'Next.'

The screen changed to a plan-view graphic of the street, spotted with coloured dots, the location of the witnesses. 'Enright was able to, ah, borrow this from the inquiry. We believe it's accurate. Perhaps you can confirm this, Carter, with your amazing gift for recall.'

I imagined myself back in the van, just before Waheed arrived. The two purple dots were the schoolgirls down the street on the opposite pavement, a blue pair indicated the couple with the umbrella saying their goodbyes. A single pink dot inside the outline of a car was the driver of the lowered Honda, a red was the woman with the recycling box and a cluster of three more dots – two green, one yellow, showed the two hooded youths and the old lady.

Trent swivelled round and faced Enright. 'And you know where to find them all?'

He nodded.

'So who's the happy snapper?'

I looked at the diagram and back at Trent. 'None of them.'

I got up and went over to the screen. 'Can we have the image back?'

Enright put up the photo again.

'The angle of the shot is head high; the point of view is the opposite pavement from where we were parked, the same side as the clinic.' I nodded at Enright who put up the diagram again. Trent turned and looked at Enright. 'You said this was comprehensive.'

'That's what we believed.'

'Great. Fucking great.'

'These are all the witnesses that were spoken to.'

'What about Greg? Have you asked him?'

Trent turned and glared at me. 'What use would he be?'

Bird in the scarf. Greg's words.

I pointed to the space beyond the schoolgirls where the photograph must have been taken from. 'A woman, white, late twenties possibly, leather coat, blue scarf, laptop-sized bag under her arm.'

Trent looked at Enright who shrugged.

'So she legged it. Brilliant.'

Trent's gaze settled on me again. 'An individual out there who happened to be passing, whose photograph has found its way to Saudi intelligence; what is it about you and trouble, Carter?' He gave another heavy sigh. Then he noticed the unfinished burger, reached for what was left of it and put it all in his mouth. There was another silence while he finished chewing, his eyes closed. He wiped his mouth with a paper napkin and stuffed it in the box.

I needed some air. I started to get up. Anne put a hand on my arm. 'If I might just come in here, Jack.' She adjusted her face into a caricature of concern as she turned to me. 'We do appreciate you have experienced unimaginable trauma and that this should be a time for reflection.' She turned to Trent. 'In view of Dan's – changed circumstances, perhaps it would be appropriate to discuss the support package—'

Trent cut her off. 'OK, OK. Anything you want?'

My wife and kids back please.

He opened his arms as if preparing to hug a bear. 'Extra cash? Totty?'

Anne's grip tightened. I eased my arm away and moved towards the door.

'We've sorted you some secure accommodation.'

'I'm going home.'

'We don't think that's wise.'

'My car's in Long Stay. If there's no lift I'll walk.'

Trent's man dropped me by the Range Rover. I waited for the Merc to pull away, then I got out and walked back into the terminal.

Lost Property had a large crowd in front of it. A group of furious Americans were remonstrating with a courier, her eyes drooping from compassion fatigue. She had her arms spread wide. Whatever she was promising to do it wasn't enough. One of the American ladies held her forehead and looked at me, somewhere to project her despair. 'Everything lost. Gone. What happens now?'

I nodded in sympathy. *I know just how you feel.*

I rang the bell at the desk. A man appeared, a different one from the last time. He looked warily at the group who all stopped talking and turned our way. I smiled – which must have been a rare sight at this counter, but it only made him even more wary. He avoided my eyes.

'I understand you have my passport.'

'You have ID?'

His accent was East European. I showed him my driver's licence. He studied the details. 'One minute.'

He disappeared behind through the frosted glass door, then returned with a small transparent folder like a police evidence bag. He slid it across the counter. The passport was inside. I stared at it. If it hadn't gone missing I'd have been on that plane.

'Do you have the details of who found it?'

He looked blank.

'Whoever handed it in, they'd have had to fill out a form – time and place the item was found and so on.'

'We don't give out no details.'

'I'd like to thank them.'

'You can leave note. We send it on.'

'There's a reward.' I put two twenty pound notes on the counter. 'For the form.'

He disappeared into the back again and returned with a ring-binder. He flicked through the forms, opened the lever arch and handed me the sheet.

'Not passenger. Cleaner. It was in Ladies', in toilet bin.'

Thirteen

Ross's eyes were closed; an oxygen mask covered his face. He looked ten years older. The machine by his bed hiccupped and sighed. A monitor drew jagged lines that faded like vapour trails. He was alone, with a ward to himself.

I took his hand, and squeezed it.

His other hand slowly rose and lifted the mask. His voice was no more than a whisper. 'Not gone yet.' He turned his head in my direction. The lids of his eyes parted enough for me to see a glint behind them. 'Helen told me.' He shook his head. 'I know how it is.'

'Know what?'

'How it is.' His eyes opened wider and he nodded.

This was already uncharted territory for us. We had always maintained radio silence about our families. It was the way he wanted it and I went along with it. In the outside world, that would have seemed strange. Not in the Scheme, where nothing was strange because everything was.

I looked at him and shrugged. 'I can't get my head around the idea of them not being alive.'

His head moved almost imperceptibly from side to side, his voice a dry whisper. 'Anyone tries to tells you you'll get over it; they're either lying or ignorant. You get used to it. After a while, it stops being a shock every day you wake up. That's the best you can hope for.'

His head sank back deeper into the pillow as if it was about to engulf him.

'Things are happening that I don't understand.'

His eyes opened a fraction. He beckoned me closer.

'What I learned – trust no one. No exceptions. Whatever's going on, stay alert.'

I wanted to tell him everything, the passport, the chalet for two, the breakers,the case of champagne, the photo, lay it all out like the bits of an engine, see if we could fit any of it together. But this wasn't the time.

There wasn't going to be a time.

His eyes opened again. 'Someone came. Asked about you. Pushy.'

He nodded at the flowers by the bed. Under the vase was a card.

John Frankland

He smiled faintly. 'Stay ahead of them. Don't let them catch up with you.'

He drifted off. In the bed he was tiny, like a bird. The sinews in his neck stood out like buttresses under his chin. The skin on his forearms lay in flaps on the covers of the bed. Fine downy stubble had sprouted on his cheeks.

I still had hold of his hand. 'All this time – what's kept you going?'

He took a breath. 'Remembering them.' He lifted his other hand and waved a finger at the cabinet beside his bed.

In the drawer with his sponge bag was a dog-eared leather wallet. I took it out and offered it to him, but he was too weak to take it. 'The picture.'

Inside, a curled edge of a photograph protruded from one of the compartments. I tweezered it out with my fingers. A small faded snap, perhaps thirty years old, the colours washed out. A woman and two boys sitting on the bonnet of a Ford Cortina. Behind, Ross, thick black hair, laughing as I had never seen him.

He gave a nod. 'Just believe me when I say, I know how you feel.'

He took the photo and lifted it up. His eyes widened for

a second. Then they closed. I thought he wanted to hold on to it but he passed it back. I reached for his wallet to but he shook his head. His forearms shuddered as they rose. He took the photo and pressed it into my palm, then folded the fingers over it. 'Remember them for me. Will you do that?'

Then he closed his eyes. For a while I watched him, counting the tiny breaths, and the longer intervals in between them.

Fourteen

I felt a hand on my shoulder. My head had dropped onto the bed cover.

I looked up. A pretty nurse, her eyes almost as dark and beautiful as Sara's, filmed with tears, smiled down at me.

'He's gone.'

A sheet covered his face. At least he hadn't died alone. That was something.

Outside it was just starting to get light. I didn't feel ready to face the house. I drove down to the seafront. On the beach, his boat hauled up on the shingle, a fisherman was sorting his catch, picking up a cleaver every few seconds to sever a head. Some gulls hovered nearby, waiting for entrails.

'Good dovers, cod fillet. Feed all the family for a fiver.'

I smiled and shook my head. 'Not today.'

A milky sun was trying to work its way through low grey cloud. The tide was right out – Charlie and Emma's favourite. A huge expanse of wet sand, the water just inches deep at the edge, safely shallow for fifty metres.

I stood for a while on the drive, absorbing the empty, shuttered house. This was how we had first seen it; bigger and fancier than anything either of us had known. Sara was starting to show, and I consoled myself that at least it was somewhere we could hide out and nest.

As I approached, one of the security lights flashed on. I put the mortise key in the lock and turned. Then I tapped a code onto the keypad and I heard the bolts spring back. The door made a glutinous *shlick* sound as it swung away from the tight seals, which kept all draughts at bay. I hovered on the doorstep as I had many times in a previous life, on the threshold of some supposedly deserted building, ready to expect the worst.

Inside it was very still. The chequerboard tiles stretched away towards the kitchen where they met blonde wood. In the darkness, just the pinpoint glow from the alarm sensors, blinking like small red eyes. I touched the switch. The tungsten spots warmed up and bathed the hall in light. For a moment I didn't recognise the figure in the mirror – stubble and bloodshot eyes from nights of damaged sleep. I focused on the shape on the stairs and felt my chest tighten. Emma's sleepsuit lay there like a recently sloughed off skin. *Not there. In your room. Now, please!* Sara's voice so clear.

On its roof like a stranded upside-down tortoise was one of Charlie's toy cars. I picked it up. Felt how cold it was.

I stepped into the kitchen, still a mess. Small islands of cereal floated on a scummy lake in the sink where I had left the children's bowls soaking. There was a smell of old milk from an open carton.

Sara hated mess. She tidied constantly, channelling her energy into keeping the house in order.

I made a coffee. There wasn't much to eat in the fridge. Sara had run supplies down in anticipation of our holiday. I lit a cigarette. The first time I'd smoked indoors.

I took the coffee into the back room and sat down at the big oak table, the scene of our one attempt at a dinner party. Another of my initiatives, a chance for Sara to play at normal life. I'd had to lean hard on Stuart to get the OK, but only after all the guests, people we had met through the kids' nursery, had been vetted. I looked round the empty chairs. On the left had sat the Hamers, Jocelyn and Mark from three doors down. He managed a building society. Clive and Erica Ardley; opticians with a sea view apartment. When Erica drank her voice got louder and she took offence when Clive tried to shush her. Felix Crick and Debbie Osberton, him twenty years older, a mineral trader fantastically pleased to have changed his old wife for a new one – though it pissed him off that she clung to her maiden name.

'... We're celebrating. Justin's got into Ferndean.'

'God you must be relieved.'

'I slept my first full night.'

'... The night before we were due to exchange, they put the asking price up fifty grand!'

'... All the turf had to be scraped off. This time I watched them every step to make sure they rotavated.'

'... They're both being tested for dyslexia and dyspraxia. It's our worst nightmare.'

'... And the train was full of brokers, snorting coke off the tables – the children didn't sleep a wink. And then there was no bus to the chalet. Guess how much the taxi was. Go on, guess?'

Their remembered voices echoed around the empty room. I imagined their reflections in the polished wood. Even when the conversation veered on to cars, any meaningful exchange was strangled at birth.

'... French cars are shit. I had a Renault once. Couldn't park it.'

'... These hybrids – you know they cost a fortune to recycle. So much for being ecologically correct.'

I'd had my story all ready, as close to the truth as possible, that's what we'd been advised. I could talk about Afghanistan, and army life. *It gives them a reason, if they ever think you're a bit strange.* Sara had the kids to talk about. As it turned out the most probing question we faced was where we'd got the dining table.

It confirmed what I'd always thought, that this wasn't the

life for me. But Sara was happy. She lived the part, drank up the attention. Her cheerfulness seemed indestructible then. Afterwards, drawing me to her, putting her hands round my face, she kissed me and grinned. 'I've got all I want. How many people can say that?'

What happened to her? What changed?

I paced the room as I'd seen animals do in zoos, unable to be still, as if stillness would be some kind of admission of how alone I was. The empty house seemed to echo with the absence of children's voices. How long before I got to Ross's stage, of needing a photograph to convince me they'd ever lived?

I poured a tumbler of Scotch. The smell of it reminded me of Jane on the cruise ship. Her words: *You can't trust the dead.*

I sat down on the sofa, took out the passport and laid it on the coffee table. I stared at it in the vain hope that it would give up the secret of its passage from our bags to an ST bin in a ladies' toilet.

It got dropped? Someone picked it up, went into the ladies', and decided to throw it away? Someone stole it, hid it there for someone else – but it got found? Or they got cold feet and ditched it?

I unlaced my shoes and lay down.

I was outside the house, in the street, but in full gear, gun raised, safety off, a round in the chamber. Everything green in the night-sight. Coming from inside, the sound of the children crying and Sara's voice, trying to be calm in front of them but full of fear. 'Dan, please help.' I shouted through the door, 'It's all right. I'm here.' I pressed the doorbell. Heard the buzz. No answer. I buzzed again. I took aim and blasted the lock. The front door flew open. A blinding light, ferocious wind. When my eyes adjusted all that was there was sky, and the sea far below.

I was on my feet before I was properly awake, gulping for breath, forehead dripping with sweat. I went into the kitchen and splashed my face with cold water. I heard the buzzing again. The doorbell. A cruel spasm of hope – for a split second I thought it was Sara. I went to the door and looked at the security screen. Standing beside an old Mondeo, gazing at the street, was Frankland.

Fifteen

'I know about this house.'

Perched on a stool in the kitchen, Frankland looked smaller, despite the bulk of his overcoat. He had a light dusting of stubble and his few spikes of silver hair stood up on his crown. He gazed around him, taking it all in. I put a mug of coffee down in front of him.

'Belonged to a shipping agent named Braine. Braine the brain. With a sideline in heroin. He's somewhere in Northern Cyprus now, fending off extradition. Had the security screens fitted after his wife got kidnapped.'

'Did he get her back?'

Frankland smirked. 'Don't think he wanted her back. Divorced her not long after. Hygiene freak, employed a pair of cleaners full-time. That was how they nailed him in the end. Wired the house. What's it like to be home?'

'I've never thought of this as home. Certainly not now.'

He sipped noisily, as if he had no one to remind him not to. I heard Sara's voice clear in my head reminding the children: *no slurping.*

'What brings you here?'

He scratched his neck, his fingernails rasping against his stubble. 'I was in the area.'

'How did you find Ross?'

'A man of few words.'

'I meant how did you *find* him?'

He smirked. 'There's a database of properties leased by something called Security Welfare Services. Not a lot of people know about it. You need police clearance to access it. Next to each of the properties there's a box marked *Purpose*. You get some great euphemisms: your premises in Shoreham are down as *Occupational Welfare*. For some reason, maybe tax purposes, they'd inputted your cover names.' He blew on the surface of his coffee, rippling it so it sparkled. 'You knew his real name?'

I shook my head. 'He was Ross to me.'

He sighed. 'Poor chap, his threat level was actually down to zero. All the people who might have come looking for him are long gone. Some kind-hearted soul must have realised he'd been on the Scheme too long to come off. You know the saddest thing?'

'Do I want to?'

'He never knew it, but it was his wife who shopped him. Thought it would protect the kids. Didn't do her any good. The IRA got them all. The bodies were never found.'

'"You can't be too paranoid."'

'What?'

'Nothing.' I pulled out my wallet, examined Ross's photograph.

'What's that?'

'Just a picture.'

He looked mystified.

'Don't you carry any pictures – of people you loved?'

He tapped his temple. 'It's all in here.'

I put the picture away. 'Did you know your wife well?'

He frowned.

'I mean, really know her?'

He wrinkled his nose. 'Strange question.' He thought for a second then shrugged. 'Not as well as I could have, I suppose.' He slid off the stool and wandered over to the window. Charlie's plastic trike was outside, on its back, its front wheel pointing heavenward.

'How did you find me?'

He turned and smiled to himself. 'The Scheme's far from

perfect. It's impossible to get all the agencies to play ball. The NHS won't have people appearing and disappearing off their files. The DVLA don't like it either. So there's a programmer in the bowels of the Home Office who matches the new with the old data for those who need to know. Make all the right official noises, show you've done your homework and she'll give you access to the original NI and licence numbers ...' He spread his arms. 'And then it's hello Dan Carter.'

He grinned, his eyes blazing.

'So how far have you got?'

He rested his chin on a fist. 'Let's see. Army sniper, fresh from Afghanistan, gets married, books a honeymoon, doesn't go; instead he finds himself in the Scheme with a whole new ID.' He faced the garden again, as if addressing an invisible team. 'There are different reasons people go into the Scheme. There's your grasses who need protecting from whoever they've shopped, there's bystanders – ordinary witnesses who saw something that's pivotal to the outcome of a case. Then there are those who've served their country in some special way we aren't supposed to know, who need a fresh start. Where they can't be got at.'

'Is that it?'

'Pretty much. I can't see you being either of the first two.'

'And if I'm one of the third lot, it begs the question whether what I did might give someone a motive for blowing me up?'

He didn't answer. A couple of crows had landed in the garden and were pecking in the grass. He turned and came back to the kitchen counter. The newspaper was where I had left it. He focused on the headline and smiled to himself.

'Didn't take much to match up the dates.'

He unfolded the paper and smoothed it out. '"New broom". We'll see.'

He glanced up at me, waiting for a reaction. I didn't have one.

'They're putting in a fresh team. Whitehall's going to have to come to terms with the idea that they may not be so ... compliant this time around. The Met are fed up of carrying the can for intelligence cockups.'

The picture of me with the gun. How long before he would see it?

He refolded the *Mail*, settled back on a stool and sipped his coffee, waiting for me to fill the silence.

'You think I did it, killed Waheed. And someone tried to wipe me out by blowing up the plane four years later?'

He shrugged. 'It's a theory.'

'The plane didn't blow up. If it had, the debris wouldn't have been clustered together like we saw it. It would have been spread out over twenty miles.'

His eyes widened. 'I take it you're a supporter of the hypoxia theory.'

'I'm not a supporter of anything. Have you got any more details?'

'I'm getting there, but like everything to do with this plane and its passengers, it's all twice as hard.'

'Which increases your suspicion.'

He nodded. 'Exactly.' He put his mug down. 'What's "Shimmer"?'

I shrugged. 'Never heard of it.'

He gave me a long look. 'Nor has anyone else, apparently.'

He reached for the sugar and stirred some into his coffee, then helped himself to a biscuit from a half empty packet. 'Just for the hell of it, I had an old FBI chum input your name – your real name, into their database. Their geeks have got very good at deep data mining. Not much gets past them. They've got smart gear that can crawl all over, worm its way under firewalls and all the clever barriers people have to protect their secret stuff. If you feed in a keyword, it'll bounce back if it recognises it and tell you the source. Are you keeping up?'

'I'm trying.'

'Good. So there's a thing called the International Combined Operations Complex, ICOX to the cognoscenti, the result of some sudden rush of blood to the head by the CIA post-9/11, the thought that it might just be a good idea if so-called Free World security services pooled useful intel.'

He let out a sudden derisory laugh. 'As if anyone's going to share their precious secrets. So it became a sort of dumping ground for all kinds of material. Smaller countries use it assiduously, uploading all their data, while the big guys just dump their low-grade stuff. But because there's no agreed standards for tagging or cataloguing, and no proper archiving of the material, its impossible to tell what's what, or where anything's from. Unless you know what you're looking for.'

'Fascinating.'

'"Shimmer" is in there. And your name's in it.'

Frankland's eyes were alight; he was in his element now. He sipped his coffee and pressed on.

'It's housed in a completely separate data universe from anybody's regular files. No country ID, no links to military, surveillance, terror databanks, shows no clearance level. It just sits there, seemingly un-openable except to those who know it's there and have the passcodes. All you can see with the FBI's kit is the traffic – how often it's been accessed and the dates.'

'And?'

'It starts last September, nothing before that, then ramps up right around the week the plane went down.'

He rubbed his thighs with this palms. 'My chum was intrigued. So he made an innocent inquiry to the CIA in Langley about the status of Shimmer, just a standard information exchange request. He figured they must know something about it. Twenty minutes later he was hauled into his Director's office. Langley had been on wanting to know the purpose of his inquiry. He fobbed them off with some excuse; all the same they didn't like it.' He shook his head. 'Nothing changes. Each organisation guards its most valuable information jealously. You'd think after nine-eleven they'd have learned.'

He gave a long mournful sigh and observed a moment's silence for all the incompetence in the world.

'I'm sorry, can't help you.'

'Can't as in not allowed or because you don't know.'

'Don't know.'

He pursed his lips and glared at me. Then he dunked another biscuit in his coffee and put it all in his mouth. I could see how he must have been in his working life, wearing his team down with his relentlessness, nothing else in his life to distract him.

His gaze drifted back to me, eyes still gleaming.

'Bet the Army must have been sorry to lose you.'

I didn't answer.

'You got glowing reports. "Extreme calmness and clear thought processes in the field ... Ability to contain and manage emotion ... High resistance to stress ... Likely to be effective under close interrogation".'

'If I'd stayed in I wouldn't have survived.'

He stared off into the room. 'You quit while you were ahead. My mistake – to leave it too long.' His expression softened, his guard briefly down.

'I'm getting the impression you've not quit at all.'

He scratched his nose. 'When all else fails you fall back on what you know best. Isn't that right?'

He studied my face as if he genuinely wanted confirmation.

I put my mug down slowly. 'You'll get to the bottom, as you put it, of why the plane crashed. And if it turns out to be simple technical failure or a mechanic's error, you'll make sure whoever's responsible gets punished. Good luck to you. I mean it. I want to know too. But if there's more – what then? Suppose there is something bigger behind it, something more than you can take on. What will you do then? When are you going to grieve?'

He gave me one of those looks that he must have deployed in interrogations past. 'I expect you must be asking the same of yourself.'

'You want a culprit, someone you can blame, and bring to justice. But what happens if there isn't one?'

He was quiet for a few seconds digesting the thought, blowing on the surface of his coffee so it rippled with the light from the window.

'Got any plans?'

I shrugged.

Sara and the children had been my domestic fortress. Inside their world I'd been good. Alone – that was another matter.

I looked at him. We were a pair. No wife, no children. All dead.

'How long have you been a widower?'

He rested his elbows on the counter. 'Years. But we'd already divorced and she remarried so it probably doesn't count.' I waited to see if he had any more to say. He dipped another biscuit into his coffee. 'It got too much for her.' He chewed for a few seconds. 'The job – not conducive to family life.'

'How come?' It was my turn to be nosy.

'You had to keep the work to yourself. She wanted to know how my day went. What could I say? She didn't like that.'

'What?'

'The secrecy.' He nodded and slurped more coffee. 'She said it had a corrosive effect on the marriage. I've never forgotten that.' He slapped his knee. 'Anyway, it's all in the past.'

I wondered if I would say that someday. Sara and the children still felt very much part of the present. I still expected the three of them to spill through the door any moment. We drank in silence.

'You didn't come back with the group.'

'I needed some space.'

'You bunked off to Tobago. Then a plane was diverted to bring you back. You know how difficult it is to do that?'

'What?'

'Have a commercial flight diverted. You must have some very influential people to call on.'

'Wasn't my decision.'

I sipped my coffee. Frankland took out a pack of cigarettes. 'May I?'

He lit up and took a long drag, like it was his first in a long time.

'The young lady on the ship, Ms Cochran.'

Her card was still in my pocket.

'Asked where you'd gone. Seemed quite concerned about you.' He searched my face for a response. I didn't give him one. He slid off his stool. Having exhausted that line of questioning he ambled over to the fridge and examined the pictures. He peered at a photo of Sara, laughing with the children when they were smaller, one under each arm. 'Attractive woman.' He studied it for a while. She had that effect. People turned to look at her. 'Not much of a life for an active young couple. Bit of a marriage-breaker too, I'd imagine, living like this.'

'We were very committed.'

'Oh I'm sure.'

He continued to peer at the pictures. 'Of course, you could do it all again.'

'What?'

'Start over. With someone else.'

I felt my muscles tense. He still had his overcoat on, as if he knew he might need to make a quick exit.

'You've no idea, have you?'

'Just being practical.'

He kept his eyes on the pictures. 'You have anyone else?'

'Is this a wind-up?'

'I imagine the pressures of living your life must have taken their toll.'

He coughed into his fist and tucked a thread from a frayed shirt cuff into his coat sleeve. I felt my face heating up. He stood up, took a few paces away and turned. 'Miss Cochran: You spent the night with her.' He put up his hands in mock surrender. 'Oh, I know you may have a perfectly harmless explanation. But what I'm trying to get across to you is how this all *looks*.'

He drew in a big breath and let it out slowly. 'You know what I think you are?' He swatted some biscuit crumbs off his coat.

'I'm all ears.'

'Floss.' He pinched his forefingers and thumbs and made a teeth cleaning gesture. 'You ever heard that term? Maybe they only use it when the likes of you are out of earshot. "Use once and discard". You do the dirty jobs everyone wants to forget about after they're done. Except in your case, something went wrong and they couldn't flush you away.'

He had recovered, hard and unforgiving again. 'As long as there are things you're not telling me, you're going to be on my list.'

I didn't doubt that. He had the gleam of obsession,

which certain situations demanded. For him this was one. He leaned forward and studied my face.

'I don't envy you, Carter. If you don't know the full story of what the hell's been going on, then I'm sorry for you. But until you start talking, you're going to be everyone's favourite suspect.'

Sixteen

Helen's receptionist gave me an apologetic look. 'Sorry, Mr Carter, Doctor Lockyer's back-to-back.'

The waiting room was empty.

'On house calls.'

I smiled. 'Then I'll wait.'

I sat down on a bench and reached for a magazine. She looked at me and sighed then took out her mobile and sent a text. Ten minutes later, Helen came through the door, clutching her bag, phone pressed to her ear. Her hair was pulled back, professional mode.

She swept past without acknowledging the receptionist or me and disappeared into her room. When she finished the call she appeared in the doorway. She looked tense. I went in and closed the door. She put her bag down on her desk and glared at me.

'We've got a possible jumper on a multi-storey in Hove. Cops are picking me up in ten minutes.' She put her face in her hands and gave out a long sigh. 'How are you?'

I didn't have an answer to that.

She let her hands fall to her side. 'I'm so, so sorry.'

'Thank you.'

'When did you get back?'

'Yesterday. I was with Ross last night.'

She glanced at the window, the sun catching the lines round her eyes as she squinted towards the sea. A moment's silence for him.

Her face tensed again. 'There was a cop here, yesterday. Frankland.'

'Ex cop.'

She snorted. 'Once a cop ...' She folded her arms.

'What did he want?'

'In a roundabout way he tried to threaten me. He knew we'd been for a drink together which he seemed keen to make something of.' She shook her head. 'Where's he been the last thirty years? He seems to have a picture of you as part serial philanderer, part terrorist lunatic.'

'He thinks the plane's to do with me.'

Her face was taut with contained anger. 'I'm carving out a life here, being a goody-goody. And he just swept in ...'

I stepped forward but she put up her hand.

'He asked me a lot of questions about your marriage.'

'Like what?'

'If either of you were cracking up. He said he'd got access to Sara's records.'

'Which records?'

She sat down.

I leaned forward and put my hands on the desk. She looked frightened.

'I'm not able to say.'

'Because you can't or you won't?'

'Both.'

She glanced at her watch. Then her face softened. 'Dan, most people on the Scheme are on their own for a very good reason. If she hadn't been pregnant with the twins ...'

'They'd have tried to split us up?'

'Aside from the cost, couples don't fare well.'

I felt a hot pain shoot across my chest.

'I know you'd had your problems.'

'She talked to you?' I heard my voice rising. 'You didn't mention this before.'

'I've got a duty to my patients.'

'After they're dead?'

There were tears in her eyes now. She sat on the edge of

the desk. 'You look terrible. Please, *please* talk to someone. I can arrange it.'

'I'm talking to you. Tell me what she said.'

She shook her head and looked away.

I moved so I was in her line of sight. 'Something changed – about six months ago. It wasn't that sudden or obvious. Something in her look, a sort of blankness, and the way she – touched me less. Before, she was always looking on the bright side – whatever, always cheering me up. Hardly anything got under her skin.'

Helen sighed. 'Doctors don't get to see the good times. It's not when we're needed.'

I went over to the window. On the beach a fisherman was dragging a bucket of fish guts down towards the sea. Above him was a funnel-shaped swirl of gulls. 'I just thought it was the Scheme finally getting to her. What did she tell you?'

'That she'd got rid of the nanny and packed in her job in a shop. She didn't want to leave the house so much.'

'Did she give you a reason?'

'She said it was because the kids were getting older, they were more aware of her not being around all the time.'

'But they were at nursery.'

'She said she wanted to be there – "in case". If they needed her.'

I came back towards the desk. 'Why did she come to see you?'

'She brought one of the kids, but I could see that was just an excuse, there was something wrong. When I quizzed her she was very defensive, actually quite hostile. Then she just broke down, and once she'd started she couldn't stop. But she wouldn't say what was on her mind. I wondered if she'd been pressured by you – to stay at home.'

'Oh come on. I encouraged her to have the job. I wanted her to have a more normal life. I didn't want her to let the nanny go. The children liked her. They were actually quite distressed when she left.'

Helen let her hands drop into her lap. 'The second time, she asked for antidepressants. I asked her why. She wouldn't say.' She shook her head. 'Thought I'd just get my pad out and write a prescription. How likely is that? She was stressed up to the eyeballs. I tried to get her to talk. All she would say was she was having panic attacks. I explained that the rules of the Scheme stipulate that any mental issues have to be referred on to the approved shrinks. Then she tried to leave. She wasn't in a good way.'

'What sort of panic attacks?'

'She didn't tell you?'

'No.'

'You weren't aware of them?'

'She was unhappy. Are you surprised?'

'Dan, I don't have the exact details of why you're on the Scheme. It's not for me to know. But did you ever talk to her about it?'

'No. That was part of the deal. Why are you asking?'

'Because when I tried to get her to sit down and talk all she'd say was she was scared about what was going to happen.'

'That it wouldn't end?'

She shook her head. 'More like that it would end badly.' She pressed her hands on the desk. 'Look, the Scheme isn't kind to people. It's a pressure cooker. You know how it is, not being able to see friends, no family contact. There's not a couple on the Scheme who haven't had to deal with this kind of thing. You're one of those blokes who think they can withstand anything. But when you've been banged up like this, it pushes you to the limit and spouses tend to get the brunt of it. And we have to take the heat out of it.'

I glared at her. 'You're making me out to be some kind

of wife-beater. Sara had nothing to be afraid of.' I winced at the sound of my own indignation.

She frowned. 'What about before?'

'Before what?'

'Before you. Her previous life. You were married, what, about three days before you wound up in the Scheme?'

'Why are you asking?'

'Why are you so paranoid? I'm trying to help.'

'We'd only met five weeks before.'

'Whirlwind romance.'

I ignored the comment. 'Sara never had anything to do with her family. It was a bad situation she didn't want to talk about. I thought she'd get round to it when she felt ready. And if not, that was fine with me. She'd always said that as far as she was concerned we were the only family she had – me and the kids. There didn't seem to be anyone she missed being in touch with.'

'And that suited you?'

'What's that mean?'

She swallowed. 'You didn't mind – or you didn't want her having other people in her life.'

'Why wouldn't I? You're trying to make out I'm some kind of monster.'

Helen looked away. From down the coast road I heard an approaching siren. She scooped up her bag.

I watched her face. A flicker, a tiny movement of a muscle near her mouth.

'What is it?'

She didn't answer. I felt my face heating up. 'Something you're not telling me.'

'Sara came back a third time. She asked me if she con- tacted someone – a friend or relation, without permission, and it was found out, what could happen? I told her that any breach of the Scheme conditions was a very serious matter, that all contact requests have to be referred up quite high. The scheme has some quite "unusual" people in it. Not all of them are heroes. When things get rough, so can they.'

'She *met* someone?'

'She didn't say if she had or not – or who. She was in a bad way. Very fragile.' Helen looked away. Her voice was almost inaudible. 'I tried to cheer her up. I told her that sometimes under extreme circumstances, exceptions could be made but they would have to be cleared by Stuart. She looked terrified. I asked her what was wrong. She said she couldn't speak to Stuart in case it got back to you.'

'Who was it?'

'We didn't get as far as that.'

The siren was getting louder.

'She's dead, for fuck's sake. What does it matter to anyone else now?'

My voice echoed in the room. The door opened a fraction. The receptionist peered in. Helen waved her away.

'It's all right, Philippa.'

I lowered my voice to a whisper. 'You're not helping here.'

'I told her there was nothing I could do. It was more than my job was worth.'

A police car came to a halt in the middle of the road outside; the driver hooted a couple of times, as if it was a minicab. Helen came round the desk and took my hands in hers. 'When people die, everything changes. You know this. After they've gone, you find yourself doing a kind of audit of your life together, part of the grieving process. Unfinished business tends to come to the surface. You have to let it. My mother died in a car crash the day after I told her she was a meddling cunt for trying to get me into rehab. Imagine processing that.'

'Who did she want to see?'

She came up close, lowered her voice. 'As far as I know,

it never happened. She must have changed her mind. That's all I know.' She put a hand on my cheek. 'Be careful.'

'Of what?'

'Of yourself. You're wound up like a spring. You're probably far angrier than you even realise. You're going to have to let it out, and when you do just be careful no one's in the way.'

Seventeen

At a junction I watched a woman pushing a buggy through the rain, her hood pulled tight round her face. Sue – the children's class rep. The little boy skipping beside her looked up and waved. Charlie's friend, Milo. I opened my window and smiled at him.

'Can Charlie play?'

His mother lunged at him, grabbed his arm and pulled him back. 'Of course he can't!'

Milo started to whimper.

I looked at her. She couldn't know. We had told no one that we were going anywhere.

She frowned while Milo struggled in her grip. 'Sorry, only I thought ...' She didn't have an end for the sentence. Her eyes darted around. I was used to dealing with people fishing for information. I knew all about how to deflect searching comments and questions, but now I was the one who was curious. 'You thought what?'

She huffed. 'Well, frankly it's been jolly difficult. The costumes ...'

I switched off the engine. 'What costumes?'

She hesitated. 'The Easter play.' Then her words came in a rush. 'I told your – Sara, she should come and get the fabric and the pattern. I reminded her a few weeks ago and she said she'd forgotten, but she *still* didn't bother to come and she could have warned me because now we're having to rearrange all the dances.'

'Warned you of what?'

Her eyes widened, her hand went up to her mouth. I

continued to smile at her, waiting.

She looked down at the child in the buggy, adjusted the hood.

'Well I, I imagined, I just thought … that she was going …' She pressed her fingertips against her mouth as if to try to stop the words, her eyes moving anywhere they could to get away from mine.

'Going where?'

Her face froze, as if her brain had just crashed, her mouth half open. Milo, sensing trouble, was staring up at her. 'Well, I don't – she didn't look …' She closed her eyes and let out a long sigh. '… very happy.'

Her face contorted into a caring smile that didn't look like it quite belonged with the rest of her features, then she backed away and marched Milo off down the street. I watched her as the rain came down harder.

Eighteen

I sat in the car, staring at the road.

Why did it change?

When I first spelled out what the Scheme was going to mean for us, Sara had absorbed it without complaint. We hadn't made any plans. 'It doesn't matter where we are, so long as we're together.' She held me tight as if to confirm what she felt. 'My life is with you.'

Instead of wearing her down, the pregnancy seemed to increase her energy. She filled her day with exercise; she decorated the house and spurned my attempts to help her. We walked to the sea and along the sand, imagining ourselves with the children paddling, digging. She rehearsed for the part of the perfect mother. She read every parenting book, watched every DVD. I loved her for her focus and commitment, as if this was the role she had been preparing for all her life.

'You're going to be so proud of me.'

She wanted a natural birth, to be in charge, but when it came to it, after a draining twenty-eight-hour labour, the twins were delivered by emergency Caesarean. She wasn't even conscious. When she came round and I held them up for her to see, she grinned. Nothing was going to get in the way of her sense of achievement.

The first three months we barely left the house. I wondered how normal people with jobs ever managed. The babies seldom slept or fed at the same time. Colic, jaundice, thrush, all came in quick succession like challenges on an assault course. When they weren't putting on weight, she substituted bottles and I took turns to do the feeds. Some nights I persuaded her to let me take them both and give her a night's sleep.

It took a year for her to get back to where she wanted to be, but she did it, doggedly, like a battle-hardened platoon commander reclaiming lost ground. She reasserted her authority and imposed a series of routines around which life in the house ran. And I loved her all the more for her commitment and determination. She started jogging, pounding the streets and the sand until her body was lean and taut. She put more and more time into keeping the house immaculate, undaunted as the twins followed in her wake, creating fresh chaos. I wondered how she would keep it up.

One day I came back to find the twins clamped to the kitchen table in their seats, red faced, bawling in unison. The floor was scattered with tiny shards of china. The size and spread of the pieces indicated that the bowls had met the floor at high velocity and had been thrown with a force much greater than a toddler could achieve. Up one wall was a streak of something green and pureed.

Sara was outside drawing on a cigarette. She glanced at me through the smoke.

'OK, so I'm not perfect.' But even then she managed a laugh.

I asked Stuart to get us a nanny. Karina was the daughter of Cold War defectors. Her early life had been lived in the Scheme, so she knew the ropes. Sara was wary of the intrusion but Karina embedded herself in our lives with a minimum of fuss, giving Sara a break from the relentlessness of the twins as they started to walk. I also insisted Sara had something that took her away from the house. I badgered Stuart and he gave in. She found a part time job in a shop, which had to be cleared by the Scheme.

She was nervous at first, after spending so much time with the children, but it gave her an outlet for her natural sociability. I had saddled her with this life; the least I could do was make it as painless as possible.

The rain on the windscreen turned the road into a blur of greys.

Sara. Talk to me.

The huge void in front of me echoed with questions I couldn't answer. After my mother died, I used to hear her voice in my head as clear as if she were right beside me. But Sara was silent. I was even having difficulty seeing her face, as if she had already been gone a long time. There were things about her I didn't know, was never going to know. Helen's words came back to me.

Who did Sara want to contact and why?

I fired up the engine and put on the wipers, floored the accelerator so the wheels spun as it pulled away.

Nineteen

The street had been paved over and a couple of trees struggled out of creosoted planters made from old railway sleepers. Tables and chairs were laid out in front of one café as if in resolute denial of the weather. Three teenagers, a pale-faced boy and two girls sat at one of the tables, their hoods up, smoking. One of the girls whispered to the other and they both laughed. The boy focused on the cigarette butt between his fingers, trying to look like he didn't care.

Mick and Maria's place was just next door to the café: *Sensory Perceptions* – the lettering of the sign in the style of a Rorschach inkblot test. In the window was an elaborate indoor water feature that Sara told me they'd had to switch off because it made customers want to pee.

A chime echoed from the back of the shop as I opened the door. The aroma of scented candles curdled in my stomach. Maria and Mick's shop was a mix of imported goods from developing countries and alternative health remedies. A poster in the window said, *Balm yourself with ambient fragrances that protect you from the corrosive influences of modern life.* Perhaps they had something for plane crashes.

Maria appeared from behind a bead curtain. She was holding a small embroidery frame in one hand. The other was clamped over a collection of bangles as if she was trying to stop them banging into each other. She floated towards me, her trademark dreamy expression fixed on her face. A jet-black lurcher followed.

'Dan. How nice.'

She seemed to speed up as she got closer, as if she was about to offer a cheek to be kissed, but stopped a metre away and ran her fingers through her long hair, bangles jangling. The lurcher gave my legs a routine sniff.

'Gandalf. No!'

'It's OK.' I scratched the top of the dog's head. He ambled back to the rear of the shop.

'She looked past me. No Sara?'

'Not today I'm afraid.'

Her shoulders sagged. A purple batik smock was gathered at the waist by a big leather belt with a bird-shaped buckle. She was probably forty but her long brown hair was fifteen. She straightened herself again and took a breath, rediscovered her smile.

By the till was a stack of cards featuring two photos of Mick: one being presented with a garland by an elderly man in a salwar kameez, with a huge beard; the other with him gazing at something high up, his chin jutted forward, a hand held as if shielding his piercing eyes, or possibly blessing a large throng. I picked it up and turned it over. On the other side was a list of *Therapeutic Experiences*. I put it down and selected a big turquoise marble from a small basket, something Charlie would have liked, and weighed it in my hand. *Can I, Dad? Pleezopleeze?*

Maria let out a long theatrical sigh. 'We do miss her.'

I nodded.

I had been doubtful about them, but Stuart pronounced them ideal as Sara's employers. They were much too self-obsessed to notice anything unusual about her or me. What's more, he said, 'The strongest substance they inhale is sea air.'

Maria's hair was draped over her shoulders. A broad crocheted band studded with what looked like tiny mirrors kept it off her face. She combed it again with her fingers, then clutched the clanging bangles again, twisting them round the axle of her wrist.

I hadn't been there since Sara left six months ago. She'd gone suddenly, without giving notice. 'I just don't want to go there any more,' she told me in a tone that indicated she didn't want a discussion. I'd asked if something had happened. She had ignored the question.

'Where's Mick?'

She looked away then back to me. 'At the Post Office.'

I hadn't thought about what I was going to say or why I had gone there at all, other than to follow Sara's tracks. Whenever I had come to pick up Sara from here I timed it so I didn't have to hang around. Maria's husband had a seen-the-light fire in his eyes that reminded me of peace campaigners. Upstairs he ran something he had chosen to call 'R&R classes'. *Re-bond with your mind and body, Relax and rediscover yourself.*

'That's three Rs,' I'd pointed out to him when I made my first visit to the shop. He'd fixed me with a messianic stare. 'We'll give you a discount. You look like you could use it.' I'd politely refused and he'd given me a reproving look. We were never going to hit it off.

I tossed the marble from one hand to the other.

'Did you find anyone to replace her?'

Maria looked down. 'Sara was so good with the customers. They always left with twice as much as they meant to. Takings went down after ...' She twisted the bangles again.

'I couldn't understand why she left.'

Her dreamy smile faded.

'You're surprised?'

Her face flushed, she looked away, did some more finger combing and bangle twisting. 'Mick said it was to do with you.' She let out a nervous laugh, and a flash of terror crossed her face as if she had overstepped a mark.

I laughed as well. She looked relieved. 'He thought you didn't approve ...'

'Why wouldn't I?'

She waved her hands at the shop as if conducting an invisible orchestra. 'Oh, you know. All this.' More laughter. 'You being – well, military.'

I laughed an *oh now I see* laugh. 'And stiff arsed? Uptight?'

Her head gave a little shudder. She wasn't sure where this was going. Nor was I.

I put the marble back in its basket. Chose a pink one this time.

Go on, Dad, one each. Pleeezz!

'She's away, with the kids.'

'Oh, bless.' Mentioning the children was like putting a light on inside her. 'I couldn't believe how they'd grown.'

Something in my face made her smile vanish.

'When was that?'

The bangles clashed together. She looked like she lived in permanent fear of saying the wrong thing but had no way of stopping herself.

'She popped in. It was so nice to see her.'

I gazed back at her, matching her smile-for-smile and left a silence I knew she would feel compelled to fill. She did another quick finger-comb.

'She wanted to send an email. When your server was down. She said she would have gone to the Internet café but she had the kids with her ... And she knew I'd love to see them.'

Maria had gone dreamy again, too unfocused to notice the colour change in my face or the pulse in my neck as a surge of blood pumped into my head.

Then she focused again, worried. She put a finger up to her lips and mouthed *Mick doesn't know*. She gave a bird-like high octave laugh. 'Hates anyone touching his computer.'

I nodded, understanding. She blinked a few times and blushed. 'Your secret's safe with me.'

She looked awkward again and dropped her gaze to her hand, still twisting the bangles. I let some time elapse while I figured out what to do next.

'Was that what you wanted?'

'What?'

She nodded at the marble in my hand. I gave her a look as if I'd only just remembered. 'Well, actually it's the same problem. It's down again. The server.'

The colour drained from her face. 'But he's due back.'

I beamed. 'I'll only be a second. I'm very fast.'

She opened her mouth to protest. I took her by the elbow and guided her to the rear of the shop. 'Trust me.' I looked at my watch. 'It's lunchtime. There's bound to be a queue. Maybe you could make me a cup of tea. That way it won't look strange if I'm in the back with you.'

I held the bead curtain for her. The dog lifted its head briefly then let it sink back into his basket. An ancient roll-top desk was piled with receipts and invoices, clamped in bulldog clips. Amongst them was a laptop, a new Sony.

'Please be careful. It crashed after Sara used it. He got all this spam ...'

'It'll be fine. Don't worry.'

The Scheme mainframe held the strictly limited directory of approved contacts we could communicate with. They didn't work on outside computers. She would have had to use another ID and another mail service.

I brushed the touch pad with the side of my thumb. 'What's the password?'

She looked at me.

'You must have given it to Sara?'

There was an edge in my voice that I couldn't disguise. The dog lifted its head again.

'The sooner I do this the quicker I'll be out of here.'

She bit her lip and glanced at the dog.

'Gandalf?'

She clutched at the fabric of her skirt, like I had seen Emma do. 'With a small g.'

She turned away and filled the kettle. I clicked on search history.

'Do you remember when it was that Sara came?'

'A Wednesday, because that's Mick's Brighton day.' She gestured toward the bead curtain. 'I'll just go and keep a lookout.'

'Was she here long?'

'About an hour. Charlie and Emma were absolute darlings.'

I clicked on search history and scrolled down the list.

Holistic Resource Network
Natural Emotional Healing
Chakra Realignment Option
Carnival of Healing
Pranic Awareness
Life Source Digest
Emotional Healing
Chakra Alignment Forum
Reaffirmation Retreat

I remembered what Frankland had said. A whole character profile just from someone's searches. But I wasn't interested in Mick's character. I was looking for a webmail service. Several more searches were for merchandise for the shop. Rainforest Products, Ethical tea lights, Guatemalan Smockworks, GeoGems, Stones4u, and a few less exotic like Brighton Film listings and Shoreham Minicab.

The chimes for the front door jangled. Maria jumped so suddenly Gandalf leaped to his feet and started barking. I ignored them.

Maria peered through the bead curtain. It was a customer. Whatever they were looking for she didn't have because the door opened and closed again a few seconds later. Gandalf returned, his tail slapping the side of the desk.

'Dan, please.'

I glanced through the beads. Maria was in the shop window craning round the switched-off water feature.

'One more minute.' I clicked back to the main page. Mick had a Yahoo account. I clicked on Switch User. No other names came up. So I went back to Search history and scrolled down the list again. There were several names that meant nothing. Marique, Vardemen, Premiera, ChemeX.

'Daaan!'

I clicked on Marique. It took several seconds to load. A gemstone distributor. Vardemen supplied Thai tableware. The last two would have made Frankland smile: Premiera offered 'Massage for discerning clientele in the Surrey area.' ChemeX was a distributor for 'Generic Viagra.'

I heard the chimes. Gandalf leaped up and crashed against Mick as he came through the beads.

Twenty

Mick stood in the doorway. He had on a knitted cap and a mustard-coloured duffel coat. A leather bag with a thick strap hung from his shoulder. His chin jutted forward, the I-am-the-One gleam in his eyes somewhat dimmed by the sight of me sitting at his desk. I offered him my hand. He didn't take it. He glanced at the laptop. The lid was closed, just as he left it, its secret still inside.

Maria stood beside her husband, biting her lip, the dreamy smile long gone. He ignored the mug she held out to him. I took a sip from mine. It tasted of nothing I recognised.

'May I ask what you're doing at my desk?' He sounded like a headmaster who'd caught a pupil in his study.

Before the Army I was in trouble – regularly. Each time slightly worse, slightly bigger than the last, incrementally building to something that I knew I would regret. Random vandalism, bike theft, joyriding, each time a stab of regret the next day, especially when I saw my mum the next morning. Nothing said. Just a look. *You can do better, but it's going to be your choice.* And then she wasn't there any more – gone to hospital, never to come home. I needed saving from myself. I couldn't do it alone.

The Army filled my days and nights. There was no time for anything out of order. It sucked up all my surplus energy so I craved sleep at the end of a day instead of trouble. When we deployed, it took me on adrenalin trips I'd never imagined. It taught me control, the power to choose how to behave, whatever the situation. Power to look down the scope, see a face and squeeze the trigger. And do it again.

Until I couldn't see the point any more. And then I was useless and it was time to get out. Since then I had tried my best to cling on to the good stuff, and keep a lid on the rest. Sara, Charlie and Emma – they were my new army, demanding my attention every day and every night. Not any more.

Without them I was back somewhere I never intended to return to. Like a kid, caught red-handed.

I looked at him. 'Maria and I were just talking.'

He sighed wearily. 'If this is to do with Sara, we can't help you.'

'What were you thinking I might want help with?'

He sighed again. 'Sara was a valued employee – more than an employee. A friend. After she – left us, we tried to maintain the extended hand of friendship.'

I mimicked his grave expression. 'Yes, she's had to fend off a few hands of "friendship".'

He gave me a pitying look. 'It's always been clear to me from your body language that aggression is your default mode of communication. It is a trap men fall into all too readily.' He glanced at Maria whose eyes were bulging with panic but he pressed on.

'Sara was grateful that we respected her privacy and didn't try to intrude, despite her evident torment towards the end of her time with us. Perhaps on reflection we should have made a difference, been more proactive.'

'How would you have done that?'

He knitted his fingers together. 'Offered her sanctuary.'

I got up slowly, incoherent rage rising in me like nausea. Maria moved behind Mick, backing into the bead curtain. She gripped his arm.

I put my face very close to Mick's and spoke quietly. 'Sara's dead. So are the children. The plane that crashed ...' I watched his face change as the words sunk in. 'If there is anything you want to tell me, now's your chance.'

But my hand didn't give him a chance. It clamped round his neck, knocking his head against the doorpost. I lifted him so he was on tiptoes. His face went purple. He blinked rapidly, his mouth opened and closed, dribble coming out of a corner. The dog was barking.

Maria's voice rang out above the noise, her words spurting out. 'She borrowed the shop. On the half day, to meet someone.'

I let Mick go and stepped back. He doubled over, retching.

'Who?'

Maria spoke from behind her fingers, which were pressed against her face. 'She wouldn't say. She asked us to leave her alone here, the whole time.'

'Was this after she used the laptop?'

Maria glanced guiltily at Mick. 'Before.'

Mick got back on his feet. He picked up his hat and straightened his coat. 'You need help.'

Twenty-one

It was getting dark. The security lights came on as I turned onto the drive, bathing the front door in a ghostly green glow. This was how we had first seen it. I'd sat there, my chin on the wheel, thinking *I can't connect with this*, then looking at Sara beside me, hands pressed against her face, a gasp of delight. 'This is so grown-up!'

I pressed the remote and the garage door slowly lifted. I reversed in and waited for the door to come back down.

I had only been in the house a minute when the bell went. It was Andy Rudney from across the road. I opened the door. He stood on the threshold. 'Er, thought I'd just tell you there was a car outside your house late last night.'

'An old Mondeo?'

He shrugged. 'A BMW X5 – black.'

'Thanks, anyway.'

'We all have to be vigilant.' He nodded gravely.

'I know. Thanks.'

We exchanged concerned looks.

'How was the windsurfing?'

He started back down the drive. 'Good. You should come along next time.'

I pressed the master switch by the door that closed all the shutters. The house whirred with the sound of fifteen electric motors.

I went into the kitchen and poured myself a large Scotch. It burned my empty stomach. The last thing I had eaten were the biscuits I'd shared with Frankland. What else had he discovered? Perhaps he was already ahead of me, remotely downloading a message Sara might have sent from Mick's laptop.

Our Major used to call it 'the Cloud' – when there are several pieces of intelligence, from different sources, none of which connect. 'You get sidetracked trying to join it all up because you think it'll tell you what's going to happen. All your mental energy goes there. But you're fucked because half the intel doesn't mean what you thought anyway, the other half is out of date and what you should have been doing all along was watching your arse.'

I was in the Cloud. Nothing made sense.

I finished the glass, poured out some more. Felt the buzz of my phone in my pocket. *Number Withheld*. I pressed Accept.

'It's Jane – from the ship.'

I heard a couple of sharp breaths then her words came in a rush. 'Gosh, I'm really so sorry to call like this out of the blue, but ...' There was a pause as if she was searching for a way to finish the sentence. 'It's just so good to hear your voice.'

I laughed. 'All I've said is "hello".'

She laughed as well. 'Oh God, there I go.' She sighed at herself. I could imagine her wafting the air and shaking her head, forever trying to erase what she had just said. 'You disappeared. I was worried.'

'We hardly know each other.'

She let out an indignant snort. 'You saved my life. You watched over me all night. You heard me say things I've probably never said out loud even to myself.'

'How did you get my number?'

'Your policeman friend.'

'He thinks I did a bit more than watch over you.'

She let out an embarrassed laugh. 'Is it difficult – being back?'

'Kind of.'

'Have you seen anyone?'

'It's been busy.'

She went quiet again, but I could hear rapid soft breaths as if she was pacing a room. 'Look, I can tell that you probably don't want to talk right now and really, I do apologise for calling like this. I just … It would be really good to see you again. There's no one … And you were so understanding … Oh God here I go. I'm sorry. It's so selfish of me, I know. I can't begin to imagine what you're going through there.'

I looked out into the gloom of the house. Like a spent cartridge – the energy gone from it. Dead, just like them.

'Are you still there?'

'I'm sorry, I'm a little drunk.'

'Would you – come over and visit? You've got my address. Just get in your car and drive over. We could talk some more; I could cook you a meal … I'd really like that.'

She stopped again. The silence that followed seemed to transmit a profound loneliness, the kind that would send grown men running, despite her looks. Had she been this tragic before? Then I felt a sudden stab of fury that an almost complete stranger should be saying the kind of things I'd wanted so much to hear from Sara.

'"You can't trust the dead", why did you say that?'

She laughed. 'God did I? I must have been so out of it. Just forget whatever I said that night. I'm much better really. I owe you, I really do.' There was that same undertow of desperation in her voice, maybe a fear of being alone.

'Look, this is very kind of you but I've drunk far too much to get in a car, and I think enough people have died already.'

She sighed. 'I'm sorry. I'd so like to talk some more. If

you change your mind though, call me, OK?'

I topped up the Scotch and carried the glass and bottle into the small windowless room behind the stairs, the one the children called Mummy's Den. I put on the desk light, an Anglepoise, which always delighted Emma with its habit of slowly lowering its head on to the desk as if it was grazing. On one wall was a big pinboard covered in the kids' artwork, animals, flowers, spaceships, some photos taken at the nursery, Charlie with Milo, his mother in the background looking slightly wary. It was one I'd taken. She'd never been sure about me. Maybe she'd been right.

The desk was super tidy, more like a display in a shop than a real space used by a real person. Sara liked things that way. She hated piles, just as she hated any half-finished task. Recently she had become more fanatical. If the washing machine cycle had ended, it had to be emptied, if any ironing got started, it all had to be completed. If there was one dirty fork in the sink, it had to be washed.

I hovered by the chair, unable to touch it. Everything was as she had left it and disturbing it would diminish what remained of her presence. I swallowed some more Scotch and told myself to get a grip.

I lowered myself into her chair; half hoping that it could transmit some signal of what she had been thinking the last time she sat there. Let me glimpse inside her mind.

Sara must have taken her diary, the one she kept all the children's dates in. There was nothing on the desk except an A4 pad, a jar of pens and pencils and a half used pad of yellow stickies, Sara's favourite medium for communication which she transported round the house and stuck in prominent places. *Haircuts, Sat 10, Sophie's party 4.30, Tues. Nit comb.* She even carried a swatch of them in her bag.

I opened the top desk drawer. There were big pads of

paper, spare small spiral-bound notebooks, mini-packs of crayons that she always had with her so the children could be occupied, a pack of pens, unopened, more packs of yellow stickies.

There were no mementoes; nothing connected with the past was allowed in the house. The children's stuff was all on the pin-board. On a shelf was Sara's collection of décor magazines. I looked in the waste bin. There was one screwed up ball of paper. I hesitated before I opened it. It felt ludicrous what I was doing, a violation, breaking the bond of trust I thought we shared. But that was already broken. She had broken it – or had she? I didn't know. Would knowing make any difference?

I unscrewed the piece of paper and smoothed it out on the desk. It was a letter about uniforms from the school the children had been due to start at in September. *Please complete the form below and return.* She hadn't. The tear-off section at the bottom was still there. She knew they weren't coming back.

I stared at it for a while until the light did its trick, the shade gradually falling to within a couple of inches of the desk, settling beside one of the Post-it note pads. I heard Emma's laugh in my head, as clear as if she were sitting on my knee. How long would I remember that sound? I reached to lift the light and hesitated. The low angle of the beam caught an indentation on the top leaf of the Post-it pad, a zero and one of Sara's characteristic crossed sevens. I raised the light a fraction so it illuminated the rest of the number. I took out my phone and dialled it.

'*You're through to Premiera. I'm sorry, we're unable to take your call at this time. But we do operate a round-the-clock personal outcall service. If you'd like to be contacted please leave your name and number after the tone, or contact us via our website.*'

I rang off. I stared at the phone trying to digest what I'd

just heard. Premiera, the massage service in Mick's search history. I switched on the computer. It was the only one in the house, which the children explored games on and Sara used for ordering stuff from approved suppliers. The email address we had been given was for 'domestic use only'. Our connection was routed through a Scheme mainframe. Any attempt to communicate outside the agreed list of addresses would trigger a warning – sent to Stuart. 'I know it seems heavy-handed, but really it's for your protection.' We were allowed to use Search. 'Just don't try to sign up for anything.'

I logged on and opened Outlook. There were two messages. One from Ocado said that our fortnightly order was overdue. Another from the nursery reminded us that there were only three more days to order copies of the class photos. I opened the attachment. A group photo with *SAMPLE* stamped across it. Charlie and Emma were in the middle of the shot grinning at the photographer. I closed it.

I clicked on the Search history.

There were a few general searches: New kids' games, Boys under five. Charlie was just beginning to veer away from the non-gender specific games into more boy stuff. There were specific sites: Webkidz, Surfari, Animalaction, Minikidz, Wickidz, Gloworld and, inevitably, a search for zebras, his favourite animal.

I scrolled down, paused, drained the glass of Scotch and refilled it, and carried on until I realised the list had started to repeat itself. I scrolled down again, more slowly. Once, to test the system, I'd typed the name of a gun site I had heard of into the search box. A message flashed up on the screen. You are accessing an unauthorised site which is blocked. This action has already been logged. Please discuss with your handler.

No Premiera. But this could have been a pad from Sara's bag. If she had looked at the site on Mick's laptop she might have noted the number down there, then left the rest of the pad here on the desk later.

My phone buzzed.

'Thought you'd like an update.' It was Frankland.

'Go on.'

He was panting slightly as if he'd hurried from somewhere to tell me his news.

'You're in trouble.'

'You amaze me.'

'Waheed – there's a picture of a gunman at the scene.'

I didn't answer.

'You don't sound bothered.'

'I'm past bothered.'

'Are you drunk?'

'Possibly.'

'Makes the Met look like pricks. I'd expect a knock on the door. And if they gave you an easy ride before, they won't this time.'

I let him have some more silence.

'Carter – am I getting through to you? If that's you in the picture, and someone's ID'ed you, there's a lot of people out there going to be on your tail.'

I listened to his short eager breaths. Eventually he sighed. 'Look, this would get a whole lot simpler if you opened up.' He had softened his tone. Good cop, now.

'You haven't. Why should I?'

'I'm not with you.'

'You've seen my wife's medical records.'

There was a pause before he answered. 'I might have.'

'Why?' I felt the heat in my face rising. 'No, don't answer that. I know. You're scratching around every corner of our lives looking for some dirt that will help you build your case that I'm either a mass murderer or a target.'

He sighed. 'There was nothing there.'

'Good.'

172

'You're not hearing me. There was no file. All gone, wiped. Nothing before the Scheme either. It's like she never existed, nor the children.'

Twenty-two

I picked up Emma's sleepsuit and folded it. My hands were shaking.

The floor creaked in the way it did when Sara got up to check the children. It used to be such a comforting sound – her routine night patrol, which she almost always conducted around one a.m. and again at four. Wasn't that strange? Or did all mothers do that? Why was she up? What was happening in her head that I didn't know?

Helen was right. Shutting down was my default position whenever there was trouble. Divert any emotional fallout into some mental holding bay.

On the landing were Charlie's pyjamas and one of the flip-flops he wanted to wear on the journey. I felt my limbs slowing down; probably the Scotch. Just get to bed. The bed I'd occupied with Sara for every night of the last four years.

The door to the children's room was slightly open, Charlie's toy zebra holding it ajar. I reached down. *A gift from Zebraland.* His favourite soft toy. He'd have missed it on the flight.

I put my hand near the doorknob. It was shaking ludicrously. *This doesn't happen to me.* Eventually I gripped it and stood there frozen. As if challenging myself, I opened it and stepped into the gloom. My movement rattled a mobile of paper butterflies. The duvets were thrown back, as if the children had been snatched from their beds. Spread on each half of the low table that separated them were their collections of precious things. On Charlie's side a lump of glass I had found on the beach, worn and rounded by the tide, several cars and a ten-piece jigsaw called The Deep, of an underwater scene. And on Emma's, a meticulously laid out tea party for Sylvanian rabbits.

On the chest of drawers a second-hand dolls' house, one of Sara's finds. 'You could give that a makeover as well,' I'd suggested, when it first appeared in the house.

'I like it how it is,' was her reply.

Above the front door a child had painted *Dream House*. I looked inside. I'd never studied it before. A group of miniature family, mother, father and two children, were seated at a table with tiny plates. There was a little TV, an old one with a round-cornered screen mounted on tapered legs. A miniature cat sat beside the hearth. Above the fireplace – as if it was a painting, someone had stuck a postage stamp, the serrated border forming the frame. A picture of a bird. *Blue-Grey Tanager*. And in the bottom corner, *Tobago 50c.*

I downed the rest of the Scotch and listened to the sound of the empty house.

I peeled off my clothes in the dressing room and stuffed them in the basket. I went through the bedroom, closed the door to shut out the silence. I turned on the shower in the bathroom. *En suite! How cool is that!* Sara loved all the smart features of the house. I stood under the stream of water. I dried myself, pulled on a fresh pair of pants and lay down. The pillow smelled of her. Straight away, sleep sucked me in and I felt the relief of drifting away.

I was reading in bed with the light on when I heard Sara's step on the stairs. I chuckled to myself at the nightmares the mind can conjure up. How stupid to imagine her and the children dead! I could even hear their snuffly breaths coming from their room. She'd be here with me any second, undressing and sliding in beside me. Order restored. Back to normal.

I sat up. It was all black. No Sara. Her steps were a dream. She was gone and so were the children. I felt like screaming at the cruel trick my own mind had played. My head dropped back on to the pillow. I listened to the darkness and the steady pulse in my head, courtesy of the Scotch.

Out of the silence came another step. No dream this time. I flicked the switch on the bedside light. It didn't come on. I leaned across and fumbled for the one on Sara's side. Nothing.

I leapt to the door and locked it. All the internal doors had mortise locks, courtesy of Mr Braine. I tried the main light. Nothing. Moving was like swimming. I cursed the Scotch. I heard another tread. A dull crack of light showed briefly under the door. I groped my way to the window and the switch for the individual shutters. For safety they were on a different circuit. No response. I went into the bathroom. The door had warped. I shoved it to with my shoulder. The lock didn't work. There was a small circle of night sky. A round window, too small for a shutter, which didn't open. I paused. Was this for real? I'd heard a step, seen a light, the electricity was off. I felt around for something I could use to smash the window. Nothing. It would have to be my elbow. It took several blows before it shattered. A blast of night air rushed in, reminding me of my near-nakedness. With a towel wound round my fist, I cleared as many of the shards as I could from the window frame. Splinters of glass on the floor needled my bare feet. I knelt on the lavatory cistern and put my head out. Below was the roof of the garage. A three metre drop at least. I tried to push myself through the window. Too narrow. I put one arm through and pressed my hand against the cold brick for leverage, the glass shards in the window frame scoring the flesh on my other shoulder. I was hanging half out of the window, trying to screw myself through the tiny aperture like a cork that wouldn't go back in a bottle. I heard a sharp crack from inside the house. The frame and the glass pulled at my underpants and for a second I was preoccupied with keeping them on – as if that would make a difference to my survival.

Another muffled thud, like a silenced gun, gave me a fresh charge of energy that propelled me through. I fell head first onto the roof. The angle of it half broke my fall and I spun round, my feet sliding towards the gutter. There was a skylight. I could get to the car. The keys were still inside. I'd have to ram the garage doors. I clawed at the skylight. It was jammed shut. I got into a crouch position, gave it one more heave, lost my grip and rolled down the rest of the roof.

I landed on all fours; glass cuts in my feet exploding with pain. Forget the car, just run. I vaulted a hedge into the next garden then came out on to the road, crouched. No vehicle. I crossed over to Rudney's side, went up his drive, crouched again in the shadow by the side of his garage. His house was dark. His car gone. They were out. No chance of shelter there.

I watched our house for a few seconds. There was no movement, no light. But whoever was inside would have heard my escape. They'd have to have transport somewhere which they could call up. I had to get out of here. I went down Rudney's garden to the back fence, climbed over into the adjoining garden of a house on the parallel street.

I could have rung a bell and begged for help, but doubted anyone would open their door to a badly cut semi-naked man in the middle of the night.

I ran down the street, keeping to the grass verges to spare my feet. I stopped when some headlights came towards me. A Jaguar. I recognised the personalised number

177

plate. I stepped on to the road, waving. At the wheel, was Clive, fellow nursery parent and one of our dinner guests. His wife, Erica, beside him had nodded off. They were in evening gear. She jerked awake as he braked and their faces formed the same frozen surprise. His window was an inch open. I leaned down, put a hand on his wing mirror.

'Thank Christ.'

His face didn't move. I gestured at the rear seat. 'Could I?'

I heard the *thunk* of the central locking. I stared at them. A few weeks ago I'd picked their whiny kids up from nursery. We'd sat next to them at the nativity play. Now they were staring at me like I was a serial killer.

The engine revved and the car streaked away spraying my legs with gravel. They wouldn't even have heard my *Fuck you.*

I kept going down the street, no plan yet, but moving was better than being still in this cold. I heard a car behind me, moving slowly, and glanced over my shoulder. Only its sidelights were on. Beside some tennis courts was a track I knew led to some lock-up garages. I turned down towards them sticking where possible to the grassy edge. My feet were so painful I was past worrying about treading on anything sharp. The wind coming off the sea had numbed the scrapes on my shoulders and thighs.

Two rows of garages faced each other. I tried every door. All locked. I found a piece of pipe a few feet long and used it to force the handle of one. It gave easily. Inside was a van. Locked. The next door had a big fat padlock. I tried the third. It was rusted tight. I used the pipe to lever the fourth. Eventually it snapped with a loud crack. I lifted the door and stared into the gloom. It was full of household stuff, a washing machine, an old television, a wardrobe. I felt along the walls hoping for a coat or overall. There was a loud scuttling and a dark blur shot between my legs and out of the garage. I tumbled against a bike. Not locked. It had no saddle but the tyres had some air in them.

On the floor was an empty plastic bin bag. I tore some arm and neck holes and put it on. At least it would be a bit of protection from the wind.

I wheeled the bike out and set off up the track. The road at the end was lit by headlights. I paused. The outline of a tall car, some kind of SUV, turning, the low burbling growl of a V8. I threw myself into the undergrowth beside the track. The car came past, turned into the area between the garages. I got back on and pedalled up the track and turned left.

Just go to the police. Tell them who you are, get on to Stuart. And give up what was left of my freedom? Not yet. Not if I was going to find out more about Sara. I wanted to make that call to Premiera.

My balance wasn't good and I had to keep my arse up in the air, and the pedals chafed my feet, but these were the least of my problems. I rode on to the main road, straight into the headlights of a police car, blue lights flashing. It blasted past on to some other emergency.

By the time I reached the Shoreham wharf I was stiff with cold. Where the coast road ran close to the water the wind came straight at me. At least it numbed the pain. A fine rain was falling and the low cloud pressed down over the dull orange of the street-lit night. All I wanted to do was get into our building and get dry. I felt my energy starting to drop. The cold, the pain and lack of sleep were overloading my system. I needed another surge of adrenalin.

Two ramps ran down to the wharf, on either side of a cluster of boarded up warehouses. I was a couple of hundred metres from the turning for the first ramp, just a glide down to our building.

A BMW X5 was parked on the road, just the other side

of the first ramp, facing away from me. Not the sort of car anyone who knew the area would leave round there. There were no lights on, the tinted glass too dark to see inside. I stopped and watched. The rain on the rear screen. A different pattern in the half-moon shape where the wiper had travelled.

I waited.

The wiper made one stroke across the window. Someone was in there. I imagined their view. A figure on a bike, no more than a silhouette in this light.

A sniper watching a street looks for any unusual movement. A pause, a change of pace or direction, even a look from left to right or hands dipping into pockets. Anything static which should be on the move. The best camouflage was consistent motion.

There were no side roads or buildings to disappear behind. If I carried on I would be in plain view. Only one thing to do – keep going towards them.

I put on a bit of speed and rode right by them, head down a little, not too much. But they would see me turn down the ramp. I rode on, kept going until the curve of the road put me out of their line of sight then turned left on to another ramp down to the adjacent wharf. As I glided down to the quayside, I allowed myself one look back to see if anything was following – just enough time to overlook a lump of concrete in my path. I saw it as I went over the handlebars. I landed on my back. More pain. A security light came on and a dog started barking on a houseboat. I had ridden past one problem and straight into another. I picked myself up. The bike's front wheel was knackered. A light came on inside the boat, a door opened, then a torch beam. The dog stopped barking. Its owner stooped over it. Then it was off, growling as it ran, its toenails clicking on the tarmac as it ran towards me.

I looked at the water. In the daytime a film of oil and

other chemicals made metallic patterns on the surface. At night it was just black. Nothing else for it. I pulled off the bin bag, walked up to the edge and dived in.

The shock of the temperature made me want to gasp but I forced myself not to. I covered as much distance as I could before I broke the surface, got my bearings and a fresh lungful of air and went back under. Our building was on a separate quay. I tried to stay under water for as long as possible but the cold was shattering and forced me back to the surface.

Keeping close to the quay put me out of view of the road or anyone who was near our building. The thought of Sara and the twins under the water flashed up, but the adrenalin and the cold chased it away. The more urgent thought exploded in my head of someone walking to the edge of the quay, looking down on me and taking a shot. A sitting duck. I hugged the quayside, keeping my limbs below the surface as much as possible to minimise noise. I paused and grasped at a ledge while I got my bearings. It was soft and mobile. There was a series of small sniffing noises. I looked where they were coming from and caught pinprick gleams in the small black eyes of about a dozen rats huddled on the ledge. Some of them dropped into the water. I swam on.

Our building had a flue that dropped vertically from the workshop floor. Somewhere under the water it did a ninety-degree turn. The exit was under the remains of a wooden dock. It was high tide so the exit would be underwater. It was a good way to get in unseen, but I had to find it first.

I inched along under the joists, which held up the dock, feeling the stonework under the water with my toes for the opening. When I found it I dived. It was deeper than I expected and narrower than I remembered. A brief battle went on in my head, half my brain questioning the wisdom of swimming up an underwater pipe too narrow even to turn round inside. If I was wrong or it was blocked, I'd have to navigate my way out feet first. The cold was starting to numb my brain. I thought about Charlie shrieking with delight, 'Cold, cold!' as he ran in and out of the sea, and of lifting Emma out of the bath and wrapping her up in a radiator-warmed towel.

My head smashed into the wall where the flue turned upwards. I pushed myself up, lungs bursting – not enough air left to get back if it was blocked. The water seemed to go on and on. I kept reminding myself it was high tide, trying to calculate the depth from the haziest recollections of the only time I had examined the flue. I broke the surface just as my lungs were about to give in. The chamber filled with the echoing noise of my own gasps. The cold had eaten away my strength. I had to take several breaths to revive my shrivelled muscles. Slow down, think. At least I was out of sight.

Ross had placed a sheet of MDF over the opening so no one would step into it. But that wasn't my only problem. The flue was built for dropping things down, not for climbing out of. The sides were smooth. I hadn't factored that in, and for a moment I entertained the thought of having come this far only to have to swim back out. That gave me the necessary surge of determination and I worked my way round the sides feeling in the darkness for crevices I could get a purchase on. Each time the water moved it gave off a smell that shot straight to the back of my throat. I bumped against something, touched it tentatively. Fur and something jelly like. A decomposing animal. Nothing to do except ignore it. I found a slot in the brickwork where some pointing had come away. Just enough to get a few fingers in while reached for the top. I touched the MDF sheet, then dropped back. Prayed that Ross hadn't parked a pile of tyres on top of it. I reached again and with my outstretched fingertips gave it a prod. Again, harder and higher. It shifted. A small chink of grey light appeared. I prodded it a few more times until it moved enough for me to get my fingers through and grip the floor of the workshop. I hauled myself up, butted the sheet aside with my head and elbowed my way onto the hard dry floor. I lay there for a minute, looking up at the night through the skylight.

I felt myself drifting. The cold and the pain were winning. That was no good. I groped my way to the stairs and got myself up to the office. I couldn't risk the fan heaters. Too much noise. There was an old bar heater under the desk. I reached among a thick nest of cobwebs, found the socket and plugged it in. The sight of its pink glowing bars and the smell of baking dust was beautiful. I filled the kettle and switched it on, holding it between my hands. I pulled off my wet pants and tried to dry myself on a pair of overalls, but the water was so slimy the fabric slid right over the moisture.

I put three spoons of instant coffee and three more of sugar in a mug and filled it with hot water. It tasted disgusting and wonderful all at the same time. The pain of the salt in the cuts on my feet cancelled out the throbbing where the window glass had gouged my shoulders and hips. I eased on the overalls, the rough seams snagging on splinters of glass that were still embedded in my skin. I zipped it up. It was Ross's. Too small. There was nothing for my feet so I toasted them by the bar heater while I drank the rest of the coffee.

I looked down at the cars in the gloom below. Nearest the door was a Porsche 911, finished and perfect except that it was up on stands. The wheels had been sent away to be shot-blasted and re-enamelled. Next to it was a silver Alfa Spider. The big tasks like the engine and drive-train had been done but that was all. Apart from one temporary seat and the basic controls, the cockpit was an empty hollow.

No windscreen, no dash, no trim and no hood, but four wheels. On the bench beside it was a new battery, still in its plastic.

I tore up a rag and wrapped the strips round my feet, hobbled down the stairs and went over to the Alfa. I opened the fuel filler and jogged the car to see if there was anything in the tank. A tinny sloshing sound suggested there was only enough for a few miles.

Despite my objections, Ross had adapted a large oil drum as a petrol tank. Not only was it a safety hazard, there were petrol stations two hundred metres down the road. I'd made a point of never using it. I said a small prayer of thanks to Ross.

I found a jerrycan and positioned it under the tap Ross had welded on near the bottom of the drum. The tap wouldn't move. My fingers were sore and weak from the climb up the flue. I looked round for something to help it move. A wheel mallet was lying on the bench. I had to risk some sound. The first blow bounced off, the clang reverberating round the building. I aimed again. This time the tap moved a fraction. Petrol started to drip out. I hit it again. Too hard. The whole assembly bent to one side, rupturing the tank. Petrol gushed onto the floor and over my bandaged feet. I caught as much as I could in the can and stuffed the hole with a wad of rag. Then I hefted it over to the Alfa and poured some in. I grabbed the battery, tore off the plastic, lifted the bonnet and dropped it into place. The terminals were corroded so I tapped them on with the wooden handle of a brush. There was no key or starter button. It would have to be hot-wired. I fumbled around the steering wheel. There was a tangle of wires. I needed light but I couldn't risk the fluorescents. I felt through them methodically until I found the two thickest and touched them lightly together. A jolt and a fountain of sparks: I had power.

The workshop door was on a roller and lifted from the

ground. It was electrically powered but could be manually overridden with what looked like a ship's wheel to the right of the door. It made a loud groan. Nothing I could do. The Alfa only needed a bit more than a metre to slide under. I gave it a few more turns and it groaned some more. I climbed back into the cockpit, felt for the choke and pulled it out to maximum, then groped again for the ignition wires, pumping the throttle pedal to prime the carburettors. Another shower of sparks. I tried not to think of them hitting the spilled petrol on the floor. The starter whirred for several seconds. *Come on.* I looked up. In the gap under the door, the legs of two figures, silhouettes, walking this way.

At last the engine exploded into life. The garage filled with oily exhaust. With no silencer the noise was worse than a low-flying bomber. I shoved the gear lever into first and let the clutch out; the engine hesitated, backfired and caught again. I ducked down as the Alfa shot forward out from under the door. I didn't see the two people, they must have got out of the way. I didn't pause to look. I aimed the car at where the ramp started, still accelerating, turned almost too late, the nearside wing mirror disappearing as it clipped the brickwork and snapped a drainpipe.

At the top of the ramp I didn't stop. As I turned east I took one last glance at the way I'd come. The X5 was gone.

Twenty-three

I drove fast through the empty streets, running red lights and slamming onto roundabouts hoping that whoever was in my path was alert enough to avoid me. The night air flailed my face. I kept my hands low on the wheel, below the bodywork, but it didn't make much difference. The wind was whipping around the cockpit. I had to keep blinking away tears that collected in my unprotected eyes. The engine thundered – at least it was a warning to other traffic I encountered. Some drunks who had spilled into the road leapt out of the way as I closed in on them. In built-up areas, having no lights was not a problem. There was so much coming from shops and signs and streetlights. No real darkness, nowhere to hide. When I reached open country I slowed. Where was I going? There was no plan. I'd been running on instinct. Escape and survive.

But for whose sake? There was no one. The debris from the plane floating on the surface of the sea, Sara's cushion, just a cushion. I had no bodies to bury, no tangible proof of my loss. In my head I knew they had to be dead. Yet one small pulse of doubt kept me going.

Even the dead kids I had seen in Afghanistan, I still had to touch their corpses, just to be sure. How could I be sure about anything any more?

Hope was driving me. Hope that there had been some mistake, hope that it was a bad dream, that there would still be something at the end of it.

I pulled over and stopped the engine. The only sound was the ringing in my ears and blood thudding in my temples.

And my chattering teeth. What was the sense in it? I was going nowhere.

I gave myself a couple of minutes to let my pulse slow then got the car going again. Drove on until I saw a phone box on the edge of a village.

I called the Scheme main line, reversing the charges. Ursula was on duty.

'It's Dan. I need Stuart.'

'He's off duty. I'll put you through to someone else.'

'No! Only him. It's an emergency.'

She sighed, 'Scheme policy—'

I cut her off. 'Only him or the phone goes down.'

Her voice was flat, weary. 'I can't without prior author-ised—'

'*Do it.*'

The line went dead for a few seconds, then Stuart's voice came on.

'Dan, what's happened?'

I gave him a rundown.

'Jesus. You sound terrible.'

'I've been better.'

'Hold on. You saw these people?'

'Two figures outside the workshop.'

'And in the house?'

'For fuck's sake, I heard steps. The power had been cut. You think I'm making this up?'

'I just want to be absolutely clear. Did you see anyone in or near the house?'

'I didn't exactly wait around.'

'Outside the workshop, did you see anyone get out of the car?'

'It was occupied. I saw the wipers move. Who sits in an unlit car with the engine off at two a.m.?'

He was silent for a few seconds. 'Where are you now?'

'As far away as I could get.'

He sighed. 'Dan, listen to me. You've been through a terrible, terrible time, you're in shock, you can't have had much sleep. We'll come and get you.'

I didn't answer. I replayed it all. I had no proof. Now that I'd stopped the adrenalin had ebbed away. Sleep was tugging me as the cold tightened its grip around me. I leaned against the side of the phone box. The light was dead, the number invisible.

'I don't know where I am.'

I heard my voice, blurred.

'Have you been drinking?'

'Trent showed me the picture.'

Stuart sighed. 'I'm sorry it had to come from him. Don't worry. We're going to sort it.'

'What's Shimmer?'

'Haven't the foggiest. Dan, we'll come and get you.'

I held the phone away from my ear, tried to think. Premiera: I had to make that call – find who Sara had met in the shop and get to them somehow. If I let Stuart's people pick me up, that would be a problem, another negotiation.

I put the receiver to my ear again. 'I'll get back to you.'

I drove another ten miles until I saw another call box.

The operator wouldn't take a reverse charge call to a mobile. So I dialled Greg's number myself and hoped he would be curious enough to ring back if he heard it.

He did.

'Hey, what's up?'

'You at home?'

'Affirmative.'

'I need your help.'

He snorted. 'What are friends for?'

He gave me directions. I headed back to the A27, the swooping road that runs east–west across Sussex. It was raining again. I was doing well over seventy. I squinted through slitted eyelids; it was like being pelted with tiny stones. I aimed myself at whatever tail lights I could see ahead. In my path was a small white van with a Golf ahead of it. As I pulled out to overtake, so did the van. I was too committed to change or brake so I crossed into the oncoming lane just as a motorcycle appeared over the brow ahead. I heard the van brakes scream as I passed through the closing space between it and the bike and allowed myself a glance behind to see if they had all made it. I felt a grim surge of satisfaction.

The track from the road was overgrown. Brambles scraped the sides of the car. I ducked to avoid them whipping my face. I killed the engine and rolled towards the buildings, my ears still ringing from the noise. The Downs rose steep and black behind the farmhouse. Last summer we had been to a farm near here with the children. Emma had fallen in love with a lamb. I had a hard time separating her from it. 'You can have your own when you're older,' I'd said, but she wasn't convinced. 'But what if I die before then?'

The place looked deserted except for an ancient ex-Army Land Rover parked in the yard and a dull orangey light in the downstairs windows. I tried to reach for the car door handle but my hands were frozen and claw-like from holding the wheel. A security light blasted me and a door opened. Greg's silhouette.

'Fuck, you're a mess.'

Twenty-four

I crouched by the fire in an ancient armchair, a parka draped over my shoulders, sipping a mug of tinned soup through cracked, burning lips. My head was still buzzing with adrenalin. My sight was still blurred from the drive and my eyelids, which I'd smeared with Vaseline, were swollen and raw. In front of me was a first aid kit. I found some tweezers and pulled out the bits of glass in my feet before lowering them gratefully into a plastic washing up bowl of hot water.

Greg watched, leaning back in a rocking chair, smirking and shaking his head.

'You joyriders never learn ...' He raised his can of lager and winked. 'To old times.'

'I'll need some new wheels.'

He wagged a finger. 'You're not going anywhere like that, sunshine.'

I used to be the one telling him what to do. He was revelling in his new role.

'Read my lips boy: R - E - S - T.'

The room smelled of woodsmoke and an unfamiliar, animal smell I traced to the pheasants hanging by the old-fashioned cooker. A couple of shotguns were propped by the door, along with an ex-Army SA80 and a sniper's L96 with a night filter on the sight. Various items of Army surplus clothing hung from a row of pegs in the porch and on the hearth, two identical pairs of mud-caked boots were propped up against a neat pile of firewood. The only evidence of his earnings from Trent was a giant flat-screen TV in one corner, and an expensive looking music system on the counter. A small laptop was open on the table.

Under it, on an incongruously bright rug with red and orange stripes, were feathers, evidently from the half-plucked bird on the table. Above the sink hung a row of menacing looking knives and on the draining board, an unexpected touch: a drying rack containing some decent looking antique plates. He saw me notice them and a half pleased, half defensive look came over his face as if he feared I might make fun of him.

'Picked 'em up for nothing in a charity shop in town. The old dears wanted a quid. Beat them down to forty pence.' He saw my weary expression and laughed. 'Amazing what people give away to these places though. Look at this.'

He reached into a drawer in the side of the table and produced a knitted woollen tea cosy, blue and green striped, the sort no one used any more.

'Remember?'

I shook my head.

He tut-tutted. 'Just like your mum's.'

I started to get up. 'You got a bike?' I asked. 'Or any other motor?'

He motioned me to sit. 'Not telling.' He smirked. 'You're the one always said, think before you move. Just relax for a minute, will you. You just got here.'

I tried to let go but all my muscles seemed to be engaged, like a car jammed in gear.

I went over the events of the last few hours.

OK. They had some way of getting in the house. They knew where to look for me at the wharf. Was that a smart guess or was there a team? Still the question though: *Who were they? What did they want?*

Greg listened, alert. There was a time when he would have been drunk or stoned by now, and I had never known him to reach his bedtime sober. Now he fixed me with a piercing gaze as if he could draw the answer out of me.

'Who've you talked to?'

'No one.'

'Well, someone knows where you live and where you play with your toys.' He sat in silence for a few minutes and then he chuckled. 'Not like you to land yourself in the shit, though. That used to be my job.'

'Yeah well ...'

'You didn't see them?'

'Just the two when I drove out.'

'And the Beemer?'

'Parked on the road. I don't know if it was the same car came down the garage track.'

'I fancy one of them. Top spec guzzler with the five point three V-eight global warmer. Cheap as chips these days.'

Suddenly he leaned forward and gripped my arm, face all serious. 'I'm sorry about your kids. Bet you were a good dad to them.'

There was a look in his eyes I didn't recognise, as if there was something more he was about to say. Then he suddenly got up, went to the fridge and got out a six-pack. He twisted off a can and waved the rest at me. I shook my head. He put them back.

'Trent showed me a picture.'

He looked blank.

'By Waheed's car, me with the gun.'

'Still don't get why you did that.'

I felt a sudden stab of anger. 'Didn't want it to get into the wrong hands, did I?'

He looked stung, and turned towards the fire, drank from his can. I changed the subject. 'How's it been – work?'

He took another long swig then examined the can.

'Can't complain.' He nodded emphatically as if trying to convince himself of his own words.

'What sort of jobs?'

His shoulders twitched. 'The regular stuff, close protection, driving. Good money and plenty of kip.' He jabbed a finger at me. 'You don't know what you've been missing.'

'Thought you were after some action?'

He waved the can. 'Yeah well, there's a time us old soldiers got to settle down.'

He had never been a great soldier – prone to moaning, frequently in trouble; the sort who needed structure but was always at odds with it. The sort who don't adapt to life back home. But he'd had a go, made a pact with normality. The tea cosy was a start, and the plates. It was more than I expected of him, but that hadn't been much. Compared to where I was right now ...

Looking at him, though, I felt that same old mix of impatience and compassion that had been the theme of our friendship.

I glanced at the windows. The rain had stopped.

'I've got to get moving.'

He wagged a finger.

'Stay. I've got more Heinz in the cupboard. Choice of flavours.'

Despite the jokey tone, he was revelling in this self-appointed parental role. He might not get the chance again.

I picked at the palm of my right hand where a small shard of glass was still embedded. 'I need a shower and some clothes.'

'And get some kip. You look like shit.'

The water that ran off me was a dirty pink from all the dried blood. I was crusted with fresh scabs and blotched with purple bruises and my feet still stung. In the bathroom was an x-shaped rack of clean clothes. I helped myself to a hoodie, sweatshirt, combats and thick socks. Nothing was my size, but they would do. I found a belt to hold up the combats, threaded it through the loops.

There was a pair of trainers on the landing. I pulled them on, my feet protesting. Outside an owl hooted. I needed sleep but the adrenalin was still pumping. Couldn't shut down yet.

When I came back to the kitchen Greg was at the table. He looked me up and down, in his gear, and grinned.

'We could be twins.'

He pulled out the contents of a jacket pocket and spread them on the table. Lighter, Rizla papers, tobacco, phone, a small bag of dope. I sat down at the other end of the table. He laid out four papers and licked the edge of each one.

'Should've seen more of each other. Since you were so near.'

I shook my head. 'Scheme rules.'

He nodded, but didn't look convinced. He knew I wasn't the rule-keeping kind, probably knew I had only come because I was in a fix. He stuck the papers together so they made one large sheet.

I pulled the laptop towards me.

'Nice piece of kit.'

'Dubai: duty free.'

I stroked the touchpad and it sprang to life. I typed Premiera into the searchbox.

Down one side of the page was an image of a woman, her face in shadow, partially clad in a lace basque.

OUTCALLS IN THE CROYDON AREA 24/7

Hi Guys. I'm Kika, five feet five, 36D, blonde and beautiful. I offer a dedicated legal service tailored to your personal satisfaction, providing you with the best visiting service in the Croydon area. Relaxing sessions for the discerning man. Call anytime to discuss your specific requirements.

All major credit cards accepted. Online payment available.
Total discretion assured.

I stared at the page, the anonymous torso. I clicked on *Contacts*. Another page came up with a series of fields to fill in. *Name, email, phone number, message,* a red asterisk beside each of them. *All fields mandatory.*

Greg moved towards the fridge, glancing at the screen as he passed.

'I'll be fucked. So much for the grieving husband.'

I managed a smirk. This wasn't the moment to get defensive. 'I'm only human. Anyone you know?'

He peered at the page. 'Sole trader, bit upmarket for me.' He reached over me, clicked on Favourites, then Brighton Classifieds – Barbee Chicks. 'Welcome to *my* world.'

The page was dominated by a huge pair of breasts with a small crucifix hanging between them. Choose from our stable of horny new girls.

He gave a little shiver of pleasure, then clicked back to the Premiera site.

I pointed at the screen.

'What's "Message" for?'

'You know, punters write what they want done, so they don't have to say down the phone.'

'How do they protect themselves, the girls?'

He shrugged. 'Some work in pairs, text each other. The smarter ones check you out first on the phone.'

He sat back down. 'One like that wouldn't come near a place like this, not unless you were a real regular. You need a hotel room. Then they call you back on the room extension, check you're really there.'

I closed the laptop, trying to order my thoughts. I watched him as he creased the paper into a V and sprinkled in the dope. Then he paused. His face clouded.

'Stuff I need to say.' He coughed into his fist as if he was getting ready for a speech. 'I've been fine, you know ...'

'Sure you have.'

'Fending for myself. No problem.'

'Course.'

'Done it before, hadn't I? When I was little.'

I wondered where this was leading.

'You and your mum, you looked after me.'

I chuckled, trying to lighten the atmosphere. 'She liked a challenge.'

He looked at me, deadly earnest. 'No joke. Without you two ...'

This was a side of him I'd never seen, even when he was pissed.

He rubbed a thumb and forefinger across his eyes. 'I'd have been dead or in prison, the way I was going.'

I shrugged. 'You had a bum deal. You got away from it. You should be proud of yourself.'

He carried on with the joint, sealing and smoothing out the fat cylinder.

'First time I stayed at yours, I nicked a tenner from your ma's purse.' He shook his head in self-disgust. 'She spotted it right away. I said it was you. She gave me this long look. She knew. Thought she was gonna clout me. But she didn't; just looked. Worst I ever felt, well almost ... So when she was out I put it back.'

He drained his lager then leaned forward over the table. 'She was the best. You know what she said? "The door is always open to you, Greg." That was the nicest thing anyone ever said to me. Then she said, "You look out for Dan, won't you." Man, she loved you.'

'I know.'

'Another thing: When she went ...' He swallowed, closed his eyes. 'I stayed out. Didn't want you to see me crying. Cos, like, she was your mum, not mine. Not for me to cry. And I knew you wouldn't, cos that's not what you do, right? Not your style. But I knew you'd be hurting more than you could say, right?'

'OK.'

He nodded emphatically. 'And there's this. Last time I saw her you know what she said?'

I nodded. I'd heard it a hundred times. He wagged a finger. 'Not *just* that I had to look out for you. No. There was another bit. Want to know what she said?'

He had momentum now; he wasn't going to wait for my encouragement.

'"Greg," she said. And she grabbed my wrist tight – even though the strength was almost gone from her. "Don't ever let him down."' He paused, then nodded a few times. 'I promised her. Yeah. And what did I do?'

I reached over, gave his shoulder a squeeze. 'Hey, all in the past. Forget it.' He shook his head; he wasn't to be deterred. I stared into my mug, waiting for him to get it over with.

'And what did I fucking go and do?' His voice had begun to shake. 'Fucking let you down, didn't I?'

I didn't respond.

'In the van, when you told me you'd got hitched, I thought – that's payback. You let him down, now he's fucking off out of your life.'

He held his head in his hands. His face had reddened. Maybe he was more pissed than I realised. But he was saying something I had always known. From the start, if it had been my choice, I'd have preferred not to have so much of him in my life, but I knew then, and so did my mother, that without us he didn't stand much chance.

He waved the spliff in my direction, like a tiny baton. He had recovered his composure. 'But then, know what? After a bit I thought, maybe this isn't so bad. Cos now I wouldn't have you around to remind me how crap I was all the time.' He sniggered, but I wasn't sure he was making a joke.

I gave him a thin smile. 'On the crap front, I think I'm ahead right now.'

The comment seemed to bounce off him. He put the spliff between his lips and flipped the lid off an old Zippo lighter. A fat flame danced in it while he lit up, then he snapped it shut. He took a large lungful and blew a cloud into the air above him.

He looked at me again; a new-found bravado gleamed in his eyes. 'I've had some time, yeah? To think about stuff, since you fucked off.' He leaned forward, offering the joint. I waved it away.

'So it's like this. I'm sorry you had to top the kid, OK?'

His words hung in the air between us. He had never apologised before. At the time he had been too stoned to take in what had happened.

'I should of come up the ridge with you, the state I was in.'

'Someone had to stay with the bodies.'

He jabbed the joint in my direction. 'You shouldn't of left me behind.'

He had made his apology, but now it had mutated into a rebuke.

'You weren't up to the hike.'

He looked put out. 'You knew I was off my head.'

I looked at the window. It had stopped raining again. I could go now, but where?

I shrugged. 'It was all fucked up. No armour, no cover, no back-up, no radio. Stuff happens. That's just how it is.'

He wasn't listening. He sniggered. 'Good drugs, though.' He rolled his eyes and waggled his head, laughed. As usual, his thoughts skipped about, jumping tracks like a runaway train. He frowned again.

'At the hearing, what did you tell them?'

I let my forehead drop into my palm. Right now I had other things to think about.

'Go on.' His eyes widened, waiting.

'That the boy had a gun, that there wasn't a choice.'

He opened his arms. 'So you didn't have to lie.'

'Until they asked me what type of gun, where I thought it had come from, if I was sure he was aiming at me ...' I felt a flash of rage. My hand grabbed his neck. I pulled him close. 'You put your fucking gun down. You didn't even know where you'd dropped it.'

He put his hands up. 'OK.'

I let go.

He shook his head, pityingly. 'See. Still pissed off. You, you should of talked to someone. Get it off your chest like I have.'

I glared at him, pushing the rage back down. It was a distraction I didn't need. He'd touched a nerve. For some warped reason it brought him gratification.

For a few minutes neither of us spoke.

He waved the spiff at me again. 'Help you relax.'

I shook my head.

'Suit yourself.' He smoked in silence, flicking the ash on to the table and swiping it off with the side of his hand, a knowing look spreading over his face. 'Bashir. That was his name.'

I glared at him. 'What?'

'He was twelve.' He nodded. 'Twelve and a bit. I had him checked out.'

I felt everything tense. 'What for?'

'Put a name to the face. Shrink said it'd help.'

'*You* saw a shrink?'

His eyes flashed with a born-again gleam. 'Surprised? Didn't think I'd got it in me, did you? *And* I sent his family some money.' He reached for another lager. 'Thought it

199

was time to put stuff right. Remember, in the van the Yank getting ...' He made a chopping gesture against his neck. 'Kept dreaming it'd be me next. Still have the dreams, but not so often.'

He jabbed a finger in my direction. 'Should try it – what with all you've been through.' He leaned forward and put a hand on my arm. '"Shut the door, move on." That's what you said to me after your mum died.' I took that to heart, like everything else you told me.' He shook his head. 'Know what? Didn't work. It doesn't go away. Blocks up like shit in a U-bend. Got to deal with it. That's what the shrink said. Said you'd be worse off cos you were the one slotted him.'

He popped the can. Some froth spurted onto the table. He waved it in the air. 'To old times.'

There was still an impish glint in his eye, as if there was more to come. I glared at him.

A fox screamed somewhere in the woods up on the hill. He held the can in mid-air, listening. There was a second cry. He looked at his watch. Then he strode over to the fireplace and picked up the gun with the night sight.

'Back in a sec. You get some kip.'

A sharp gust of night air rushed in as he left.

A digital clock radio on the counter said 03.10. The fire had sunk into the grate, the remaining logs glowing a dull orange. I put a couple more on from the stack on the hearth. A breeze stirred some tree branches outside. I could just make out the line of the Downs, black against a dark grey sky.

I got up and tried to stretch but sat down again, the strength gone from my legs. Bashir. A name for the face. And knowing the name seemed to bring the face into even sharper focus. I was back in the valley, the smashed Land Rover, the bodies of our crew, Greg – and Bashir, his olive skin, smooth as Charlie's, his eyebrows furrowed with concentration. There were others, watching from behind some half destroyed buildings. Someone shouted to the kid to come back but he wasn't listening. He had seen the gun. He had to have it. The look on his face, as if this was the moment he'd been waiting for all his life. Seeing the opportunity and grasping it with both hands. I knew just what was going on in his head – because that's what I'd have done.

In his own warped way Greg was right. I'd never dealt with what happened. I knew I'd had no choice. I was doing my job. I'd killed before, more times than I cared to count …

I blinked and the image was gone. I stared into the fire. Greg's words chimed with what I was having to face now, about myself, about Sara. 'Move on, keep looking forward.' That had been my mantra. I'd shared it with Sara. Now everything I thought I had got away from had chased me down. I was cornered. Nowhere to run or hide.

If I had talked to Sara, like Helen had suggested, talked about the difficult stuff, would it have made any difference? The last months, Sara had gone blank, unreadable. Would that have happened if I had told her everything? I thought I was a safe haven for her, someone she could count on without question. It hadn't been enough. When she was hurting, I couldn't reach her.

The air was thick with smoke: from the fire, from Greg's spliff. I needed to get out. I made another effort to stand. All the cuts and gashes pricked with pain as if I'd been rolled in nettles. I heaved on the parka and stepped out into the knifing cold. At least it sharpened my senses.

The yard was empty. A track led between the house and the barn up into the steep field behind.

He had started up the incline. He didn't look round when he heard my steps.

'Thought I told you to rest.'

'I can't sleep.'

At the top of the field was a row of scrubby trees. I walked behind him, wincing with pain. There was no moon or stars, just the dull glow from the town on the other side of the hill. There were no sounds except our breathing and the crunch of the undergrowth under our feet.

I watched his black form ahead of me, moving with incongruous stealth.

Suddenly he stopped, dropped to one knee and aimed. The sound smashed into the silence of the night, its echo bouncing off the Downs. Several metres away a small dark shape scuttled away into the trees.

Without turning round he spoke. 'He had guts, that kid … And I just ran …'

He cradled the gun in the hook of his elbow, pulled a squashed pack of cigarettes from his jacket and put one in his mouth. I tried to think of something to say. 'It was him or you.'

The look he gave me was one I didn't recognise. 'Should have been me. Not him. I was the one deserved it.'

He lifted his lighter. It wouldn't spark. His hands were shaking.

I stepped closer, took it from him and lit it. His face shone in the glow – it was running with sweat. The cigarette flared. He sucked hard on it. I stepped back.

His voice shook. 'I'm just a fuck-up. You and your mum, shouldn't of let me in your lives. Never. I wasn't worth the bother.'

'Why all this now? What's happened to you?' I put a hand out and grasped his shoulder. He stepped away nearly toppling. He gripped the gun.

A mile beyond the house, down the valley, a pair of headlights was moving fast along the road out of Lewes.

Greg's mouth was moving but nothing was coming out.

Tears were running down his face. A warning signal in my brain.

I heard the growl of a V8. The car slowed, disappeared behind some trees.

He swayed a little then moved his legs slightly apart as if bracing himself against the effect of the joint and the lager.

The car was nearer, slowing, the lights turning. I swung back to Greg, a sudden flash in my head like two wires touching. 'You knew it would be me. When I phoned from the call box, you said, "What's up?" You were expecting me.'

He made a whinnying sound like a scared animal. Then he raised the gun. His lips were slightly parted, his jaw tensed. His look told me he was somewhere else now, as if the sum total of everything bad in his life was crawling into his soul and taking control of it.

His words came in a rush, his voice high and shrill. 'I didn't have a choice. They said they'd take my fucking head off. They meant it. Just like the Yank on the film.'

I kept my eyes on him.

'Is this Shimmer?'

His mouth hung open. He held the gun chest high, the barrel shaking wildly.

'Who are they?'

There was sound of a door slam somewhere beyond the buildings. I turned to look, so I only saw the muzzle flash out of the corner of my eye. The sound wave nearly blasted me off my feet.

He toppled sideways. The gun still pointing up at his chin. Before I got to him a second blast tossed him in the air, the echo bouncing off the Downs. He lay flat on his back across the muddy track. He had missed his throat but the side of his head was glistening. His breath came in short hisses like a snuffling puppy. His eyes wide and wild.

I touched the side of his head but it was as soft as a trifle.

He grabbed at the parka and pulled me down, so my face was close to his. He tried to speak but couldn't. He coughed a spray of blood. 'Run. Go. Now.'

'What's Shimmer?'

His voice was just a whisper but there was no mistaking what he said.

'You. You're Shimmer.'

Then his hand dropped onto his chest.

Twenty-five

I hovered for a moment over Greg's body. The expression on his face was suddenly boyish again, as if the torture in his soul had left. I had always feared his life would end badly, that whatever demons he'd tried to vanquish as a soldier would find him and finish him, despite his dreams of attaining some semblance of a normal life.

I lifted the gun and checked it. Three rounds left, one in the chamber. I felt his pockets. No wallet, but a small pistol, a Beretta. He loved his guns. I took both and half-ran, half-stumbled up the hill to the edge of the trees. I vaulted a fence and flattened myself in the longer grass behind it, twisting round so I faced the house. I surveyed the house with the scope. Nothing. I kept it trained on the space between the house and the barn, murky greens and blacks.

A minute passed. I kept watching. A head appeared round the corner of the house at crouch level, then another, too far to see faces. One of them pointed at Greg's body. They were about twenty metres from it.

There was no point in running. I'd give away my position and in my condition I wouldn't get far. If they came nearer I could fire a warning shot to try scaring them off, but there was no guarantee it would. Or I could do what I'd been trained to do, and take them out. The first one would be easy. But the second would back out of sight and most probably run. Besides, there was another problem. I'd given up killing.

*

One of them came forward and checked Greg. He returned to his partner and they crouched down in a huddle, conferring.

I had to figure out what I wanted, what was driving me. All the people who mattered in my life were gone. What was left? My own animal self-preservation? The disinclination to submit to whoever was hunting me, and give them that satisfaction? Vestigial pride? Obstinacy? A glimmer of hope of something impossible?

All of those, and the need to know about Sara.

Lying here in the wet grass wasn't going to get me nearer to that. There was no knowing what the guys at the bottom of the hill would do, or if there were more of them. They might not leave before dawn. If I was them I would lie low, hoping that I'd eventually come back for nourishment and transport. If I was going to get away from them I was better off making the most of the darkness.

I ditched the rifle – moving with it was going to be a problem, so I unscrewed the scope and put it in a jacket pocket. Behind me, trees covered the brow of the hill. I wormed my way back into the undergrowth until I was well out of any line of vision, stood and headed straight up the hill. It was slow going through bramble and thick undergrowth; as the adrenalin subsided all the pain came back. Nothing to do but ignore it. Except for a dog barking somewhere in the distance there was silence. No wind, no movement. As I got higher the trees thinned out. I tried to pick up some speed and fell face first into some leaves, their cold wetness on my face almost soothing. I felt the temptation to stay there. Sleep was calling, but so was hunger. I got up again and kept going. My eyes were adjusting, even though they still stung like fire from the drive. I found a track that led up the side of the hill. I jogged to the top and came out into the open again. I glanced back. I could still see the house, so I kept going in the opposite direction, pausing only when my heaving lungs begged me.

Over the other side of the hill, the undergrowth became thicker again. I came to a barbed wire fence. Beyond was a field sloping down to a cottage. There was a dip behind the remains of a fallen tree, which had filled with rotting leaves. It was damp but soft and inviting. I unlaced the trainers and eased my feet out, but the pain was more pronounced so I put them back on. I curled myself into a foetal position to conserve what warmth I had and told myself to try and rest. As soon as I shut my eyes the last hours replayed themselves frame by frame. The weight of all these thoughts pressed me into a short troubled sleep.

It was still dark when I woke. A misty rain was falling and I was already shivering. I hadn't eaten properly for more than twelve hours. I was also thirsty and soaked. I had no money and no phone. There was no point staying put. I had to move if only to get back some warmth. I looked out at the field.

I patted the pockets of Greg's parka. No cash, just a scuffed pack of chewing gum. I took out a strip. The different taste in my mouth was welcome. I carried on down until I hit a track, which led to the lay-by of a narrow road. Then I headed in the direction of Lewes. It was raining steadily. Large drops fell from the edge of the hood and ran down my face. I tightened the trainers but even so my feet slid about inside. The glass cuts twinged with every step, and there was a stabbing pain in the ball of my left foot where a blister must have formed and burst. The road dropped down through an estate of brand new houses, some of them still not occupied. I was tempted to find shelter in one, but I needed to make the most of the darkness.

A chilly gust of wind dumped more rain into my face. I kept on into the town. In a pedestrianised street were benches, bike racks, and a bin, overflowing with polystyrene fast-food cartons. I was hungry, and thirsty. I could see the remains of a bag of chips and immediately my mouth filled with saliva. More urgent was the state of my left foot. Every step was like treading on fire.

I sat down on the bench and took off the trainer. The sock was soaked in blood. I peeled it off carefully, put it in my pocket and examined the foot. There wasn't much I could do except let the air get to it.

The childish sniggers made me think of the kids. But these weren't kids. I looked round. There were three of them. Two were about twenty, the third was older. He had a belly which pushed his football strip out so the hem flapped like a skirt.

'Filthy fucking junkie.'

I caught a gust of alcohol breath. I concentrated my attention on my foot. *Don't engage. Give them nothing back, they'll just carry on.*

'Look at the state of him. Look at his clothes. Hanging off 'im. That's smack for you. Pathetic.' They gathered round me. I ignored them. Suddenly I was on the ground, my right cheek in a puddle. I didn't see which of them thumped me, probably the fat one. This wasn't robbery. I had nothing they needed. This was entertainment.

'Get up, you fuck.'

The fat one grabbed the hood of the parka and hoisted me into a kneeling position and stepped back to take aim with his boot. Although the fall had disorientated me, the blow triggered a fresh burst of adrenalin, cutting through all the blur of fatigue and shutting off the pain. I focused on the trainer that was coming my way, jerked left so it shot past its intended target – my head. The momentum unbalanced its owner and he fell on his arse. I was weak but he was drunk. We were even. I had also accumulated a vast arsenal of rage.

He roared as he staggered to his feet. He was the fiercest of the three, the pack leader, but he was also my best bet. And if I damaged him the others would probably run.

When he came back at me I grabbed the trainer with both hands while it was still in the air and twisted it with all the force I could find. There was a loud *snap* from somewhere in his leg. Then he too was on his knees, bellowing like a gored bull. But I'd underestimated the two younger ones. One grabbed my head and smashed it against the bin. I heard a couple of teeth crack. I put an elbow into his stomach and he doubled over. The fat one struggled to his feet but was having trouble standing. The third one's blows were wild, badly aimed pummels. The bad thing about fighting with fists is it damages your hands. One of his blows missed me and went into the concrete post that held the bin. As the fist recoiled I caught it with both hands, separated the little finger and snapped it sideways like a twig. His squeal was loud and high-pitched and only when he paused for breath did we all notice the siren. They decided to run, but I wasn't finished. The fat one wouldn't have been my first choice but he was the straggler, hopping and stumbling on his good leg. I brought him down with a kick in the lower back. He didn't have time to shield his face and I heard his nose crack as it slapped the pavement. I turned him over and went straight for his pockets. A hand darted up and grabbed a hunk of my hair, pulling me down, and then the other, smeared and slippery with the blood from his nose, clamped on my ear. I used my weight to headbutt his nose. The fat one's hands retracted to his bloody face, his eyes bulging at me. The pain should have neutralised him but it did the opposite: two fists came my way again but I was out of reach. I fumbled for the pocket and pulled out Greg's pistol. When he saw it the fists unfolded into shielding hands. I pressed the barrel between them and right into his mouth. The look of dismay was grimly gratifying. This was a new experience for him. Maybe he thought he was just having a drunken bad dream. It was tempting to pull the trigger and discharge some of my rage.

'Phone and money. Now.'

He brought out a grubby mobile and a fistful of notes, held them towards me, the hand shaking wildly. I stepped back and grabbed them.

I looked at his trainers. My size.

The siren was close now. I tore the trainers off his feet, then put as much distance between us as I could manage.

Twenty-six

It was gone four a.m. The bus station was no more than a row of stops and small transparent shelters. A group of students were huddled in one, sharing a joint. Every few seconds they erupted with laughter. I positioned myself in the shadows, spat on a hunk of T-shirt and tried to wipe my face. Then I eased off the remaining trainer and checked both my feet. I tried on the fat man's trainers. Better. I laced them tight in the hope they'd rub less but both feet were still humming with pain. I had the Beretta tucked into a pocket in the combats. A police car cruised past slowly and the students watched it pass. When it had gone they laughed again. I stayed out of sight until the bus appeared. It said Brighton. That would do.

The driver gazed at me wearily as he passed me the ticket and change. 'Any trouble – you're off, OK?'

The bus headed down the A27, the road I had driven up a few hours before. I watched what traffic there was. The bulky silhouette of what could have been a BMW X5 shot by at about eighty and disappeared into the night.

The rest of the passengers were good cover. They were mostly revellers disinclined to observe the no-smoking signs and in the mood to cause a distraction. The driver ignored them. A couple of cans rolled and skittered across the floor each time the bus changed direction.

Near the Brighton bus station was a public lavatory. It looked like it was locked, but someone had forced the gate. It stank of vomit. Enough light from the street found its way in for me to examine my face in a scratched metal mirror. No wonder the bus driver was wary. A small dribble of water came out of the cold tap, which I used to wipe off some more of the caked blood and dirt. My lip was badly swollen. I felt round my mouth. Some jagged edges from chipped teeth.

The man behind the counter in the all-night café showed no curiosity as he took my order, but wanted paying up front. A big group of Chinese language students filed in and for the next half hour, while one interpreted the menu, each of them ordered minutely different breakfasts.

The food was hard to eat with my mouth in the state it was. But I was too hungry for it to matter. I ate the lot, pushed the plate away, lay my head on my arms and fell asleep.

The sunlight was almost horizontal. Beyond the palms the rim of the sea was pale blue. Their faces glowed gold. Charlie was running among the zebras while Emma fed one a fistful of grass. Sara turned to me and waved. Emma looked up. 'Daddy. Hurry up.'

I shot awake.

It was light outside. The clock behind the counter said eight. I ordered another coffee and some more toast. Then I took out the fat man's phone. Three bars up the right hand side of the display, half its power was gone. How long before the rightful owner got it blocked?

I dialled the Premiera number. Two rings and it was answered.

'Hello?'

A woman, maybe early thirties. I tried to fit the voice to the torso on the site, imagine her face. She was hurrying, hard rapid clicks of heels. A siren blotted everything out for a few seconds.

'Hi.'

'How can I help?' Bright, friendly, an undertow of efficiency, ready to ring off if I didn't sound right.

'I got your number off the web ... I've not done this before.'

She warmed up. 'That's no problem; you'll soon catch on. You understand that this is a personal massage service, strictly legal. The standard rate is a hundred pounds.'

I said that was OK.

'When were you thinking of?' Brisk again.

'Today?'

'I've only got one till two thirty. Whereabouts are you?' Her tone was so matter of fact, like fixing a dental appointment.

'I'm coming up from Brighton.'

'I only do outcalls, no private addresses, hotels only.'

'Can I call you back when I've got a reservation?'

'OK ... Text me when you're there and I'll give you the instructions. Can I have a name?'

'Dave.'

'OK, Dave, text me when you're fixed up.'

'And yours?'

'Kika.'

The café clock said it was nearly ten o'clock. I paid for the coffee and toast and counted out what was left of the fat man's money – eleven pounds. Hardly enough for a train ticket, let alone a hotel room. I went out onto the street, every part of my body protesting with dull aches and sharp stabs of pain. I shuffled into a chemist. The pharmacist gave me a wary look. I would need a makeover before anyone would let me have a room. I bought the strongest painkillers they would let me have and swallowed twice the dose.

Benjy's place was about a mile, up in the back of Kemp Town on the east side of Brighton. I tried to walk purposefully, trying to blend in with people heading to work, imagining a sniper's scope scanning the crowd, looking for anything abnormal, until I remembered my image in the toilet mirror. I didn't look like someone with a purpose.

He had just opened up. The carcass of a dismembered Lotus grinned out of the gloom of his premises. Bonnets, wings and other bits of bodywork either leaned against the wall or were stashed above in the rafters. A mound of small items, dynamos, alternators and carburettors, were heaped in the rear, as if a tsunami had washed in and piled flotsam up against the back wall. 'Order does my head in,' Benjy had explained when I first saw inside. But he'd been a useful source of spares and expertise.

He reared up from under a bonnet and glared at me, an unlit cigarette clamped between his teeth. He surveyed my face and clothes.

'They send you back to Astrakhan?'

Geography wasn't his strong point.

'Got into a bit of bother.'

He shrugged. 'What can you do?'

He rummaged in a pocket of his leather jacket and pulled out a lighter.

'Your wheels come up good.'

He beckoned me further in. The wheels from our Porsche stood in a neat stack, the alloy of the top one gleaming with fresh lacquer; I ran my hand round the rim.

'What would they fetch on their own?'

He wiped his nose with the back of his hand, the cigarette drooping from it. 'The set? Maybe a G.'

'Interested?'

He snorted. 'If I had the cash.'

I nodded at the worn-looking Yamaha he had just arrived on, ticking as it cooled, a crash helmet perched on the saddle. 'How about that instead, plus the hat?'

'For real?'

I nodded. 'And a few notes, whatever you've got on you.'

'You all right in the head?'

'Good question.'

He had done a stretch for fraud, and had probably got away with a lot worse. He knew better than to probe, just shook his head.

As well as the helmet, he threw in a padded jacket and gloves. He only had sixty pounds on him and some change.

I wheeled the bike out onto the pavement.

'Forks are bent, and it vibrates like fuck over eighty. Try not to get stopped; it's not taxed.'

A fine steady rain slicked the road. The helmet and gear made the run a lot more civilised than the dash in the Alfa but I had to concentrate hard as the bike pulled to the left at speed.

I kept to the slow lane, overtaking only to get past fountains of spray thrown up by trucks. As I passed Gatwick I caught sight of the roof of Trent's building.

The motorway dissolved into an A-road. I weaved through the morning commuter traffic; blank faces of people getting on with normal lives, muffled sound of radios and music behind rain-sprayed glass. A life that had eluded me.

I stopped at a Tesco's, bought a toothbrush, paste, cotton wool, antiseptic cream, some foundation make-up, a pair of lightly tinted sunglasses – the sort that some people wear all year round, a plain blue shirt and a local map with a list of hotels. I locked myself in a disabled toilet, put on the shirt and set about trying to make myself look more presentable. The bruising had spread across from my left temple. The gash on my chin was shallow. I applied a thin layer of the cream, then daubed on the foundation and spread it with the cotton wool. The result wasn't great, but with the glasses and the new shirt I didn't look so home-less.

It was twelve forty-five. I rode past the Hotel Clarion and circled back. It was big and busy. Two coaches had just emptied their cargo into the reception. I phoned first. They had rooms for forty pounds.

I texted Kika. *At the Clarion.* She called back straight away.

'Are you checked in?'

'Not yet.'

'I'll need a room number first.'

'Why's that?'

'That's how it works. You text me the number when you're there and I call you straight back on the room exten-sion. Just a precaution, OK? Get yourself ready and have a nice thorough shower, please, before we begin.'

I left the bike near the entrance, took off the helmet, checked my appearance in the bike mirror and put on the glasses.

At the desk, three receptionists manned computer termi-nals. A pretty Chinese woman looked at me blankly as I asked for a room.

'Certainly, sir. Single or double?'

'Single.'

She put out her hand. 'Your card?'

A bulky man towing a wheeled case came up alongside and flopped against the desk. Over his shoulder was a suit carrier. He was sweating. The tags on his bag indicated he had just flown in.

'Reservation for Holger,' he announced to all the recep-tionists at once. He was American.

A ginger-haired youth with a Trainee badge on his lapel got to work on his keyboard.

I smiled at the Chinese woman. 'Will cash be OK?'

She didn't smile back. 'I'm sorry, sir; we need a card for

registration, it's hotel policy.' She immediately shifted her eyes to a woman on my left.

'I can pay in advance.'

'Sorry, sir; as I said, it's hotel policy.'

I glanced at the clock. Twelve-fifty. My plan was evaporating. Ginger was preparing Holger's key card. 'I'm afraid your room's not quite ready, sir. If you wouldn't mind giving it fifteen minutes.'

There was a gust of stale breath as Holger let out a low groan. 'Oh great. And I got a meeting at two, I need to nap and get washed up.'

'I'm sorry, sir, if you'd like to take a seat in the Brasserie, I can arrange a complimentary drink.'

Ginger slotted the key card into a paper wallet and scribbled the room number on the inside: 641.

The Chinese receptionist glanced at me again. 'I suggest you try Yellow Pages ...' I thanked her and backed away into the throng, another plan taking shape.

The sixth floor had an L-shaped landing. Rooms 600 to 620 were to the left, 621 to 665 to the right. 641 was right on the corner. The cleaner's trolley was parked outside it. The door was open. I walked past, glimpsed the cleaner wiping down the TV. She was talking at high speed in a language I didn't recognise, an earpiece dangling from under her thick mop of black hair. I took out my stolen phone. A man loitering in a hotel corridor is strange. A man tapping a text into his phone is not.

After a minute the cleaner came out, still talking, and pushed the trolley on to the next room, leaving the door to 641 propped open. It wouldn't do as a place to meet Kika, but I could tail her. I nipped in before the cleaner turned round, went through into the bathroom. I waited. I heard her return and un-wedge the door. It closed with a heavy clunk. I checked the time on the bedside radio. Twelve fifty-five.

I texted Kika 641 and waited for the phone to ring.

It didn't.

Three minutes passed. Holger would be on his way. I phoned her number. It went through to voicemail. I dialled again. The same. The display turned from 12.59 to 13.00. *Welcome Mr Holger*, it said on the TV screen. *Enjoy your visit to Croydon.*

I went to the door and listened, heard the lift chime. I locked the door and returned to the bedroom phone. I heard a key card go into the slot. The handle turned. The card came out, went in again, then a heavy thump on the door. 'Ah, fuck this.' Holger, his day getting worse.

The room phone rang. 'Sorry, Dave. Don't worry, you'll get your full time. See you in three.' She rang off before I could reply. I put down the receiver and went back to the door. I could hear Holger's wheezy breaths. He was still out there. I opened the door.

His mouth formed a wide O.

I gave him a big smile. 'Your room's ready, Mr Holger. Enjoy your stay.'

I stepped past him and headed down the landing. He was still staring at me as I turned the corner. I walked past the lift lobby, towards the other end of the corridor, listening.

Thirty seconds later I heard the chime, then the lift doors opening. I took out my phone and put it to my ear, facing the other way. The footsteps turned and headed in the direction of 641. She was dressed in a dull-grey raincoat, flat shoes, a large bag over her shoulder, purposeful, not hurried.

I expected the encounter to be brief. She wouldn't linger once it was clear there had been a mistake. Hoaxers and time wasters were probably an occupational hazard, just something to be written off. I took the lift back to reception, found a chair with a view of the entrance and the lifts. I had just sat down when she emerged, head tilted, dark brown hair curtaining her face, a pair of large sunglasses covering her eyes, a gleam of lip-gloss.

All the noise in the reception area seemed to evaporate, like in the microsecond between the flash of an explosion and the arrival of the sound wave. I felt my whole body flinch and a hot sharp pain spread out across my chest.

She was so like Sara. Older, her face wider, more severe, but similar in the set of her shoulders, the line of her nose. She walked with short quick steps to the revolving doors. The sight of her leaving immobilised me. In the second I had wasted she was through the doors and into a white Skoda minicab.

I made a dash for the bike, pulling on the helmet. By the time I'd got going the Skoda was gone. It was a wide road, two lanes each side. I caught sight of the cab three hundred metres away at a set of lights, indicating right. The filter light turned green. I roared after it. I reached the junction just as the light went red and the traffic surged across my path. The road to the right ran uphill. The Skoda had disappeared over a brow. I shoved the bike into the oncoming lane. A Transit snaked as the driver jammed on its brakes, stopping an inch from my wheel. The Fiesta swerved and blared its horn. I was across. I felt the bike lift as I crested the brow and stood up in the saddle to give me extra height to see ahead. The Skoda was waiting at the next junction. I kept about fifteen metres between us, far away enough not to be conspicuous, close enough to keep up through any other lights. After about five minutes the Skoda indicated and slowed. I pulled in several car lengths behind. At the end of a row of shops was a tower block, surrounded by a wide barren area of grass and asphalt. Kika paid the driver and walked towards the block. I got off the bike and followed. Was this her home? Her next appointment? I had no idea what sort of reception I was going to get. Best to assume it was negative. How much had Sara told her about me? What had she said? If Sara really was trying to get away from me, had she been part of the plan? Did she even know about the plane?

In her work she would have dealt with some difficult situations. She would know how to look after herself. I needed to approach her somewhere I could control.

Ten metres from the entrance to the tower block she stopped, felt in her bag then turned back, coming straight towards me. No sunglasses now. So like Sara, but much more make-up. There was nothing to do but keep going. Three metres from me she turned and went into a chemist. I followed her in. It was my turn to look purposeful. I pulled off the helmet and strode over to a display of toothbrushes. She walked up to the dispensing counter at the back and handed over a prescription. 'For Mr Harding.'

The female pharmacist looked at her stonily, then sighed sharply. 'He was in here this morning, demanding his meds again, wouldn't go.'

Kika shrugged. 'Sorry about that.'

The pharmacist was still agitated. 'Next time – I'm calling the police, OK?'

Kika gave a placatory wave. The pharmacist turned to me and put out her hand for the toothbrush, still addressing Kika. 'Can't have that behaviour in here.'

She scanned the toothbrush, put it in a bag and gave me the change. I turned to leave.

'There's only so much we can put up with ...'

I walked out and headed slowly towards the tower block, studying my mobile again. Accosting her at her door wasn't going to work if there was someone waiting for her. I heard her footsteps behind and slowed but kept just ahead of her.

The door to the block had a security code lock on it. I

paused, concentrating on the blank face of the mobile as she went up to the door and punched in the number. I grabbed the door before it closed again just as a woman with a double buggy charged out of the lift, filling the doorway. I glanced at the babies, twins, asleep in identical positions. No choice but to hold the door while she manoeuvred the buggy. Kika was in. I let go the outer door and leaped for the lift doors just as they shut. I punched the button but I heard the whirr. The lift was already moving.

Even without glass in my feet it would have been hard to keep up, but what was driving me now numbed the pain. I took the stairs two at a time. Each floor had four doors. Each of the doorbells had a small window beside it. Some were covered over with labels, others blocked out. Some were smashed. None had names. I passed a child, wailing, a teenager with her busy lighting a cigarette. A door opened and let out a burst of TV laughter as a man emerged with a big bag of laundry. I heard the lift groan and stop the next floor up. The doors parted just as I got there.

'Kika?'

She glanced up, blank. Then she dipped a hand into her bag, pulled out a small canister. Mace. I dived out of the way as the spray arced up. I dropped the helmet and grabbed her wrist, shook the can out of her hand. A blow with her other fist came down on the bruised side of my face. My foot skidded on the can. I kicked it away and it bounced down the first flight of stairs. Her forehead crashed into my nose. She was quick. She'd had to do this before. I kept hold of her wrist and scrabbled for the other flailing arm. Her knee came up into my crotch. I twisted away and managed to lessen some of the impact but I almost blacked out. I got hold of her other arm and pinned her against the wall, both of us gasping for breath. Her bright red dress showed where a button of her coat had come away, her face was full of rage.

'I'm not here to hurt you, OK? Just a talk, then I'll go.'

Eventually her muscles un-tensed. I let go, stepped back.

'You know who I am?'

I retrieved the helmet. Her bag had slipped off her arm. I retrieved it and handed it to her.

She kept her eyes away from me, breathing hard. A tear dripped off her chin.

'She was on that plane, wasn't she?'

The door behind us opened a few inches. A big florid face appeared in the gap above the door chain.

'Just open the door, Dad.'

She looked me in the eye, for the first time, fierce. 'Nothing in front of him, OK?'

Twenty-seven

Harding closed the door to release the chain then opened it further. He leaned heavily on a walking frame so his head was thrust forward. A thick tuft of white hair sprouting from a low hairline gave the impression of a rhino preparing to charge. He glared at me with small bright eyes. 'Who the fuck's this?'

Kika gave the door a push but the walking frame was in the way.

'None of your business. Here.'

She thrust her hand into her bag and pulled out the package from the chemist. He retreated a foot and the door came fully open. Warm stagnant air wafted out. Next to the door was a long framed photograph. Men in uniform. Beside it, a picture of a teenage Sara, posed, expressionless.

Harding performed a laborious U-turn and shuffled into a room at the end of the hall where a television was blaring. I glimpsed more military memorabilia on the wall, a commode, a leg brace, a huge pile of magazines. Another picture of Sara, younger, in school uniform.

Kika nodded towards another door. 'In there.'

A large wardrobe, doors gaping, dominated the room. A sofa bed was half covered with more clothes. A mini-laptop was open on the coffee table, beside a make-up kit. She dropped her coat on a chair. Underneath was a strapless, tight fitting dress, violent red.

'Wait here.'

She was gone for a couple of minutes. I put down the

helmet and gloves and sat on the edge of the bed. When she returned the make-up was gone. Even more like Sara. She stepped across to the wardrobe, put on a cardigan. Off duty now.

She closed the door behind her and leaned against it, her arms folded, her gaze cold, wary. From behind the door came the sound of her father's TV.

Her voice was low. 'Keep it down, OK.'

'You're very alike.'

She continued to stare into the space between us, silent.

'Sara never spoke about you. I thought you were overseas.'

She snorted, gripped her forearms. Her face looked pale, almost translucent, as if the pigment had faded. There was a long silence. I waited for her to speak. She blinked a few times, more tears coming.

'You came to see her – in the shop?'

No response. She was looking at me more, assessing.

'I'm trying to find out what had happened to her. I need to know what she told you.'

'She's dead. What's it matter?'

'How do you know she is?'

'She'd told me she was going to Tobago. Where that plane was ...' She pressed a fist against her mouth to stifle a cry.

'When you saw her, what did she tell you?'

She turned away.

'I'm not going until you tell me. I'm not going to hurt you, but I have to know.' I leaned back, folded my arms to show her I wasn't moving.

Kika reached into her bag and took out a pack of cigarettes, lit one with a lighter, blew a long jet of smoke into the room and glared at me.

'Just tell me what she said.'

'That she had to get away, start again.'

I felt everything tense. 'Go on.'

'Said she was taking the children, going somewhere safe.' Her eyes flashed, full of contempt. 'She was so scared.'

'What of?'

She looked at me wearily, as if the answer should have been obvious.

My face was heating up. 'What did she say?'

Kika shook her head. 'She was frightened, that something was going to happen if she didn't get away, her and the kids. She said – it hadn't worked out and she was in trouble.'

'What trouble?'

'She wouldn't say.' Kika folded her arms, glancing at me cautiously. 'She said it had to be a secret. No one could know.'

My face burned. 'If you think I harmed her ...'

She gave me a disparaging look.

'Did you see them – the children?'

She shook her head. Tears suddenly welled up in her eyes. She ignored them as they ran down her cheeks. 'I asked if I could. She was afraid – in case they said anything to you.' Her face reddened. 'She said she wasn't allowed to see anyone, talk to anyone. I told her I wasn't having this. I was going to get on to social services ... She begged me not to. Said she'd get into terrible trouble.'

Her eyes filled with tears again. 'It's all she ever wanted – her own family. A chance to do it right.'

Her chest convulsed with sobs.

I shut my eyes for a second, trying to sort through what I was hearing. Sara had planned to go without me; she had dumped the passport. But why was she so scared? Why hadn't she confided in me? A whole side of her I didn't know, didn't understand.

'Was that the only time you saw her?'

Kika took another drag of her cigarette, her eyes unfocused.

'The time before was when she'd just met you.' She wiped her eyes and fixed her attention on something outside. 'She was so happy then, so certain. She said: "I'm going to do this. I'm going to have my own life. I've found what I want." Never saw her so happy. Free at last.'

'What do you mean, free?'

I could hear her father shuffling outside, the walking frame banged against the wall, then a curse. Kika shivered and moved away from the door. She wiped her cheeks with her fingertips, then she shut her eyes, clutching her arms. 'She never talked about him?'

I shook my head. 'Nothing.'

Her mouth opened, hesitated as if testing the words in her head before she spoke. Then she sighed and shook her head slowly. 'You wouldn't understand.'

'Try me.'

She focused on the space between us. 'Even before Mum died, he—' She took a breath. 'First me – then both of us. She was his favourite. When you don't know different you just – live with it. He said if either of us told he'd kill the other.' She looked hard into my eyes and raised a finger. '"One word …"' Then she made a cutting motion against her throat. 'He controlled everything.'

Kika sucked on her cigarette. 'Sara was the brave one. She'd just go blank. "I just act it. Like it's a part." That's what she said. "It's not me. I switch off. I'm not really there." That's how she coped.' She exhaled. 'And looking after herself. Everything she did, how she dressed, her school work – all neat and tidy. Nothing out of place. So no one would know, no one would guess. It was the same when she started acting.'

I listened, motionless, my innards dissolving, as if I'd swallowed acid.

She pushed up a sleeve and scratched her arm. 'I tried ...' She shook her head. 'My way – just to get out of it, float away. When it got expensive he started paying for my stuff.' She sniffed and wiped her nose with the back of her hand.

'So you couldn't leave?'

She nodded. 'I wanted her to get away, to have the life she deserved, for her sake and mine. Something good – at least for one of us. She always believed in the future, that there really were happy endings.' She glared at me again. 'And then you came along.'

She waved the cigarette and shook her head. 'She wanted me to meet you, but I wasn't in good shape then. Didn't want to spoil anything for her.' She sighed and wiped her face. 'I told her it had to be a clean break, no contact, no way of him finding her.' She nodded at the door. 'That I couldn't know, so no matter what he did to me, I couldn't tell, because he'd have come after her.'

She lit another cigarette from the remains of the first. 'He wasn't like that then – before his stroke. Running, training – and the drinking. When he realised she'd gone, he went mad, right off his head. Then he wanted to go to the cops.' She threw her head back and laughed a shrill empty laugh. 'Said she must have been abducted. He just didn't get it.'

As if on cue, the door burst open and banged against the wall. Harding was standing there, leaning on his frame, heaving for breath.

'Go away, Dad, we're talking.' He looked at me, his face a rough terrain of creases, a sergeant major's face, the sort that had spent a lot of time contorted with anger. He gestured with his chin. His voice was a hoarse snarl. 'You want her, use your own place.'

I stood up, moved towards him, taking control of the space. I put my face near to his, gave him a hard look. 'I'll be gone in a few minutes.' We stared at each other for a few seconds then he backed out of the door, as I closed it gently in his face.

I turned back to Kika. 'Why do you stay?'

She frowned as if she was having trouble thinking of an answer; the same dead look I had seen in Sara's eyes. 'It's a room. I've nowhere else.' Her eyes unfocused. 'We shared it when we were kids.' She gestured with her chin. 'Every night we'd go to sleep, holding hands. We had the doll's house there between the beds. Sara was obsessed with it. Four walls, no one above or below or either side. That's what she loved about it. That's what she wanted when she grew up. And stairs with carpet on. *Dream House*. She painted the name above the door.'

'I thought she'd got it second-hand.'

Tears ran down her face again. She made no attempt to wipe them. Her arms hung limp by her sides. I went towards her, but she shrank back.

'She gave me some hope. Because she got away, from all – this, found someone to be with, where she thought she could be safe ... And then, seeing her that last time, in the shop, blank – like she used to be, like she'd never got away...' Her face tensed again, contempt in her eyes. 'Turned out she'd swapped one prison for another.'

I knew I hadn't harmed Sara – but Kika had no reason to believe that. I heard Helen the doctor's voice again: *You don't talk about what you can see in your head every day; it starts to come out some other way.* If Sara had told me any of this, could things have been different? It didn't explain her actions – her need to escape from me.

I moved closer. She stiffened. I took hold of her arms, looked into her face. 'Look at me. You have to believe me; I never hurt her. Sara and the children were everything to me. She was the only woman I ever loved. I knew there were things in her past she didn't want to talk about; I respected that. Maybe that was wrong. Six months ago something happened, a change. She started to withdraw. She wouldn't talk, wouldn't tell me what was happening.'

Kika looked at me for a long time. Assessing. She twisted out of my grasp and went to the other side of the room, leaned against the window, lost in her own thoughts.

A full minute passed before she spoke. 'Last year, August, someone came here, to see Dad. I wasn't here. Told him he was from social services, for an assessment, but when I called them they denied all knowledge. He was here two hours. Dad wouldn't say what it was about, but it had spooked him. Two days later I went to a job. A hotel. Got to the room, the john was in a mask. I've had that before. He cuffed me. OK, that's what he'd specified – an extra. Cash was on the table. But instead of doing the business, he just asked me stuff. Didn't hurt me, didn't touch me. All I could feel was his breath on the back of my neck, but I knew I wasn't going anywhere till he'd got what he wanted.'

She turned to the window, her breath condensing against the glass.

'What stuff?'

'"Tell me about your family. Tell me about your father." He didn't say he knew, but it was like he did: everything. Some men just want to talk, hear stuff; that's what turns them on, but this was different. There's a rule, you don't mix business with personal. But he wasn't having that. He said, "I want the truth, and if I find out you've lied, there'll be consequences." He made me describe ... all Sara had to put up with.' She leaned against the window, a hand over her eyes.

'Do you remember anything about him?'

'Nothing to remember. Slim, medium height, kept his voice very quiet, didn't have any accent. He had the mask on and the hotel towel gown. Didn't touch me except to do the cuffs. When he left I had to keep my face buried in the pillow.' She bit the knuckle of her thumb. 'He said just what you said.'

'What?'

'"You're so like her."'

She wiped the corners of her eyes with a fingertip, gave me another wary look.

'And after I saw her in the shop in Worthing, there was a call. The voice was a whisper but I think it was the same. "I know you care about Sara more than yourself. She's going to disappear, for good this time. If you raise the alarm or make any attempt to find her, she'll get punished, like she was before. So will the children."' Her breaths came fast as if she was reliving the shock she'd felt. 'I just thought it must have been you.'

My vision blurred as if I'd been hit over the head. It was almost too painful to take in what she was saying.

A heavy knock on the front door focused me. Kika froze. I heard Harding stir outside. I stepped towards the door. 'You expecting anyone?'

She didn't answer. I pulled the door open. Harding, stooped over his frame, filled the hall. He looked round, a lipless grin. The knock repeated. I listened. A squawk of a radio.

Twenty-eight

There were two options, and a fraction of a second to choose. If I went quietly I might be safe from who ever had come after me to Greg's, but there would be questions about his place, his shooting, the incident in Lewes. Lots of explaining. Eventually Stuart or one of his people would show up and take over.

Not yet.

I wrenched the door open. Two cops, a man and a woman. I bent forward and charged, butting my way through the narrow gap between the cops. One fell back as I came up hard against the closed lift door. The WPC made a grab for my arm. It spun me round and I lunged at the stairwell, sliding and rolling down the first flight. I got back on my feet and leaped down the stairs a flight at a time, catching the banister to swing round the corners. A youth in a hoodie flattened himself against the wall as I passed. I slipped on something slimy and slid on my arse down half another flight. I could hear feet clattering behind me a few flights above, more coming from below, almost drowned by the din of blood pumping in my ears.

On the second floor the man with the laundry was on his way back. He had just emerged from the lift with his load and was opening his door. I pushed him forward so we both fell into his hall. I leapt up and closed the door. 'Sorry, I need to use your balcony.' He stared up, open-mouthed, as I climbed over him, into the living room then out through the door.

'What the fuck—'

I turned and shushed him, then swung a leg over the side and lowered myself onto the balcony below – one floor up. I looked down. There was another cop looking up. I dropped down on top of him, the air going out of him with a shout as he broke my fall.

There were three police cars, two with lights still flashing, a third, occupied. Benjy's bike was thirty metres beyond them. I could circle round, but that would eat up time. I heard a yell from inside the lobby. No choice but to head straight for the bike. The door of the police car in between opened. There was no room on the other side. The adrenalin was pumping hard, charging me up. I vaulted onto the bonnet then strode straight over the car, the bike key at the ready.

The engine clattered into life. Something wasn't right. The helmet. I'd left it on Kika's bed along with the gloves. Too bad. The cop was out of his car but got back in when he heard the bike rev. I kicked away the stand and the rear tyre screamed as it hit the tarmac.

It was a cul-de-sac, the tower block at one end, a T-junction at the other. The junction was cut off by another approaching police car. I steered back towards the flats, mounted the kerb and headed across the grass in front of the block. Another cop had emerged from the lobby and launched himself right into my path. I kept accelerating. He made a grab for my arm as I tried to steer past which made me swerve into a bench. The front tyre bounced off it, sending the wheel into the air. I used the momentum to pull the bike into a position with a clearer path, then took off again, across the grass to another road that ran behind the block, speeding between two bollards and clipping a *Pedestrians Only* sign.

I tried to keep my speed sensible. There's no point going too fast in busy streets. The faster you go the sooner and the more often you have to brake. That's what I tried to tell myself. I caught sight of the speedometer. Fifty. I looked up again and I was a few metres from a woman with a buggy, oblivious, talking into a phone. I swerved, the brakes locked, the bike went over and we parted company. I tried to roll myself up ready for the impact but my head went between my arms and I heard a crack as my cheek hit the road.

When I came to I looked round for the bike, couldn't see it at first. It had finished up half under a truck, its engine still idling. I got up, fell down again. Felt something wet dripping into my left eye. The buggy woman took a tentative step towards me. I waved her away. 'It's OK.'

I pulled myself up again, retrieved the bike and heaved it back on its wheels. The left mirror and indicator were gone. The woman's phone was on the ground. I picked it up, smearing it with blood. I wiped it on my sleeve and passed it to her. 'Sorry about the mess.'

The street behind was full of sirens bouncing off the buildings. I headed away from the sound. One of the handlebars was bent but the bike seemed to be intact. I dabbed the eye with my sleeve. Then I remembered the glasses I had bought this morning. They helped a bit. With the wet eye closed, I squinted through the other.

I didn't think about directions until I saw on the horizon the Crystal Palace pylon rearing up above the buildings. Heading into London wasn't a good idea. I took a couple of right turns until I was going roughly south again and pressed on through the network of suburban streets that run down the side of the A23. I could still hear sirens but in the distance.

I hit the M23 and wound the bike up to the point where the vibration threatened to shake the handlebars out of my grip. Thoughts started to crowd in. After Gatwick I took the route for Lewes. As the adrenalin started to subside I felt my energy drain away too. The side of my face that had hit the ground was starting to pulse with pain, like feet marching over my head. I lifted a hand to it and the bike swung across into the fast lane, almost lost it. A truck blasted its horn. A few miles on I ran a light, missing a car by inches. 'Fucking idiot,' the driver shouted. I wasn't concentrating. Too much in my head. It started to rain, hard. Kika's words came back like jolting shocks. The light was starting to go.

I pulled into a petrol station and with the remains of Benjy's money bought petrol, a couple of sandwiches and a Coke. The man on the till looked at me like I was the Terminator.

'Got a toilet I can use?'

His head shuddered. I took that to be a no. I rode on a few miles then pulled in to a lay-by, switched off and put the bike on its stand. There was a derelict bus shelter, no windows, no seat, just a roof. I went under there to eat the sandwiches, drink the Coke. I sat on the ground, elbows balanced on my knees, let my head hang between them, listening to Kika's words replaying in my head, a whole side of Sara I'd never known.

Suddenly I couldn't eat any more, spat out the mouthful of sandwich on to the ground. I felt the area round my eye with my fingertips. A rough surface of wind-dried scab had formed. There was a big tear in the shoulder of the jacket.

She'd swapped one prison for another.

Sara thought I was her safe haven, the person who would love and protect her. She'd been wrong. I'd failed to read the signals, to even begin to understand her torment. By keeping a safe distance, observing our rules of engagement, I'd lost her.

And now, with each discovery came more questions. Who was the man in the mask? What else was there in Sara's past I didn't know about? What was clear was that she had been in a desperate dark place, too afraid to confide in me. I brushed some rain from my hair. She was trying to get away – from me. Why? The place in Tobago: no place for children, how would that have worked? Was she trying to leave for good? Was she so desperate and afraid that she hadn't thought anything through?

It was almost dark. The temperature had dropped. There were no sounds except the rain and the empty hollowness of the woods. I needed shelter, sleep, somewhere to think, to put the pieces together. I was out of options. I got out the phone. It was dead. I threw it into the woods and got back on the bike.

Twenty-nine

River Cottage was at the end of a track that ran next to the village church. I killed the engine and let my ears adjust to the silence; nothing but the bark of some crows in the high, leafless trees beyond the spire. It was already almost dark, what little colour there was in the landscape drained away into greys and blacks. Either side of the road was woodland. I wheeled the bike a few metres off the tarmac and laid it down in some thick undergrowth. It sank almost out of sight. I put the bag with it, but kept the scope in my pocket.

I didn't go up to the cottage straight away. I went through the church gate and into the graveyard, walking parallel with the drive to the cottage. There was a light on over the door and another in one downstairs room. Someone came out of the church so I paused and gazed at a gravestone. Two children, brother and sister: *Gone to a better place*. The man strode past, his long coat flapping. 'Chilly tonight.'

I nodded without looking up. For the next few minutes I wandered through the graves until I was sure he was gone. Then I moved to a corner where a sycamore overhung Jane's garden. I knelt down and examined the cottage through the scope. No sign of anyone, no car but some recent tyre tracks in the gravel. I went up to the door. There was no bell, just a knocker. I lifted it and let it drop so it bounced twice. Nothing. I examined the door. A Yale and a mortise. I stepped back and scanned the front. No sign of an alarm box. I circumnavigated the cottage, checking each of the downstairs windows, all of them secured with key locks. A door into a back porch had a cat flap. I felt inside in case there was a key. The temperature was dropping fast. I was seriously chilled from the bike. Another night in the cold wasn't a good idea. I'd done enough of those in Afghanistan. They took a long time to recover from. I needed dry and warmth – soon.

There was no guarantee Jane would appear. I circled again, looking at the upstairs windows. The drainpipes were too fragile to climb and too far from the windows. I checked the garden for a shed and considered it as somewhere to rest. Nothing for warmth – and my own body heat was down. I examined what was there. A mower, garden tools, an ancient A-shaped wooden ladder for picking fruit from trees, shears, secateurs, a pair of gardening gloves, stiff and split, but gloves nonetheless. I shoved my hands in and worked the fingers.

I dragged out the ladder and leaned it against the cottage. Not nearly tall enough to reach an upstairs window. I rummaged in the darkness of the shed, groping for inspiration. A loose clump turned out to be a length of nylon rope. I untangled it and laid it out on the grass. It was in two pieces. I knotted them and paced out the length. About fifty metres. I found a shard of slate and tied it to one end, spun it above my head like a lasso, then sent it sailing over the roof of the cottage. By the back door was a boot scraper, cemented into the wall. I tied one end to it and, collecting the secateurs on the way, went round to the front. The slate was swinging about seven feet from the ground. I fetched the ladder, set it against the wall under one of the upstairs windows, worked the rope along until it hung roughly in front of the top right hand window and started to climb.

There was a crack as loud as a gun as the rung I was standing on snapped. I froze, hanging from the rope, my foot hunting for another rung. Eventually it found the top

237

of the ladder. Only room for one foot. I hauled myself up on the rope until I could grip the window sill. I felt for the secateurs and worked them under the bottom of the window frame. A small movement – the frame was rotten. I levered them further into the gap, twisting until the lock broke away. One leg of the ladder was starting to sink. It had shifted when the rung broke and was now on soft ground. I felt myself start to slide away. Not enough purchase on the sill to leave go of the rope.

And then the ladder was gone and I was swinging on the rope. I made a grab for the sill and knocked the secateurs off. I wasn't making a good job of this. As a kid I'd been fast. But I was out of practice.

The sill was just deep enough to get some grip. Maybe I could lever myself up with one hand while I got the window open with the other. I shoved two gloved fingers into the gap I had made and got the window up an inch, then two, then more – enough to get my head through if I twisted it sideways. The warm air wafting out from the bedroom gave me an extra spurt of energy. I heaved myself over the sill and flopped head first onto the carpet.

It was a small room with a single bed, featureless and unadorned, as if it had never been used. A small bookcase was empty. A couple of boxes were full of books. Next to a bathroom was another bigger room. Beside a double bed was a dressing table covered in bottles and bowls of jewellery. A large wardrobe stood open, some clothes were draped across a couch, and a few on the floor, the sort of mess Sara would never have tolerated. There was also a big suitcase, empty but open. A third room also had a small single bed and a view up the drive. I went downstairs and into the kitchen. It was small, with a low ceiling, an L-shaped counter and a folding table for two. I stood over the Aga, soaking up the heat. I found a kettle. While it was boiling I discovered a bread bin and bit straight into the remains of a loaf. And I saw a banana, which I wolfed down in four bites. I identified a tin of tea bags, took a mug from a shelf and poured in the water, splashing the counter. I added some cold so I could drink it straight away. I took it to the table, pulled out a chair, and sat heavily, the strength leaving my legs as they got the message to relax. The warmth and the sudden intake of food soaked up all that was left of my energy. My head nodded. I let it drop onto my arms.

In the dream, Sara was kneeling in front of the open doll's house. Emma was beside her holding to her chest a family of tiny dolls. One by one she passed them to Sara who arranged them around a miniature dining table ...

The light woke me. I squinted into the brightness. Jane was standing in the doorway.

Thirty

We stayed like that for several seconds, me blinking into the light, her motionless, car keys hanging from her hand. She looked different from when we were on the ship. Winter clothes. A leather coat and boots, a scarf round her shoulders, a high-necked sweater and big shoulder bag.

She surveyed the kitchen, the open bread bin, the half-chewed loaf, the banana skin.

'Sorry about the mess.'

She put her bag down and stepped closer, peering at my face.

'I came off a bike.' She glanced down at my hands, the knuckles split and scabby from the fight. She blinked a couple of times and swallowed. Then suddenly her face brightened, as if she'd come out of a trance. 'Well, I'm glad you're still alive.'

'I've been better.'

There were voices from over by the church. I stiffened.

'Choir practice. When the wind's the right way you can hear every word.'

'Are you expecting anyone?

She shrugged. 'No one comes here.'

I went over to the window. A small Mercedes two-seater was parked outside. I drew the curtains. 'Some people may be looking for me. I don't know who or why. Also I've had a bit of trouble with the police. I just need to sort myself out, get cleaned up, then I'll go.'

She didn't respond, as if her mind was elsewhere again, her eyes darting away from me and back, as they had on the ship. But her winter clothes, the bag, made her seem more grounded, less fragile.

'It might be dangerous for you. Even after I'm gone they may come here.'

She smiled faintly and shrugged, unperturbed, dropped the gnawed loaf back into the bread bin.

A phone rang in her bag. I swung round. She took a BlackBerry out, looked at the number, dropped it back into her bag.

'Your friend Frankland again.'

'He's not my friend.'

'He called this morning, said you'd vanished.' She swallowed. 'I thought maybe you'd given him the slip but when I tried your number it just rang and rang.'

'How did he know; had he been to my house?'

She shook her head. 'I didn't ask. I don't like talking to him. He's very nosy.'

She smoothed her hands down her thighs. 'You left the ship without saying goodbye. Where did you go?'

'Tobago.'

She held my gaze, waiting for me to say more.

'Then I came back.'

I glanced round the room. Taking it in properly for the first time. A small dresser of blue and white plates filled one wall.

'How long have you been here?'

'It's rented. The owners live in Italy.'

'You're moving?'

She looked puzzled.

'The boxes – upstairs.'

She turned away. 'Time to make a fresh start.'

She took off her coat. The fuzzy edges of her mohair sweater made her look slightly out of focus. She gave me a genteel smile, as if I'd just popped in for tea. 'Are you hungry? I can make you something. You could have a bath.

There's some of Howard's clothes ...' Her words came in a torrent, as if she was keen to change the subject.

The choir was getting going. Voices soaring and dying away.

'Do you believe in an afterlife?'

Her expression softened. She shook her head.

'Me neither. But it's as if Sara's trying to tell me something.'

She put her head slightly on one side, waiting for me to go on.

'What you said, on the ship. "You can't trust the dead." What did you mean?'

'Why?'

'I think you were right.'

She smiled, sad. 'I think you should get cleaned up.'

Thirty-one

The bathroom window looked out over the churchyard. The voices of the choir soared. I perched on the edge of the bath while Jane studied the side of my face. She filled the washbasin and dipped a flannel in it. I smelled her scent. Nothing artificial, just her. She squeezed the water out of the flannel, bunched it into a pad and gingerly touched it to my eyebrow.

'You looked after me on the ship. So now we'll be even – well less uneven.'

She peered at my cheek. 'There's glass and grit.' She took a pair of tweezers out of a wash bag. Her face was all concentration, her movements slow and deliberate.

'What you said, it was as if you were trying to warn me.'

She grimaced and wafted the comment away as if it were a bad smell. 'I was pissed out of my head. I wouldn't pay any attention to anything I said that night.'

'About trust: "Just one of those lies you tell yourself." That's what you said.'

She raised her eyebrows. 'I'm a bit jaded where all that's concerned.'

I felt a pulling sensation and a small rip.

'There.' She held up a thin bloodied splinter in the tweezers. I felt a trickle down my cheek. She pressed the area with the flannel pad while she reached for some antiseptic.

'What I told you about Sara and me: it was wrong. Sara was trying to leave me. She dumped my passport so I couldn't get on the plane. Someone was threatening her.'

The words hung there. Jane made no comment, showed no reaction. There were reddish-brown blots of blood on the new shirt where more glass cuts had reopened and bled.

'It's as if I never really knew her. All the time we were together. Things in her past I had no idea about.'

She squeezed the pad out in the basin. The water turned a rusty pink as she dried the area and shook a large sticking plaster out of a box. She was about to apply it.

'You said, "You can't trust the dead." How do you know that?'

She attached the plaster, smoothed the edges with small presses of a fingertip. No comment. This was a one-way conversation.

I caught her wrist. 'Every time I've asked you, you've avoided answering me. I want to know.'

Her voice sounded matter-of-fact. 'When people die, you find stuff out. It isn't always what you expect. Everyone's got secrets. It's impossible not to.'

She released her wrist and continued with the plaster. 'Done. I'll leave you to do the rest.' Then she reached over to the bath taps and turned them on. 'I'll put out some of Howard's clothes.' She smiled, brisk now. 'Take your time.'

I peeled off Greg's combats and hoodie until I was down to my pants – apart from the new shirt, the only thing left that was my own. There were large purple bruises on my chest. My feet were so bloody and blistered the socks were stuck to them. I had to get in the bath first and soak them off. Then I lay back amongst the steam while the dirt and flakes of dried blood floated off me.

The exchange with Kika replayed itself. I'd hardly known Sara at all. I put my head under the surface, held my breath.

The bath water was a rusty grey. I hauled myself upright

and hosed myself down with the shower then patted myself with a towel. In the cabinet was a foil sheet of Co-dydramol and some razors. I swallowed three capsules. While I waited for them to kick in I shaved, carefully.

On the landing, Jane had left a pair of blue jeans, some Argyle socks and a sweater with epaulettes. Officer's gear, tweedy, old-fashioned stuff, but a better fit than Greg's. I put them on and examined myself in the mirror. What kind of man would leave a woman like Jane?

I hobbled down the stairs. The kitchen table was laid for two. A candle was burning. The intimacy of the scene was unnerving.

Jane had changed into a pale grey woollen dress. Her hair was loose. She looked me up and down and smiled.

'Isn't this a bit weird for you, me in this stuff?'

'Not as weird as how you looked when I came in.' She gestured at the food. 'Eat.'

She uncorked a bottle of red wine and poured two large glasses. I laid into the food. She sipped her wine. For a few minutes neither of us spoke.

'You're the first person I've entertained since Howard left.'

'How long is that?'

'Not long.'

I looked at her.

'A month.'

She refilled her glass; her hand shook slightly. Another couple of minutes passed. I had expected questions about what had happened to me but she seemed content with the silences that punctuated our conversation. I asked her what she did. She shook her head. 'IT stuff, very dull. Anyway, I'm getting out.'

'What will you do?'

She looked at me, swallowed. 'Travel. Get right away.'

She sat upright, almost prim, handling her cutlery with a

studied precision. It was hard to imagine the woman sitting opposite me was the same one I had stopped from throwing herself off the ship, or even the one who had phoned me so breathlessly the night before. She picked up her glass and cradled it.

'Last night on the phone—'

She shook her head and waved the glass. 'Drinking alone. Not good.'

She took a sip and set the glass down on a coaster.

'Tell me about Howard.'

She sighed and looked away into the room. 'It wouldn't have lasted. I was just angry about being humiliated, being deceived.'

Her eyes flicked towards me and away. She had barely touched her food. She sat back from the table and lit a cigarette, blowing the smoke away from my direction, her chin held high, as if she'd rediscovered the certainty that had deserted her on the ship.

'What about the good times? There must have been some?'

She shrugged.

'Then what brought you together?'

'Company, peer pressure, biological clock. The usual bloody stuff.'

She stubbed out the cigarette.

'Anyway. It's all in the past, now.' Frankland's phrase. I wondered if she meant it. Whether she did or not, it was clear she didn't want to say any more.

'For me it's the reverse. The present's just a vacuum. But the past's crowding in. Stuff I never knew.'

She smiled but made no comment as if I'd just been making small talk. No curiosity this time.

I had finished my food. She pushed her plate towards me. 'Go on. I'm not hungry. You look as though you need it.'

The combination of the food and wine along with the painkillers was tugging me towards sleep. She lit another cigarette and smoked it with several short puffs, refilled our glasses.

As soon as I'd finished the second plate she reached for it, stacked the two together and took them over to the sink. I got up and cleared the rest of the table.

She stood at the sink with her back to me. Suddenly she went very still, her voice smaller. 'On the ship, in the second between letting go and you catching me, maybe not even a second, I realised I didn't want to die after all.'

She turned. Her face glowed in the candlelight. She took a couple of steps towards me. Her lower lip trembled and I felt the touch of her breath on my cheek.

'Is that why you wanted me to come, so you could say that?'

Her eyes locked on to mine. The same fierce intensity I had seen on the ship. She took another step closer. Her face inches from mine. She kissed me on the mouth then let her head rest on my shoulder.

'When you stayed with me – on the ship. I felt so safe.'

I could feel her pulse, fast.

She looked up. 'You could come with me. Right away from everything. I know how.'

I held her gently. She was still for a few moments then she shook her head, straightened up, brushing the creases out of her dress, her cheeks flushed. 'I'm sorry. Every time, I make a bloody fool of myself.'

Thirty-two

I lay on the narrow bed in Jane's spare room, the curtains open, looking out at the darkness. I hadn't the energy to undress, just let the softness of the bed suck me down into sleep, hoping my brain would shut down for a while.

Her behaviour was strange: restrained politeness punctuated with flashes of breathless emotion, as if two personalities were competing for control. The studied indifference to my admissions about Sara was as baffling as her interrogation of my marriage on the ship. She had asked me nothing about my life before and I had responded in kind, the Scheme training still in play. I knew nothing about her.

Was it living on the Scheme that had destroyed Sara and me? Or were we doomed anyway? No way of knowing now. My gaze drifted. In my head I saw, frozen like a photograph, Sara, the children either side of her, in the garden, a sea of toys around them, sun shining. Everything she wanted, except her face was set. I could see tiny muscles tensed in her cheeks as if she was pressing her teeth together. And me looking at her thinking, *I can still make you happy.*

There was a loud rustling outside. My eyes snapped open in time to see a fox on the gravel struggling to kill something almost as big, maybe a badger. I watched them until the other animal was still and the fox paused and looked around, triumphant, its tongue flickering as it panted.

I looked at the clock on the bedside table. Five ten. The fox made its way down the drive, dragging its trophy. I thought about Greg, where I had left him, dead in the wet field. He couldn't live with what he had done, or what he had agreed to do. My brain was still whirring, but I started to drift again and dreamed I was back with him in the van, my head full of the wedding night, the street filling with people about to witness the death of Waheed. Greg nudging me and pointing. *The bird in the scarf.*

A short leather coat. A laptop bag. Her hair down around her face, the long scarf, looking up, mouth open. Jane?

I sat up, bursting through the surface of consciousness. Wide awake now.

The one who took the phone shot of me, the one there was no circle for on the graphic of the police reconstruction. Absurd, but so was everything else in my life now. *You can't be too paranoid.* Ross's words, the ones he wanted on his gravestone.

There was no chance of going back to sleep now. I pulled on the rest of the clothes, lifted the latch on the door and opened it gingerly. Across the landing, Jane's bedroom door was shut. I made my way downstairs.

I stood in the kitchen, waiting for my eyes to adjust to the dark. I opened the curtains and looked out. Nothing. No wind. No sound. Jane's bag was on the counter. I opened it. It smelled of her. I went through the contents. A brush, a pack of tissues, a small make-up purse, a BlackBerry. It was off. I turned it on but it asked for a password. I turned it off again. Another phone. Still on. No password. A purse. I snapped it open and looked through the cards. Visa, Amex, all in her name. As well as some banknotes were a few receipts, from an off-licence, a shoe shop, petrol. I closed the purse. Looked in the bag again. A small leather ID case. I flipped it open. A plastic card with her photograph, a blank look. Across the picture was stamped a long number, a bar code and the words *Chilham Datasystems*. I put back the contents of the bag and went into the study.

The computer was on Sleep. I clicked the mouse. Up came the Google homepage. I typed in Chilham Datasystems.

Twenty-five pages of results. I modified the search to exact phrase only. Nothing. I went to Maps. Typed Chilham again. A village the other side of Ashford, seven miles away. I opened Google Earth and searched Chilham, Kent. Charlie and Emma loved looking at Google Earth. 'Doing journeys,' they'd called it. Seeing the world they had not been allowed out into. As I zoomed in, the squares blurred and reformed until the village rooftops filled the frame. I pulled out again so the outlying buildings were included. One square about two miles from the village stayed an opaque grey. I adjusted the frame so the square was in the centre and zoomed in. Still grey. I pulled out. The area went from a road to the top of a hill.

I clicked Close and stared at the screen for a while. Nothing proven. I went to the Search window in the tool-bar and clicked on the arrow beside it. A drop-down listed all the recent searches. The last was 'Sunkiss'. I clicked on it and opened a BBC News report.

Black boxes confirm fuel fault and pressure loss. Authorities rule out bomb.

There was a soft crack sound outside, from somewhere on the other side of the cottage. I went through to the living room, parted the curtains a centimetre and looked out. Watched for a while. Nothing, just the outline of the church and the black leafless branches of the trees. Two pictures were perched on the little window sill. The one of Howard she had with her on the ship, the other a much smaller photo in a silver frame. Jane, a teenager, laughing. Beside her, a tall man in a seventies safari suit. Her father? With them a group of men in turbans, behind them, the jagged outline of mountains.

I picked it up, took it into the study, switched on the desk lamp and held it under the light. The picture could have been fifteen years old. I sat down on the office chair. There was nothing on the desk. I pulled open the drawers. Empty.

I flipped open the lid of a packing box: more books. *The American Century*, *After 9/11*, *The Search for Bin Laden*. I delved deeper. A biography of Henry Kissinger, several books about Vietnam, the PLO. Maybe she was an academic. I didn't know. I hadn't asked. She said she was in IT. The Scheme mantra: *Don't ask what you don't want to be asked back*. Books on Russia, the end of the Cold War, Germany and Turkey. I lifted the box off the stack and looked in the second. It was full of almanacs, *The State Department Quarterly Review*, *Foreign Policy*. I opened the third box. *Afghanistan, A Military History from Alexander the Great to the Taliban*, an ancient, well-thumbed guide to Afghanistan, *Kabul, City Under Siege*, *Oil, Arms and Allah*. A crow cawed somewhere near the church. The last book had a sun-bleached green cover. A copy of the Koran. I opened it at the title page. Written in a scratchy fountain pen flourish was one word, *Amniat*: Pashto for peace. And after it a single *W*.

Thirty-three

I left the books where they were, pulled on the bike jacket, took the phone from Jane's bag, helped myself to some of her cash, unlocked the front door and stepped outside.

After the snug cottage it was seriously cold. I made my way to the bike, which I had left on its side in the undergrowth. I got it upright, ready to go if need be. Then I found myself a vantage point with a good view of the road and the drive. I scanned the cottage with the scope. No lights yet.

I pulled out Jane's phone and tapped in Frankland's number. He picked up after one ring.

'Me again.'

There was a pause before he replied. 'Carter, still at large.' His voice sounded blurred, as if he'd been up all night.

'Surprised?'

He snorted. 'Whose phone is this?'

'Stolen. How's the investigation?'

He let out something between a sigh and a groan. Perhaps his batteries were finally starting to run down.

'Let's just say there's a collective disinclination to co-operate.'

'Since when did you let that get in your way?'

'Carter, help me out. Did you kill Waheed?'

'A direct question; not your style.'

He was waiting for an answer.

'If I did, you think I'd be calling you?'

'If you did, someone avenging his death would have a motive for blowing up the plane. Why are you calling?'

'I want your help.'

He laughed drily. 'It would help if you stopped disappearing.'

'And turn myself in?'

'If the plane's down to you, why should I help?'

'"Look at all possibilities, rule nothing out." That's what you told me on the ship, remember? Think about it. What are you looking for? Justice for your daughter. Me banged up – is that going to tell you *why* she died?'

He didn't answer.

'I saw Waheed die, saw how he died. I was there. That's why they put me in the Scheme.'

He was quiet, mind whirring. 'And your wife?'

'She dumped the passport. She was trying to leave me. She wanted to take the children and get away.'

'I don't blame her.'

'That's not helpful.'

'You're not convincing me, Carter.' He sighed. 'Your old buddy Greg's dead in a field, the weapon with your prints on, you mugged three people in Lewes, assaulted your sister-in-law, plus some policemen in a Croydon tower block, nearly mowed down a mother and child; you're a one-man crime wave. Everyone in the South-East is on the lookout. The Scheme will have washed its hands of you. There's nothing for them to protect now. Far as they're concerned you've gone rogue. I wouldn't put money on your chances of lasting the day.'

'And you'd like the glory of turning me in. One last collar felt for old time's sake? I overestimated you.'

His silences were getting longer.

'What do you want, Carter?'

'Answers, same as you. What do you know about Jane Cochran?'

'You're asking me? You slept with her on the ship.'

'Just answer the question.'

253

'Got very bothered when she found out you weren't on the plane back. Asking me where you'd gone. Started making calls on her BlackBerry.'

'Anything else?'

'Didn't like me asking about the dead husband. Passport says she's British, but there's no birth certificate, or naturalisation. Everything else is a brick wall. You having second thoughts about her?'

'I get it. So we blew up the plane to get rid of our spouses and my children to start a new life?'

He let out a weary sigh. 'The kid on check-in at Gatwick remembers you pressuring your wife to get on the plane without you. A cab driver in Tobago took you to look at a chalet popular with honeymoon couples. Either way, it doesn't look good.'

'The plane. Anything more on it?'

'What are you expecting?'

'I don't know, but since we last spoke I've been chased across half of South-East England by people behaving like they might want me dead. Your idea there was a bomb on the plane for me is starting to sound less crazy.'

In the cottage an upstairs light came on. Jane was up.

Frankland yawned. 'The plane glided into the sea. It probably didn't break up till it hit the water. Cabin pressure loss could have been caused by a device that knocked out the crew and passengers but not the plane itself.'

'What about the faulty fuel gauge?'

'Reported but not rectified. However, the Gatwick re-fuelling crew who filled it up used the meter on the tanker. There was enough fuel to get to Tobago. Bermuda tower was the last air traffic contol to communicate with the crew.'

'How do you know?'

Frankland sighed wearily. 'Because there's no record of any communication after that.'

'You said Sara's medical details had been wiped. Why would that be?'

'Someone planning to start a new life. Dispensing with the old one.'

'How easy is that?'

'You need a sympathetic medical person willing to break the law. Your Scheme doctor maybe?'

'Can you check?'

'You've got a lot of questions all of a sudden, Carter.'

'That's all I've got right now.'

Another light came on downstairs. The front door opened.

'Carter?'

I pressed the red button.

Thirty-four

Jane came out of the house and made straight for the Merc. She had on a parka with a fur-fringed hood, her bag on her shoulder. She shut the door and started the car. Lights came on, full beam. I hid my face.

She came up the drive fast, throwing up a spray of gravel as the rear wheels spun, moisture on the trees glistening in the headlamp beams. She accelerated up the road. I got on the bike, fired it up and followed.

It was still dark and with the misty rain visibility was bad. All I had were her lights. I kept mine off. After two miles she turned on to the Ashford bypass. Although it was early, traffic was building up. I hung back, five cars between us. Everything slowed for a roundabout. A police bike came the other way. I glanced over my shoulder just in time to see him do a U-turn. He came alongside, flipped up his visor, tapped his helmet and pointed at my bare head.

'Stolen,' I told him. 'Got a spare at work.'

'Where's that?'

'Chilham.'

He peered at me, then looked down at the bike. 'Missing indicator, only one mirror.'

The traffic was moving again. I could see Jane's Merc speeding into the distance.

'Got knocked over when it was parked. Fell on its side. I'll get it fixed.'

His radio crackled. He spoke into his mouthpiece. "K, I'm on it.' And then to me. 'If I see you round here again without a helmet, you're nicked.'

His blue light went on, his visor came down and he took off.

Jane had vanished. I wound the bike up past sixty in the oncoming lane, weaving in and out as traffic came towards me. At a roundabout I took the A28 towards Ashford, remembering that Chilham was somewhere between there and Canterbury. The turn came up so fast I overshot it and had to backtrack. I told myself to slow down but the rest of my brain wasn't listening. I went as fast as I dared on the slimy rain-soaked roads. Farm traffic had laid a couple of tracks of mud in my path and I tried to keep between them. I came over the brow of a hill just in time to see the Merc take a sudden left into a narrow lane that dived down through some trees into another valley. Beyond the woods the land flattened out. Jane picked up speed again. The road rose then ran alongside a section of hillside that had been scooped out, probably an old quarry. On the site, surrounded by a high wire fence was a big industrial unit painted grey. Above it, on the hill behind, was a mast with some heavy-duty dishes. The brake lights of the Merc came on. I slowed as well. Jane turned and paused at a manned gate. I rode on past and watched in the mirror. The bar lifted and she drove in.

Twenty metres ahead was a village shop, just opening up. In front of it on the other side of the road was a farm track that led up the opposite hill. I parked the bike outside the shop and went inside.

'You look a bit chilly.' A young woman in pink fluffy earmuffs was laying out newspapers. I gestured at her head.

'Got any more of those?'

She laughed. 'No, but there's coffee on.'

I walked up the hill on the opposite side until I had a clear view of the building and the gate. The area it covered was no more than a hundred square metres. There was a faint scar on the slope up to the mast, perhaps where cabling had been sunk underground. A cluster of newish-looking receptors were attached to the top of the mast, along with a much older pair of antennae. Although the grey building was recent, the site and the pylon looked older, possibly once a radio transmission station carrying signals over the Downs. There was only the one entrance to the facility. Jane's Merc was parked between a Transit and a Mini. I sipped the coffee and ate a chocolate bar I'd bought.

I dialled Jane's BlackBerry. She answered after two rings. She said nothing, but I could tell by her breathing it was her.

'How many people are with you?'

There was no response.

'Answer the question.'

'I'm alone.'

'Where are the others?'

'There's only one – he does nights.'

'What about the Mini?'

'It's a pool car.'

'The Transit?'

'It hasn't moved in months.'

I examined it through the sight. One of the front tyres was almost flat.

'Any other exits?'

'Just a crawl space underground where the cables go up to the mast.'

'Leave your coat, your bag, and your phone. Drive out, park a hundred metres past the shop and walk straight up the track opposite. Keep your hands down by your sides and your palms open so I can see them.'

'And if I don't?'

I focused the scope on the guard's lapel badge. Jim Clegg.

'I've got Jim's Adam's apple in my sight. The shell in the chamber will take his head off. Do it now.'

I snapped the phone shut, sat down and watched through the scope. A minute passed. Jane came out of a side door in the building, no coat or bag, plume of breath floating above her in the cold air. She got into the Merc. At the gate she said something to Jim and he laughed. She gave him a little wave as the bar went up and she drove out on to the road. She parked just past the shop and got out, scanning the slope. The breeze wafted her hair and she brushed a strand off her face, then folded her hands under her arms.

While I watched her climb I kept Greg's pistol in my hand, balanced on my knee where she could see it. Fifty feet away from me she stopped. She frowned at the gun.

'Is that necessary?'

I waved her forward.

'You tell me. Throw the keys.'

She flung them so they landed a metre from where I was sitting. I got to my feet and frisked her while she held her arms half up. Her expression was blank, subdued, her eyes focused on the ground. She shivered.

'You left early.'

'I've not been sleeping well.'

She looked at the gun, then back at the building.

'You couldn't have hit him from here.'

'But you thought I could. I never told you I was a sniper.'

She said nothing.

'What happens in that building?'

Her eyes flicked to mine and away. Her lips parted. Curls of misty breath came from her in regular puffs.

'This makes everything very difficult.' She folded her arms tightly under her breasts, kept her eyes down.

'I'm used to difficult. Who knows I'm here?'

'No one. What do you want?'

'Answers. Everything you know.'

She glanced back at the building.

'Start with Waheed and work forward.'

She sighed. 'Not here.'

Thirty-five

We sat in her car on the brow of a hill that overlooked the valley. The fields were white with frost. I kept the engine running for warmth. In the distance was the town of Wye, shrouded in mist. A train horn sounded and, further away, an emergency vehicle siren.

Jane took her time to get started, as if she had to go through a process to unlock what was in her head.

'I carried messages.'

'Why was he killed?'

She shrugged. 'I don't know.'

I looked at her.

'Honestly, it's the truth.'

'Who ordered it?'

'No one's sure.'

'Why was he in such a hurry to get to the clinic that day?'

She shrugged again. 'There's no way of knowing. He didn't wait for his driver. Maybe he knew someone was on to him.'

'He knew you were CIA?'

She flushed.

'I thought they'd have trained you not to do that.'

She stared at her lap. 'Do you know how hard this is for me?'

'Keep talking.'

She wiped her face with her hands and pressed them against her thighs. 'His relationship with the Agency goes back to the days of the Soviet Afghan occupation. He was part of that generation of Saudis working for the liberation. He came here as an asylum seeker in ninety-eight. After nine-eleven he was sometimes used as a back channel for communication. Sometimes he gave us good material.'

'Why you?'

'He was extremely particular, always his own way of doing things. Same contact, no changes, nothing written down. No hi-tech. He didn't even use the phone. Only meetings. No one thought he was under threat.'

She stared into her cup, her shoulders hunched, deflated.

'I've seen the picture you took.'

She looked up, puzzled.

'Me with the gun.'

She stiffened, indignant. 'It was video. Eight seconds.'

'The still shows me aiming at the car.'

She shook her head. 'The whole sequence shows you pick the firearm off the ground and examine it, then you look up at Waheed and drop it when the car explodes.'

'Where is the footage stored now?'

She shrugged. 'I saw it once, later that day – after they whisked me off to Teddington for a debriefing. I guess it was filed away in the Waheed database.'

'Until someone un-filed it and took a screen grab from it, then leaked it.'

She stared blankly, the life sucked out of her.

'You want me to believe you don't know about this?'

She snorted. 'You wouldn't believe how much I don't know.'

'But you were Waheed's handler.'

She laughed scornfully. 'I was his postmistress.'

'For a Yankee spook you have a quaint way of putting things.'

'I grew up here. There's not much American in me.'

'Were you fond of him?'

'I thought he was a force for good. He hated terrorism. He was the conscience of militant Islam. That's why he's such a big martyr.'

'What were you doing on the ship?'

She put her fingertips against her forehead and pressed. No answer.

'What's your job now?'

Her hands curled into fists on her thighs. She took a couple of short breaths as if she was getting ready to make a jump.

'Don't spin this out please.'

A sparrowhawk rose up in the sky and hovered, fluttering its wings, preparing to dive.

Her voice was almost a whisper.

'You. You're my job.'

Thirty-six

I lit her cigarette for her. She opened the window a fraction to let out the smoke. Another car pulled up in front of us. A woman got out and lifted a child out of his seat, held him while he peed, screeching because of the cold.

Jane's eyes were unfocused, far away, her voice, distant. 'With Waheed dead, that was the end of the assignment. I asked for something different – away from here. But because it happened on my watch, it was as if I was tainted; it wasn't like I was going to get promoted. And as I was spare, they sent me down here.'

She took a long pull on her cigarette. 'We knew the Brits were keeping you under wraps. It might surprise you how much powers keep back from each other. We didn't let on about my phone footage. It's all "capital". Assets to deploy when there's bargaining to be done. And they weren't going to let on about why you were there. All we had was your military record and that you'd been mothballed – put on the Scheme. To us that suggested you had some deeper role, and therefore were a valuable asset.'

She turned to me, fierce. 'You do realise – it's the end for me, telling you this.'

'I can put the gun to your head if it helps. Keep talking.'

She took her time to answer. 'A decision was taken to activate surveillance.'

I looked at her. 'I hardly went anywhere.'

She shook her head. 'It wasn't outside.'

'*Inside* the house?'

'It had already been wired up by Special Branch to eaves-drop on the previous occupants. It was just a matter of adding a handful of pinhole lenses in the alarm system and a transmitter to our station.'

'When was this done?'

'Before you moved in.'

'The Scheme people knew?'

She smiled. 'They had no idea.'

I felt my face heat up. 'You had cameras recording us?'

She nodded.

I opened my window; freezing air gushed in.

'The Agency's a very anal place. They love to record stuff, just in case. "When in doubt – blitz it", is their policy. Since nine-eleven their listening capability has gone through the roof. They've got so much recording going on they can barely process it all.'

She shrugged. 'They pretty much forgot about us. It's not unusual. A small outpost, the harvest's nothing hot, agendas change, whoever initiated it gets moved on. They can overlook you for years. You just keep going with the job till someone realises they can make some savings. Or something happens.'

A couple of cyclists straining on their pedals came to a halt in front of us and admired the view, panting out puffs of cold breath. They smiled at each other, kissed, and rode on.

'When I came down here, there were about twelve watch-ing operations active, then it dwindled to three. And then just the one.'

'Just us?'

She looked down. 'The quality wasn't good and the cover-age wasn't comprehensive.' Suddenly she laughed, scorn-fully. 'We're just feeders: collect, collate, report, collect, collate, report. Helping build the intelligence mountain.'

'What happened to the material. Who saw it?'

She shrugged. 'They figured if anything significant cropped up it was down to us to flag it. No one paid any attention until last September when people came over from Langley, a team I'd never seen or heard of before. Only used their pass-names. They weren't field agents; they were more like geeks, the sort who inhabit the sub-basements, but with senior grading. They hardly spoke. I offered them a briefing but they didn't want it. They looked at less than an hour of material then went into a videoconference on a secure link. Locked the door. The next day they were gone. I guessed they were part of some rationalisation programme.'

'Why?'

'Because all they said was we'd not be needed much longer. I thought they meant you'd be out of the Scheme.'

There was a sensation in my head like cresting the summit on a big dipper. I felt my focus go for a second. Jane didn't move, didn't speak. She had delivered her bomb. She was braced.

'They said that?'

'No. Not exactly.'

'Then what?'

She fixed her eyes on something outside, but whatever it was she wasn't seeing it. Her look was as I had seen it on the ship, taut, terrified. I reached across, turned her face in my direction. Her eyes were shut.

'Look at me.'

'They wouldn't tell us.'

'You expect me to believe that?'

Her eyes were still closed. 'I didn't know. Not about the plane, nothing. Please, please believe me.' Tears welled from between her eyelashes. She reached up to wipe them.

'You kept recording?'

She nodded.

'Why?'

She shrugged. 'It's what we were there for.'

'That doesn't make sense.'

Another shrug. 'What does?'

'Sara changed. Around September.'

Her eyes closed again. No answer.

'What did you see?'

All the blood in my head was pulsing so hard I could see the vibration in my vision.

She bit her lip, tears running down her face. 'Don't make me answer that. Please.'

'It's on discs?'

Again, no answer.

'You're going to show me.'

She shook her head violently. 'I can't do that.'

'Get them.'

'They're encoded. They only play on our equipment.' She looked at me, gulping in breaths.

'Then I'm coming in.'

Thirty-seven

There was just enough room in the boot. I curled up facing the rear, gun at the ready for anyone who wanted to look inside.

At the gate Jane said something to Jim, which made him laugh again. Then he said something else I couldn't hear. The parking bay the far side of the Transit was out of his line of sight. She left the car for a few minutes. When she let me out she handed me an ID card.

'As long as this is in your pocket you won't trip any sensors.'

'What about cameras?'

'Only outside.'

Inside there were no windows. It smelled of warm electrics. The only sound was a low hum. It was just one big room, carpeted and soundproofed, half of it in darkness. There was a row of workstations, each with a pair of monitors, all but two of them shrouded in plastic covers.

'They used to run all kinds of surveillance out of here.'

Her coat was draped over a chair. Her desk was bare; just a laptop and a mug with two pens. The monitors on the other desk were decorated with toys and stickers.

'That's Bob's seat. He's the only other one left.'

I gazed at the soft toys. Simpsons figures, small animals. The sort of stuff the twins loved. Stuck to the edge of the screen was a postcard with a picture of a steel foundry on it. *Youngstown, Ohio,* the caption read. *Missing you already.*

'He's not really adjusted to being in the field.'

There was a squash kit bag on the seat.

'When's he due in?'

'He comes at four.'

Behind the desks was a wall of shelves stacked with what looked like thin books, but as I got closer I saw that they were DVD cases.

Three larger monitors were suspended from the ceiling. Jane picked up a remote and pointed it at each in turn. They sprang to life, matching screensavers of pinewood forests.

'Is the feed still on?'

'It was switched off while I was away.'

'Who controls it?'

'Teddington.'

I looked back at the shelves; each case had a date on the spine. I walked down the length of the row. Four years.

'Bob catalogues them. It's his *raison d'être*. We never missed a day. The system's old, but very robust.'

I ran my finger along them. My life with Sara and the children, all recorded. There was no sound in the room. All I could hear was my own heartbeat. I turned to Jane. She tucked a loose strand of hair behind her ear.

'You watched all this?'

She looked down. 'Some.'

'What about when I wasn't home?'

'It's all there. Bob did a log of everyone coming and going.' Her hands pressed her thighs. She swallowed.

'This why you talked about trust so much on the ship?'

Her face was blank.

'OK. Show me what I need to see.'

She hesitated then came up beside me, reached up and took down a disc. 'The cameras are there really to help ID unknowns or check for miming or any unusual actions. It's not comprehensive: there's several blind spaces. The mikes are low down in the skirting so the sound's not so good when the kids are in the room.' She flushed.

'Go on.'

She went back to her desk, slid the disc out of its case. 'This is September sixth.' Her hand shook as she held the disc.

'If it helps, imagine I'm holding you hostage. I've shot my way in here.'

She slotted the disc into the player and pressed some keys. The monitors in front of her lit up, each screen populated with dozens of tiny frames, miniatures of fisheye views of the rooms in the house. She typed in a timecode, her hands shaking. The view that came up was from the living room, looking towards the garden, everything curved by the wide angle of the lens.

'The sound's pretty bad because the French windows were open and there was a strong breeze. Also the conversation started in the garden so we don't have the beginning. You only hear Sara's voice at first.'

I stared at the screen. Sara appeared. Alive again. Leaning against the doorframe of the French windows, staring blankly into the house, her shoulders tense.

Someone else was in the garden, blurred, almost out of frame. Sara put a hand up to her mouth, her voice small. *'Why are you saying these things? You're frightening me.'*

The reply was inaudible. She put her hand over her eyes, distressed. My heartbeat raced. I wanted to step through the screen and hold her.

'Please. Why?'

She dropped her hands. Her face was tight with fear.

The other figure came into view, a silhouette obscured at first by light bouncing off the windows. He placed his hands on her shoulders, and squeezed them. A cold pain spread across my chest.

'It's for your own good.'

Stuart.

Thirty-eight

Jane looked at me. 'Sure you want to go on?'

I just stared at the screen, desolate. I nodded. She hit Play.

Stuart's voice, all concern. *'I'm only trying to protect you. You and the children. Think carefully about what I'm saying. I'm going out on a limb for you here.'*

Sara was frozen, staring into space. *'I don't understand. Why can't I just get him to explain?'*

He smiled and shook his head. *'If you do, you'll be putting yourself in danger. He's in denial. If you disturb that ... Trust me, I've seen this before. I know what happens.'*

Sara bit her fist, choking back anguish. Tears puddled round her eyes. *'This isn't true. This isn't him. I need to talk to him.'*

He held her face and turned it to him. *'It can't go any further. I'd be shot for telling you any of this. Not only that, his reaction – if you confront him ...'*

I tried to swallow. My throat was like sandpaper.

Sara gestured at herself. *'I have to stick with him. I promised. He's all I've got. We're all he's got.'*

He left her words hanging, lifted his hands from her shoulders and took a few paces back, staring at the ground, letting the silence work on her.

Eventually he spoke again. *'How has he been with you?'*

'What do you mean?'

'Any threats, violence? I'm sorry, but I have to ask.'

Sara's voice rose again. '*Of course not! Why?*'

Surprise on Stuart's face. '*Is he quiet? Remote?*'

'*He can be, that's how he is sometimes.*'

He peered at her. '*He ever talk about his Army time? Afghanistan?*'

'*Never – why should he?*'

He frowned. '*Nothing about what happened there?*'

She stiffened. '*Its all in the past.*' Her voice rose. '*It's got nothing to do with us now.*'

He shook his head, the all-too-familiar concerned expression on his face.

Sara pressed her fingers into her forehead. '*So he killed a child. Maybe it was an accident.*'

Stuart bowed his head. '*I can't go into details. We're still gathering information. But I can tell you it was no accident. The authorities there are looking into it. The indications ...*' He shook his head, then he reached out both hands and held her arms. '*It might have been ... to silence the victim.*'

I gripped the edge of the desk, choking back the rage. Jane pressed Pause and put a hand on my arm.

I moved away. 'Play. Keep going.'

Stuart stepped closer to Sara, took her hand, looked mournfully into her eyes and blinked, as if searching for words.

Sara pulled away. Her voice was small, like a child's. '*I'm so scared.*'

He took both hands this time, his voice more forceful than I'd heard before. '*Look at me. I'm breaking every rule talking to you like this. Nothing I'm telling you can get back to him, you understand?*'

She looked at him, uncomprehending. '*But he's in the Scheme, he's protected.*'

He sighed. '*We do what we do to protect you from what might be out there, but I can't protect you from what's inside his head, or whatever happens here in this house.'*

'He's said nothing – ever.'

'He wouldn't. He's very good at holding stuff back. It's almost as if he's two people. You know how some men can be like that, don't you?'

Sara flinched.

I looked away towards Jane, unable to focus. She paused the player again.

I gestured at the banks of discs. 'And he had no idea about this ...?'

'No, none. The Brits don't know we know anything about you. But he's clearly very careful, he covered his tracks well and he knows exactly what he's doing to her, as if he can tell where all her pressure points are.'

Stuart's voice brought me back to the screen. *'I can't live with the idea of what might happen. On my watch. I just can't let that happen. After all you went through with your father.'*

She jolted as if he had just given her an electric shock. He leaned forward so his lips were almost touching her hair. I couldn't hear his next words.

Tears were running down her cheeks. She put her hands over her face again. *'Stop this. Please!'*

Stuart was on the move again, pacing, a palm against his forehead. Shaking his head, letting the silence do his work. Then he turned, came up close, moved a strand of her hair with his fingertips. She held her head and slid down the doorpost to a squatting position. Stuart bent down in front of her.

This time his voice was different, more forceful. *'You do understand if it got out that I was talking to you like this ... I'd be finished. Whoever they put in my place won't have your interests at heart.'* He shook his head. *'You must understand.'* He put a forefinger against his lips. *' You've got to think of the children as well. Whatever happens.*

You've got to be strong, look after yourself. You know what to do. You managed it before.'

Jane ejected the disc and looked up at me. 'It's textbook stuff for grooming informants: create anxiety, undermine the key sources of trust in their world, turn them into threats. Hint at negative consequences, insist on secrecy, but only give evasive clues about what's happening. He's breaking down all sense of security she's invested in you.'

All the moisture had gone from my mouth. I looked off down the row of desks. Kika's tale of the masked man in the hotel room – Stuart had done his homework.

Jane inserted another disc. 'He picks it up a week later.'

'Stuart only came every four weeks.'

She gave me a look. 'From here on he times all his visits when the children are at nursery and you're at the work-shop. He must have had some sort of feed there so he could be sure you wouldn't appear. Sara never seems to know when he's going to turn up.'

She slotted in the second disc.

A different angle, looking down on the dining table. Stuart, sitting at the head, looking intense, lost in thought. Sara put a mug down in front of him. There was no response from him.

Jane paused the player again. 'Already you can see the impact he's had, how he's letting her wait on him. Not talk-ing, just being there, imposing his authority, reprimanding her. She'd had some contact – we're not sure who with – another woman.'

'Her sister, Kika?'

Jane frowned. 'He's not very nice about her.'

Sara stood beside the table, her head bowed, as if waiting for Stuart to acknowledge her. Eventually he nodded at a chair and she sat down, the cuffs of her sweater pulled over her clasped hands.

Stuart took a sip from the mug. His voice was cold. He

spelled the words out slowly. '*What were you thinking of?*'

'*I thought she could help.*'

Stuart rolled his eyes. '*She's a prostitute and a drug addict.*'

'*She's all I've got.*'

He let out a long, weary sigh. '*Have you grasped the magnitude of this? You're in way over your head. I'm gambling everything for you.*' He paused for his words to sink in, took a sip from the mug. '*Besides, you don't need anyone else's help. I'll provide everything. It's all in place.*'

'*I'm so scared.*'

'*You should be.*' He moved the mug away and drew her to him. '*The Afghanistan thing, it wasn't an isolated incident ...*'

'*What does that mean?*'

'*If it's a war crime ...*' He brought his hand down on the table hard so Sara jumped. '*I'm going to get you out of this. Till then, you've got to keep up appearances.*' He stroked her hair. '*But you're good at that, aren't you.*'

I looked away, trying to process what I was seeing. My eyes settled on the toys on Bob's desk. When I looked back, Jane was fast-forwarding.

'Stop.'

An image of Charlie, staring straight towards the unseen lens, into my eyes and yawning. Emma reached forward and put her hand over his mouth, something Sara used to do. Charlie batted her hand away, then they crouched down and continued their game. My throat tightened.

Jane ejected the disc. 'I'm so sorry.'

'Did you report any of this?'

She nodded. 'They just said to keep monitoring.'

'Did his bosses find out?'

She shrugged. 'I've no way of knowing.' She turned back to the keyboard. 'After this there aren't any visits for a while. Maybe he took her for drives somewhere or met her outside. There must have been conversations about his plans which we don't have.'

She put in a third disc. 'This is four weeks later.'

In the kitchen, Sara was making coffee, Stuart leaning against the counter, hands in his pockets, his eyes, gleaming, fixed on her. *'It's where you always wanted to go, right back to when you stuck that stamp in your doll's house.'*

She looked up at him. He smiled, knowing.

'I can't be without the children.'

He nodded, eyes closed. *'First we need some quality time on our own together. Just you and me. I've got it all fixed.'*

She turned to him. *'And after: what then? I need to know.'*

He sighed, irritated. *'You've got to trust me on this. One step at a time.'*

She tossed the coffee spoon down on to the counter, spraying it with granules, then swiped the jug onto the floor.

She covered her face. *'I can't. I just can't.'*

He looked pained, like a weary parent. Then he carefully swept the granules into his palm with the side of his other hand and funnelled them back in the jar. *'Remember what I said. Just think of the consequences, not just for you, but for Emma and Charlie.'*

The strength seemed to leave her; she leaned her elbows on the counter and held her head. Stuart came up and turned her towards him. She resisted at first, but he tightened his grip. *'You don't know him. Not really. I know what he's capable of. There isn't any alternative. Besides, you're the most important thing in my world now, Sara.'*

Her reply, into his shoulder, was muffled. *'I just don't know what to think any more.'*

He held her closer. *'Don't disappoint me.'*

She pulled back, as if the words meant something else to her. There was a look of terror on her face, like the one I had seen at the airport when we parted. He pushed her away and stepped back, his voice much louder. *'I'm risking everything for you.'* Emphasising the words like an exasperated teacher.

He strode out of the room. Sara turned, about to go after him, but a second later the front door slammed. She crouched down into a ball, leaning against the wall.

Jane pushed herself back from the keyboard and looked at me. 'He's piling on all the pressure now. He's almost got her where he wants her. He's destroyed the confidence she had in you as someone capable of protecting her and the children. He's the one controlling her destiny now, apparently the only one who can guarantee her security – and she's got the added burden of believing he's risking everything for her. She owes him big time, so she thinks.' Jane sighed. 'He saw something in her psyche, saw where she was vulnerable and just worked and worked away at it till she didn't have any sense of free will any more. I'm so sorry, Dan.'

Every muscle in my body was tensed, my hands locked into fists.

'There's one more disc. A week before the flight.'

I moved Bob's squash bag off his chair and sat, focused on the screen.

They were in the hall, directly underneath the camera, Sara in Stuart's arms. He lifted her face and brought her mouth to his. He opened his lips and kissed her hard, his eyes closed, hers open. She eased herself out of his embrace but he pulled her back and pressed her head against his shoulder. *'Not much longer now. Everything's in place.'*

Her reply was inaudible. He stroked her hair. *'It's got everything. They'll love it. You'll have nothing to worry about. Think of that.'*

She nodded, smiled back. He kissed her, she didn't respond at first. He looked pained. She kissed him back.

He pulled her closer. *'It'll all be so different when we're finally alone.'*

He whispered something in her ear. She jerked back. *'Not here, not in the house, please.'*

His face froze. He didn't speak. He didn't need to. His look was one I never imagined him capable of, as if another personality had taken charge.

Sara's face was drained of all energy, blank and empty. I'd seen her with that expression before, in the photo in her father's hallway.

Jane paused the player, looked down, smoothed the creases out of her jeans.

'What happens next?'

She quickly pressed Eject. She put her hand on mine and slowly shook her head. 'You've seen all you need to.'

Thirty-nine

You go cold. There's nothing, no emotion. You take your time, lower the gun, check around you. Look again through the scope – one check to see it's completed. That's the drill. Only later do you feel. Sometimes never. That's where I was. Cold and nothing. Helen the ex-Army doctor had called it the 'gift'. Was it a gift? Or maybe it was the curse that had led me to put up barriers around my life to protect me, which ultimately obscured what I needed to know. No matter how much I loved Sara, I had never really known her, so when she was in danger I couldn't see it, couldn't reach her.

Stuart. The buffer, the long-sufferer, absorbing our frustrations with the Scheme, softening blows, dispensing calm and reassurance, the public servant, trying to help us make the best of a shit situation, his career stuck in neutral. The sound of his voice, his hands on her, his mouth on her lips. Now I knew what the last six months had been about – the systematic destruction of Sara's feelings for me.

I stared into the room, seeing nothing, blinded by the images and the words. He had taken Sara from me and now she was dead. I felt my fingernails pressing into my palms, my chest squeezing the air out of my lungs. This was the kind of moment I had been trained for, when it goes bad in battle, when anger takes over, when you forget to think. Let go, let your emotions run riot, and you're as good as dead. That's when you have to grip on to something, some certainty in your life, someone's love for you, somewhere there is trust. I focused on the blank screen, trying to digest it all, listening to the hum of the room and my own blood pulsing round my system, my face hot. I'd already lost my future. Now the past was disintegrating as well.

I had nothing to hold on to. I was lost, tumbling into a void.

Jane bowed her head, said nothing.

'On the ship, you knew all this ...'

She looked up into the dark space above the lights, her eyes unfocused, biting her lip. Her voice was faint. 'I thought you were better off with your own memories. You seemed so certain about her.'

'You thought I was a fool because I trusted her, because I couldn't see what was happening.'

She closed her eyes and pressed them with a thumb and forefinger as if trying to erase what she had seen. 'This kind of life, it destroys you. Takes away your judgement. You live among so many lies you lose sight of the truth, of what matters.'

When they opened again, her eyes were full of tears. 'Our world is full of Stuarts, pulling strings, control freaks messing with people's lives on some pretext or another.' She shivered. 'I know how his mind works because he and I, in a horrible way are alike.'

'Why did you follow me to the ship?'

She looked down. 'My job was to watch you.'

'You did a bit more than that.'

She blinked away some tears. 'In this business, you think you're so powerful, breaking laws and rules for the good of your country. It goes to your head. Only when something happens that you think is *really* wrong – and if your moral compass isn't already completely off-beam – that's when you discover just how powerless you are to actually do anything ... because you're too well programmed.'

She turned her face to me, let the tears run. Her voice

was almost inaudible. 'Seeing you for real – on the ship, it all came home to me. I felt such a failure. I could have stopped it but I didn't. I just watched.' She reached for a tissue. 'I couldn't live with what I knew. It seemed like the only thing to do. Just end it all then.'

Sitting there, alone, surrounded by all the screens and machines, she looked small, defeated.

I paced about, thoughts ricocheting round the inside of my head. 'The geeks from Langley. You think they knew the plane was going to go down?'

She turned away.

'Well?'

'I considered it, of course. We're trained to be suspicious. But what was the motive? To take out a whole plane of innocent people, for what?'

'Does "Shimmer" mean anything to you?'

She frowned. 'The Langley guys, I heard them use it. I didn't know what it meant.'

'Then Stuart was connected to them.'

I told her about the incident at the house, and the men at Greg's. 'They wanted me alive.'

'How do you know?'

'The shot of me with the gun by Waheed's car gets leaked. It kills the suicide bomb claim. There's a culprit now. Justice to be done. I was being set up.'

She nodded at the screens. 'But this must have been Stuart's own agenda, what he imagined was going to happen to you after Sara had gone ...'

I paced the room, gazing at the neatly filed discs. More questions crowded in. The place in Tobago, above the dangerous beach, only big enough for two, the 'honeymoon chalet'. Sara's words, *I can't be without the children.* And Stuart's, *It's got everything. They'll love it. You'll have nothing to worry about.*

I looked at Jane. 'Was there anything you heard them say about the children, what he had arranged?'

She stared at the screen, shook her head. 'Nothing we recorded. Why?'

'I saw the place in Tobago. It was just for two. He must have fixed up something else for them.'

Some spark of a thought pushed itself forward, a last pulsing signal of hope. Frankland's comment on the ship about the other mourners: *Hoping that their loved ones would turn up at another airport, like lost luggage.* I was one of those now.

She turned. 'Why did you come back from Tobago?'

'Stuart found me.'

'How was he then?'

'Suitably remorseful. I gave him a hard time about putting us on a cheap flight.'

'How did you get home?'

'He had a plane diverted to pick me up.'

She frowned. 'That's some clout for a handler, someone his level. You have to pull a lot of strings to re-route a commercial flight.'

I kept pacing, gazing at the discs. *Look in the gaps.*

'Frankland said there was no record of any air traffic communication after Bermuda.'

'That's consistent with cabin pressure loss and hypoxia. The plane cruised on till it ran out of fuel.'

'But does no record mean there was no communication? Maybe someone got at the record?'

She peered at me. 'You're still hoping, aren't you?'

I turned away and followed the row of discs down to the dark end of the room. 'My father was in the Falklands, lost at sea. No one saw him die. No body to bury. My mother never completely gave up hope. I used to think it was stupid. Irrational ...'

She caught my eye and raised a finger. I heard the door. Then a male voice, American.

'Jesus, Jane, what's up with you?'

Forty

I dropped behind one of the redundant monitors. Bob's dress was shamelessly American, a tartan barn jacket, a leatherette cap with ear-flaps, baggy jeans and boots. He stood in the doorway, looking towards Jane.

'Who you talking to?'

I heard Jane sigh. 'Myself, who else?'

I could just see his face between the screens. He didn't move, staring at her through oversize glasses. 'You OK? You look like hell.'

'Thanks.' She snorted and turned back to her keyboard. 'You're early.'

He waddled over to his desk and sank on to the chair. 'Left my kit.'

He started tapping on his keyboard. While he waited for it to come to life he fiddled with one of the toys stuck to the frame of his screen. By his elbow was a zebra just like Charlie's. 'How come you weren't picking up? There's stuff going down.'

'What stuff?'

'Teddington were on. They're pulling you back to Langley, tonight. You're booked on the red-eye to Dulles. Check your mail.'

He unwrapped a stick of gum, folded the paper into a little square. 'Guess it's home time, boss. Game over.'

I couldn't see Jane from where I was crouched, but I heard the sound of frantic tapping on her keyboard.

'Hey, maybe they'll give you something nearer the fire, like Kabul. Me I'm praying for Stateside. I need to reconnect with the mother country.' He swung round so he was facing my direction. Then he reached down and picked up his bag. 'That's if the treadmill doesn't get me first.'

He heaved himself onto his feet and went over to her. She nodded at him and smiled faintly then turned back to the screen. He hovered for a moment before turning towards the door. 'Hey ho, onwards and sideways.'

Jane let a full minute pass before she breathed out a long sigh and put her face in her hands. I went towards his desk, examined the toy zebra. *A present from Zebraland.*

Charlie's words in the car going to Gatwick. 'I want to see zebras.' And my reply: *'There aren't any zebras on Tobago.'*

Jane looked up at me, drained.

'Why the recall?'

She looked back at the screen. 'Doesn't say, but it's an ASAP order. Either I'm in the shit or something's happened.'

'So you're going home.'

She snorted. 'I don't have a home. What are you going to do now?'

'There's only one person can fill in the gaps.'

She froze. She knew what was coming.

Forty-one

It had to be a public place, somewhere Stuart couldn't control.

The shopping centre was full of families. I scanned the area from a balcony. It must have been a Saturday. I had lost all sense of the days. There was a comforting smell of pizza and chips. Two coffee chains had tables and chairs set out on the main concourse.

I dialled and waited, heart hammering. Stuart would know about Greg and my visit to Kika, but not about Jane. I was a man on the run trying to find shelter, leaving a trail of trouble. No reason he should think I'd discovered his treachery.

He picked up after two rings. I said nothing.

His voice sounded strained.

'Who is this?'

I gave it a second before I spoke, thinking myself into a role. I whispered. 'It's Dan.'

'Thank Christ. Where are you?'

'Ashford.'

'Whose phone is this?'

'Nicked it.'

'You sound terrible. What happened?'

I let him listen to my silence while I imagined my hands closing round his neck. I tried to drain the rage out of my voice, to sound like I had run out of road. 'Everyone's on to me.'

'What?'

'Who wants me, who's doing this?'

'You're not making sense, Dan, let me come and get you.'

'It's Waheed isn't it? They want me for Waheed.'

'Dan, just tell me where you are.'

'No cops, no heavies OK? On your own or I won't show.'

'You have my word.' Oozing concern. 'Just tell me where you are. I'll be there in an hour.'

I gave him the location then shut off the phone. One hour.

Jane was waiting in her car. I handed her a coffee.

'He's on his way.'

She sighed. 'I don't have a good feeling about this.' She nodded at the pocket where the gun was. 'Should you have that with you? You might just use it.'

'I may need him to see it.'

'What happens after?'

'I haven't thought that far.'

'Maybe you should.' She put a hand on my arm. 'Enough people have been hurt.'

A couple in an Astra pulled up. The mother unclipped a baby from its seat and slotted it into a sling on the father's chest, then adjusted the straps for him. The baby stared at us doubtfully.

'It's a long time since I've done anything like this – field-work.' She bit her lip. Then her words came out in a sudden gush, breathless, as she had been on the ship.

'There is another way, remember – we could just vanish. I know how. I could get us what we need. You'd be less conspicuous if you weren't on your own. I can fix it.'

'Sorry, but I have to do this. I owe it to their memory. I owe it to myself.'

The corners of her eyes glistened with tears. I put my hand over hers and she gripped it.

'Talk about something else. While we're waiting, tell me how you got into this.'

She took a breath, then looked out into the gloom of the multi-storey.

'My father was in the State Department. We were based in England while he shuttled all over. Then he died. Mother went off with someone else. I stayed on at school here. It was home. Someone who knew Dad approached me. It was just after A levels. They wanted someone to befriend a Kuwaiti prince they were interested in getting on side. The money was great. I had fun, got the job done. Langley were happy, they asked me back, I thought Dad would have been proud. Before I'd really thought about it I'd become one of them.'

She wiped her cheeks with the back of her hand.

'Once you're in, it's very hard to get out.'

'And then you married one of them.'

She said nothing.

'I know he's not dead.'

She flushed. 'It would never have worked. It wasn't all Howard's fault. I could never let go with him. We were too bound up in our work. He's with someone less difficult now, more easy-going. Probably for the best.'

She looked off into the car park, her face empty. We were two people without a future. A Golf GTI with black wheels buzzed past, tyres squealing as it took a corner. Someone shouted at the driver.

'Were you fond of Waheed?'

She took a sip of her coffee.

'I respected him. He had known my father so he felt like a link with the past. He didn't like America, of course, so I think it helped that I sounded so British. But there were other things happening that he disliked even more.'

'In the car, when he was dying. He made a sign.' I put my hands together in a cup, like Waheed had done.

Her face froze. '*Kapot yadayim keurot*, Hebrew for "Cupped Hands". It was a Jewish outreach centre in Brussels. It was bombed later that morning.'

'Whoever stopped him didn't want you to know that. Right?'

She looked out of her window and shrugged.

'Is that "don't know" or "don't want to say"?'

'On a bad day, I guess I think it was someone from my own side.'

'Is this a bad day?'

'I've had better.'

Neither of us spoke for a few minutes. I ran back over what I had just seen on Jane's discs, feeling the rage rise again as I replayed the images in my head. Sara and I had entered into an unspoken agreement about the past. We paid a dreadful price. How long had Stuart been planning this? He'd researched her meticulously, right down to the stamp on the doll's house wall. He'd interrogated Kika, he'd found out about the father. He knew her better than I ever did, knew exactly where she was most damaged, most vulnerable, knew how to put her under his complete control.

'I checked out Stuart's time in Kabul, spoke to one of ours who was there at the same time. There was a woman – the wife of a politician, very close to the top. He was running her as an informer, but she got killed. These things happen, but the fact he got recalled suggests there was more. These relationships can get – complicated.'

She turned to me suddenly, reached out and held my face in both of her hands. 'Please, please don't die.'

Forty-two

I leaned on the balcony. There was a panoramic view of the concourse and the two cafés. The coffee and the adrenalin had wired my brain.

I dialled Frankland. There was a weary sigh when he heard my voice.

'Some stuff I need to tell you.'

'Bit late for that isn't it?'

'And I'll know more in a few hours. Will you meet me?'

'That's more than my life's worth.'

'I've got a witness who'll confirm I didn't kill Waheed.'

'Who would that be?'

'The person who took the photograph.'

There was a long pause before he answered. 'I think you've lost it, Carter. You should do everyone a favour and head for the nearest nick.'

'The plane was over a hundred miles off course when it ditched – due south of Florida. You said there was no ground-to-air communication after Bermuda; do you *know* that, or is it just that there's no record you've been allowed to see?'

'Make your point.'

'There's a gap. What if the plane hadn't wandered off course? Suppose it had been re-routed, was trying to get *back* on course when it ran out of fuel.'

'Why would it?'

'Enough fuel for Tobago, but not for a detour. If there had been an unscheduled stop. An unfamiliar airport, different ground crew, someone who didn't know about the gauge fault, got the fuel data wrong.'

All I could hear was his breathing.

'You said look in the gaps. Rule nothing out.'

His tone was resigned, as if talking to a wayward child.

'Goodbye, Carter.'

Forty-three

Stuart was dressed in a thin leather jacket. He had a few days' stubble and his face was the colour of putty. He looked as though he'd had even less sleep than me.

He sat down, looking around nervously. I stayed on the balcony scanning the crowd for any back-up. A man dropped to his knee and tied a shoelace. I watched him for a few seconds, then a child came running up and tugged him forward. A woman in a hoodie walked slowly, texting. Two security guards passed in front of Stuart, ignoring him.

I watched Jane come on to the concourse and sit down at one of the tables outside the other café. She was about thirty metres from Stuart. I dialled her.

'He's alone?'

'No one's with him on the concourse. Dan?'

'What?'

'I don't have a good feeling about this.'

'One more thing. Call Bob, ask him if he knows where Zebraland is?'

'Dan—'

'Please.' I rang off.

I watched the concourse for another ten minutes. Enough to be as sure as I could that he was alone, though I realised that part of me didn't care. I'd come to the end of the road. What happened next – I couldn't see beyond the fog of rage and despair. There wasn't a plan, or an agenda, just a toxic mix of adrenalin and rage. And I didn't give a shit about the consequences.

He smiled his usual smile as I approached, a look of relief as well. I lowered myself into the seat facing him. He put out his hand. I stared at it for a few seconds, as if I'd never seen one before. His eyes focused on the grip of Greg's gun, tucked into my belt, just visible. I rested my fingers on it.

He gazed at me, pityingly. 'My God, you look dreadful.'

I examined his face. It was tight, as if the skin had shrunk. The whites of his eyes, always slightly bloodshot from the constant flying, were almost pink, as if someone had held them open and applied a hair drier to them.

My head swam with emotion and anger, clouding all coherent thought. With my free hand I gripped the edge of the table. Stuart laid his outstretched hand on it. It felt cold and clammy, like a piece of liver.

He let out a short, shy laugh.

'I'm so relieved you called. I thought we'd lost you for good.' He shook his head and peered at the graze on my forehead. 'You have been in the wars.' Then he leaned forward, confiding. 'Look, things got way out of hand.' He shook his head and pushed the hair off his forehead. His fingernails were bitten right down. 'The plane, the photo ... I know you've got a lot of questions, believe me, I would. But there's something much more important.'

All the saliva had gone out of my throat. The images of him with Sara flashed in front of me like lightning. He nodded towards the exit.

'Shall we go?'

I laughed.

'Why would I want to do that?'

He smiled a version of his familiar caring smile.

'You're needed.'

I didn't say anything. I let my gaze wander across the concourse. Jane was holding her phone to her ear.

I looked back at Stuart.

'At Gatwick, Sara almost stayed behind. She didn't want to get on the plane without me. She pleaded.'

He kept smiling, but his eyes narrowed a fraction.

'I persuaded her. I didn't want them to miss out.' I leaned forward. 'You should have seen the look on her face. And she didn't even know the plane was going to crash.'

He blinked, but that was all. I glanced over at Jane. She was frowning, the phone still pressed to her ear.

I waited for whatever thought would come next but none came. My brain felt as if it was boiling in its own fluid. I couldn't think. I touched the gun in my belt. I knew what I needed to do.

Something wasn't right. I had a gun; I'd let him see it. I could kill him any moment. I was ready; I had every reason. But he was calm. Too calm.

He had something.

I glanced at Jane, still on the phone, now looking in my direction, shocked disbelief on her face.

Stuart suddenly came into focus, so sharp I could see every pore, all the moisture that had collected in the corners of his mouth, which had curved up into half a smile.

Then it was like the sound wave from a blast, hitting every part of my body in the same second. My heartbeat hesitated; confused by the chaos of signals it was receiving. For a moment my vision went blank, like a faulty TV.

I managed one word:

'Zebraland.'

His smile curved up some more. 'It's an old Cold War facility, right down the bottom end of Florida. Where they used to send the families of defectors, to get them used to the American way. It's on a base so it's nice and secure. And of course there are the animals ...'

I stiffened as he reached into his pocket, but he pulled

out an iPhone, dabbed it with a fingertip and pushed it towards me.

I focused on the screen. There was the tinny sound of cicadas. An image of a lake and a boathouse. The image was burned out by bright sun, the shapes of animals moving, hard to distinguish until one came out of the shade. Then it swung round to a face. Karina, the children's former nanny.

'OK, so here we are in the sunshine today. We have been making paintings and then soon we are going to get ice cream, isn't that right, kids?'

The image blurred then Charlie's face came into view. He frowned into the lens for a second before the screen panned past some grazing zebras and settled on Emma at a table with crayons and paper, her head lowered.

'Look at the phone, Emma. Let's have some smile!' *Emma looked up, her face serious.* 'Not so happy today?' *Emma didn't respond.* 'Show the picture you're making.' *Emma held up a drawing of giraffes.*

Charlie moved closer to his sister. They were wearing identical T-shirts with Zebraland *in striped letters. Karina's voice again:* 'What about you, Charlie? Let's see yours too.' *He put his hands over his face and giggled.* 'Come on, Charlie, don't be shy now.' *It was of a car and a caravan. They both looked different, tanned by a kind of sun that had never shone on them before. Emma was rocking slightly which she always did after she'd been crying. She turned away.*

The screen went black.

I couldn't breathe. The sudden rush of elation blotted everything else out, the pent-up emotion of the last days haemorrhaging. My children. Alive. I looked at Stuart for confirmation. He grinned and nodded. I tried to stand but my legs had lost all strength. I looked over at the other café. Jane was gone.

Forty-four

Kids, they make cowards of us. The words I'd heard in Kabul. *You can never be fighter and a father; love will cloud your judgement.*

This was a time to heed those words. But my mind was gone, blinded, overpowered by the shock. I'd never given up hope and my hope had been rewarded. I had to get to them. That was all that mattered. Stuart was on his feet. 'Time's ticking on. You need to be in the air in an hour.' He turned and, without looking back, started towards the exit to the car park. He knew I'd follow. There wasn't any question of that. All I could see was Emma and Charlie.

He moved briskly through the crowd. I followed. In the car park was a black Espace, its engine running. There were four men inside. A door slid open. One got out and gestured at a middle seat. I hesitated.

Stuart waved me forward. 'Can't take any chances at this stage. Need to get you there in one piece.' The interior stank of tobacco. He slammed the door shut, stepped back and raised his hand.

The driver floored it and the wheels shrieked on the car park surface.

'If you don't mind, sir.' One of the heavies opened the front of my jacket and removed the gun. 'Don't want any accidents, do we?'

We stayed in the fast lane all the way to Gatwick, a steady hundred and ten. Security waved us through the gate to the perimeter road and we threaded between a series of hangars,

296

their doors open, floodlights on. Inside, planes were being turned around for the next day's flights. I recognised Trent's plane from the picture in his brochure: *on-call rescue and repatriation* ... It was all white, no livery. A single set of steps dropped down from under the tail where a woman was standing in a long coat. She smiled as we pulled up.

'Good evening, Mr Carter, I'm Paula.' She had to shout over the engines, which were idling in readiness. Two of the men from the Espace followed me on board.

'I'll take you to your seat. We're ready to go.' Her smile reminded me of the sort I had seen well-meaning teachers give the children.

A fixed partition divided the fuselage. In the rear section there were eight individual seats. The door in the partition was closed. There was a strong smell of cleaning fluids as if the cabin had just been sluiced out.

'Take whichever seat you like and strap yourself in. We should be away in a few minutes.' She pulled down all the window blinds then disappeared through the door into the forward part of the fuselage. I heard the stairs being retracted and two men from the Espace came through the cabin and followed Paula through the door, closing it behind them. The engine revs rose and I felt a small jolt as the undercarriage brakes were released. The plane taxied out to the runway. There was no queue. It turned left, paused, brakes on while the engines climbed to full power, then let go.

I was going to my children.

The Army was a mixture of following a routine and surviving on your wits. Sometimes it was chaos, so you cursed and shouted to get things sorted. Then there were the times when everything was perfectly arranged and all you have to do is follow instructions. That's when you rest your brain, switch off. Recharge your batteries. This should have been one of those moments. For the past days I'd been living on the extreme edge of my wits. It had taken its toll; my whole psyche was battered. I'd failed Sara; I'd never given her the security she craved because I never knew what drove her, or what she feared. We were kindred spirits, each with our secrets. We'd made a deal; together we would create our own future. How naïve that seemed now. How disastrous. But now I had something to cling to – the children were alive. I had a focus and a future after all.

But the questions kept coming. Get to the children. That's what mattered. And then, maybe some answers.

The air in the cabin was dry. I opened one of the blinds and saw the lights below. The plane had taken off to the west and was in the process of performing a long slow turn to the right.

I watched the ground fall away. The wide body of water below looked like the Solent. That would be on the flight path. But it was too long for the Solent. I saw the bridge that carries the M25 over the Thames. Private flights sometimes have to detour round the commercial air lanes. The plane gained more height. Wisps of cloud rushed past below. It was hot in the cabin. Paula appeared with a tumbler of sparkling water.

'Sorry it's so stuffy.' She shook her head apologetically and set the water down on the armrest. 'Back in a minute.'

I took a sip. It tasted faintly metallic.

The plane climbed into cloud. I stretched, told myself to rest. There was nothing else to do. I needed to be fresh for what was ahead.

On the ground, I pretty much always know what direction I'm headed, without thinking about it. I've got my own inbuilt compass. In the air, it's easy to get disorientated. I'd heard of pilots who had flown hundreds of miles in the wrong direction, convinced they were on the right course. I wanted to be right about where I was going.

The clouds parted and I was looking down on the Zuiderzee, the unmistakeable body of water that takes a big bite out of Holland. I could even make out the dead straight dyke that bisects it. The plane twitched slightly to the right. We were going east.

Pauline appeared again with a small leather case.

'Are we making a stop?'

She smiled. 'A stop?'

'That's what I said.'

She carried on smiling. The two men from the Espace came through the door to the forward cabin. She opened the bag. I felt for my seat belt but before I could unbuckle it the men reached down and clamped their hands over each of my arms. One put a hand over my face and forced my head to one side. Paula yanked down my collar and I felt the needle sink into my neck. There was a second before I blacked out, all my muscles melting.

Forty-five

First there was the smell: grilled meat and paraffin. Too particular, too specific to be imagined or dreamed. And then sounds: the whirring of a starter motor struggling to turn a reluctant engine, the bleat of a goat and the higher-pitched reply of its kid. Then, far off, the swooping boom of a fast-moving jet fighter, and all the time, the wind banging a shutter.

Before that, the sensations were less particular, threaded together with long periods of blankness. I tried to put what I could recall into some order: being in the shopping centre, then a smoky car interior, the crackle of a radio, the roar of a taxiing jet, and, after a long gap, the ponderous throb of a helicopter.

There had been nothing to see, only black, regardless of whether my eyes were open or closed, except for fleeting fragments of blinding light and burned out images – a white tailplane, an overhead air nozzle, orange fabric on my arm, a woman's face, then a blank, as something was slid over my head; no coherent picture, just scraps.

More than once, as consciousness returned, there came a jab in my arm followed by a plunge into somewhere that felt a relief to be, where thoughts just melted away into a formless sludge.

I was going to see the children. That was the agreement. They would take me to them. The images came back. The tanned faces, the unfamiliar T-shirts. Were they in heaven? I'd already decided there was no such place. Maybe I was dead and these were just the last flickering pictures as my batteries expired.

The meat smell was real. I concentrated on that, and the profound hunger it provoked. You don't feel hungry when you're dead. Meat and paraffin, the sound of jets, the goat. A long way from home, yet all so familiar.

When I opened my eyes nothing changed. My eyelashes brushed against fabric. The same when I moved my cheeks and jaw. I tried to reach up, but there was no strength. I tried again and my hands only came up so far, a metallic chink signalling the limit of possible movement. I moved my hands down as far as they could go, felt the bulk round my middle, under the surface of the garment. A giant nappy. I adjusted my legs. Something tightened round my ankles. Just those small movements were exhausting, as if I had been submerged in oil.

It wasn't just my muscles that were weak. My brain had slowed right down. I tried the alphabet, lost my way round L. Tried again. Got to S. Times tables? Kings and Queens of England? Forget it.

So I stayed focused on the smell of the lamb, as if inhaling it would bring nourishment and with it, consciousness. Charlie and Emma were there in my head – something that pleased and excited me, but something else that tormented. Not distinct enough to engage with.

I was horizontal, folded into a semi-foetal position. If I tried to move there was a plasticky creak, like the sound of the children's old changing mat. Another specific memory. Another reason to believe I was conscious. The shackles, the orange fabric, the covering over my face – something I remembered from Afghanistan, at an American base where our chopper had to make a forced landing: shackled, hooded people being herded up into the belly of a transport, shuffling, big bottomed, orange-clad.

A door opened, letting in a gust of cold air tinged with

another distinct smell: burned rubber. A scrape of boots, a click of knee joints and the lower half of whatever was covering my face lifting – as it did, a strip of dull light coming up my face.

'Drink.'

A tube was thrust in my mouth, the smell of the fingers that held it, smoky. I drank. The water was heavily chlorinated. A few sips, and just as abruptly the tube was extracted. The boots went away.

Some time later there were two sets of footsteps. They came up close to my face as if I might be kicked. I tried to curl myself into a ball. A big hand shook my shoulder.

''K, pal. Going upright for a shower.'

American.

'Lift him. On his feet.' Another language, not English, but one I understood.

They kept the hood on me, and the shackles. One each side, they stood me up. I couldn't support myself. Something had numbed the muscles.

The clothes came off, not the normal way, but almost all at once, with much ripping of Velcro. The cold bit into my chest and limbs. Something was removed from round my waist and fell to the ground with a dull moist thud. I felt the sudden cold air between my legs.

'Thank fuck for that.' The American voice again.

The nappy was clean, just heavy with piss.

On a radio somewhere, the tinkling sound of high-pitched singing rose and fell. Tepid water slopped onto my shoulders and someone applied what felt like a rough sponge. I still had some form of footwear on and the water ran down into it.

'The boots off?' A different voice, still in that foreign language.

'No.'

The towelling down was cursory, and I was left standing, shivering for a minute. Then the American spoke again.

'Not the suit. It stands out.' And then, in English. ''K, Bud. No diaper this time. You wanna go, you say, OK?'

They laid me down and put on a pair of what felt like fatigues, then the shackles came off, a combination, no key, and then a vest and something else came over my head, a sweater maybe. Then the shackles went back on, my wrists once again in chains attached to a belt round my middle.

'OK, we're done.'

They walked me backwards and lowered me onto a chair with a wobbly leg. 'Keep still else you'll fall into the kitty litter.'

The meat smell was stronger now, and nearer. The saliva started to leak from the corners of my mouth, the animal urge to eat obliterating everything else. Then the hood came up slightly and I could see the dirt floor, rubber boots like wellingtons on my feet, the floral and check pattern of the mattress where I had lain. Even though there was little light, my eyes stung with the unfamiliar glare.

I felt the warmth of a bowl in my lap. A utensil was put in my hand and the hood adjusted so only my lips and nose were exposed.

'Buon appetito.'

By dropping my head as low as I could, the spoon just reached. The taste of the food exploded in my mouth. Chewy lumps of meat in an oily gravy. I swallowed after barely chewing the first three mouthfuls then told myself to slow down, feeling the effect of the food spread through my body, bringing it back to life. How long I had been without food – days?

When I couldn't get any more out with the spoon I ran my fingers round the bowl, feeling for any missed pieces. Then the bowl left my hands and the hood was pushed down again.

With the food, more of my brain started to wake up, images loading, focusing.

And then it came, each one like a jolting explosion in my head, the pictures on the phone, the shudder of panic. Emma and Charlie, alive.

As I got up, the chair I had been shackled to crashed against my legs, and a new noise now, all around me, going on and on, until more feet and something hard smashed against my head.

'Man, shut the fuck up!'

I was back on the ground. The sound stopped. It had been coming from me.

'They were taking me to them!'

I tried to get up. Another slam, and then nothing for a while.

It was time to focus. Save the rage for later.

The breathing was nearby.

'Any chance of having the mask off?' I tried to sound polite, compliant.

'Later.'

'Where are we?'

'Nowhere.'

I could hear my own breaths coming faster; panic fighting reason, then the sound of a zip, the small pop of a plastic canister opening. One sleeve went up, a jab, and then nothing.

Forty-six

A small vehicle engine was idling, very close by, the exhaust acrid from its unserviced engine. The other sound was the American, talking loudly.

'Six hours if there's no checks. Ten if there are ... Yeah, yeah. Yeah, he's good to go.'

A convoy of vehicles passed by, their suspensions jolting and squeaking. It drowned out the voice. When they were gone the speaking had stopped.

The engine died. A door opened and all the exhaust fumes were blasted away by a gust of freezing wind. It smelled fresh though, dry mountain air. High up. Nearby, several voices talking in hushed tones.

Two sets of hands lifted me on to my feet, then propelled me forward. Icy air surrounded me. We were outside. The voices all stopped. The only sound was the wind. Someone coughed and spat. A third pair of hands fiddled with the string at the bottom of the mask, then it was off. I was blinded by the sudden blast of daylight. My eyes shut tight against the glare. All I saw was the outline of several men in turbans. There was a murmur and someone shouted something I didn't understand. From behind me the American shouted in Pashto – I recognised the language now – close to my ear. '*Keep back. No damage.*'

I tried to turn my head to see him but the hood came back down. Then I was moving again and into a vehicle that stank of sweat and diesel.

'Where am I going?'

'Over the hills and far away!'

The door beside me slammed, and so did several others in another vehicle somewhere ahead. A convoy? Whoever my face had been shown to – perhaps they were coming along. Someone got in the seat in front and the American – I could tell by the smell of hash on his breath – reached across and put a seat belt round me, over my arms.

'Let's move on out.'

The road was straight to start with. The first pothole smashed my head against the roof.

'Head down, Bud. A whole lot more of them to come.'

'It's Dan.'

'What?'

'My name, Dan. Yours?'

There was no reply.

'Where's Stuart? Stuart Holder, is he here?'

No answer.

I ran through some options. Trying to find the door catch, throwing myself out. In shackles? The seatbelt was across my arms. Forget it. Feigning a fit, choking, throwing up? That might get me out of the hood. Demand to take a shit. I might see them undo the combination, see something, anything. Any straw to clutch.

They'd brought me this far; the Yank didn't want me damaged. If I had an opportunity to run they wouldn't shoot to kill. More likely to wound. Where would that get me? I remembered some advice from training, what to do if captured. *Go with the situation, appear passive, allow your captors to drop their guard. Look out for any opportunity. Drain your mind of agonising about your predicament. Squash your anger. Watch, listen, wait and think.*

To keep me alert I thought about Emma and Charlie. Alive, with Karina. At least they liked her. They had been sad when she left. I tried to hold on to that thought, but what kept breaking through was the slicing agony of them wondering where their parents were.

We slowed right down. There was a lot of shouting and bleating. We left the road and bounced over a rocky verge to get round what must have been a herd of sheep. Then speeded up.

I lay against whatever I was sharing the seat with. A bag, some boxes. No clear idea what was happening or where I was going. Whatever it was, I needed to be alert. But whatever they had injected me with was still working. I slipped away into a chemical sleep.

Forty-seven

The blast jolted me awake. It was up ahead, maybe fifty metres, big enough for the draught to swipe our truck off the road. Next came the roar from the American, and with the guy beside him screaming the cab was full of noise as the vehicle bucked and rocked. We bounced a few metres over rough ground, lurched to one side, then slammed into something hard that pitched me half into the front seat.

Nothing happened for a few seconds, then the American spoke. 'Fuck. Shit.' He opened his door.

Out of the silence, some distance away, I heard moans. The other man stayed in the cab. He was muttering to himself, a prayer. Then I heard two shots. The moaning up ahead stopped but the praying near me got louder and more desperate.

The door again. The American was back. 'Shut the fuck up. *Silence.*'

The praying stopped. The truck lurched as the American got back in. He tried the starter. The engine fired, then stopped. The second time the starter whirred and stopped, whirred and stopped.

'Fucking great.'

A hand shook my shoulder. 'You OK?'

My head had slammed into something. I could feel a trickle inside the hood. 'What happened?'

'Land mine.'

The other one started speaking again, fast and indecipherable, panicking.

'Shut up!'

308

I tried to sound calm. 'Whose mine?'

'Old one most like. There's no one active up here.'

'What's up with the engine?'

He didn't answer.

'Why's it not firing? Is it the pedal?'

'What?'

'The gas pedal? Sounded like you were stamping on it. Is there no resistance?'

'What are you, Triple A?'

'The engine fires on what's left in the feed from the pump, but if the throttle cable's gone there's no more being pumped.'

He sighed.

'You take the hood off, I could look.'

He laughed. 'You kidding?'

'You got a better idea?'

No response. The other one muttered something.

'He's a mechanic. He'll fix it.' He said something I couldn't decipher which deteriorated into English, ending in '... fucking do it!'

The passenger side front door opened. Cold wet air rushed in. Then the sound of the bonnet opening, ungreased hinges shrieking their protest.

Nothing happened for a minute. Just the sound of the American's lighter and the smell of tobacco.

'The others: are they all dead?'

He grunted a reply, which I took to be a 'yes'.

'Who were they?'

No answer.

'Before we set off, why did you show them my face?'

He sighed. 'No more questions, OK?'

I tried to picture him. Taller than me, because of the angle his voice came from, strong, judging by the ease with which he manhandled me onto my feet and into the cab. A weariness in his tone that suggested something mundane about what he was doing. No fear, or if there was any, it was well concealed.

'Where are we headed?'

'Right now, nowhere.'

The road had climbed a lot; I'd heard low gears whining.

'Are we near the border?'

He snorted. 'No borders up here, Bud. This here's the badlands.'

'Why am I here? Is it for some kind of trial?'

'Hey, can you just not talk, all right?'

A couple of minutes passed. The chemicals were wearing off. Apart from the wind, it was completely quiet. Too quiet. The American exploded into action. He was out of the cab and calling, screaming, his boots scraping on rocks as he moved about around the truck. His sidekick had legged it.

I didn't speak. He'd need time to think. I allowed myself a ration of hope.

He came back to the cab.

'This is so fucked up.'

He thumped something, his breath coming in hisses. Then my door opened. 'OK.'

The damp air smelled of burnt fuel and rubber from the exploded vehicle. He stood me against the truck, slowly eased off the hood, the chill slicing into my cheeks as the fabric came away from them. I bowed my head, screwed up my eyes, letting light in slowly as they adjusted. For a moment I thought there was something wrong with my sight. There seemed to be nothing but blank grey. Then a gust of wind lifted some of the cloud.

It was a brutal landscape. Nothing green, no trees. Just sharp jutting crags disappearing up into the low hanging cloud. Fifty metres away a few flames flickered from the remains of the other truck.

It was all horribly familiar, as if my life had travelled in a circle and deposited me back where I'd intended never to return. I didn't need any confirmation of where I was, as the last sliver of futile hope that this was all a bad dream faded away.

The American grunted. 'Welcome to Afghanistan.'

I turned his way. A short leather coat hung off him over quilted Soviet fatigues. Cowboy boots jutted from under muddy cuffs. An AK-47 was slung over his shoulder; a grey, soiled baseball cap pulled down over his brow. He had a full growth of beard that disguised the lower half of his face.

I had seen him just once, for no more than a minute, four years ago. But it had been a long minute, when I had thumped the life back into him in the street outside Waheed's clinic. Skin stretched over prominent bones, the gash on the bridge of his nose. There couldn't be two faces like that in the world.

His eyes flitted towards me and away. He remembered too.

Forty-eight

'You going to tell me your name now?'

He stared off into the gloom of the surrounding hills. I examined his features: the high cheekbones, the small, deep-set eyes, the scar running through his eyebrow. No question, no doubt. Eventually he met my gaze and shrugged. There was a moan from the other vehicle. He walked a few metres towards the wreck, pulled a small pistol from his fatigues and put a bullet in the groaning man. The body jerked, then went flaccid.

'Kyle.' He let out a long breath. 'You gonna fix the truck now?'

I raised my shackled hands. He came towards me, the barrel of the AK lowered in my direction. He turned my face away while he twisted the combination lock. The shackles came apart. I tried to stretch my arms out. They were stiff with cramp. I looked down at the chain between my ankles.

'And these?'

'Don't need legs to fix a truck. You even try to walk, I shoot.'

'You want me alive, though.'

'Maimed is fine.'

'What's the plan?'

He shook his head. 'I'm just the delivery man.'

Everything under the bonnet was covered in a thick sludge of grease and dust. I scraped some of it away round the throttle linkage. The bead had come off the end of the cable.

'Is it fixable?'

I didn't know. I didn't know what lay at the end of this journey. I wasn't in a hurry to find out. But being stuck here wasn't going to get me anywhere.

'I can try.'

'Yeah, good idea. You try.'

'Got any tools?'

He rummaged in the cab and pulled out a canvas bag from under the seat. He tipped the contents on the ground. A pair of pliers, scissors, an adjustable spanner.

He surveyed the landscape. 'We so need to be out of here.'

I looked at him. I remembered him on his back in the street outside Waheed's clinic, his face coming alive, his eyes snapping open, the brief sense of elation as the life came back to him. He glared at me. 'Like now.'

'Tell me what this is about.'

'Fix the truck.'

With the point of the scissors I managed to undo a self-tapping screw that held the earth wire to the bulkhead.

He edged closer, watching.

'You're in my light.'

He stepped back, patted his pockets for a cigarette, shook one out of a flattened soft pack and lit up. I rethreaded the cable through the hole, which articulated it to the pedal, then tried to screw the self-tapper into the same hole to jam the cable in place.

I glanced up at him. 'Why you?'

He snorted. 'Keeps it in the family, I guess.'

'Tell me about Waheed.'

'Call came on the day. Get up, get out there, take him out, a crash job. No briefing. Nothing about you or your surveillance.'

'CIA, right?'

He picked some tobacco off his lip. 'They wanted him

313

down whatever – no matter where or who saw. Just get it done. And if I didn't get to him before the drop, to go right in and take out the handler as well.'

I stopped. 'But she's Agency too. Waheed was in a rush to get to her. He had something.'

Kyle gave me a weary look. 'CIA's a big old outfit. Happens sometimes the left hand doesn't always want the right to know what it's got.'

'Gunning someone down in the middle of London? They must have been desperate.'

He gestured at the engine. 'Don't talk, work.'

It was hard trying to make the screw turn with just the scissors. I abandoned them and tried grabbing it in the jaws of the pliers. The thread started to grip. I kept turning. Kyle watched from the other side of the truck. I'd saved his life. And now this.

I kept turning, my hand shuddering from the grip I was trying to keep on the pliers. I paused to let the strength return.

I looked up at him, searching his eyes for any trace of humanity I could get a grip on. 'If I hadn't brought you back, I'd be home with my kids and my wife would still be alive.'

He looked away. After a second, he shrugged. 'Life's full of ifs.'

I tightened the screw as far as it would go. 'OK. Now try it.'

He got in the cab. I watched my improvised assembly as he depressed the accelerator. There was a loud *ping* as the screw gave way and bounced against the radiator.

He got out of his seat, roared with exasperation.

'There is another way.'

Up the road, the cloud had descended over the remains of the other truck.

'The cable in that one may be intact.'

He refused to take the leg shackles off so the journey up the hill was slow. Where he imagined I would run if I could, I didn't know. What was nearby? Would there be anything of use to me? I was better off sticking with him for now.

Wafts of smoke rose from the remains of the other truck, heat still coming off them. In the rocks around the wreck glinted the small items – rings, watches, pens, change, arranged in a circle as if for some kind of ceremony. It was all so familiar, something I'd hoped never to see again.

I looked at what was left of the dead. 'Who were they?'

He didn't answer.

'Before we set off, you showed them my face: why?'

'Fix the truck.'

I opened the driver's door. It was already half off its hinges. It leaned drunkenly, then fell on the ground. The driver, the back of his head gone, was splayed across the blood-drenched seat. An AK beside him. Kyle leaned in and picked up the gun, put the safety on.

I reached into the footwell, moved the driver's leg and tried the throttle pedal with my fingers. Still plenty of spring. I noticed a glint of metal in his pocket, the handgrip of a small gun. Kyle was watching me. I came out then slid underneath the vehicle to reach the pedal box. The back of the truck had taken the brunt of the blast. All the rear axle assembly was gone. Oil dripped from where the clutch had split away from the flywheel. I used the pliers to undo the joint between the cable and the pedal.

'Good job they're the same model.'

I opened the bonnet and undid the attachment to the carburettors. I got up, went back to the cab, reached into the footwell again, loosened the other end of the cable and pulled it through. I looked over my shoulder to check Kyle's position. He was collecting another AK from near another of the bodies. I slipped my hand into the driver's pocket, lifted the small pistol, an old Soviet Makarov. I shoved it into the top of my left boot then stood up, holding up the cable like a dead snake.

A sat-phone bleeped. Kyle hoisted it out of his jacket and answered, waving me forward like a traffic policeman. He kept the AK pointed at me as he backed away a few metres. I tried to listen but the wind had picked up again. I watched him gesticulate as he spoke. An argument.

'Was that Stuart?'

He tapped the bonnet with the muzzle of his AK. 'Just fix the fuckin' truck before we both freeze to death, OK?'

Forty-nine

The cloud swirled around us. The wind was stronger now, whipping rain and sleet around my face. My hands trembled; the tips of my fingers were numb. Kyle watched me all the time. Since the phone call, his attitude had changed.

While I worked the cable into place I tried to think through some options. If nothing else, it kept my spirits from plummeting any further. I might have an opportunity to shoot him. But then what? He had the phone. He'd have some cash. This wasn't the sort of place people took cards. But I had no idea where I was. If I found a British or Coalition position – would they help? Could I trust them? They'd hand me over. I'd end up back with Stuart.

I'd call Frankland; he'd have to listen now. But what could he do? At least I could tell him about the children. What would happen to them if I didn't get out of this? I pushed that thought away – too painful. Jane: she'd made the call, then vanished. Why? Kyle's orders had been to take her out if necessary. Was she still a target?

I was alone. There was no one. Ross's words came back to me, the ones I should have heeded: *You can't be too paranoid*.

Burning rage surged through me – mingled with self-disgust. I'd found Stuart out; I'd had my chance to punish him, to destroy him. If nothing else, I would have got some grim satisfaction from revenge. But he knew my weaknesses just like he'd known Sara's. The images of the children flooded back.

'Hey, you done?' Kyle prodded me with the gun. 'What's going on?'

I had come to a stop, cold, fatigue and despair slowing me to a halt. My face twitching with rage, blood on my torn fingertips as I tried to tighten the last nut on the throttle assembly.

'Try it. It should work now.'

He stared at me, as if something had happened to my appearance. Then he shook his head. 'Never saw so much anger in a man's face.'

He shoved me to the ground. I thought he was about to put the boot in but he just knelt on my abdomen, snapped the shackles back on my wrists and attached the chain to the belt round my middle.

I felt the gun in the boot, against my ankle, out of reach now.

Fifty

I had escaped the hood. That was something. He gave me a bottle of water and a piece of Hershey bar. I was in the back as before, shackled and belted. He drove with the AK propped up on the dash. The road was rough and narrow. Several times we had to pull over as big, heavily laden trucks with equally overloaded trailers struggled up the incline, gears whining.

Whenever we got to a straight section he speeded up so we bounced inside the cab like skittles. Despite ducking, my head crashed against the roof. We passed herdsmen, AKs slung over their shoulders. No one went unarmed here. A pickup truck full of men and bristling with guns hugged the centre of the road. When Kyle eventually passed them they all stared.

The cloud didn't lift and steady rain blurred the view. I kept looking for landmarks, something that I might remember from before. Kyle wasn't going to tell me where we were.

'What would you have done if I hadn't fixed the truck?'

'What the bandits do, taken the next one that came along.'

'You been here a while?'

'The Waheed thing made Europe difficult to operate in.'

'You're freelance?'

'Better that way. More choice.'

'Where's home?'

He didn't answer.

'Any family, kids?'

No answer. I let a couple of minutes go by. The road started to climb again, twisting.

'Stuart tell you I've got two kids? He had them taken away from me. They're somewhere in Florida. He screwed their mother and now she's dead.'

He slowed almost to a halt, turned and looked at me, weary. 'You want the hood back on?'

We pulled up at a sprawling breezeblock structure, a petrol station. Beside it was a parking lot full of burned out trucks. The rain was coming down harder. He locked the doors and walked across to a shop where a dull light burned. A man came out and filled the tank while Kyle watched, looking up and down the road. Was there any way of turning him into an ally? I had nothing to bargain with, and no reason to trust him. Only the possibility of appealing to some vestige of humanity in him. He didn't look like he had any left. He was just doing his job. Just the delivery man.

The gun was too far down. I could feel it in my boot but no matter how much I bent over, I couldn't reach it.

I thought of Greg. Dead in the wet field, his own bullet in his head because he couldn't live with himself. What had they offered him to hand me over? Or what was the penalty if he didn't? *They said they'd take my fucking head off. They meant it. Just like the Yank on the film.*

He always feared the worst, couldn't help himself. In the van, his glazed fascination with the video on his laptop – the beheading of an American soldier. *Could have been one of us.*

Kyle came back to the truck, counting paper money, his wallet open. A picture: a woman and a small child.

The rain came down harder. Kyle lit a cigarette and the cab filled with smoke. Better not to go straight in, try circling around the subject. This far from home, men either want to talk about family in huge detail, or not at all. I guessed he was the latter.

'Were you in uniform before?'

'Navy Seal.'

'You toured here?'

''o2 to four.'

'Where's home?'

No answer.

I kept talking, about leaving the Army and working with Trent, getting married, the twins. Then I told him about Stuart, how he'd turned Sara. I could hear the desperation creeping into my voice, imagining I could appeal to the humanity in a contract killer. He didn't respond, just stared at the road ahead. But he didn't tell me to shut up. That was something.

'I could talk to them.'

'What?'

'On your phone. I could call my kids. Let them know I'm still alive.'

He didn't answer. Nothing was getting through.

Fifty-one

It was hot inside the cab. I felt the sweat oozing out of me and then cooling on my skin, itching where I couldn't reach to scratch as it collected around the belt.

It was getting dark. We passed through a village. A group of children all holding hands stared up as we passed. I looked down at the chain, tried to curve my hands round to reach the lock. They wouldn't reach.

'I saved your life. I made the truck work. One call.'

No answer.

'Come on.'

'All calls are monitored. You should know that. Anyhow, what you going to say to them?'

He shook his head at the road. My face was hot, tears I couldn't wipe away filling my eyes. All the unexpressed grief rearing up like a tidal wave threatening to engulf me.

'You're a father, you know how it is.'

He sighed. 'Look around you. This is a war. You start thinking too much about the other guy, you're fucked, right?'

'Is this a war, here inside this cab?'

He shrugged. 'I'm just doing the job. I got my instructions. You know the score.'

My breaths were coming so fast I could hardly speak. 'One call.'

He sighed, pulled over, put the hand brake on and turned round, looked me in the eye. A moment of hope. Then an explosion as the grip of his gun smashed against my face.

Some time later I came to. The hood was back on.

Fifty-two

I sat shackled to a low bench, my knees bunched up in front of me. My head lolled near my hands so the tips of my thumbs just touched the outside of the hood. There was a smell of paraffin heaters, but the space was cold. Kyle had led me from the truck, across a road and through a metal door, which made a big echoing clang when it shut. A garage or warehouse.

'What happens now?'

'You wait.'

'Wait for what?'

He hadn't answered. I'd heard his boots and the door, some kind of lock. I was alone.

For at least an hour there was nothing, just the noise of my thoughts in my head. I tried again to reach the pistol in my boot, my wrists grinding against the shackles chained to the belt. The best I could do was brush the handgrip with my index finger. I reminded myself to stay focused, to keep alert to any opportunity. But it wasn't working. The adrenalin I'd been surviving on had run out. I was cold, thirsty, hungry and sore. A new voice was trying to get my attention, mocking me, for getting on the plane, for walking into a trap, for ever thinking there was light at the end of the tunnel. The children were thousands of miles away. What was going on in their little heads now? A whole gallery of faces passed in front of me: Greg's bulging eyes, half his face gone as the life left him, Ross drifting into his last sleep, Sara, the terror in her eyes as we parted at Gatwick, Bashir, as I aimed and fired.

From some distance away came the call to prayer, so familiar I could have joined in.

God is most great. God is most great.

God is most great. God is most great.

Two hours after sunset. I'd lost count of what day it was. I tried once more to reach the gun and rolled off the bench onto the cold floor.

I testify that there is no God except God.

I testify that there is no God except God ...

A different engine, a V8, a scrunch of stones as the vehicle stopped outside.

Come to prayer, come to prayer.

Come to success! Come to success!

God is most great. God is most great.

There is none worthy of worship except God.

I managed to push the hood up slightly so the gap below my nose widened. The top half of my face throbbed from the pistol whipping. I looked down. There was a dull light, maybe from the heater. I could see the concrete surface of the floor and a couple of cables. I struggled towards the cables and bumped into something that toppled over with a loud aluminium clatter.

The door scraped open. Kyle and someone else, a lighter step, a man's scent, clashing with sweat. The second person circled round me, stopping at whatever it was I had knocked over and righting it.

A sigh, irritable. Enough for me to identify Stuart.

'Long way from Florida.'

He didn't answer.

The cuffs bit into my wrists. 'You like diverting planes. At least this one didn't run out of fuel.'

I felt the hood being loosened. He pulled it off. There was almost no light in the room. His face was a ghostly glow. No smiles now. I focused on his gaze, gave him a long look. 'Sara's somewhere you can't get at her; that's something. What did you have in mind after Tobago? Were you just going to take my place in their lives?'

He took a few paces away into the gloom, let out a long weary sigh. 'Dan, understand that neither of us are in a position to negotiate. What this is about is so much bigger than you and me. The world knows how Waheed died; the photo's out there. There's no covering it up any more. Our masters need closure, a gesture that will end this mess. If I go home empty-handed it's the end of the line for me. And that's not in your interests, Dan, whatever you think of me.' He turned. 'There are the children to consider.'

He leaned down so his face was close to mine, his voice almost a whisper. 'I can't mend what's happened, but at least I can see that Emma and Charlie are provided for. We get this wrong – who's going to be there for them? Focus on that, will you?'

I pushed everything down. I didn't want to give him the satisfaction of seeing my rage or my pain. 'I want to speak to them.'

'That depends on whether you cooperate.'

'I cooperated for four years. Much good that did me.'

He gripped my chin and lifted it up. In spite of the cold, his face was damp with sweat. 'Don't make this any more difficult.'

From behind, Kyle pressed his hands down on my shoulders. Stuart moved a small table in front of me. Then he stepped back and switched on two lamps. The light was fierce, stinging my eyes even when I shut them tight. I waited for them to adjust. What was the hurry? When I opened them again the room was a grey blur, but between the lamps I could just make out the lens of a camera and a tripod.

Stuart laid a sheet of paper in front of me. 'In a few seconds I'm going to give you something to read. I want you to recite it out loud. After that, you can speak to the children.'

'This some kind of court?'

'You just need to say the words.'

My pulse was thundering so hard in my head it almost obliterated all thought. I looked at the sheet in front of me. The words came into focus.

I, Dan Carter, former soldier of the British Army, do solemnly confess to the murder of Waheed al Amarir. I admit that I committed this act of assassination alone and without aid or interest from any other party, acting out of the same desire to kill Muslims, as I had in Afghanistan as a soldier, where my targets included a child, Bashir al Mazar. I ask for the forgiveness of blessed almighty God for these acts and that he may punish me accordingly for these crimes.

Stuart's voice came from somewhere behind the camera.

'OK, start please, nice and sincere.'

Play for time, create some incident. Spin things out. When there's nothing left, keep hoping for something.

'The phone call first.'

'Dan you're in no position—'

'Phone!'

My eyes were becoming accustomed to the light. I looked round. The room was getting clearer. No windows, just a grille. A couple of silver equipment boxes lay open on the floor. A cable snaked from the camera to a console and then up through the grille.

Kyle appeared from behind me and went over to Stuart. I couldn't hear their exchange.

Kyle came back, holding a sat-phone.

'The number's punched in. You just press green.'

I snatched it up too fast so it dropped to the floor.

'Sorry.'

He handed it back to me. I pressed a button and listened.

'Nothing.'

A weary hiss from Stuart.

'It's OK, I never forget a number,' I said.

I dialled and waited for the pickup, my heart ready to smash its way out of my ribcage. I heard Sara's words to Kika loud and clear as if she were shouting them inside my head: *Just act.*

I held my breath until I heard the voice on the other end, then I started to speak the lines I'd already rehearsed. 'Karina, it's Dan. Hi. Long time no speak.' Trying to sound upbeat.

I paused. 'I know. I know. Are they there?'

Tears were flowing freely down my cheeks. I fixed my eyes on Kyle.

'Hello, darling. Yes it's Daddy … I know darling, I'm so sorry … Really, yes … Have you? Fantastic … and will they let you feed them?' I wanted to keep my voice as level as I could but it was impossible. 'That's wonderful, precious … and they don't try to nibble your hand? Tell me are you being a good girl?' I waited for the answer. 'Really? I bet you are.'

I covered my face with my hands. 'Let me speak to Charlie … yes you too, darling … yes soon … promise … yes always and always … no I'm fine, it's just a bumpy road doing that to my voice … Bye, darling, bye bye … yes always … I love you.'

Kyle's eyes were in shadow, but I kept looking his way. I let a few seconds pass, then continued. 'Charlie! Hi, big boy … you're kidding … real ones? Real proper ones with lots of beautiful stripes? … Fantastic … yes I know … yes … yes … and Karina's very good to you isn't she … yes … soon … yes I know, I'm sorry … no … not much longer now … that's right … I love you too … I love you …'

I threw the phone away from me, roaring with pain and grief, as if all the pure emotion that had accumulated over years of control and restraint burst out of me like an alien thing I had been nurturing all this time. I shoved the table away so it toppled forward onto the camera. Kyle came forward and moved it out of the way. He smacked my face twice with the flat of his hand.

'Careful.' Stuart came up close and put a hand on my shoulder. 'Right, Dan. Do the words.'

The whites of his eyes were a dirty pink. His breath smelled of a mixture of something acidic, his mouth hung open. It was as if all pretence of propriety had finally left him, exposing the empty space inside him.

I froze. This was my last chance. I didn't want to think about what would come after. I looked down at the cuffs. Blood had gathered where they had ground into my wrists. The chains running from them to the clasp on the belt. Another one attached to the bench. I was trapped and tethered like an animal, defenceless. And the gun, in the boot, pressing against my ankle. Out of reach.

'The words, please. Don't spin this out.'

I started to read them in an unhurried monotone.

'Off by heart, Dan, just like you did the day you met Sara.'

Stuart stood behind the camera. He had collected every detail about us, then used what he'd learned to undermine us. He'd destroyed Sara; now he had the destiny of my children in his grip. His power over me was absolute.

I spoke the words at the camera, with the minimum of feeling. Then I twisted round to see where Kyle was. On the wall behind me was a giant poster of Waheed. I translated the Arabic. *Brothers of the Martyr*. It was all clear now: the camera, the poster, the confession. Just like the video on Greg's computer in the van. Out of the past, a warning.

I'd come to the end. I knew what was next. I focused on Kyle. 'I saved your life. Remember that?'

I couldn't see his face at all now. In the camera light his

shape was just a black silhouette. And a reflection bouncing off a serrated blade.

He stepped forward, his hand came down and clamped on to the back of my head, twisting it round. No eye contact. No more appeals to whatever humanity he might have left in him.

His fingers gripped my head and forced it hard down between my knees. As he pushed I straightened the fingers of my left hand and used his force to help ram them into the boot. I felt the handgrip of the Makarov. I made a last wish for some bullets in the clip. Even just one. One, for Emma and Charlie's sake.

A hot, blinding pain spread out across the back of my neck. With all the force I could pump into my thighs and calves, I thrust myself back against Kyle's hand and brought the gun out raising it as far as the shackles would allow. There wasn't any time to aim but the aim was crucial. I squeezed the trigger and hoped. What felt like a whole second passed and then the gun exploded close to my face.

Fifty-three

Kyle released his grip. Something toppled over and one of the bright lights went out with a crash as it hit the floor. I felt something warm running down my neck and back. Blood.

I flopped forward, taking the bench with me. I twisted onto my back so I was aiming straight at Kyle. His eyes locked on to mine. He was saying something but there was no sound. My ears were numb from the gun blast. Nothing happened.

We stared at each other. His small recessed eyes gleamed out of his face like two black-headed bullets. He looked like the killer he was, a gaze of cold commitment that left no space for compassion. Then he wavered, held up the knife as if ready to drop it.

I shook my head. 'Pick it up.'

With the gun, I waved him toward where Stuart was. All I could see was a heap and, further behind, against the back wall, the upturned camera lying on its side, its tripod legs in the air like a huge dead fly.

I couldn't move much, but I had the gun in both hands now. I kept it trained on Kyle. I had no idea how many bullets were left. There could be one or more, or there could be none.

Stuart started to move, heaving himself up onto his elbows, a blood stain spreading across his groin. He looked dazed. He was saying something I couldn't hear. He raised a hand. I thought it might be in surrender but he used it to wipe a strand of hair hanging over his forehead.

Kyle moved, watching me, the gun in my hand, reading my mind. My life had gone into reverse. I was back in a place where self-preservation ruled, where split second decisions dictated everything. No time for reason or evaluation. Just action.

Stuart started to get to his feet, scrabbling like an overturned animal. I had winged him but that was all. His eyes bulged. His mouth worked but I couldn't hear anything. I was glad. I had heard all I ever wanted from him. He could be as sorry as he liked. It didn't matter. Kyle hovered near him. Stuart's mouth was still going, negotiating, pleading.

I waved the gun at Kyle's knife. 'Do it.'

Part of me would have preferred to look away. After all, he was someone's son. Someone had loved him, maybe not well, but loved him all the same. But I didn't. I watched. He had tortured me in ways I could never have imagined, and now it was his turn.

The look of affronted panic on his face as Kyle bore down on him was grimly satisfying. His lips were still moving, a hand went up to shield himself.

Kyle swiped the blade across his neck and a fan of blood sprayed upwards. Stuart dropped back and his face flopped sideways, his eyes staring at me, frozen for ever in permanent dismay.

My neck was bleeding fast. I risked a glance down. There was a lot of blood under me. I had appealed to Kyle before and got nowhere. I looked at him again but my vision started to blur. I weighed the gun in my hand and suddenly it felt much heavier. He stared at me, the same look, empty.

I kept the gun up, but I could feel myself going. He stood and watched, the knife hanging from his hand, as my options drained away like the blood running down my back. I lowered the gun, laid it down on the floor beside me.

Fifty-four

I stared into the darkness for some time before I decided I might be alive. There was no sound except wind, no light. I was on my back, wrapped in heavy blankets. No shackles, my hands folded on my chest. Under them, something squashy. I looked down – a drip bag, and beside it the sat-phone and the Makarov. I held it up, detached the clip. Five bullets. The back of my neck was partially numb, something strapped across it. I looked up, and again there was nothing. Just a clear night sky, and a few stars.

I couldn't move my neck so I tried rolling on to one side to look around. A flat clearing on an otherwise steep hillside. No buildings, no people or animals. I could have been on the moon. The effort of moving made me dizzy and I flopped back. In the distance came the throb of a helicopter.

It blasted me briefly with a searchlight and I covered my face as a whirlwind of grit and dust rushed round me. It landed just metres away, the engines thundering while four men scooped me on to a stretcher. And then we were away again. Someone was holding me, and then a woman's voice.

'It's OK. You're safe now.'

Fifty-five

Several times my sleep was interrupted by groups of figures in white. I didn't think they were angels but some of the drugs I was on got me thinking that way. Once I was lucid, I asked what they wanted. One of them gestured with his clipboard. 'We've never seen a partial beheading.'

I was strapped down, my head in a brace. 'Just while the tendons heal,' someone explained. They kept me pumped full of sedative. I knew why. They didn't trust me to stay put. I asked whoever came in about the children. Each time the same answer, 'It's OK, they're fine. Let's get you right first.'

'How long?'

'Soon.'

I asked for something to read. And I wanted to see what had been reported. The same answer: 'Soon.'

It was night. The main lights had gone out. I'd just woken after another druggy sleep. A figure on the end of my bed, just a silhouette, a woman. For a second my mind played a mean trick. It can be a cruel place, the imagination. She twirled a strand of hair between two fingers. I breathed and recognised the scent.

When Jane saw I had opened my eyes, she leaned forward and kissed my forehead.

'How long have you been there?'

She shrugged. 'I keep feeling the need to check that you're still alive.'

'That's nice of you.'

She took a breath. 'They'll be here tomorrow. Their flight gets in at eight.'

My pulse raced. I was wide awake now. 'I'm going to meet them.'

She opened her mouth to protest, then realised it was futile.

Neither of us spoke for a minute. She took my hand.

'It's over?'

She nodded. 'Yes.'

She put on the bedside light. There was a newspaper on the bed. She held it up for me to see the headline. *Waheed assassin killed by supporters.*

Then she passed me an envelope. 'The papers here won't publish this, but it's all over Arab websites.'

I opened it. Inside was a screen grab from a web page. It was all in Arabic, but I didn't need to read the text. In the centre was a photograph, slightly fuzzy, of a severed head, held by a hand in front of a poster: *Brothers of the Martyr.*

'I guess Kyle owed you a favour.'

I looked again at the head. The eyes half closed, the jaw slack, the hand holding it up in front of the poster gripped the same strand of hair Stuart had so often swept from his brow.

'Al Jazeera received it at 03.50 GMT that morning, which was about the same time we picked you up. He must have gone back and filmed it after he sorted you out.' She shook her head. 'The guy's a piece of work.'

I put the picture back in the envelope and smoothed the flap down. 'Where is he now?'

Her shoulders lifted a fraction. 'Somewhere no one can find him.'

'His instructions were to kill you as well if Waheed got to you first.'

She sighed, a grim smile on her face.

'The geeks I told you about – they were building an über hi-tech eavesdropping system that would dispense with field agents. Four years back they'd used up their budget, they were losing traction, so they figured they needed something that looked like a traditional Intel failure to win back internal support.'

I made the cupped hands gesture, like Waheed had. She nodded. 'The Brussels bomb would do the job, they thought. But then Waheed found out about it so they had to stop him. Being geeks, they'd not factored in the fallout from him being martyred.'

'Nice colleagues you have.'

'They're gone now. There've been some changes.'

'But it was Stuart who leaked the photo.'

She nodded. 'After that, the Saudis demanded closure. An inter-agency summit was convened, us and the Brits. Stuart floated the idea of pinning it on you. Apparently the whole room went quiet. No one wanted to go down as sanctioning it.'

'But someone did.'

She glanced at the window. Darkness changing to grey.

'You left the shopping centre in a hurry.'

She sighed. 'Once Bob confirmed Zebraland, I knew I had to take this higher. I told them it would blow up in their faces if they didn't stop it.'

'How?'

'The picture of you with the gun by Waheed's car? I got Bob to search for complete footage. He found it, got it copied.'

'And?'

She looked down. 'Let's just say it got leaked.'

'Who to?'

She bit her lip. 'A retired policeman.'

Frankland.

336

She smiled. 'The Agency got cold feet. The operation looked like a train wreck. They wanted out. Told me to do whatever I could.'

Suddenly her eyes filled with tears. 'I flew out that night. Not to Dulles, to Bagram. But we couldn't find you. The Brits were denying everything. We'd had a trace on Trent's plane and a position from Stuart's phone when he made one brief call, but most of the time he kept it switched off and the battery out. He wasn't taking any chances. I was frantic. We'd got everybody mobilised.' She shivered. 'And then you dialled my number.'

She paused and dabbed her eyes. 'While they were getting the fix on your location, your voice was patched through to the ops room speakers. You, pretending to talk to your children. Thirty guys listening, hardened operatives, tears in their eyes. You could have heard a pin drop.'

She held both my hands, lifted them to her lips and kissed them.

'I never forget a number.'

Fifty-six

It was only seven a.m. but the terminal was packed. I hadn't slept much and I'd been given an extra dose of painkillers before they let me outside. The brace holding my neck was itching. I'd covered it with a scarf. I wanted to try and look as normal as possible, but it made all my movements look robotic.

Frankland kept a firm grip on my arm as if he'd just made an arrest. He wasn't talking much, which was unusual.

He sipped from a large paper cup of tea. I watched his face for a few seconds, a look on it I hadn't seen before.

'So, how's it been?'

He glared at the crowds.

'Now there's nothing more to find out.'

He shrugged. 'There's always more.' But the energy had gone out of his voice. The job was done and he knew it.

'When you ended our last call, you thought you'd washed your hands of me,' I said.

He didn't answer.

'Rule nothing out. Isn't that what you said?'

He flapped his free hand. 'OK, I was wrong. I misjudged you. Happy now?'

He sipped his tea. The arrivals doors opened and a group of travellers flooded through. I glanced at the board for the Florida flight listing. *Baggage in hall.*

Frankland was lost in thought. I turned and looked at him. 'Thanks for coming today. This must be hard for you.'

He rubbed his nose. 'There's a bit of land, not far from

you, just below the Downs. I thought we could plant a couple of trees for Sara, and Rachel, you know, my daughter ...'

For the first time I saw tears in his eyes. He stared down into his cup as if reading a tealeaf. 'It might help your kids ... you know.'

He took another sip. 'They still don't know, do they?' His voice was cracking.

'About Sara?' I shook my head. 'I'm going to be as straight as I can.'

'Just give them time, lots of time.' He looked up at me, fierce again. 'And while you're at it, make the most of them.'

Passengers were flooding past, a traffic jam of trolleys. I felt my mobile buzz in my pocket. I took it out. A text. *Look up.*

From the balcony above, Jane waved and smiled. I smiled back, but then I heard a squeal at the Arrivals door. Two small blurs had broken free from their escort and were streaking towards me.

Acknowledgements

For fantastic comments on the manuscript, my thanks to Joanna Briscoe, Olivia Lichtenstein, Richard McBrien, Patrick Tatham, and Liz Hatherell for her diligent copy-editing.

For invaluable technical and specialised advice, James Castle, Justin de Lavison, Pascale Gillet, Jason Hartcup, David Neuberger, Andy McNab and Martin Rudland.

Huge thanks to my agent Mark Lucas, who never flinched from saying the things that needed to be said, my brilliant editor Bill Massey and, also at Orion, Natalie Braine and Jonathan Weir.

For all round support, Sophie Doyle and Katarina Petruscakova.

And my wife Stephanie Calman and our children, Lawrence, who withstood having lumps read out to him, and Lydia, who was so good about the expired passport that nearly did her out of a trip to Tobago – the original inspiration for *Just Watch Me*.

About the Author

Peter Grimsdale is an award-winning filmmaker and television executive whose work has appeared on all the main British TV channels. He is married to author Stephanie Calman. They have two children. He is the author of one previous novel, *Perfect Night*.